THE DEVIL'S GRAVEYARD

Dear Reader,

It is never safe to make assumptions.

In particular, it is never safe to make assumptions about things that may or may not appear to be safe.

Almost certainly, they are not.

<small>Anonymous</small>

By the same author:
This particular 'Anonymous' is the author of *The Book With No Name* and *The Eye of the Moon*, in which the reader will find the further adventures of the Bourbon Kid (with a few rips in the fabric of time).

THE DEVIL'S GRAVEYARD

A novel (probably)

Anonymous

Michael O'Mara Books Limited

First published in Great Britain in 2010 by
Michael O'Mara Books Limited
9 Lion Yard, Tremadoc Road
London SW4 7NQ

A CIP catalogue record for this book is available from the British Library.

Papers used by Michael O'Mara Books Limited are natural, recyclable products made from wood grown in sustainable forests. The manufacturing processes conform to the environmental regulations of the country of origin.

ISBN: 978-1-84317-472-1

1 3 5 7 9 10 8 6 4 2

Designed and typeset by www.glensaville.com

Printed and bound in Great Britain by Cox & Wyman, Reading, Berks

www.mombooks.com

One

Shee-IT! Sure was true that there ain't no substitute for cubes. The big-inch mill in this mutha could pull . . .

Johnny Parks was finally fulfilling a lifelong dream. Driving down a desert highway in the early morning, at over a hundred miles an hour, was exhilarating. The fact that he was in a police squad car pursuing an infamous serial killer in a black Pontiac Firebird just added to the buzz.

The car radio crackled into life and the Chief's voice came through loud and clear for the third time in the last two minutes.

'Repeat, all units pull back. Do *not* pursue fugitive into the Devil's Graveyard! Acknowledge – that's a goddam order!'

Johnny's partner in the shotgun seat, Neil Silverman, reached down and twisted the volume control on the radio until, one by one, the sound of the other officers acknowledging the message died away. The two cops shared a smile and a nod. As they did so, they sped past a giant sign at the roadside. It read:

Welcome To The Devil's Graveyard

Johnny watched in his rearview mirror as the other seven squad cars strung out behind them stopped, turned tail and drove away. *Gutless bastards.* This was his moment – *well, his and Neil's*, he supposed. Neither of them would normally have been involved in such a high-profile chase, but so many other officers had been killed that morning, they had been called into action. Both men were in their early twenties and had graduated from the Academy together just six months earlier. Neil had been the best shot on the pistol range, and was definitely going places in the force. As for Johnny, he was just excited to be driving the ace marksman along the highway. This was his big chance to make a name for himself. If anyone was going to take down the driver of the Firebird it would be his buddy Neil – which was why Johnny was so eager to keep up the chase a little while longer, even though it meant defying the Chief's order.

With the harsh glare from the desert sun in his eyes, Johnny was struggling to keep control of the car as they inched up to the Firebird. Navigating the highway, with its drifts of sand and gravel, while trying to intercept a madman who'd rammed at least three other vehicles off the road that morning took all the skill he had.

If Neil was the best young marksman on the force, then Johnny considered himself to be the best driver. He had been a fanatical stock-car racer as a teenager, practising for hours on a specially built dirt track at his father's farm, and winning many races at the local track. It was his driving skills that had landed him his fiancée Carrie-Anne, the head cheerleader at his high school. They were expecting their first child any day now. So if Johnny could capture the fame and fortune that would come with being part of the double act that took down the Bourbon Kid, then his soon-to-be-born child would have a father to be proud of.

'*Come on, Johnny!* I can't get a clear shot from here!' Neil yelled, aiming his revolver out of the open window. 'Get closer!'

Johnny put his foot down on the accelerator and tried

to pull the front of their squad car level with the rear of the Firebird.

'You aimin' for the tyres?' he shouted above the roar of the engine noise and the wind blowing in through the open window.

'Nah. The driver.'

'Ain't you supposed to aim for the tyres?'

Neil took his eyes off the black car just ahead and looked over at him.

'Listen. If I nail this guy, we're gonna be fuckin' legends, Johnny. Think about it – you'll be able to tell your kid you took down the biggest mass murderer in history!'

Keeping one eye on the road, Johnny grinned back at his partner. 'Yeah. That'd be pretty cool.'

'I can see it now. We'll be openin' supermarkets, doin' after-shave ads, the whole nine yards.'

'I could do with some new after-shave.'

'Well, jest you keep the car steady, 'cause I'm about to make it happen.'

'Can you just wound him, though? Couldja do that? Huh?'

Neil shook his head impatiently. 'What the fuck d'ya want me to do? Blow his fuckin' nose off? I'm good, but I ain't that good. No one is.' He leaned further out of his window and added, 'Don't forget, this bastard killed at least ten of our guys this morning. Good men. Men with families. *Happy Halloween, the boogeyman's in town!*'

That it was Halloween was not lost on Johnny. The local inhabitants – the few that there were, that is – never set foot in the Devil's Graveyard at any time, much less at Halloween. There were always rumours doing the rounds in bars and diners about what happened out there each October thirty-first. It was said that busloads of innocent fools were driven in every year, never to be seen again. Most people believed it. It was the local town's dirty little secret. Johnny had already driven past the signpost that signified they were on deadly ground. It was foolish enough to be in a high-speed car chase with the serial killer known as the Bourbon Kid, but to be conducting that chase in the Devil's Graveyard on Halloween... well, that was about as foolhardy as a bungee jump with no cord.

'Okay, Neil, I gotcha. Just hurry up and take this sonofabitch down. Then let's get the fuck outta here!'

'You got it, buddy.'

The road stretched ahead endlessly towards the horizon, shimmering like a mirage in the early-morning heat. As far as the eye could see, there were no buildings, no other traffic. Again Neil leaned out of his open window and pointed his handgun at the Firebird's blacked-out driver's window. The wind blew his normally perfectly combed blond hair up high above his head.

'Come to Daddy, you sonofabitch,' he whispered.

A millisecond before Neil fired, the Firebird's driver hit his brakes, bringing the cars level. Neil had already committed to squeezing the trigger. The bullet missed its mark, flying past the front of the other car. Johnny was also braking hard, but before he could process what was happening, the Firebird's driver's-side window lowered. The twin barrels of a sawn-off shotgun appeared. It was pointed at both of them. Johnny opened his mouth to yell at Neil to duck, but –

BOOM!

It happened so fast Johnny barely had time to blink, let alone get the words out to warn his partner. The heavy charge of buckshot blew off most of Neil's head and splattered it all over the side of Johnny's face. Blood, hair and chunks of brain flew into his open mouth as he squealed out an agonized 'Oh, fuck!' The shock of it caused him to lose control of the car. The Firebird swerved across him, its front wing knocking into the cruiser's at high speed. Johnny hit the brakes again, but it was way too late. He had already lost control of the steering wheel, which spun wildly in his hands. Out of the corner of his eye he saw the Firebird fishtail three or four times as its driver fought to control the skid, then straighten up and race off down the highway. Tyres screaming, the squad car careered off the road and into the rock-strewn desert wasteland. It hit a boulder and flipped over, rolling in the air, tossing Neil's lifeless body out of its seat.

Johnny found himself upside down in mid-air. Instinctively, he crouched sideways and grabbed the base of his seat, pulling hard against it. It was the first thing he had been taught to do if his car overturned during a race. If the roof of the car was going to crash into the ground, Johnny had to be pulling himself away from the impact by gripping hold of the seat and holding on for all he was worth. He heard the roof crumple as it smashed down on to the desert ground. The dented metal missed his head by less than an inch. Three more times the car flipped over, each time leaving him more and more disoriented. Eventually it landed on its side with Johnny pinned against his window, staring at the sandy ground. The car wobbled a few times before finally settling to a stop.

What was left of Neil slumped on top of him. His dead friend's remaining eye was staring blankly at him, and specks of blood were dripping down on him like early spots of rain. He heard the tick of cooling metal, and caught the acrid tang of escaping fuel.

A second before passing out, Johnny made a conscious decision to quit the force.

Two

The morning of Halloween was unlike any other in the Devil's Graveyard. Joe opened up the gas station at eight o'clock sharp as he always did, but everything else about the day was just a little bit different from the usual routine. He spent less than ten minutes out in the fresh air unlocking the padlocks on the two gas pumps and switching on the power. Even the lizards, snakes and assorted vermin that frequently slithered or crawled along the dusty wasteland were not in evidence. If they had anywhere to hibernate for a day or two, then it was a safe bet that's where they were.

Sleepy Joe's Diner was the only stop on the desert highway that led to the Hotel Pasadena. It doubled as a gas station, and since there were no other fuel stops within a hundred-mile radius, most people travelling that way stopped by for a refill. And on the days leading up to Halloween, sales were at their peak.

Joe looked forward to the festival almost as much as he dreaded it. All kinds of weird characters dropped by to fill their gas tanks and their stomachs. Ninety per cent of them were fruitcakes; the other ten per cent could be politely described as naive. So far, for the twelve years he had owned the gas station and diner, Halloween had delivered exactly what he had expected. This year was unlikely to be any different.

After making sure the pumps were primed and ready, he headed back inside to the sanctuary of the diner. He knew only too well that the peace and quiet outside was merely the calm before the storm. He knew from experience what was headed his way, and he was grateful for the fact that when things turned horrifically wrong later in the day – as they would – he had a tornado-proof cellar in which to tuck himself away.

In the kitchen area out back of the diner, he put on a pot of coffee in readiness for Jacko's annual visit. Then he set about the early-morning chores while it brewed.

At about eight-thirty a van pulled up outside, as it did every morning, to deliver the papers. Most mornings Joe exchanged pleasantries with Pete the delivery guy and chatted briefly about the local news. On this morning, however, Pete didn't even step out of his van. He simply wound down the driver's-side window and threw a stack of newspapers bound together by a string out on to the forecourt. The bundle landed on the ground at Joe's feet, blowing up a small cloud of sand and dust.

'Mornin', Pete,' said Joe, tipping his cap.

'Hey, Joe. Runnin' late this mornin'. Gotta be goin'.'

'Can I interest you in some coffee? Just put a pot on.'

'Nah, thanks all the same. Gotta lot to do today.'

'Well, I oughta settle up with you. Reckon I'm a week in arrears.'

In the van, Pete began winding the driver's window back up. It wasn't difficult to tell that he had no intention of staying around this morning.

''S okay, Joe, I know you're good for it. You can settle tomorrow. Or later in the week, don't matter.'

'You sure 'bout that? I can go fetch the money outta the till.' But he might just as well not have spoken.

'See ya tomorrow, Joe. Have a good day.'

The van window closed completely and Pete pulled away with a quick wave to Joe. Soon he was out of sight, heading towards the Hotel Pasadena.

Most days, the banter between the two men would last for about five minutes. Pete was normally pretty friendly, as well as grateful for the mundane conversation, but on Halloween morning he was always eager to get on with his deliveries. In the Devil's Graveyard, there were only two places to deliver to – Joe's and the Hotel Pasadena – so Joe took no offence at Pete's eagerness to get going that morning, even if he was a little disappointed.

By eight-forty-five, he had the diner up and running and ready for business. Feeling relaxed and ready to face the day, he poured himself his first mug of coffee and took a seat at one of the round wooden tables to look at the newspapers. There were only eight tables in the diner, each covered with a uniform red-and-white-checked tablecloth. To any new customer walking in for the first time, it wouldn't have been obvious that Joe was the owner. He wore the same blue denim dungarees every day, washing them only once a week. His thinning grey hair was always concealed beneath a fifteen-year-old red baseball cap, save for a few tufts sticking out around the ears. Silvery-grey stubble prickled his haggard, sagging old face, and he looked as miserable as sin, regardless of his mood. Even as a young man it had been joked that he looked like the wind had changed when he was in the middle of a face-pulling contest.

The front-page headline on the first paper he picked up read 'WANTED DEAD OR ALIVE – REWARD $100,000'. Beneath the bold black 72-point type was a grainy photo taken from some local CCTV footage of a man with greasy, shoulder-length dark hair dressed all in black and wearing a pair of dark sunglasses. According to the article that accompanied the headline, this man had committed a series of armed robberies in a nearby redneck town. In the course of these, he had killed a number of local law-enforcement officers as well as innocent members of the public. The death toll was up past thirty, but the cops expected to find more corpses over the next few days. The article also dared to suggest that the perpetrator might be the urban legend known as the Bourbon Kid. Everyone knew about the Bourbon Kid. But they also tended to lump him in with the likes of Bigfoot and the Loch Ness Monster.

Joe, contentedly reading the paper, considered the possibilities of picking up the reward for catching the Bourbon Kid. Would he use the money to buy a new car? Or maybe go on a vacation? Move to a better town, even? Then again, would he even have the guts to capture the Kid? The answer was an emphatic *no*. But what about shooting him in the back if the opportunity presented itself? Yeah, that had potential. It was cowardly, certainly, but it was in the interests of the public. And the public would be eternally grateful for it. For that reason alone, he figured if he claimed the money, he wouldn't move to another town. No sense in being a local legend if you're not around to hear the applause.

He was taking a sip of black coffee from his favourite chipped white mug when, right on cue, Jacko, his annual visitor, arrived. Putting thoughts of becoming a local hero to the back of his mind, Joe reminded himself that the appearance of Jacko was about as exciting as his life was ever going to get.

As the newcomer pushed in through the door, the small bell above it chimed gently, announcing his arrival. He was a black guy in his mid to late twenties. And every year he came to the diner dressed as Michael Jackson from the days of the *Thriller* video. He wore a red leather jacket, matching red leather pants and a blue T-shirt. His black hair was short and held in a tight perm.

Every year Jacko spent the entire day in the diner chatting with Joe, drinking copious amounts of coffee and hoping to hitch a ride to the *Back From the Dead* singing contest at the Hotel Pasadena. Every year he failed miserably in his quest. Yet it never seemed to deter him, for, sure as eggs was eggs, he returned each Halloween to try his luck once again.

Joe watched him walk in and take a look around. Pretty soon their eyes met and both men smiled at each other. Jacko spoke first.

'Still here then, Joe?'

'Still here. You want your usual?'

'Yes siree.' He paused, shifting uncomfortably from foot to foot before adding, 'You know I don't got no money though, right?'

'I know.'

Joe's rickety wooden chair creaked loudly as he got up and headed back towards the counter at the back of the diner. On the wall behind it was a wooden shelf, set just below eye level. It held a row of white mugs identical to the one from which Joe had been drinking. He picked one out from the middle of the row and set it down on the counter. Then he picked up the coffee pot from a sideboard next to the kitchen doorway and began to fill the mug. By the time he had finished pouring Jacko had seated himself in Joe's chair. He was reading Joe's newspaper, too. The older man allowed himself a wry smile. *Same routine every year.*

'How's business?' Jacko called out, not looking up from the paper.

'Same as ever.'

'That's good to know.'

Joe made his way over to the table and placed the mug of coffee down in front of Jacko, just to the side of the newspaper. He stood over him, watching him reading the front page.

'Wadda ya think your chances are this year?' he asked.

'I feel *really* good about this year.'

'That good, huh? Well, I got five bucks says you don't get a ride again.'

Jacko finally looked up, to reveal a perfect smile, a smile full of optimism as well as bright white teeth, a smile the likes of which a young Michael Jackson would have been justly proud.

'You have such little faith, Joe. God will send someone my way this year. I can feel it.'

Joe shook his head. 'If God's sending anythin' this way, it's trouble, my friend. You get in a car with anyone round these parts and I'm pretty sure I won't be seein' you again next year.'

Jacko laughed. 'I dreamt it last night. I had a premonition that God is sending a man to grant me safe passage through these parts. It's my day of destiny.'

Joe sighed. Jacko was so full of shit. And he talked in a language wholly unlike anyone else from hereabouts. It did make him kind of endearing, though.

'Any idea who this guy is that God's sendin' for ya?'

'Not yet.'

'Any clues as to what he looks like?'

'Nope. None at all.'

Joe reached out a hand and ruffled Jacko's permed hair. Then he smiled. 'Fair enough. Breakfast'll be 'bout five minutes.'

'Thank you, sir,' said Jacko in a manner far too polite to be wasted on such an establishment as Sleepy Joe's Diner, for which the adjective 'shitty' might have been coined.

Its owner went out to the kitchen and started cooking Jacko's breakfast. He knew it by heart. Two slices of bacon, two sausages, two hash browns and an egg, sunny side up. Four slices of white toast were already buttered and ready to go.

Getting the makings from a battered old fridge, he set a pan on the stove and threw in a chunk of fat, followed by bacon slices and two fat sausages. After a while, he pulled a rusty metal spatula from a drawer beneath a sink opposite the grill and began flipping the sausages. The cold meat sizzled as it landed in the hot grease and the aroma of cooking food floated up to Joe's nostrils. When he sucked in the flavour he knew the day was fully under way. Feeling a sense of anticipation of all that was to follow, he called out to the dining area. 'Lotta strangers headed this way, y'know. An' accordin' to the paper one of 'em might be a serial killer. You ever heard of that Bourbon Kid fella? He drops by here, then I'm recommendin' you don't want a ride in his car.'

Jacko shouted back from the diner. 'I'll ride in anyone's car. I ain't fussy.'

'Guy's a killer, Jacko. Doubt very much he's a man of God.'

'Men of God come in many different guises.'

'They carry enough ammo to conquer Mexico?'

'They might.'

'Well then, maybe he's your man.'

There was a pause before Jacko called out again. 'Coffee's good, Joe.'

'Yeah. I know.'

The two of them exchanged idle chat for the next hour or so as Jacko ate his free breakfast and then sat around reading the newspapers while Joe sat on a stool behind the counter. He was on his third mug of burned coffee when a car finally pulled up outside. Joe had seen it drive past a little earlier at high speed. There was a signpost at a crossroads about half a mile down the road that gave directions to the Hotel Pasadena, but every year on Halloween the sign went missing, and any driver who passed by the diner invariably returned a few minutes later to ask for directions.

Joe knew the drill. He had to act confused if anyone came in wanting to know where the Hotel Pasadena was. This would ensure that Jacko could offer his services as a guide in exchange for the ride he so desperately wanted.

The car was a sleek black number with a long hood. From the size of the hood, it was a safe assumption that an extremely large and powerful engine lay beneath it. The engine roared pretty loud at idle, too. In fact, it roared in a manner that suggested the driver wanted the idling-speed revs kept deliberately high, rather than any suggestion that it was in need of a service. This was a powerful car, and no doubt the driver wanted people to know that. It was covered in sand and dust from what had almost certainly been a long journey across the desert. Being a cynical old bastard, Joe wasn't one to give any indication that cars impressed him. He had a shitty old pickup truck and resented anyone who owned anything better. Truth was, he would have paid the black car no attention at all if he could, but unfortunately for him, Jacko wanted to know a little about it.

'What kinda car is that, anyway?' Jacko asked him. Joe, pretending he hadn't noticed it, cast an exaggerated glance out of the dirt-covered window. He knew the model straight away.

'Pontiac Firebird,' he grunted.

'A what?'

'A Pontiac Firebird.' This time he elaborately stressed each syllable: 'Pon-tee-ack Fye-er-burd'.

'What's a Pontiac Firebird? I ain't never heard of it.'

'Bad guy's car.'

'Whadda ya . . . ?' Jacko cut his question short as the bell chimed, announcing that the driver of the car had entered the diner.

Joe knew straight away that his prediction was right. This *was* a bad guy. That much was obvious from the aura that surrounded him. The man had a powerful presence. Anyone within screaming distance would have picked up on it. Except maybe Jacko.

The stranger wore black combat pants that hung over a pair of well-worn black ankle boots, with a heavy black leather jacket, which, incongruously, had a dark hood hanging at the back of it. Underneath the jacket was a tight black T-shirt. His eyes were concealed behind a pair of dark polarized sunglasses with gunmetal frames, and his hair was thick, dark and lank – greasy even. It hung almost to his shoulders, but it hung in no sort of style. The guy looked effortlessly cool, like he slept in his clothes and didn't give a shit.

As he walked over to the counter, most likely with the intention of asking Joe for directions, he glanced over at Jacko and nodded in acknowledgement. There was no doubt about it; this was the guy in the photo on the front of the newspaper. Joe felt his palms sweat. *Was this a sign?* Only a short while earlier he had been considering what to do if he was ever faced with the serial killer from the newspaper report. And now, as if to test him, God had sent this very man his way. Joe thought about the one-hundred-thousand-dollar reward. Did he have the courage to carry out his plan and shoot down this wanted murderer if the chance presented itself? Without doubt, here was his once-in-a-lifetime opportunity to make some real money. While he was caught up in a trance, weighing up the risks of doing anything about claiming that money, the man spoke. His voice was gravelly in tone, with a unpleasant, even sinister element to it.

'You people round here not heard of road signs?' he asked.

Joe shrugged apologetically. 'Normally only local folk round these parts, mister. Don't need road signs.'

'I look local to you?'

'No, sir.'

Right on cue, from where he sat at the table to the man's left, Jacko grabbed his opportunity to butt in. 'I can give you directions, mister.'

The man turned, raised a finger to lower his sunglasses a little and peered over them at Jacko, looking him up and down.

'You don't look local.'

'I ain't. But I've been here before.'

'An' somehow you know where I'm headed?' The voice rasped, like small stones shifting on a blighted river bed.

Jacko grinned. 'Hotel Pasadena, I reckon. If I could hitch a ride with you, I could point you in the right direction.'

'Why'n't you just point?'

Joe felt edgy on Jacko's behalf. Had he not realized that this guy was a serial killer – and not, therefore, the kind of guy you jump in a car with?

'Well, I'm headed to the Pasadena myself,' said Jacko cheerily. 'So in exchange for the directions, I could really use a ride.'

'Just point.'

'Well, you see I ain't never exactly sure 'til I see the roads. I wouldn't wanna give you the wrong directions, y'know?'

'No. You definitely wouldn't wanna do that.'

'So, okay for a ride then?'

The man pushed his sunglasses up half an inch, concealing his eyes again. He seemed to be taking a long, hard look into Jacko's eyes. As he was doing so, Joe made a choice.

A hundred grand reward was too good to turn down.

Slowly, without any obvious movements, he reached for a small wooden drawer at waist height beneath the counter. He kept a small nickel-plated revolver in there in case of trouble. All he had to do was pull it out and shoot this new customer in the back while Jacko had him distracted. *A hundred grand in the bank.* Nice work. Thank you very much. With a steady hand that belied his advancing years, he inched the drawer open and reached his hand inside. His fingers touched the cold metal of the revolver. His heart pounded against his chest, but *he had time.* The guy at the counter was still looking the other way, apparently mulling over Jacko's request for a ride. Eventually, just as Joe got a solid grip on the butt of his pistol, the stranger responded to Jacko's suggestion.

'Okay, you can have a ride. But get me two bottles of bourbon from behind the counter.'

Joe watched Jacko grimace as he stood up from his chair. 'Er, I don't, like, have any money.'

The man sighed, then slipped his right hand inside the left side of his black leather jacket. From it he drew out a heavy grey pistol. Turning back to face the counter, he extended his arm and pointed the gun at Joe's throat. Joe's eyes bulged, but he pulled his own weapon from the drawer as quickly as he could and aimed it at the guy in black.

What followed was a loud bang that would have been heard for miles around. The white mugs on the shelf behind Joe's head were suddenly splattered scarlet with the blood that spouted from a gaping hole in the back of his neck.

The day's killing was well under way.

Three

Sanchez hated bus rides. Truth be told, he wasn't a big fan of any kind of travel, but a seemingly never-ending bus ride with no apparent destination was near the top of the list of things he never wanted to do. Only drinking his own piss topped it. This particular bus trip had followed a three-hour flight. He wasn't a fan of flying, either. Fact was, he wouldn't have been there at all if he hadn't won a mystery two-week vacation, all expenses paid.

Sanchez was renowned as a tightwad in his home town of Santa Mondega, so it had come as no surprise to anyone that he'd taken advantage of the free first-class flight and accommodation in a mystery five-star hotel somewhere in North America. For all he knew he could be headed to Detroit (or some equally terrifying place), but he didn't much care. It was simply a relief that the trip had taken him out of Santa Mondega on Halloween, a night when the place tended to be even more evil than usual. Which was saying something.

It had happened because, a while back, he'd filled in a survey for an online dating agency, which had offered the vacation as a prize for the most eligible single person in each town of his region. Yet somehow, to Sanchez's dismay, there had been a tie for most eligible singleton in Santa Mondega. Annoyingly, the other winner had been seated next to him on the plane, and was now in the seat beside him on the bus. And it was someone who got right on his nerves, bigtime.

Annabel de Frugyn, or 'the Mystic Lady', as she preferred

to be known, was the local fruitcake. She was a fortune-teller by trade, and an abysmal one at that – in Sanchez's opinion, at least. Within a minute of taking off she'd predicted that they would crash into a mountain. Then she'd pointed out a couple of potential terrorists sitting a few rows in front. They had overheard her, and from then on Sanchez had been convinced that they had it in for him simply because he was sitting next to her. The only thing she had foreseen correctly was that they would be seated next to each other on the bus as well as the plane. And now she was predicting something that Sanchez found even more terrifying.

'The spirits are telling me that you and I are going to end up spending a lot of time together over the next few days,' she said jovially. She was smiling her hideous gap-toothed smile and there was an unnerving twinkle in her eye.

For fuck's sake, thought Sanchez. *She's at least sixty. And a total dog.* She was indeed sixty, exactly twice his age. Not at all the kind of female company he had been hoping for on his free vacation.

There wasn't an empty seat on the bus, and it was noticeable that there were no couples. Everyone on board appeared to have won his or her ticket through participation in the same survey that Sanchez had taken. So, crammed into the seats were fifty-five single people, none of whom seemed to be under the age of twenty-five. Without doubt, though, the oldest and ugliest was the Mystic Lady, sitting next to Sanchez.

I gotta ditch her early on, he thought. If he wasn't careful, people might start to think he liked her, and that could potentially ruin his chances with any of the other women on the bus, all of whom he considered to be candidates for his irresistible charms. In particular, there was an attractive Portuguese woman two seats in front on the other side of the bus. Either she'd been checking him out for most of the journey, or she had a lazy eye. Either way, he wasn't bothered;

she was definitely a better proposition than the old hag next to him.

Time to head any misunderstandings off at the pass, Sanchez reckoned, and with that in mind he turned to his companion. 'Guess you know what these mystery trips are like, Annabel,' he said, his voice almost drooling with insincerity. 'We'll probably get separated early on and not see each other again until the journey home. If at all.'

'Nonsense,' Annabel laughed, slapping him on the thigh. 'Since we don't know anyone else, we must stick together. So much nicer to be with someone you know when you're in a strange place, isn't it?' Her hand remained on his thigh. He was wearing a pair of brown knee-length shorts in one of the cheaper synthetic fibres, and they'd been creeping up his ass somewhat during the journey, so her hand was perilously close to touching flesh.

The letter accompanying his winning ticket had suggested that he dress for warm weather, so above the shorts Sanchez was wearing a red short-sleeved Hawaiian shirt. As a precaution he had a brown suede jacket on top of it, but judging from the weather they'd encountered so far he wouldn't need it. Although the first thing to discard would be Annabel. Forcing a polite smile, he responded to her enthusiastic rambling through gritted teeth.

'Oh, yeah, sure. Of course. Trouble is, I get lost real easy when I'm away from home. Seriously. One minute I'm right there, next thing you know, you've turned your back for a second and I'm nowhere to be seen.'

'Well, I'll just have to make sure I don't let you out of my sight then, won't I? Don't worry, honey – I'll make sure you don't get lost.' Once again, Sanchez felt her hand squeeze his thigh, and inwardly shuddered. Unlike him, she hadn't heeded the advice about the warm weather, and had swaddled herself in a long black dress beneath two cardigans. One of these was dark blue and worn underneath a hideous flea-infested dark green one. Much of her long grey hair hung down over the front of these fetching garments, no doubt acting as a ladder for fleas to climb up and down from head to clothes. Sanchez would have swatted her hand away from his thigh, but the sight of her yellow fingernails and wrinkly hands repelled him. They would, he thought, have shamed a leper. Fortunately, after an inappropriately long time, she removed her hand herself and pointed through the window at something ahead, close to the road's edge.

'Oh look,' she said excitedly. 'There's a road sign. See what it says.'

They had been on the bus for two hours. On their arrival at an airport named Goodman's Field, Sanchez had been surprised to find that there were no tour guides; in fact no one to tell them where they were headed. He'd asked around, but none of the other passengers was any the wiser. Even the Mystic Lady, with her dubious talent for seeing into the future, had no idea. And everyone was complaining that there was no signal for their cell phones. So a signpost truly was worth a look.

Since leaving the airport, they had been driven along a deserted highway through an arid and almost featureless desert. The bus driver had spoken to no one and refused to acknowledge, let alone answer, any questions concerning their destination. Rude indeed, but he was a big bastard so no one was inclined to make an issue of it. And up to this point in the journey there hadn't been a single signpost to tell them where the fuck they were.

As the roadside billboard drew closer, Sanchez peered through the window to see what it said. The sign stood out in front of the miles of desert wasteland, framed by a distant vista of orange-coloured mesas and cliffs. It was a big black sign at least ten feet high and twenty feet wide. Five words painted in a dark red colour across became visible as they neared. The sign read 'WELCOME TO THE DEVIL'S GRAVEYARD'.

'Nice,' Sanchez thought out loud. 'Ain't exactly the fuckin' Bahamas, is it?' Annabel, certainly more excited than him, showed it by squeezing his thigh playfully again with one hand and slapping her own thigh with the other.

'Aren't you just thrilled?' she asked. 'I haven't been out of Santa Mondega for years. Isn't this fun? Boy, I could use a drink to calm my nerves.'

Sanchez sighed, then reached inside his jacket. He pulled out a small silver hip flask.

'Here,' he offered glumly, unscrewing the stopper and handing the flask over to Annabel.

'Oh my! What's this then?' she asked, her eyes lighting up with alcoholic glee at the possibility of some liquor.

'It's my own homebrew. Been saving it for a special occasion.'

'Oh Sanchez, you are such a gentleman.'

'Don't mention it.'

Annabel took the flask and poured a mouthful down her throat. A second or two later she began choking. She pulled a hideous face (even by her standards).

'*Ugh!* That's *horrible*! What on earth is it?' she asked, retching.

'It's kinda an acquired taste. You gotta persevere with it. By the time we get where we're goin' you'll be addicted to it.'

The Mystic Lady didn't look convinced. Within ten minutes of her first sip of Sanchez's finest, she had locked herself in the confined space of the bus's lone restroom. Her alleged ability to predict the future had not helped her to foresee that Sanchez might serve up a flask full of his own piss.

Even more importantly, she hadn't foreseen the evil that lay ahead for their brief stay in the Devil's Graveyard. A place with an even greater undead problem than Santa Mondega.

Four

In almost the same second, the Bourbon Kid tucked the pistol back inside his leather jacket, sliding it into a snug holster below his left shoulder. As if in slow motion, Joe's still-vertical body began to sway. It was a sequence of events all too familiar to the Kid – the victim's knees were about to buckle beneath him. Right on cue, after a count of three, the body wobbled a bit, then crumpled in on itself and fell to the floor like a rag doll. The old man's face crashed into the hardwood counter on the way down. All that was left on display was his blood. An elegant spray of it speckled the long row of white mugs on the shelf behind the counter, while a few errant drops splattered a selection of candy bars by the till. *A work of art indeed*. If the Kid chose to add a signature to the piece, it could be worth a fortune.

To his left, the Kid had seen the customer in the red leather suit jump to his feet in shock at what had just happened. The guy said nothing. Instead, he walked slowly over to the counter to take a look at the dead body of the diner's owner. Normally people tended to exit pretty quickly once the Kid started blowing people away, but this guy seemed to have forgotten that the killer was still present. The Kid watched him lean over the counter and wince at the sight of Joe's corpse. After a few seconds of staring at the body of his friend, the guy suddenly seemed to remember that the Kid was there. As was his gun. Slowly he turned to face him. The Kid waited for his reaction. More importantly, he waited for the guy to go fetch the bottles of bourbon the Kid had asked him for shortly before shooting Joe in the throat.

'You killed him,' the guy said, stating the obvious.

'You think?'

'Why would you do that? Joe's a good guy.'

'Was.'

'Huh?'

'*Was* a good guy. *Now* he's a dead good guy.'

'He didn't do anything to you.'

'He pulled a gun on me, case you didn't notice.'

'You pulled *yours* first!'

'Wanna see me do it again?'

'Not really.'

'What's your name, son?'

'Jacko.'

'Right. Jacko, you listen up, and listen good. If you ain't grabbed me the two bottles of bourbon I asked for by the time I count to three, my gun's comin' out again.'

Jacko nodded. 'Yeah. I gotcha.' He walked tentatively around the counter checking the floor, mostly to make sure he didn't tread in any blood. 'Bourbon, huh?' he mumbled.

'That's right.'

'Comin' right up.'

'Get me some cigarettes, too.'

'What kind?'

'Any kind.'

The Kid picked up a Texan chocolate bar from the display on the counter. With his forefinger, he flicked a piece of what might have been bloodied gristle off the wrapper and then ripped the bar open at one end. He took a bite and, deciding that the taste was acceptable, left Jacko to pick up the rest of his shopping list and headed back out to the car.

The Kid had strong instincts when it came to sniffing out danger. They had served him well when, from the corner of his eye, he had seen Joe reach below the counter for something. It could have been a doughnut, but there was an outside chance it was a weapon of some kind. As it turned out he'd been right, so the bullet he'd used to blow the old guy's throat out hadn't been wasted. Now those same instincts were telling him that an evil moon was coming. That wasn't much of a surprise on Halloween. He'd learned that the hard way. He'd killed for the first time on Halloween, a decade earlier. Since then, he'd killed hundreds of people – some had deserved it, and some hadn't – but not one of those killings had been as hard as the first.

Dispatching his mother with six rounds to the heart at the age of sixteen was never going to be anything other than traumatic. Even though she had been bitten by a vampire and had turned into one in front of his very eyes. True, it was only when she had attempted to kill *him* that he had realized that he had no choice but to kill her. But, unsurprisingly, it had been a defining moment in his life. One intertwined with drinking his first bottle of bourbon.

And now? Well, here he was on Halloween, ten years later, in an area of the desert known as the Devil's Graveyard, about to give a ride to a hitchhiker dressed as one of the cast of the *Thriller* video. And he was down to his last two bullets. He still had plenty of weapons, just no ammo for the guns, having used his last 12-gauge shell on the rookie cop in the fast cruiser. His own fault for killing so many other people earlier in the day. Could just be a tough day ahead. He toyed briefly with the idea of taking Joe's gun and whatever ammo he could find, but discarded it. He didn't like small-calibre pistols at the best of times, and that one had looked like the definitive Saturday-night special, accurate only to about six feet and as liable to blow up in your hand as to take down a target.

The Firebird's seat was still warm when he sat back in it and peered out through the dirt-covered windshield. The wipers had cleared enough of the muck away so that he could see where he was going, but the areas of the windshield outside of the range of the wipers were caked in sand, dirt and mud. Undeniably, the chase through the desert had taken its toll, but the car hadn't let him down. It never did. The custom-built engine was not only powerful enough to outrun most other road vehicles, it was also very dependable.

He turned the key and fired up the engine. As he did so, Jacko came out of the diner carrying a few bottles he had snagged from behind the counter. The Kid leaned over and part-opened the passenger-side door. His new travelling companion climbed in and placed two bottles of Sam Cougar and two bottles of Shitting Monkey beer on the floor by his feet. Pulling the door shut, he opened the glove-box in front of him and tossed two packs of cigarettes in before closing it again. The Kid was impressed. Not many people had the guts to get into his car. Not willingly, at least. And to do so after he had just seen the Kid gun down an old man in cold blood – well, that took some nerve. Jacko did look like a total jerk in his red leather outfit, though.

The Kid stared at Jacko from behind his sunglasses, waiting for him to offer up some directions to the Hotel Pasadena. Instead, the Michael Jackson wannabe started with some questions of his own.

'Reckon you're the Bourbon Kid, ain'tcha?'

'What gave it away?'

'I have a real sixth sense for these things.'

'Good. Your sixth sense had better be workin' real good from here on, too. 'Cause, make no mistake, we take one wrong turn, I'll kill you.'

'Okay. When you get to the crossroads up ahead, take a right.'

The Kid released the parking brake and slammed his foot down on the gas pedal. The car raced away from Sleepy Joe's and back on to the highway. The wheel-spin from the screeching rear tyres created an almighty kick-up of sand and dust. By the time it had settled, the diner-cum-gas station was long out of sight.

At a crossroads half a mile down the road, the Kid slid the Firebird into a right turn as Jacko had instructed. The car was half-covered in dirt already from the journey thus far, and this particular shitty concrete road, with its gravelly surface and frequent potholes, wasn't going to improve things any time soon.

'So whatcha doin' round these parts anyway?' Jacko asked.

'Mindin' my own fuckin' business. It strike you that you should do the same?'

From his response it shouldn't have been difficult to work out that the Kid didn't have much use for small talk. Jacko, however, seemed oblivious to this.

'I'm hopin' to enter that singing contest at the hotel, he continued. 'Y'know, the *Back From the Dead* show?'

The Kid didn't respond or even take his eyes off the road ahead. Jacko carried on regardless. 'Y'see, I'm a Michael Jackson impersonator.'

The Kid took a deep breath through his nostrils, held it for a few moments then breathed out slowly. He was trying to keep himself calm, something that he often struggled with, never more so than on Halloween. At last he took his eyes off the road and glanced over at Jacko. His words, when he finally spoke, were surprisingly reasonable.

'Seein' as how he's dead, there's gonna be thousands of Michael Jackson impersonators at this show. All tryin' to cash in on his fame. Why'n't you just be yourself?'

'You gotta be impersonatin' a famous dead singer. And in case you ain't noticed, I ain't dead . . . or famous.'

'I can make you both of those things.' The gravelly edge had returned to the other's voice.

Jacko raised an eyebrow. 'Guess you don't really mix too well with others, do you?'

'Got no need to.'

'Yeah? Well, you're gonna meet lots of people like me at this hotel, and they tend to be friendly sorts. You might wanna brush up on your social skills.'

There was a profound silence. Even the Firebird seemed to hold its breath, until the Kid grated, 'And you might wanna practise keepin' your mouth shut.'

'I would,' Jacko replied happily, 'but I need to be tunin' up my voice.'

'Not in my car you don't.'

'Aw, come on, I gotta practise. I'm gonna sing "Earth Song" for my audition in the show. Wanna hear it?'

The Kid tightened his grip on the steering wheel. 'You sing so much as one word a that song, I'll make sure the screamin' part in the chorus goes on for a long long time.'

'I see. I could do "Smooth Criminal" if you prefer?'

The Kid hit the brakes. Tyres smoking and squealing, the Firebird fishtailed to a halt. 'Get out,' its driver rasped.

Even Jacko could see he meant it.

'But there's a couple more turns still to take from here,' he protested. 'You could get lost without me.'

The Kid took some more deep breaths as he deliberated on whether or not to pull out a weapon and kill his travelling companion. Eventually he decided, Yeah, the guy deserved to die, but what to kill him with? Bare hands? A blade? Or a beating over the head with a gun butt? As he was reaching inside his jacket for his pistol, his passenger made a wise decision.

'Let's not talk any more. I'll just give directions. How's that?'

'You'll live longer.'

'Cool.'

The Kid put his foot down on the accelerator and the car sped off again down the dusty highway, kicking up another cloud of dust, sand and smoke behind as it went.

'There's a fork in the road 'bout two miles from here,' said Jacko. 'You wanna kinda hang a right when you get to it.'

They carried on down the highway for another couple of minutes until the fork in the road came into view. The Kid did as suggested and headed off down the road on the right. The peace and quiet in the car suited him just fine, but he could sense that his passenger was finding the silence uncomfortable. The knowledge that this imbecile might start jabbering again was enough in itself to irk him. Eventually, just as the Kid expected, Jacko spoke again.

'You gotta radio in this car?'

'Can't get no tee-vee or radio or cell-phone signals in this shithole desert. Place is totally cut off. Just how I like it.'

'Well, I could whistle some tunes. Y'know, keep us entertained for the rest of the journey.'

'Not with a broken neck you couldn't.'

Jacko opened his mouth as though about to respond, but, suffering a sudden attack of common sense, decided against it. The two men didn't speak for the rest of the journey, other than one last direction Jacko offered when he advised the Kid to turn left at a T-junction. Half an hour's silence later, the black Pontiac Firebird pulled into the long concrete driveway that led from the road up to the Hotel Pasadena. There were surprisingly few other cars around as he cruised up to the front of the hotel. A young valet with thick dark hair greeted them at the foot of the steps that led up to reception. People were busily hurrying back and forth outside, and there were a lot of rich-looking people visible in the foyer through the glass double doors at the hotel entrance.

As the car came to a stop right outside the front of the hotel, the valet approached. He was in his early twenties, and his uniform consisted of a white shirt with a red vest and black pants. The Kid looked over at Jacko, who was reaching for the door handle to get out of the car.

'You. Stay in the car. Make sure the valet doesn't crash into anything.'

Jacko nodded. 'Okay.'

'And hand me a pack of cigarettes.'

Jacko reached into the glove box and pulled out one of the packs of cigarettes he had tossed in there earlier. He threw it over to the Kid who caught it and tucked it into an inside pocket of his jacket. As he opened the driver's side door, he issued one last instruction to his passenger. 'When the valet's finished parking the car, make sure you squeeze his knee.'

''Scuse me?'

'Squeeze his knee, just once. It's a custom in this place. You don't do it, they get really offended.'

Jacko looked baffled. 'Jeez, thanks. I had no idea.'

'Sure.' The Kid stepped out of the car and pulled a hundred-dollar bill from his hip pocket. He slipped it into the valet's right hand. The young Latino's face lit up.

'Say, thanks, mister.'

The Kid nodded at Jacko in the passenger seat. 'See him?' he asked.

The valet peered into the car and saw Jacko with his tightly permed black hair and his red leather suit, grinning back at him. 'Yeah. I see him all right.' He sounded wary.

'He touches your knee, punch him in the goddam face.'

As he walked up the steps to the hotel's front entrance, the Kid had a feeling he would see Jacko again before the day was through. His instincts were telling him that there was something about the Michael Jackson impersonator that wasn't quite right.

He just hadn't figured out what it was yet.

Five

The Hotel Pasadena was as impressive up close as it had looked from afar. The desert sun glinted from the many windows on the forty-storey building, giving the impression from a distance that they were approaching a giant mirror. The closer the bus got to it the more magnificent it looked. The bus took a right turn off the highway through a sturdy set of solid iron arched gates set into a white concrete wall that ran along the perimeter of the hotel's grounds. There was a sign across the top of the gateway with a name in bright red metallic lettering.

HOTEL PASADENA

No shit, thought Sanchez.

A smooth concrete driveway almost a quarter-mile long led up to the front of the hotel. As the bus headed round to the back, Sanchez stared open-mouthed at the sheer magnificence of the place. Maybe this wasn't such a bad deal after all. In Santa Mondega there wasn't a single building that could even come close to matching it. The local museum was impressive, but looked old and decrepit in comparison to this brash beast of a building.

The bus parked up at the rear of what was already an extremely busy parking lot, in contrast to the marked lack of cars at the front. After grabbing his luggage from the trunk of the bus, Sanchez headed quickly (by his standards) round to the lobby at the front of the hotel before Annabel the Mystic Lady could latch on to him. Four wide white marble steps led up to a set of large glass double doors. Sanchez took them two at a time before darting through the automatic doors, which parted for him as he reached the top step.

The lobby was vast, too. The ceiling was almost forty feet high, and at its centre hung a magnificent chandelier, light gleaming from its thousands of cut-glass pieces. The floor was made up from polished squares of alternating grey and black marble, and made Sanchez feel that he should remove his shoes to avoid scuffing it.

But, boy, was it busy. Half the free world appeared to have just checked in. Everywhere there were people with suitcases, making all kinds of noise. Sanchez wasn't overly fond of other people at the best of times, and after a long journey spent sitting next to someone whom, in his more charitable moments, he considered to be a demented old crone, meant that he was feeling particularly intolerant. The constant bustle before him made his heart sink. About a hundred people were milling back and forth around him in the lobby. It was plenty big enough to accommodate everyone, but its circular shape meant that every sound bounced off the creamy white walls and straight into Sanchez's ears.

Fortunately, Sanchez saw, there were plenty of porters, busboys and receptionists to deal with the guests as they all jostled for attention. Which was just as well, since checking in was one of his least favourite activities in life. It ranked right up there with having his thigh squeezed by a repugnant old fortune teller.

He quickly realized that to waste time gawping at the sheer size and opulence of the place would likely cost him his chance of being served quickly. Already a few people had darted past him towards the reception desk. Seeing this, Sanchez shifted up a gear and headed for one of the six female receptionists. They were sitting in a row behind the chest-high oak desk, each with a monitor on in front of her. Five of them were already busy, but fortunately the best-looking one seemed still to be free.

Sanchez scuttled over to her and set his large brown suitcase down on the floor. Grinning like a fool, he peered over the desk at her. A quick glance down the line at the others confirmed he had struck gold. Undoubtedly he'd picked the best-looking one. This was only fair, of course. A man of his distinction and sophistication shouldn't have to waste his charms on just anyone. She was a petite young woman in her early twenties with long dark hair scraped back into a ponytail that had been brought forward to hang down over her left shoulder. Like each of the other receptionists, she wore a smart vest in some shiny red cloth, with a pristine white blouse underneath. The vest had a gold emblem sewn on to the left breast. Staring at it for an inappropriately long time, Sanchez worked out that it was some kind of a fork. *Odd choice for an emblem,* he thought. *But hell, there ain't no accountin' for taste.*

'Can I help you, sir?' the receptionist asked, in an accent that betrayed her origins in the Deep South.

'Sure. Sanchez Garcia. I won this competition.' Sanchez fumbled around in the inside pocket of his brown suede jacket for a few seconds, before finally pulling out the now somewhat tatty letter confirming he had won a stay at the hotel hosting the rather exciting sounding *Back From the Dead* singing contest. He handed it over to the receptionist who took a look at it and began tapping away on a keyboard in front of her. As he waited for her to confirm his stay and offer him his room key, he heard the voice of Annabel de Frugyn behind him. He prayed she wouldn't spot him and come hovering round, giving the receptionist the false impression that they were together.

'Ah, there you are, Sanchez, I thought I'd lost you.' There was a horrible cooing tone to her voice, somehow.

Fuck! He turned round and saw the ludicrously badly dressed, silver-haired old witch standing behind him with a luggage cart on which her three suitcases had been piled.

'Yeah. We seemed to get split up back there,' he said. 'Figured I'd look for you here.'

'Well I'm here now.' She smiled, in what she fondly imagined was a coquettish manner. Fondly, but inaccurately; the effect was, in fact, nothing short of grotesque.

'Maybe we should split up again? I was enjoyin' the thrill of lookin' for you everywhere.'

Annabel gave him a playful shove in the back and rolled her eyes at him.

'Why, Sanchez! You're such a tease.'

The receptionist next to the girl serving Sanchez had just finished with her latest customer and called over to Annabel, 'Can I help you, ma'am?'

'Yes. You surely can, young lady. Annabel de Frugyn. I won this competition.'

Sanchez, relieved to see Annabel head over to the other receptionist, turned his attentions back to the young woman dealing with his arrival. She was regarding him with an apologetic 'I'm sorry, sir' look on her face. A look Sanchez had seen far too many times in his life, especially from pretty girls. Something was wrong. He could sense it.

'I'm sorry, Mister Garcia,' she said, 'but we seem to have no record of you on our computer.'

'*What*?'

'For some reason we don't have a room reserved for you. Your letter is definitely valid, but we don't actually have a room booked in your name.'

'But you have spare rooms, right?'

'I'm afraid not, sir. The hotel is fully booked.'

Sanchez could feel himself grinding his teeth. 'So what the fuck am I supposed to do? This is the only fuckin' hotel around.'

'Sir, could you please refrain from swearing?'

'If you can refrain from being an unhelpful bitch.' His

voice was rising, too, in both pitch and volume.

A hush descended upon the lobby as it became evident that there was a dispute in progress, one with every chance of escalating. To add to Sanchez's discomfort, Annabel leaned over from her place at the desk next to him and whispered in his ear.

'You can always share my room with me, if you want?'

'Bite me,' he snarled back.

The receptionist cleared her throat. 'I'm afraid that will be your only option.' She paused before drawling an insolent 'sir.'

Sanchez sighed and ran his left hand through his greasy dark hair, squeezing a clump of it tightly as if he was about to pull it out. 'Oh for fuck's sake. This just ain't happening.'

Just when it appeared that all was lost and that he was going to be forced to agree to share a room with an elderly fortune-telling sex pest, a voice he recognized spoke out from behind him.

'Yo, Stephie. Guy's a good friend a mine. Get him a room.'

Sanchez's eyes lit up and he released his grip on his hair. He turned, and was overjoyed to see the coolest guy he knew. Coolest guy on the planet. It was Santa Mondega's most feared hitman, Elvis. Whether or not Elvis was his real name was unknown, but he travelled by that name and dressed accordingly at all times. Today he was wearing a sharp, bright gold suit jacket with black pants and a black shirt that was buttoned up only about halfway. As always he was wearing his trademark supercool gold-rimmed shades, and had his thick, dark hair slicked up and back from his forehead, Presley-style.

Sanchez loved this guy, and was always pleased to see him. Which, given that Sanchez was almost never pleased to see anyone, was a pretty big social advance for the Tapioca's owner. Elvis had a knack for showing up at just the right time, too. One notable incident, exactly ten years earlier, had seen Elvis arrive in time to gun down a gang of vampires that had swooped on Sanchez and a bunch of other innocent folk during a church service. The King had been booked to perform a song-and-dance routine for the churchgoers, but when the vampires had started terrorizing the congregation, he'd begun swivelling his hips and pointing his guitar at them, firing silver darts into their black hearts from the end of it. All while singing James Taylor's 'Steamroller Blues'. So it was understandable that Sanchez now greeted the King with a beaming smile.

'Hey, Elvis. Like, whatcha doin' here?'

'Here for the *Back From the Dead* competition, man.'

'You're singin' in it?'

'You bet your ass I am. Million-dollar first prize, ain't it? Couldn't pass up the opportunity, now could I?'

'Cool,' said Sanchez. His vacation was picking up at last. 'So, can ya get me a room here? Some shit 'bout how I ain't on the goddam computer.'

'Sure. Stephie will sort it out, won'tcha, Steph?'

The pretty receptionist didn't look overly enthused about the idea. On the other hand, the look in her eye suggested that she was quite smitten by Elvis. The guy had a way with women. They just seemed to melt when he looked at them. And he had virtually hypnotic powers for getting them to do things to please him. A skill in which Sanchez was severely lacking.

'He just called me a bitch,' she pointed out, nodding sulkily at Sanchez.

Elvis pursed his lips. '*What?* Sanchez, you didn't call her a bitch, didja?'

'Uh – I guess I may have.'

Elvis slapped Sanchez across the back of the head. 'Well, ya'd better dam' well apologize, an' if you're lucky Stephie might just find ya a room.'

Sanchez ventured what he thought was an apologetic smile at the receptionist. The effect was of a corpse suddenly grimacing. 'I'm sorry I called you a bitch,' he offered in a surly mumble.

Stephie faked a smile back. 'Don't mention it. Okay, there is one room. A guy called Claude Balls was due yesterday, but he hasn't shown up yet. You can have that one.'

'Uh, thanks. Thank you very much.' Aware that he had just been reprieved from a night with Annabel de Frugyn, his gratitude was at least sincere.

While Stephie began completing the paperwork and locating a room key for him, Sanchez turned back to his friend. 'Thanks, Elvis. Really appreciate it.'

'Don' worry about it.'

'Well, I'm definitely in your corner for the singin' contest. What time are you onstage?'

Elvis appeared not to hear him. 'Hold up. See that guy?' he said, pointing at a man in his early forties, wearing a white suit. 'That's the hotel owner, Nigel Powell. Chief judge in the competition. An' a multi-millionaire, too.'

Powell strode confidently over towards the reception desk, with two heavily built security guards following closely behind. Beneath his bright white suit jacket, he wore a black T-shirt, which succeeded in giving off the rather outdated *Don Johnson, Miami Vice* look. He had slicked-back black hair, improbably white and even teeth, and a fake orange tan that positively glowed against his white suit. The two security guards wore identical black suits with black T-shirts beneath. Both had short military flat-top haircuts, and both looked to be the kind that follows orders without question. Everyone in the lobby watched in a kind of awe as the trio made their way up to the second desk at reception and came to a stop behind Annabel.

'Miss de Frugyn?' Powell asked politely, his voice, deep and resonant.

Annabel's body language suggested that she thought she'd been caught checking in with a stolen credit card (which was not altogether unlikely). She turned slowly to face the manager and his two heavies.

'Yes,' she trilled nervously. 'Can I help you?'

'Miss de Frugyn, my name is Nigel Powell. I have the honour to be the owner and manager of this hotel. Might I have a word with you?'

'Why – certainly.' Her body language spoke now of the startled jackrabbit.

Reaching out, Powell took a hold of Annabel's hand and politely shook it. 'My colleagues here will take your things to your room for you. Please, come this way.'

Sanchez and Elvis watched as the multi-millionaire led Annabel away through a set of glass double doors on the right-hand side of the circular lobby. Although they didn't know it, he was taking her to a private area of the hotel.

'Was that the Mystic Lady?' Elvis asked Sanchez.

'Yeah. Been sat next to her on the plane and the goddam bus. Fuckin' useless annoyin' old hag,' Sanchez muttered.

'Hear she's kinda good at foreseein' shit.'

'Nope. She's kinda good at talkin' shit.'

'No, man. I reckon she could probably predict who's gonna win this show.'

'You sure got high hopes,' said Sanchez sarcastically.

Elvis smiled. 'You like a gamble, don'tcha, Sanchez?'

'Yeah.'

'Well, there's more'n just the singin' contest goin' on this weekend. They also gotta casino on the lower ground floor here. Reckon ol' Mystic could be a useful friend to have in a place like that.'

Sanchez contemplated what the legendary hitman was saying. The Mystic Lady might actually be a useful ally in a casino. Except that, if the management knew of her alleged skills, they might not want her around.

Maybe that's why she had been escorted elsewhere by the owner?

Six

Emily was not overly thrilled at having to share a dressing room with four men. Still, she kept reminding herself that it was only for one day, and the possible reward at the end of it would be life-changing.

She was one of the five singers Nigel Powell, chief judge of the *Back From the Dead* singing contest had pre-selected as finalists. Emily was a little uncomfortable that the public auditions hadn't taken place yet, and that all of the other hopefuls who were now showing up at the hotel remained oblivious to the fact that the five finalists had already been chosen. But then she remembered every dive bar she'd ever had to perform in, the years of struggle, what this meant to her and to her mother. For the reality was this: they were the five finalists because they were the best tribute acts on the club circuit. So what if the show was rigged? Wasn't everything nowadays? That, at least, was what she kept telling herself, anyway.

Besides, it wasn't as if she'd won yet. She still had to beat the other four.

The five contestants sat in a row at individual dressing tables, each with its own mirror lit by small bulbs around the top and both sides. The dressing room was fairly poky, being about thirty feet long but only about eight feet wide. The walls were a calming pink colour, as were the tables. Emily's was the only one that had any make-up on it. She had spent some time making sure she looked exactly how she wanted, whereas the guys had mostly sat around scratching themselves. Typical.

The four guys were all sitting at the tables to Emily's left. Nearest to her was the Otis Redding impersonator. Aside from being black, he didn't really look much like the late singer at all, but he had a magnificent voice, and was wearing what looked like an extremely expensive black suit with a red silk shirt beneath it. He was, Emily thought, liable to be quite a threat in the final.

Next to him was Kurt Cobain. He not only looked very much like the real Cobain, he potentially smelled a lot like him, too. He had on a grubby grey pullover and ripped jeans. His hair was blond and greasy, the lower half of his face was covered in two-day-old stubble and, to round off the grungy image, he appeared to have avoided soap for a few weeks. Maybe he was trying to smell like teen spirit. The resulting stink was more like teen jockstrap.

To his left sat Johnny Cash. Emily had figured out early on that this guy was taking things very seriously. He had changed his name legally to Johnny Cash, and did his best to live his life exactly as the much lamented singer had done. On his tribute tour, he'd played in almost all the same venues as his idol. His outfit consisted – to no one's surprise – of a black shirt and black pants, and his black hair was greased up in a quiff. Without a doubt he had the most charisma of all the male contestants, and Emily had already decided that if she didn't win the competition, then she would rather he won it than any of the others. But she really didn't want to lose.

The final contestant, sitting at the far end nearest the door, was the James Brown impersonator. Unquestionably an oddball, he wore a purple suit with a blue shirt, mostly unbuttoned, underneath it, showing off a smooth brown chest and a chunky gold cross that hung from a chain around his neck. A permanent white smile beamed brightly across his face, and he sported the same wavy, unstyled hair that the Godfather of Soul had worn in his later years.

It was deathly quiet in the dressing room. Only the sound of Kurt Cobain's nasal breathing broke the monotony. Emily decided to break the ice.

'Does my hair look okay, do you think?' she asked Otis Redding.

His response was instant. 'Oh yeah, baby, you look fine,' he said, with a reassuring nod. Johnny Cash, who had been busy preening his own hair in the brightly lit mirror before him, leaned round to get a look at Emily's hair.

'He's right. You look right on the money,' he said with a smile and a wink.

'Thanks,' said Emily, smiling back at him. Encouraged by their friendliness, she said, 'Guess I'm starting to get seriously nervous now. How's everyone else doing?'

Relieved that the silence had been broken, the four men spoke almost together. The general consensus was that they were indeed all nervous. James Brown summed it up perfectly. 'Reckon I'd be less nervous if I didn't know I was already through to the final,' he said standing up from his chair. 'Now we got all this pressure of knowin' that, even if we suck in the heats we're still gonna be put through by the judges, an' everyone will know that the show is rigged.'

Emily nodded vigorously in agreement. 'Definitely. I barely slept last night, worrying about fluffing the audition stage. Seems to me there'll be less pressure in the final.'

Johnny Cash spoke again. 'Yeah. Truth is, though, I'd sooner earn my place in the final legitimately. This feels like cheating really, don't it? Whyn't they just allow us to try an' get through on our own merits?'

Otis Redding was the only one to reply. ''Cause it's only a one-day competition.'

'Yeah? An' what difference does that make?'

'Well, numbnuts, when you get to the final you're not gonna be standin' there singin' on your own. You're gonna have the house orchestra playin' along to your song.'

'So?'

'So the orchestra needs to know days in advance what music they're gonna be performin', don't they? If a fuckin' Jimi Hendrix impersonator gets through to the final – unexpected, like – and says he's gonna sing "Voodoo Chile", I betcha anythin', the orchestra'd be fucked. Imagine trying to learn how to play that and four other songs in about an hour.'

The light finally dawned in Johnny's brain. For all his charisma, charm and talent, he wasn't the sharpest tool in the box. 'I get it,' he said slowly. 'I never thought of that. So that's why they wanted to know in advance what song I'm gonna sing?'

'Yeah. That's why.' The 'Bozo!' Otis added was just loud enough to be heard by them all

Emily smiled. She'd figured it out fairly quickly. Truth was, there were a number of things to consider about the competition, none of which had probably occurred to Johnny. One in particular had been preying on her mind for a few days. Now seemed a good time to air it.

'I wonder,' she mused, 'what would happen if one of us five fell ill, so that one of the other contestants made it into the final?'

James Brown had stood up from his seat and was heading for the door, but as he reached out for the door handle he turned back to answer Emily's question. 'I'm sure they'd just go with four finalists.'

'Maybe,' Emily said carefully. 'But what if something happened to three or four of us? Say we all got food poisoning and couldn't perform. What then?'

Brown opened the door of the dressing room, ready to walk out into the hall. 'Well now, that would make for a real interestin' final, I reckon,' he said.

'Where you goin', man?' Johnny Cash called after him.

'Goin' outside to the parkin' lot for some fresh air. Smells like somethin' died in here.'

Instinctively, everyone glanced at Kurt Cobain. He picked up on their unwelcome glances and blushed a little. Then he aimed a defiant comment at Brown as he walked out into the hall.

'Watch out for speedin' buses in the lot, man. Be a shame, you got squashed and there was only four of us in the final.'

Seven

More than ever, Sanchez was rooting for Elvis to win *the Back From the Dead* show. Not only had his friend come through for him by persuading the receptionist to give him a room originally reserved for someone else, but now the King was carrying Sanchez's suitcase up to the room. They had taken the elevator to the seventh floor and then walked down a long corridor for about fifty yards. The corridor was wide enough for six people or so to stand next to each other. Its walls were covered in cream-coloured wallpaper, and there was a thick, soft, green carpet underfoot. It was evident that the owner of this hotel took great pride in the place. By comparison, Sanchez's bar, the Tapioca, looked kind of shitty when you walked in, but once you were past the slightly shitty area, you found yourself in the very shitty part. This place was smart all the way through.

'This is it,' said Sanchez, pointing to a door on the left-hand side. It was painted white, with small black numbers at eye level reading 713.

'Fer fuck's sakes open it, then. This fuckin' suitcase weighs a ton,' Elvis snapped.

Mumbling an apology, Sanchez pulled a key card from his shorts and slipped it into the card reader on the door. A tiny red light on the reader turned green and a gentle click followed. He turned the handle on the door and pushed it open.

A very spacious room greeted them, with a double bed

standing at its centre. There was a wooden dressing table on the far side and another small table beside the bed with a lamp on it. Over in the far left-hand corner was a door that led through to the bathroom. Sanchez was pleased with what he saw. Place was better than home. He was so struck by its cleanliness that he didn't pay much attention to where he was walking. As he gazed around the room his right foot trod on something lying on the carpet. He heard a crumpling noise and looked down. Beneath his right foot was a large brown envelope, an ordinary-looking thing measuring about twelve inches by eight. He stooped to pick it up and walked over to the bed. In the meantime, Elvis, who had followed him in, was closing the door behind them. By the time he'd turned round Sanchez was sitting on the bed, picking at one corner of the envelope.

'What the fuck you got there?' demanded Elvis.

'Ain't sure.'

'So open it up.'

'I am, goddammit!'

Sanchez's chubby fingers were pawing at the sealed end of the envelope. The flap had been stuck down with Scotch tape, with more tape used to seal the sides of the flap. He ripped the tape off, then tore off the end of the envelope. He peered into it. There were a few Polaroid-sized photographs inside, and something else, bulkier, tucked right down at the bottom of the envelope.

'What the fuck is it?' asked Elvis.

Sanchez frowned. 'Looks like photos.' Gripping the end of the envelope tightly to stop the item at the bottom from falling out, he tipped it up and allowed the contents to slide out on to the bed. Elvis dropped Sanchez's suitcase to the floor and walked over to take a closer look at the photos. Sanchez picked up the photo nearest to him and took a look at it. It was a five-by-four-inch colour photo of an unshaven white guy with greasy blond hair.

Elvis peered over his shoulder. 'Who the fuck's that?' he asked.

'Dunno.'

'What's that piece of paper?'

'Where?'

'There.' Elvis pointed at a small square of white paper that had slipped out of the envelope with the photos. Sanchez picked it up with his other hand and took a look at it. Written on it in blue ink was a list of four names. He compared the names with the photo in his hand.

'What's it say, man?' Elvis asked.

'I think this guy is Kurt Cobain,' said Sanchez, waving the photo at him. He then flicked through the other three. 'These are photos of four of the contestants in the show, I reckon.'

'Gimme that,' said Elvis, snatching the piece of paper out of Sanchez's hand. He took a look at the list of names and then peered down at the photos Sanchez had spread out on the bed. 'This is bad,' he remarked, after a long pause.

'I don't get it. The fuck's this all about?' Sanchez pondered out loud.

'You know what I do, right, Sanchez? Like, for a job?'

'Yeah. I know. Everyone knows. You're a hitman.'

'Right. And this, my fat friend, is a *hit list*. Guy who was meant to be stayin' in this room was s'posed to get this envelope. Then these four singers were gonna get wasted.'

'Holy shit!'

Sanchez had little enthusiasm for the idea of staying in a hotel room that had been reserved by someone who planned to carry out four killings. If the guy showed up, there could be trouble. For Sanchez.

Elvis thought for a moment, then offered his advice. 'I was you, I'd take this here envelope down to reception an' leave it there for whoever the guy is, in case he shows up later.'

'Shouldn't I give it to the police?'

'Well, that's one idea, yeah. Personally, though, I reckon if someone is plannin' on killing off these four singers, then it'll boost my chances of winnin' the goddam show.'

'That's kinda harsh, ain't it?'

'Always look for the positives in any given situation, Sanchez. Besides, in case you hadn't noticed, there ain't no police in the Devil's Graveyard.'

'Oh, yeah. Right.' Sanchez sat on the bed and thought about what to do. He could see the sense in Elvis's plan. 'Okay,' he sighed, 'I'll try an' reseal the envelope, an' then take it down to reception.'

'Cool.' The King glanced at his watch. 'Look I better get goin', buddy. I'm due onstage for my audition in about half an hour. Make sure you're in the audience. I need all the support I can get.' He grinned, and added, 'Even though I'm fuckin' brilliant.'

'Yeah, sure. Catch you later, man. Good luck, an' thanks again for carryin' the case for me.'

Elvis folded the piece of paper with the four names on it, handed it back to his friend and walked out. Once the King had closed the door behind him, Sanchez took another look inside the envelope to check out what he thought he'd seen. Sure enough, tucked inside at the bottom was a thick wad of cash. He had kept a tight hold of it to stop it falling out when he had emptied out the other contents. After all, if Elvis had seen it he might have wanted a share. And since the envelope had been in Sanchez's room, technically that meant it was his. Sanchez pulled out the money and, with his stubby finger trembling, counted it out on the bed. Hundred-dollar bills. Two hundred of them.

Twenty grand.

Time to head to the casino.

Eight

Annabel de Frugyn was shepherded into Nigel Powell's private office. It was a smart room with a thick, springy royal-blue carpet and plain white plastered walls. There was a large wooden desk at the far end of the room, set in front of windows concealed behind a pair of bright red curtains that clashed horribly with the carpet. Powell gestured for her to seat herself in a small black leather-upholstered chair at the desk. He walked round and sat behind the desk in a much larger chair, also in black leather. On the desktop was a fairly organized jumble of stationery and framed photos, the latter all facing Powell. There was also a large white, rather old-fashioned telephone on the desk just to the left of his chair.

One of the two security guards who had escorted the hotel owner to the lobby earlier had followed them into the office. He took up a place standing at the door, which he had closed behind him. Still standing, she smiled her hideous smile at him, but in true military fashion he stared straight ahead, ignoring her. Unfazed, she sat herself down in the chair opposite Powell. In her lap she held, tightly, the handbag that she carried with her everywhere. She may have allowed the hotel security to take her luggage to her room, but no one was getting their hands on her dirty old brown leather handbag.

'So, Miss de Frugyn, you're probably wondering what you're doing here,' Powell began, sitting back in his chair, smiling.

She couldn't help but smile back at him. The man had a

devilish charm, and clearly took great care of his appearance. Despite being in his early forties he didn't have a wrinkle on his face. No doubt the result of plastic surgery and regular injections of Botox.

Annabel's smile was the complete opposite and revealed a vast number of lines and creases on her face. 'You want me to use my psychic powers for something, don't you?'

'Very good. Impressive. And absolutely correct. I'll be honest with you, Annabel, if I may call you that?' She simpered back at him, a sight, if anything, even more revolting than her hideous smile. 'It's no accident that you're here at this hotel. I kind of rigged it so that you would win a ticket to the show.'

'I sensed something was amiss when I received the letter telling me I had won.'

'Really? Your psychic powers told you that?' Powell sat up straighter, suddenly more alert.

'Yes. That and the fact I hadn't entered the competition to win a ticket in the first place.'

He smiled politely. 'Let me cut to the chase. I've heard many good things about you. A friend of mine recommended you after visiting you for a reading once, a few years back.' He paused, assuming a more solemn look. 'And today I need your services for a matter of grave importance.'

'You want me to tell you who will win the singing contest?'

'No. It's more important than that.'

The Mystic Lady was determined to divine what he wanted before he told her. 'You wish to know what you're getting for your birthday?' she ventured.

Powell threw a look over her shoulder at the security guard by the door. A look that suggested he wasn't wildly impressed by Annabel's mystical powers. She still had to convince him she was worthy of the title 'Mystic Lady'.

Sensing his scepticism, she tried to reassure him 'I work a lot better when I have my crystal ball,' she told him.

'Ah. I see. And do you have it with you?'

'Yes.'

'Please do get it out.' There was the hint of an order behind the suave delivery.

Annabel unzipped her handbag, but before reaching inside she frowned. '*Wait*,' she said with a gasp. 'I'm seeing something.'

'What is it?'

'I see you handing me five hundred dollars.'

Powell sighed. Annabel never worked for free, and she made sure that everyone knew it. Her reputation had spread far from Santa Mondega, so Powell had known what to expect. He reached inside his jacket and pulled out a thick brown leather wallet. Opening it, he counted out five one-hundred-dollar bills. Then he slipped three of them over the desk to Annabel, who snapped them up and quickly concealed them somewhere about her person.

Powell kept one finger on the two remaining bills on his side of the desk. 'Three hundred now,' he said coldly. 'Two hundred more if you tell me what I need to know.'

Annabel pretended to contemplate his offer. In truth, though, there was no way she was going to refuse. Normally some haggling would take place, but her request for five hundred up front had been a somewhat optimistic one. The fact that he was willing to pay the whole five hundred made the three hundred up front more than acceptable to her. So, with another nightmarish smile, she delved into her bag and pulled out a small crystal ball, an object far cleaner than the dirty receptacle that held it. She set it down on the desk in front of her and looked up at the man sitting opposite her.

'So tell me what you want to know.'

'Well, Annabel,' he said, leaning over the desk and offering his own dazzling smile, 'a few weeks ago I was approached by a rough-looking Mexican fellow named Jefe. Claimed to be an assassin or bounty hunter of some sort.'

'I think I know him,' said Annabel.

'You should do,' said Nigel. 'He's the one who recommended I speak to *you*.'

'About what?'

'He told me he'd been offered a substantial sum of money to kill some of the contestants in this year's show. He had accepted the job via a third party, only then to be told that the contract had been given to someone else.'

'I see. And you want to know who that someone else is?'

'Yes. I also want to know who it is who's hiring these people, and why.'

'Jefe didn't know?'

'No, but he said you might be able to help with that. That's why you're here.'

'Okay. Anything else?'

'That will do for now. Think you can manage it?'

'Well, let's see, shall we? Can you dim the lights?'

'Sure. Tommy, dim the lights, please.'

The black-suited security guard turned a switch by the door and dimmed the overhead lighting until it was sufficiently dark to see that Annabel's crystal ball was beginning to glow a gentle white colour. This was her cue to lean forward and begin waving her hands over the enigmatic sphere. After a few seconds, a swirling white mist appeared inside it. Powell had the good sense to remain quiet as she went through some rather dubious gesticulating with her arms. Eventually, after staring unblinkingly into the glowing glass ball and concentrating hard for just under a minute some insight seemed to come to her.

'The man you seek,' she intoned, 'is in the hotel already. He has a list of people he plans to kill.'

'Can you see what he looks like?'

'I see two men together. One of them is a contestant in the show. The other is a merciless killer. They plan to kill off their main rivals so they can win the show.'

Powell reached a hand up to his chin and began rubbing it as if he had an infuriating itch.

'Who are they?' he demanded.

'Wait. I'm seeing something. It's – it's a room number.'

'Go on.'

'This room is on the seventh floor.' Annabel, staring fixedly into the crystal globe, was beginning to sweat with the effort of concentrating. Powell, too, was staring into it, but could see nothing other than the white mist swirling around inside. Again the old woman spoke, her voice now a monotonous drone, her words interspersed by short pauses.

'It's room number – thirteen on the – seventh floor. That's where – you'll find the – assassin you're looking for.'

'Wow!' said Powell, sounding surprised. He was impressed in spite of himself. 'That's very precise. Do you have a name for the occupant?'

Annabel slowly shook her head. 'No. There's confusion over this man's name. I can't work out why.' Her speech was beginning to sound normal again.

Shit! thought Powell, but he kept it to himself. 'Okay,' he said gently. 'Can you see anything else?'

'Yes, there is one thing. But I suspect you already know this.' She sounded hesitant now.

Powell raised one eyebrow quizzically. 'And what is that?'

'This show is cursed.'

'Excuse me?' If he was surprised, he did a remarkable job of concealing it.

'There's some kinda curse on this show. I can't figure out exactly what it is, but if I was a contestant, I don't think I'd want to win.'

The show's owner and promoter waved a dismissive hand and smiled at her. 'I'm not worried about curses. Or what happens to the person who wins the show. I just want to be sure the show goes ahead without any glitches.'

'It's your call,' said Annabel. 'But I reckon a more appropriate name for your show would be *The Hex Factor.*'

Powell sighed. 'I think we're done here. Tommy, turn the lights back up, please.' The white mist within the crystal ball began to dissipate and Annabel sat back in her chair, looking a little tired, and, if anything, even older. The security guard turned up the lights again and Annabel watched with unconcealed pleasure as Powell tossed the remaining hundred-dollar bills over the desk to her.

'Thank you, Annabel. You appear to have done well.' He looked across at her and added, 'Of course, if we need you again for any reason, we know your room number.' There was a note of subtle intimidation in his voice, and Annabel had no doubt that if even one of her predictions proved false, then her five hundred dollars might just be repossessed. She snagged the two hundred-dollar bills and quickly concealed them within her clothing with the other three, then picked up her crystal ball and placed it back in her bag.

'It's been nice doing business with you,' she said, getting up from her chair. She was not altogether insincere – five hundred bucks was five hundred bucks.

'Yes, hasn't it? Thank you, Annabel. I wish you a pleasant stay.' Powell reached over the desk and shook her hand again, before adding one last question. 'Did you work out who's going to win the singing contest yet?'

The psychic grinned. 'If I was a gambling woman, I'd say it's someone whose name begins with J.'

Powell and Tommy once more exchanged a glance and then the security man opened the door for Annabel to leave. When she was gone, Powell picked up the receiver of the white telephone on his desk and pressed several buttons. The call was answered within one ring. A woman's voice spoke.

'Reception. How may I help you?'

'Hi, this is Mister Powell. Can you tell me who is staying in room seven-thirteen, please?'

'Yes, sir. One moment please.'

Tommy walked over and sat down in the chair across the desk from his employer. A second later, the receptionist gave Powell the name he was seeking and he replaced the handset on the phone.

'So, was the mad old bitch right, or not?' asked Tommy.

'Well, I'm told she only ever gets fifty per cent of her predictions right, but that's not a bad ratio. As long as she's given us the right room number for this hitman, then I'm happy.'

'So who is he?'

'According to reception, his name is Sanchez Garcia. Send some guys up there to find him. And make sure they're armed. If he really is a hitman he could be very dangerous.'

'What do you want them to do?'

'Interrogate him.'

'And if he is here as an assassin?'

'Find out who he's working for and kill them both.'

'And if he's not the assassin?'

Powell shrugged. 'Just kill *him*.'

Nine

Having finally arrived at the Hotel Pasadena, the Bourbon Kid had made straight for the bar. He had a lot to reflect on. And as a man who didn't generally like to indulge in reflection, he allowed himself just one day a year to remember the past and dwell on how things might have been if, ten years earlier, Halloween had panned out differently.

He had picked the quietest of the hotel's bars, a lounge just off the lobby, and was sitting on a stool at one end of the bar, staring into a half-filled glass of bourbon. The barmaid, Valerie, a diminutive young woman with dark hair tied back into a ponytail, had wisely sussed out within a second of laying eyes on him that he wanted no small talk. His body language spoke volumes. He deliberately gave off a hostile vibe (although most days he did that unintentionally anyway). She had poured his drink quickly, and with minimum fuss had set it down in front of him on a coaster on the bartop.

There were no more than twenty people in the bar. As if picking up on his sour mood, none of the other customers had taken a place at the bar. They were all seated at the tables set artfully around the room, engaged in polite, hushed conversations. This was not the usual kind of lowlife hangout the Bourbon Kid was used to. It was a bit too classy and its customers too well-mannered. But in his present mood, that suited him just fine.

He had headed to the Devil's Graveyard for a number of different reasons. Getting drunk was the first order of business. That way he wouldn't remember so much. It was ten years to the day since, as a sixteen-year-old, he had killed his mother. On top of that, that same night he had left his teenage sweetheart, Beth, at the local pier with a promise that he would return before the witching hour was up. That had been before he had discovered what was left of his mother. It still regularly gnawed at him that he hadn't been able to make it back to Beth that night. He'd had more pressing matters to attend to, like finding a home for his distraught younger brother, Casper. Casper had been born with severe learning difficulties, and the news that his mother was dead had sent him into a hysterical fit. To make a bad situation worse, the Kid, who was known as JD back in those days, had also broken Casper's father's neck later that night in a fit of temper. The two brothers had been fathered by different men. JD hadn't liked his own father any more than he liked Casper's, he just hadn't got around to killing him yet.

Yet it was Beth who filled his thoughts for most of the time, on the rare occasions when he allowed the past to come back to him. Just on this one day each year he let himself remember her exactly as she had looked when he kissed her for the first time. They had been to a Halloween party together at their high school in Santa Mondega. JD's mother had made him a scarecrow outfit to wear, and although it wasn't exactly his kind of thing, he knew she'd gone to great trouble to make it. It had turned out to be an unintentionally brilliant choice because when he arrived at the Halloween disco, he had found Beth there dressed as Dorothy from *The Wizard of Oz*. Seeing this as a good omen, the two of them had ditched the dance to head to the pier. The road there wasn't exactly made of yellow brick, but that hadn't done anything to dampen their mood. Events later in the night had done that.

The Kid stared at his reflection in the glass of bourbon and allowed himself a slight smile. In his mind's eye, he could still clearly see Beth skipping along the school corridor singing

'We're off to see the Wizard, the wonderful Wizard of Oz'. He'd cut her off pretty quickly, so that she never made it to the end of the first chorus. Given the chance, he would have loved to go back to that moment and this time let her sing the whole goddam song. Even if she had looked silly. She wasn't much of a singer, either, as he remembered. Yet it was such simple imperfections that had made the memory of her so precious to him.

The Kid had plans to go back to Santa Mondega one day and find Beth, in the hopes of – what? Of rekindling a relationship that had never got under way? He had stayed away from the place for much of the last ten years in the knowledge that she hadn't been there either. On that screwed-up Halloween night ten years earlier, Beth had been arrested and charged with murdering her stepmother. The Kid didn't know the details of the case, but it looked like she'd been framed by a local cop named Archibald Somers. Beth had ended up in jail, sentenced to twenty years for first-degree murder. If she was still the sweet, demure girl he had known back then, there might be a chance she would be released early for good behaviour. Matter of fact, that was something that might be due to happen any day now.

Nothing in the Kid's life was quite as black and white as it seemed on the surface though. His problem with Beth was that even if she was released, he couldn't go looking for her, for the same reason he couldn't go to visit her in jail. He had way too many enemies. If anyone knew he cared about her, she'd be a target for any number of murderous creatures, be they vampires, werewolves or just rotten slimeball humans.

He rolled the whiskey glass in his hands. For a split second he saw reflected in it the grinning face of the vampire that had destroyed his mother. The image made him grip the glass tightly and he quickly relaxed his hold on it to avoid shattering it in his hand.

There was one main reason why the Kid was spending

Halloween at the Hotel Pasadena. Truth was, he liked nothing more than a good, old-fashioned, Halloween killing spree. On a trip through Plainview, Texas, a few weeks earlier, he had discovered during an arm-wrestling bout with a guy named Rodeo Rex that the Devil's Graveyard was rife with the undead. Particularly on Halloween. During the match, Rex had tried to throw the Kid off his stroke by bragging about heading to the Graveyard to do a job on behalf of God, killing off the undead. By then it had looked like the bout might go on for ever because the two of them were so evenly matched. So, although he hated to lose any kind of contest, the Kid had let Rex win. After allowing the giant biker to slam his arm down and claim victory, the Kid had then made a point of squeezing his opponent's hand crushingly hard and breaking every bone in it, to ensure he wouldn't be able to keep his appointment in the Devil's Graveyard. The task of killing the undead would now be all his own. Having put Rex out of action, he had headed into the Devil's Graveyard to generate some carnage.

A Sid Vicious impersonator walked past him and out of the bar, towards the vast theatre that took up most of the hotel's ground floor. The sight of him snapped the Kid out of his black reverie. The *Back From the Dead* show had brought a whole bunch of interesting faces to the hotel. People pretending to be dead singers were everywhere, and, as the idiot Michael Jackson impersonator had proved beyond all doubt earlier, they were a bunch of freaks. All of them. And all of them had the same simple quirk in common. They felt more comfortable in someone else's skin.

The Kid had not removed his sunglasses since entering the hotel. His eyes were most likely bloodshot and bleary from the hours on the road, and the drinking and lack of sleep preceding his arrival. The shades also did a good job of keeping strangers away. No one could make eye contact with him, and no one was going to misinterpret the dark lenses as an invitation to make small talk. With his trademark black clothing, the sunglasses were doing a fine job of maintaining his 'leave-me-the-fuck-alone' look. It certainly worked on the staff, who stayed well away at the other end of the bar when they weren't serving anyone near him.

On the bartop, next to his glass of bourbon he had placed an unlit cigarette taken from a recently opened pack, which he had set down next to a small silver tray intended for tips. He knew that the bar staff were praying to God that he didn't light the cigarette, because that would mean they would have to ask him to put it out. To a casual observer, it may have looked as though he had no intention of lighting the cigarette, or had simply forgotten that it was there. To anyone who knew of his reputation, however, it was clear that it was there to provoke an argument with someone who didn't like smokers.

After twenty minutes or so of staring at his half-filled glass, he picked it up and downed the contents in one. He slammed it back down on the bar hard enough to catch the attention of Valerie, the barmaid who had served him earlier. She scuttled nervously over to him.

'Same again, sir?'

He nodded, and she poured him another half glass of Sam Cougar. In return for her pouring the drink without offering any conversation, he tossed a crumpled twenty-dollar bill on to the bar.

'Keep the change.'

'Thank you, sir.'

As she was ringing up the sale in the till at the back of the bar, a man's voice called out from behind the Kid.

'A bottle of your finest champagne, Valerie,' it said cheerily. It was deliberately pitched at a level so that everyone in the bar would hear. And, its owner hoped, be impressed.

He was obviously a man the barmaid recognized and loathed, for she turned immediately and forced a fake smile. One that suggested she didn't like him, but had no choice but to kiss his ass if she wanted to keep her job.

Slightly to his surprise, the Kid recognized the man from news reports. His name was Jonah Clementine, the former chairman of a high-profile international bank, which had recently been liquidated after more than a hundred years of lucrative trading. Thousands of hard-working employees had lost their jobs with little or no severance pay, but Clementine had survived the scandal with his fortune, if not his reputation, enhanced. After years of awarding himself and his fellow senior partners bonuses in excess of twenty million dollars a year, he had then contrived to walk away with a thirty-million-dollar payoff shortly before the bank went publicly, and very messily, bust. He was exactly the sort of customer that the hotel staff would most hate. He would treat them as inferior beings almost beneath his notice, and they would no doubt have to smile and give him preferential treatment. Which appeared to be what Valerie was doing.

Clementine also had a reputation as an international playboy. A blonde model in her early twenties clung to his arm. She had an improbably large pair of (mainly silicone) breasts tucked into a tight white T-shirt, which she pressed tightly against her companion's upper arm. Her long legs, tanned a perfect golden brown, were on display almost all the way up to her waist, just south of which disappeared into an abbreviated pair of gold hot pants. She was, in short, the perfect foil for Jonah Clementine in his three-thousand-dollar hand-tailored grey Savile Row suit. Since the scandal about his profiteering had broken on virtually every news service, he had obviously had time to employ the services of a personal-fitness trainer. Despite being in his early forties, he had a physique that was no longer that of an office drone. He had a muscular upper body, which, coupled with a sharp orange tan that was surely fake, made him look quite the handsome hunk. He wore a cream silk shirt under his suit jacket, with a red-and-black-checked neckerchief tied loosely around his neck. Unlike the sort of customers the Bourbon Kid was used to sharing bars with, he was clean-shaven and smelled of expensive cologne, while the short, spiky styling of his black hair looked as though it had taken an hour in front of a mirror to perfect.

'Sir, how many glasses would you like?' Valerie asked him in response to his request for a bottle of champagne.

'Just two please, Valerie. Get yourself a drink too, though, won't you? I'm on a lucky winning streak today.'

'Aren't you always?' the barmaid joked politely as she headed to a fridge at the back of the bar to fetch the champagne.

While she was picking out a bottle of Diamant Bleu (a rich man's drink if ever there was one), the millionaire was eyeing up the Bourbon Kid. The Kid had picked up his unlit cigarette and slipped it into the corner of his mouth, where it hung idly for a moment before it suddenly lit itself. It was a trick that had impressed many people over the years. It would not impress Jonah Clementine, however. He was the type of guy who was only impressed by things he could control. A flake like the Bourbon Kid was only ever going to get under his skin. And that was exactly what the Kid intended to do.

'Excuse me, you're not permitted to smoke at the bar.' The words were reasonable enough, but were clearly intended as an order.

The Kid ignored him.

'Hey, you! I'm talking to you.'

The Kid took the cigarette from the corner of his mouth with his left hand and looked over at Jonah Clementine. Then he blew a lungful of smoke in the playboy's direction.

'What the fuck's the matter with you?' snapped Clementine. 'There are other people here besides *you*. Not everyone wants to breathe in your second-hand smoke.'

'What's your point?' A more cautious man than Clementine, one less used to getting his own way, would have noted the gravelly tone to the words. Noted, and maybe reflected on what it might mean. But he blustered on, astonished that anyone should defy him.

'My point is, put your goddam cigarette out, or I'll have you thrown out.'

'Nope.'

Clementine raised both eyebrows. 'Nope? *That's it? Nope?*'

'Yep.'

'Okay. You're giving me no choice. Valerie, call security and have them throw this guy out. *Now.*'

Standing behind the bar, the girl visibly cringed. On some level she was probably pleased that Clementine had made the call about the guy smoking for her, because she didn't want the man in the sunglasses to blame her for his imminent removal from the bar. But she still dreaded the unnecessary commotion that was about to descend on the place.

Set out of sight beneath the bar was a security-alarm button, placed there for just such occasions. Valerie leaned down and pressed it, hard. Within forty-five seconds a burly member of the security team arrived through the main entrance to the lounge and made his way to the bar, looking for any visible signs of trouble. His name was Gunther, and at the age of forty he was one of the oldest security men on the hotel staff. Tall and well-built, he had a short, flat-top military haircut, which he had kept as a reminder of his time in the army. He wore smart black chinos and a black T-shirt that showed off a set of well-defined muscles. His face was well worn, suggesting that he had taken his fair share of punches in his time.

'Whassup, Valerie?' he asked.

'I'll tell you what's up,' Clementine intervened. 'It's this clown over here. Won't put his cigarette out. Making life unpleasant for everyone else.'

'I see.' Gunther turned to the Kid, who was sitting unconcerned on his stool, taking a drag on his smoke. 'Sir, I'm going to have to ask you to put that cigarette out.' The words were polite, but there was a steely edge to the security man's voice.

'So ask.'

Gunther took a look at Clementine, and nodded. He obviously felt the same way about this flake smoking in the bar.

His tone hardened. 'Okay, bud. C'mon, let's take a walk.'

As he spoke, he reached out and grabbed the Kid's right shoulder. His intention was to pull him, gently but firmly, off the stool in the hopes that he would come easily.

He didn't.

With his own right hand, the Bourbon Kid reached up, grabbed Gunther's massive paw and squeezed his fingers together hard, almost crushing them. As he did so, he lifted the security guard's hand away from his shoulder without moving from his stool.

'Don't touch me again.'

He released his grip and the security guard stepped back, wiggling his fingers to ensure they all still worked. Satisfied that his hand wasn't broken, he took a closer look at the Kid. One long, hard stare later, his face revealed the recognition that he'd gotten off lightly.

'I know you,' he said.

'Good.'

'Enjoy your cigarette.'

'I will.' He took another drag and added, 'One more thing 'fore you go.'

'Yeah?'

'I'm gonna kill that fuck in the suit in a minute. Send someone down here to clear up the mess.'

Jonah Clementine heard the threat and reeled in outrage. 'Who the *hell* do you think you're calling a fuck?' Turning to Gunther, he barked, 'You! Get this lowlife outta here now or you can kiss your fuckin' job goodbye.'

'He's okay. Leave him be.' With that, Gunther turned and walked away. Valerie and the other customers watched him go in silence, all wondering what would happen next, and all trying not to stare at the dark figure casually smoking a cigarette at the bar.

It was many years since anyone had disobeyed one of Clementine's orders, and besides, he hadn't got to be the man he was by giving up. Visibly seething, he took up the issue himself. He was a man of great power and wealth, and even greater self-importance, so to be publicly defied by a mere security guard like Gunther, as well as insulted by barfly scum, was something he wasn't used to. And he had his blonde bimbo to impress.

Staring at the Kid, he barked again, 'Put that cigarette out *now*.'

A few painfully long seconds passed before the Kid duly did as ordered, stubbing the cigarette out in the silver dish that Valerie had left on the bartop for tips.

'Thank you,' said Clementine triumphantly, his mouth twisted in a malicious sneer. 'That wasn't so hard, was it?' The Kid ignored him. Instead, he reached over to the pack of cigarettes on the bar. He pulled another one out and placed it in the corner of his mouth.

Clementine reared up. His blonde girlfriend rubbed his back to help spur him on. He and the Kid were no more than a yard apart and the bimbo looked like the confrontation was turning her on.

'Oh you're a fucking comedian, aren't you? Ha-ha-fucking-ha,' Clementine sneered. Lowering his voice menacingly, he hissed, 'You light that while I'm here, I'll have you taken out to the desert and shot like a dog.'

The Kid took a long look at Clementine through his sunglasses. For a few seconds the two of them stared at each other, motionless. Then Clementine lunged out to snatch the cigarette from the other's mouth. The Kid grabbed his arm with his left hand, stopping its forward motion stone dead. Then, with his clenched right fist, he punched Clementine in the face. Hard. All without even getting off his stool.

The businessman swayed gently on the spot, a look of complete bewilderment on his face. Blood began to seep out of both his nostrils, pouring down to his mouth. After a painfully long couple of seconds, he fell backwards in a heap on the floor. There was an unpleasant noise as his skull connected with the hardwood boards.

The blonde in the gold hot pants threw her arms in the air and squealed.

'*Oh my God, Jonah!* Are you okay?' She bent down and leaned over him to see if he was all right. Her six-inch stilettos and the weight of her enhanced breasts made it difficult for her to keep her balance, so she pressed a hand down hard into Clementine's chest to balance herself. He didn't react. After a few attempts at patting him on the cheek to try to rouse him she looked back up at the Kid. 'He's unconscious,' she said accusingly. 'You've knocked him out.'

'He ain't unconscious.'

'He is. I'm telling you. He's out cold!'

The Kid sucked on the end of his unlit cigarette and it lit up brightly before he responded. 'If he was unconscious,' he growled, 'he'd still have a pulse.'

The bimbo stared open-mouthed at Clementine's body for a moment. It took her a while, but she eventually realized that he wasn't breathing. Again, she looked up at the Kid, who had now turned back to his half-filled glass of Sam Cougar.

'Oh my God!' she said. 'How d'ya light up like that? That's, like, *so-o-o cool*.'

She stood up and walked over to him. She placed a hand on his shoulder and whispered in his ear. 'So, d'you wanna buy me a drink?'

'Beat it, skank,' he snarled in a voice like wave-washed

gravel. Then he looked over at Valerie the barmaid and nodded at his drink. 'Miss?'

'Yes, sir?' The girl's heart was racing so fast that she was surprised she could speak at all.

'Fill the glass.'

Ten

Sanchez was a man with many flaws. One of the worst was a weakness for gambling. It was a pastime that had cost him a fair amount of his wealth over the years, but the lure of a bet and the opportunity to make money without breaking sweat was, for him, powerful and seductive to resist.

From the second he had laid eyes on the money in the envelope he had found in his hotel room, he had been concocting all kinds of plans about how he would speculate with it. And in spite of Elvis's warning that the envelope had been intended for a contract killer, name and identity unknown, Sanchez couldn't pass up the opportunity. So he headed straight for the hotel's casino. He had the envelope containing the photos and the twenty thousand dollars tucked away down the front of his shorts, cleverly concealed by his red Hawaiian shirt, which hung over them. When he'd bought the shirt, the shop assistant had informed him that, wearing it, he'd never be able to hide anything. Well, she'd been wrong.

Being a tolerably honest sort – by his estimation, at least – Sanchez was fully intending to hand the envelope in to the reception desk. After all, it didn't belong to him. And when he handed it in, it would still have the money in it: right amount, right number of bills in the right denomination. But before he did that, he was just going to use twenty thousand as stake money in the casino. As soon as he'd made a decent profit, he would slip twenty thousand in hundred-dollar bills into the envelope, seal it and drop it off at reception. No one would be any the wiser.

When he had first decided on this plan, his intention had been to play it safe and make only a small profit. But by the time he actually made it down to the casino on the lower ground floor, he had decided that he would only quit once he'd doubled the stake money. Twenty thousand for Sanchez and twenty thousand for the hitman, whoever he was. It seemed only fair. His palms were sweating as he stepped out of the elevator and into the casino area. One good bet, and his vacation would be off to the best possible start.

The casino was straight out of one of Sanchez's dreams (well, leaving aside that the croupiers weren't monkeys in red suits and hats; Sanchez's dreams had their odder moments). It was vast and opulent and the lighting made the whole area glow a bright golden colour. The carpet was deep crimson in colour, not dissimilar to the red of the waistcoats worn by croupiers and waitresses. And there were customers everywhere. The sound of rolling dice, cards being slapped down on baize-topped tables, roulette wheels spinning, cheers from winning gamblers, sighs from losers, coins rattling into trays, it was all there.

Sanchez was in heaven.

To his left were rows of slot machines, mostly being used by elderly people. Directly ahead was a bar fronted by rows of stools on which a few losers sat drowning their sorrows. Over to his right were the roulette and blackjack tables, about twenty of them in all. Each table had a croupier and two or three gamblers seated at it, so there was plenty of room for Sanchez. He could pick any table he wanted, but what game did he fancy? Blackjack, poker, craps, roulette?

What he needed was a sign. He was not overly superstitious, but he did believe in good luck. Some kind of omen would set him on the right path, he felt. And he spotted one almost at once. There was a roulette table near the centre of the room at which three players sat taking their chances. One of them was the self-styled Mystic Lady, Annabel de Frugyn.

Jackpot! Despite his personal distaste, right now she was just the person he had hoped to see. If the rumours were true, then this crazy old crone could see into the future. So who better to stand next to?

Sanchez made his way over to the table, heading for Annabel. She was seated on a stool between two tiny middle-aged Chinese women. Each of them had huge stacks of chips in front of her suggesting that they were all winning. Or that they had only just started playing. Sanchez grabbed a free stool from another table and manoeuvred it in between the Mystic Lady and the smaller of the two Chinese women, nudging her to one side so he could squeeze in to the left of Annabel. The sight of him sidling up next to her had the desired effect. She was pleased to see him.

'I knew you couldn't stay away, Sanchez,' she said, winking at him with quite horrible coyness.

'Ha ha! Yeah, that's right,' he replied with a shameful level of forced enthusiasm. 'So, you havin' any luck?'

'Oh my, yes. I'm on a real winning streak, Sanchez. The hotel manager gave me five hundred dollars and I've tripled it already.' Well, she had received five hundred bucks from Powell. Sanchez didn't need to know how she'd earned it.

Sanchez reached down to the envelope tucked into the front of his shorts. He'd wedged it in good and proper, and he provoked a number of odd glances from the others as he tugged at it three or four times before it came free. The sudden release made his arm shoot back and he accidentally elbowed the small Chinese lady in the face, knocking her off her stool to land on her back on the floor. *Shit!* Thought Sanchez. *Still, no time for an apology. She'd be okay, one way or the other.*

Recovering his composure, he opened the envelope, pulled out the thick wad of bills and casually tossed it over the table to the croupier. The latter's face gave away nothing. He was a bald, olive-skinned young man in his late twenties, and he had an impressive poker face when it came to showing a complete lack of interest or surprise when large amounts of cash were thrown at him.

The tiny Chinese woman climbed back on to her stool muttering angrily and looking about ready to fell Sanchez with a karate chop. But when she saw the wad of cash she seemed to change her mind, and even attempted a wan smile at the bar owner. Everyone liked a guy with money. And for once, Sanchez was that guy. Smiling himself, he called over to the croupier. 'Chips please, good sir.'

The croupier picked up Sanchez's money, expertly counted it, and replaced it with a pile of red, yellow and blue chips of corresponding value. Sanchez could sense that his female companions were mildly impressed by his apparent wealth.

Annabel confirmed it. 'Hey, Sanchez, that bar of yours must be doing really well!'

'Sure. I'm a pretty astute businessman,' he bragged.

'Reckon we should go into business together,' suggested Annabel. 'With your business sense and my foresight, we could make a killing.'

'Sure. Let's start now. You tell me red or black and I'll lay down the money.'

'Oh, this one is definitely gonna be red.'

'You sure?'

'Absolutely.'

She did sound incredibly confident. More telling, to Sanchez, she placed a stack of chips down on red.

'Last bets, please,' prompted the croupier. Although his request was aimed at everyone at the table he was looking directly at Sanchez, daring him to prove he had the balls to gamble more than just one chip on his first bet.

Sanchez weighed up his options. He had to make a decision quickly. *Oh, what the hell? It's all found money anyway,* he decided.

And he placed all his chips on red.

Eleven

In the time that had elapsed since the Bourbon Kid had punched the former bank boss Jonah Clementine in the face, killing him instantly, no new customers had come into the bar for a drink. The leggy blonde glamour model who had, until very recently, been hanging off Mr Clementine's arm had left almost immediately, most likely heading to the casino in the hopes of finding a wealthy substitute before they all got snagged by other gold-diggers. Slowly and unobtrusively, the other drinkers in the bar had followed her out. None of them had made sudden movements to get up and leave, but they had all discreetly finished up their drinks and conversations and, one by one, made their way out of the bar.

Valerie the barmaid had no one new to serve, but tried to busy herself wiping down parts of the bar as far away from the Kid as possible. All the other staff had been closer to the exit behind the bar and had dashed through it before Valerie got the chance. With the hotel having a policy that one member of staff had to be available behind the bar at all times, she was stuck there until one of them plucked up the guts to return. Which wasn't likely to happen any time soon.

For the first twenty minutes after the killing the only people to enter the bar were two guys from the security team. Gunther had sent them along after the Kid had warned him that a corpse would need disposing of. Soon. The two men had slipped in quietly and lifted Clementine's lifeless body from the black hardwood floor, which now had a pool of his blood settling on it. They carried it round behind the bar, at which Valerie threw a fit.

'You can't bring that back here!' she moaned. 'It ain't hygienic!'

The security officer at the back holding Clementine's legs shrugged. 'Gunther's orders. Wants the body hidden away until the ambulance gets here.'

'Well stash it in the kitchen, then. I don't want it back here.'

'That's what we're tryin' to do. If you could just get the fuck outta the way, it'd help. Look now – there's blood spillin' all over the goddam floor.'

Valerie stepped aside and watched as they struggled through the door at the back of the bar through which all her colleagues had disappeared a short while earlier.

'An' don't expect us to clear the blood up after you,' she yelled. 'You can do that yourselves!'

From his seat at the bar, the Bourbon Kid heard one of the security guys shout back *'Aw, go fuck yourself!'* from the kitchen. Neither of them had dared to take a look at him on their way past him, but they were quite happy to mouth off at a young barmaid. In their defence, they wouldn't want to piss him off. There had been enough about him on the news in recent times for people to have learned that it was wise to avoid him. He killed without motive whenever it suited him. And he didn't care who he killed, man, woman or child. At least, that's what the news reports were saying. Who would want to put that theory to the test? Sure there were bigger guys than him – tough guys, too – staying in the hotel, but the aura of evil and unpredictability that surrounded him ensured that no one, no matter how big, would deliberately set out to antagonize him.

Valerie was desperately looking for an excuse to duck out into the kitchen area. She didn't want to be anywhere near the Bourbon Kid, but unfortunately she was the nearest person to him. Until, that is, a lone figure walked into the bar. A man brave enough to sit with the Kid. He had been passing through the main hall adjacent to the bar and had caught sight of the people hurrying out. Valerie saw him stop on his way in and quiz a young couple about what had happened. She pretended to be busy wiping down the bar, but watched as the couple nodded towards the Kid, obviously explaining to the man what they had seen unfold when the Bourbon Kid had met Jonah Clementine. Then, apparently undaunted, this man sauntered into the place and headed over to the corner of the bar where the Kid was sitting.

The Kid had just finished his third glass of bourbon. The man approaching him had chit-chat in mind, the kind that he hoped might interest the killer. Valerie recognized him as one of the singers from the *Back From The Dead* show. His name was Julius and he was a fairly innocuous-looking middle-aged black man with a smooth bald head like a pool ball. At full height he was no more than about five-feet eight-inches tall, but he was slenderly built and extremely light on his feet. The pomp in his walk and the suit of purple velvet made him look a little like a pimp, ready to offer the Kid one of his whores.

In fact, he was a James Brown impersonator, in the hotel to win the singing contest. The single-breasted purple suit jacket he wore hung open to reveal a bright blue shirt underneath. His pants were flared below the knee, giving the suit a very seventies look. He took up a place at the bar on a stool just a yard to the left of the Bourbon Kid. Once he'd made himself comfortable he called out to Valerie.

'Yo Valerie!'

She had been doing her best to stay away from that end of the bar, hoping that it would encourage any new customers to walk down to the other end. But now Julius was sitting there right next to the man who was causing Valerie (along with everyone else) to steer well clear.

'A beer for me, and whatever my friend here is drinkin'.'

The Kid clearly responded immediately in his usual gravelly tone. 'I ain't your fuckin' friend,' he growled, not even looking over at his new companion.

'You could be,' Julius suggested with a smile, which was ignored.

'But I won't be.'

Valerie picked up the bottle of Sam Cougar from the back of the bar and made her way over to where the two men were sitting. She filled the Kid's empty glass. Straight to the top. Without being asked.

You had to hand it to the guy, for Julius was clearly undeterred by the Kid's unpleasant manner. 'I know who you are,' he said.

Valerie's hand was shaking as she replaced the lid on the bottle of Sam Cougar, and she was relieved that she had to return it to its place on a shelf at the back of the bar. After setting it down next to a bottle of vodka, she took a deep breath and headed off to a fridge at the far end to fetch the beer that Julius had ordered.

The Kid took a drag on his cigarette and finally turned to look at the black man with the beaming white smile who had seated himself next to him at the bar.

'You know who I am, huh?'

'Yeah.'

'Good for you.'

'You're the Bourbon Kid.'

'So they say.'

Julius continued smiling like someone who'd just won big in the casino. Then he let out a small laugh. 'Oh, you don't disappoint. Do you know who *I* am?'

The Bourbon Kid took another drag on his cigarette and blew the smoke into Julius's face. 'Let me guess. You're Gandhi, right?'

'Hey! That's funny. You're a funny guy, y'know that?'

'You do know I'm about to kill you, don't you?'

Valerie interrupted by placing a bottle of Shitting Monkey beer on the bar in front of Julius. She cleared her throat and stammered 'That's twelve dollars, please sir.' She looked at him pleadingly. *For Chrissakes don't start another incident,* she thought, desperately hoping that, somehow, the advice would penetrate his brain. Before a bullet did.

Julius pulled a twenty-dollar bill from the hip pocket of his purple pants and placed it on the bar. 'Keep the change,' he said with an increasingly confident smile.

'Thank you, sir,' she blurted, picking up the note and scurrying to the till at the other end of the bar.

Still grinning like a politician at a photo opportunity, Julius turned back to the Bourbon Kid, whose patience was by now on the verge of snapping. 'I have a job offer for you. How'd you like to earn yourself fifty grand for a day's work?'

The Kid took another drag on his cigarette and then picked up his half-pint glass of Sam Cougar. He poured damn near half the contents down his throat in one swig, then placed it back on the bar.

'Gimme the money now.'

'I can't. I don't have it yet.'

'I want it now.'

'I know that, but I already paid another guy up front and he hasn't showed up. So you're my plan B.'

'I'm *plan B?*'

'Hey, if I'd known you were gonna be here you'd have been *plan A*, but you're a hard fella to track down. So I went with another guy.'

The Kid's eyes were still hidden behind his sunglasses, which made it difficult for Julius to gauge what kind of impression he was making. He ploughed on regardless.

'Look, I'm in this singing contest today. You know the one? The *Back From the Dead* show?'

'I'm aware of it.'

'Well, I *have* to win it. You help make that happen, you

get fifty grand out of the prize money.'

'How much is the prize money.'

'A million dollars.'

'Then I'll take half.'

Julius shifted uncomfortably on his stool. 'Look. If you knew the reasons behind why I have to win this competition you'd do it for free.'

'No. I wouldn't.'

'You know, there's a lot more at stake than just a million dollars here. People's lives are in danger.'

'People's lives are always in danger.' There was an extra rasp to the gravel now. Julius was uncomfortably aware that he probably counted as 'people'.

Julius picked up the bottle of Shitting Monkey and took a sip. He swilled the drink around in his mouth for a few seconds before swallowing hard and placing the bottle back down on the bartop. 'All right, listen up. Here's the thing. I'll tell you the whole story, but you ain't gonna believe it because it's kinda *out there*.'

'Yeah?' A world of indifference permeated the word.

'Yeah. But this is *so* outrageous you'll probably think I'm makin' it up. It involves, like, supernatural stuff an' all sorts.'

The Kid blew another lungful of smoke in Julius's face. 'You know,' he said softly, 'ten years ago today my mother turned into a vampire and tried to kill me. I doubt anything you say is gonna shock me as much that, so why doncha just get the fuck on with it?'

Julius fiddled with the beer bottle on the bar, turning it around until the label with its picture of a defecating monkey was facing him.

'Okay. Well, you know that guy, Nigel Powell, owns this hotel?' He spoke in a hushed voice, even though there was no one within earshot. 'D'you know how he got to be the owner?'

'No.'

'He signed a contract with the Devil.'

'And?'

'And, well – this hotel is built over the gateway to Hell.'

'*And?*'

'Powell *sold his soul* to the Devil. In exchange, the Devil gave him this hotel and all the wealth that came with it.'

The Bourbon Kid took a much smaller sip of his bourbon before responding. 'Sounds like a sweet deal.'

'Sure. But here's the thing. No deal with the Devil is ever gonna be that cut-and-dried. This is kinda like a rolling one-year contract. Every year on Halloween, Powell has to get someone new to sell his or her soul to Satan. *A different person every year.* If he fails to do that, then he's broken his contract.'

'Meanin' he goes straight to Hell for all eternity, I suppose?'

Julius shook his head. 'Worse'n that. This *whole* hotel will crumble and sink into the depths of Hell at the end of the witchin' hour tonight if he doesn't get someone new to sell their soul to the Devil and take his place.'

The Kid sighed. 'I don't believe a fuckin' worda this shit. Why'n't you admit it: you just wanna win the show, doncha?'

'You interested, or what?'

'Just tell me who you want dead.'

'I'm one of five singers liable to win this competition. I need the other four eliminated. Way it is, the winner of this contest gets a million-dollar contract from Powell. But that contract is not with Powell, it's with the Devil. If the winner signs it, they will have sold their soul to Satan.'

The Kid looked at Julius suspiciously. 'I ain't buyin' any of this bullshit. You just said you want me to help you *win* the show. Why'd you want to win and sell your soul to the Devil?'

Julius had a smug look on his face. 'I have my reasons.'

'Which are?'

'You don't need to know.'

'Fair enough. Be simpler, though, if I just threaten this Nigel Powell an' make him let you win.'

'No.'

'Why not?'

''Cause that'd let him off easy.'

The Kid shook his head. 'Yeah? I can make these things real unpleasant when I'm in the right mood.'

'Listen, mister, just trust me on this. All you gotta do is kill off my four main rivals in the show. That will leave me as the only singer in the final who's practised his song with the house orchestra. I'll be nailed-on favourite to win.'

The Bourbon Kid raised an eyebrow and looked at Julius to see if he was serious. It seemed he was. 'So this whole fuckin' show is rigged?'

'Well – yeah. Ain't they always?'

The Kid took one last long drag on his cigarette, then stubbed it out on the bartop. 'I s'pose. And what happens when you've won?'

'I give you your fifty grand.'

'Five hundred grand.' The gravel suddenly sounded as though it had been flash-frozen.

'Sure, whatever. If you're as good at killing as people say you are, it'll be money well spent.'

'No shit.'

'So we have a deal?'

'We have a deal. But hear this: you break it, I'll break your neck.'

Though the Kid had made up his mind that he'd take the job, he was still suspicious of Julius's motives. The guy was liable to try and weasel out of paying up when all this was done. He was definitely not to be trusted.

Julius reached inside his jacket and pulled a small brown envelope from one of the inside pockets. He placed it on the bar and looked at it for a moment, then slid it along the polished wooden surface towards the Kid.

'The details of the job are in there. Four names. I need them dead. *Real* quick,' he said, nodding at it.

The Kid picked up his glass of Sam Cougar and downed the rest of it. He then pulled a ten-dollar bill out of his pants pocket and tossed it on to the bar next to the butt of his extinguished cigarette. Turning to face Julius, he picked up the envelope and stood up from his stool, ready to leave.

'One other thing gotta you know,' said Julius.

'Yeah?' The Kid sighed. There was always one other thing.

'One of 'em's a woman. You okay 'bout killin' women?'

'I killed my mother, didn't I?'

With that unanswerable remark floating in the air, the Bourbon Kid walked off, leaving the James Brown impersonator in the purple suit to finish his beer alone.

Twelve

Sanchez had done some pretty stupid – yeah, okay, some dam' stupid – things in his time. Usually they had involved women or gambling. His latest involved both, although the woman concerned was not of the sort that usually induced an act of stupidity. The women over whom he usually made an asshole of himself tended to be young, attractive and devious. The Mystic Lady was old, ugly and stupid, in Sanchez's eyes at least. What in the hell had he been thinking?

The twenty thousand dollars from the brown envelope was now gone. Blown in a moment of madness that had seen him lump the whole lot on *red* at the roulette wheel. All because he'd listened to that mad old hag Annabel de fuckin' Frugyn. *Some fuckin' fortune teller she'd turned out to be.* If she ever decided to set foot in Sanchez's bar in Santa Mondega, the Tapioca, she'd be getting another sample of his famous homebrew. Useless old bitch.

So now he was faced with an awkward predicament. He had to take the envelope and hand it in at reception, ripped open at one end and minus the twenty thousand dollars. He should have told Elvis about the money straight away, when he first saw it at the bottom of the envelope . They could have split it between them, and then he'd have had Elvis on his side if anyone came looking for it. It was too damned late now to admit to Elvis he'd held out on him. He wasn't even sure if taking the envelope and handing it in at the reception desk was a good idea. If the intended recipient showed up asking for it and found it opened and the money missing, he would probably come looking for Sanchez. The only positive thing that he could see in this goddam mess was that handing in the envelope would ensure that the receptionists might also come under suspicion.

The alternative – not handing in the envelope – would most likely result in its intended recipient tracking down Sanchez anyway. If the envelope was found in his hotel room, he'd be in all kinds of trouble. So he had convinced himself that handing it in to the reception desk kind of made sense.

He was relieved to see that the hordes of visitors checking in had now gone. The oval-shaped reception hall was fairly quiet. He circled it a few times, still wondering whether or not he was doing the right thing, but by the time he'd strolled nonchalantly past the desk four or five times he reckoned it was beginning to look like he was stalking the receptionist. And since that was the one and only Stephie, whom he had earlier called a bitch, he guessed he was starting to look creepy. So eventually, before she reached for some kind of panic button, he approached the desk. It was definitely the right thing to do, not least because he'd promised Elvis he would hand in the envelope, and right now he wasn't keen on pissing the King off too much. Elvis was his only ally.

'Hi again,' he said, offering Stephie a disingenuous smile.

The receptionist had seen him strolling back and forth, occasionally staring over at her, and was understandably creeped out by it. The very large number of guests arriving had meant that she'd had a busy morning; physically and mentally drained, she was not in the right frame of mind to take any shit from Sanchez.

'I really, *really* hope you're not about to ask me out,' she said, looking at him with barely concealed contempt.

Bitch, he thought, but he forced his best smile and slapped the envelope down on the reception desk.

'Found this in the room you kindly got for me. Thought

I oughta hand it in, y'know? – case the guy it was meant for shows up lookin' for it.'

Stephie looked down at the envelope in front of her. 'Oh sure,' she said sarcastically, 'Though I see you've opened it.'

'Nah. It was like that when I found it.'

'Of course.' She snatched it up and stood, tutting quietly under her breath just loud enough for him to hear. 'I'll go stick this in a safe-deposit box out back, just so it doesn't open itself again.'

'Uh, thanks,' said Sanchez, maintaining his horrible fake smile. 'Oh, and er, like, if the guy does come lookin' for it . . .'

'Claude Balls.'

''Scuse me?'

'Claude Balls. The man whose room you took.'

'Yeah, him. If he comes lookin' for it, mebbe you could give me a call in my room? Just so I'll know he got it okay? It'll help me sleep better.'

'I'll bet.' Throwing him one last disapproving look, Stephie disappeared with the envelope through a door at the back of the lobby. One of the other female receptionists passed her on the way. She was a short, rotund woman in her fifties with a face like a bulldog chewing a wasp. She took up a place at the desk next to Stephie's and smiled at Sanchez. Time to make a hasty retreat, he figured. Elvis was shortly due onstage for his audition for the *Back From the Dead* contest. Sanchez wanted to be sure he was there so that he could win some credit with the King by applauding loudly afterwards and complimenting him on his performance.

As he headed to a set of glass doors that led out of the lobby and down towards the theatre, he heard a booming voice from the lobby behind him. It sounded like it belonged to a very large and domineering man.

'Hello, miss,' it said, politely enough. 'Do you have a room reserved for me? Name of Claude Balls.'

Sanchez felt the hairs on the back of his neck stand on end. *Please*, he thought. *Don't let this man look as nasty as he sounds.*

Dreading what he might see, he turned around. His worst fears had been realized. For there, standing at the reception desk, was an absolute giant of a man. He stood around six-five, and wore a long grey trench coat. His thick, unwashed red hair was dragged back into a ponytail that reached down below his shoulder blades. He had a goatee to match, hanging down almost to his chest in a thin plait. Beneath the coat, he was wearing what looked to Sanchez like military gear. A former soldier, perhaps? A deadly assassin? Judging by the contents of the envelope Sanchez had opened, most definitely.

The worried bar owner would not have been reassured to learn that the man claiming to be Claude Balls was actually a well-known hitman round those parts. In fact, he was better known as Invincible Angus because of his incredible endurance. He'd been stabbed, shot, maimed, maced, bludgeoned, you name it, but he always got back up. And he always got his man.

Sanchez didn't need to stare at him for long to know that it was time to get going before one of the receptionists told their latest guest about the envelope that had been tampered with. Just then, sensing that he was being watched, Invincible Angus looked over at Sanchez and gave him an evil glare.

'The fuck you lookin' at, fatso?' he snarled.

There was no need for a response. Sanchez simply turned and rushed off to find Elvis.

Thirteen

Over the years, Luther's impersonation of Otis Redding had earned him many admirers. But it was the approval of the three judges in the *Back From the Dead* competition that could make or break his future. If he won this competition, he would get a contract with the casino and he'd never have to do 'real' work again. As a travelling performer working the night-club circuit he barely made enough money to scrape by from week to week. This once-in-a-lifetime opportunity could change all that. As long as he kept his cool.

The first thing a tribute act would be judged on was its appearance. And Luther had taken great care to look his best. First impressions were crucial, and he wasn't about to let any stone go unturned in his search for fame. He had had an eye-catching shiny black suit and a sharp red shirt made especially for this show. The suit had the name Otis stitched in gold on the left breast pocket, and across the back in much larger letters. *Tacky?* Well, maybe slightly, but important? *Absolutely.* Being instantly recognizable as the performer in question was vital. Luther had learned that lesson early in his career. It helped him to create the illusion that he really was Otis Redding.

As he strode out on to the stage he saw himself on a huge television screen set above a raised area at the back of the stage. Because of that, the entire audience would be able to see every bead of sweat on his brow.

Standing up onstage in front of an audience of thousands

in the hotel's main hall was the most nerve-racking moment of his career to date. In front of him, the auditorium looked absolutely huge, bigger than any other he had ever performed in. The rows of seats went back at least a hundred deep, rising all the way to the back, and were split into three sections. The middle segment spanned thirty seats across and the two side sections had another fifteen seats in each row. And right now every one of the seats was filled.

Up above was a gallery that ran from each edge of the stage to the centre, where there was a glass-walled sound booth. A deejay, who also doubled as the lighting engineer, sat inside it. Luther glanced up and saw the deejay picking his nose. He immediately looked away and tried to erase the image from his mind.

The auditions for the final had been under way for half an hour. The early contestants were the real hopefuls, the ones who had no idea that the show was rigged and had travelled from miles around in the hope that their dreams would be realized. Some were exceptionally good, undeniably worthy of a place in the final. Others were pitifully bad. But now, half an hour into the show, Otis, the first of the five contestants who had been secretly pre-selected for the final, was up to perform. All he had to do was make sure his perfomance didn't suck.

On the stage directly in front of him he could see the panel of three judges watching his every move. It felt as if they were checking his temperament, watching for weaknesses. He could feel their eyes burning into him even more fiercely than the bright lights from above. He only recognized one of the judges. The panel was composed of a black woman, a white woman and, seated between them, a man with skin tanned a curious shade of orange. This was Nigel Powell, the head judge, and the deviser and owner of the competition.

They sat behind a silver-panelled desk that ran along the front of the stage with their backs to the audience and the orchestra pit below them. Before each of them was a glass of water and a pen and notepad, should they decide to make any notes.

As the lights dimmed and the spotlight fell upon him, making the watching audience virtually invisible to him, Luther felt a sudden last-minute surge of confidence. He was going to be incredible. He was certain of it.

After briefly introducing himself and being quizzed by the show's host, Nina Forina, he mentally braced himself and prepared to sing. Feeling more nervous than he really needed to, he waited until the orchestra began the introductory bars, took a deep breath and launched into the opening line of 'These Arms of Mine'. It felt odd, singing in front of such a large audience without a backing track, but he nailed it. The crowd below showed their immediate approval by applauding loudly, which boosted his confidence even further. For the next ninety seconds, until Powell called for him to stop, he owned the stage. None of the singers who had gone before him had been allowed to sing for more than thirty seconds, but to make sure the audience remembered Luther's performance it had been secretly agreed that he would be allowed to sing for longer. By the time he had finished his audition he was receiving a well-earned standing ovation from the crowd, and even a pair of oversized white panties from one of the women near the front.

But it was the judges' acclaim that counted. The first judge to speak was Lucinda Brown, a successful singing coach from Georgia who had trained many soul singers in her time. She was a slightly overweight black woman wearing a low-cut, yellow silk dress. Her dark hair was tied up in a mad 'bird's nest' style on top of her head. Her most positive quality was undoubtedly her natural warmth. She probably knew exactly what the contestants were going through, as she'd undertaken numerous auditions herself in her younger days. Certainly she looked the most sympathetic of the judges, and seemed immediately to be trying to put Luther at ease.

'Honey, how old are you?' she asked.

'I'm twenty-five,' Luther answered. He was now more nervous than he had been in the build-up to performing. All of a sudden the fear that he might have taken his place in the final for granted was gnawing at him. He started taking deep breaths to calm himself, anxiously awaiting any criticism or praise that might be coming his way. He could feel a bead of sweat sliding down his forehead as he melted under the heat of the lights, but he dared not reach up to wipe it away. All he could concentrate on was his breathing.

'Child,' the yellow-clad judge began, 'if Otis Redding coulda sung like you when he was twenty-five, you can bet the sweet Lord Jesus that God wouldn't have allowed him to die in any ol' plane crash. Boy, you was *good*. If ol' Otis is watchin' from up above, I bet he's sayin', *Please Lord, I have been reborn!*' She paused, before adding, 'You *own* this place.' She was wagging the index finger on her right hand vigorously as she spoke, which helped enormously in exciting not only herself but also the watching audience.

Lucinda's praise was all that was needed to send the crowd wild. Many of them jumped to their feet and clapped excitedly. Luther just breathed a huge sigh of relief. He knew he'd sung brilliantly, but he also knew that judges could be idiots. But he had done exactly as Powell had asked. He'd performed a song to the best of his ability, and he looked *good*.

So, yeah – Lucinda, the first judge, had taste.

On to the second.

The white-suited man in the centre nodded to his left to signal that the other female judge should offer her opinion next. She was a Barbie-doll clone in her early forties named Candy Perez, and her claim to fame was that she had once had a top-ten hit in Mexico with a catchy summer pop song that was more famous for the gimmicky dance that went with it than for any singing ability that its performer might have had. Now she smiled broadly at Luther. The smile didn't create a single wrinkle on her face, despite the fact that she would never see thirty, or even forty, again. Like Nigel Powell, the woman was all Botoxed-up, and dam' proud of it. She had big curly blonde hair and wore a classy white leather jacket that was halfway zipped up, squeezing her ample breasts into an impressive cleavage. She didn't appear to be wearing anything beneath the jacket, so it had to be hoped for her sake that the zip could take the considerable pressure.

'Luther, I thought you were great.' She turned a dazzlingly white and entirely insincere smile upon the anxious singer. 'The best I've seen so far. Congratulations. I think you've got a real chance of winning this competition. You done real good, sweetie.'

As more wild applause filled the auditorium, Luther wanted to punch the air and shout 'YESSS!' but chose instead to show some dignity and restraint.

'Thanks – uh, thank you so much,' he muttered humbly.

And so to the third judge. The one whose opinion really mattered. Nigel Powell.

Powell knew how to work the audience, and he was in any case the undoubted star of the show. Being the show's deviser, owner and chief judge meant that his opinion mattered above everyone else's. And he loved to be noticed. That much was obvious from his outfit. The smart black shirt underneath the pristine white suit was fairly tasteless, but it got the man noticed. And the women in the audience loved him. He knew it and they knew it, all of them. Every woman he met seemed to fall under his spell. The man oozed charm, but he also exuded an aura of money and power. So Luther needed him on side, not just to grant him safe passage to the final, but to convince the audience that he could win it when he got there.

The chief judge was milking the crowd too. His body language gave nothing away about his thoughts on Luther's performance, but after solemnly pretending to ponder his response for a while he eventually spoke up. His voice was deep and measured, and his tone verging on the serious.

'Luther,' he said, nodding confidently to himself, but always maintaining eye contact with the now suddenly nervous Otis Redding impersonator. 'Luther – tell me, how much do you want to win this competition?'

'It means everything to me.' The singer's nerves turned his reply into a hurried squeak.

'Really? And do you think you've got what it takes?'

'Yes.' The questioning was nerve-racking, even though the answers were obvious. It felt like Powell was testing the character of his contestant, just to show off.

'And do you think you could get up and perform like that five nights a week? In my hotel? And be that good every time?'

'Yes, Nigel, I know I could. If you just give me the chance. I'll do whatever it takes. This means so much to me.'

Powell sat back in his seat and smiled his bright white smile at Luther.

'Good, because I think you've got a great chance of winning this whole thing. I see real star quality in you. I'm pretty sure we're going to be seeing you again in the final later on. Well done.'

The audience began whooping and cheering, now not just standing on their feet, but literally bouncing up and down while applauding. The emphatic ovation went on for quite some time and was still going strong as Luther made his way offstage via a set of steps on his left that led backstage. The applause was still echoing in his ears as he headed into the waiting room set aside for the contestants who had yet to perform. His four dressing-room companions had all gathered there, and were the first to greet and congratulate him.

'Well done, man,' said Johnny Cash, slapping him on the back. 'Great fuckin' vocals, y'know? Reckon you'll definitely make it to the final.'

'Thanks.'

The compliment was all for show, of course. A few other contestants, unaware that Luther's place in the final was already guaranteed, also wished him the best of luck. He did feel a slight twinge of guilt, knowing that a bunch of people whose hopes and dreams were resting on their success in this show had no idea it was rigged. The feeling soon passed, however.

Glad to have finally gotten his first performance out of the way, he left the large backstage waiting room and stepped out into the corridor, where he headed to the elevator at the end of the hall. He was looking forward to getting back to the dressing room on floor eight and having it all to himself for a while. He felt that, really, he ought to stay to support the other four, but they had all been given instructions earlier in the day to head straight back to their shared dressing room once their performances were over.

When he finally made it to the end of the long yellow-walled corridor his legs were just beginning to regain some of the strength that had been drained out of them during the judge's comments. Even so, his heart was still pounding heavily in his chest as he reached out one hand and pressed a small, round, grey plastic button on the pale yellow wall next to the elevator. To his relief, the silver doors opened straight away and, with no one waiting to come out, he stepped into the elevator and pressed the button marked '8' on the keypad to his right.

Before the doors could close, a man dressed entirely in black, wearing sunglasses and with the dark hood on his jacket pulled up over his head, appeared from around the left side of the entrance. He stepped into the elevator and stood beside Luther, staring back out into the corridor.

'What floor?' Luther asked.

'Doesn't matter.' The voice was not exactly a growl – more a rasp, like gravel being stirred.

The singer wasn't quite sure what to make of the stranger's

response. Maybe the guy just liked riding in elevators? Then the doors closed and, with a slight lurch, the elevator carriage began to move upwards.

Luther was dead before he reached floor two.

Fourteen

Sanchez weaselled his way through the backstage area and stepped on to a part of the stage behind the performers. He found a vantage point just behind a large, heavy red curtain that ran from floor to ceiling. He'd made it there just a minute or two before his friend was due to perform.

In the show, Elvis had the misfortune to be scheduled to appear after the highly impressive Otis Redding impersonator. A tough act to follow. Sanchez kept his fingers crossed that his buddy wouldn't hit any bum notes. Then, when the performance finished, he applauded vigorously, and loudly enough for the King to hear him and know that he had watched and approved.

Elvis had performed an excellent rendition of 'Kentucky Rain' and the audience showed its approval with wild applause and more than a few wolf whistles. Everyone – young, old, male, female – seemed to love him. The guy just had charisma. To Sanchez, he was the coolest dude on the planet. Not that he'd ever admit that to him. That would be uncool.

The three judges hadn't been quite so enthusiastic about Elvis's performance as Sanchez or the rest of the audience. In fact, their comments seemed to be designed to temper the enthusiasm of the watching fans. Sure, Sanchez was biased, but he had Elvis down as being every bit as good as the Otis Redding impersonator who had gone before him. Elvis thought so too. But the only judge to offer any real praise was Candy Perez. Elvis gave her a wink and kept his cool, carefully avoiding calling the two other judges dumbass muthafuckers.

In high style and with great dignity he strutted offstage towards Sanchez, waving to the audience and blowing kisses as he went. As soon as he was out of sight of them, the smile on his face turned to a scowl. Sanchez, seeing his friend's face, reckoned some reassurance was required.

'Yo, Elvis! You were great, man. Reckon you're a dead cinch to make it to the final,' he blurted out. He meant it, too.

'Bull-*shit*! Fuckin' show's rigged, man,' Elvis snarled. He wasn't a man to take criticism lightly. Or at all. And in this instance he had a point. He knew how to work a crowd, and he had his impersonation off to perfection. Anyone who said otherwise was a fuckin' liar.

'Yeah? You really think it's rigged?' Sanchez asked.

'Sure. Didn't you see the way the judges gave that Otis Redding guy great comments, even though he wasn't anythin' special? Anyone can do fuckin' Otis Redding,' he added dismissively.

'You were better than him, that's for certain.'

Elvis nodded his agreement. It was clear that despite his almost super-human self-confidence, a few compliments from Sanchez were more than welcome.

'Thanks, Sanchez. 'Preciate it. Still reckon I'm fucked though. An' you know somethin' else? When I was out there – singin', you know – somethin' hit me.'

'Shit, man. I didn't see anythin'.'

'No, numbnuts. I mean somethin' dawned on me. That Otis Redding impersonator? Well, he was one of the guys in the photos you had in that envelope, wasn't he?'

Sanchez thought for a moment. He had only caught the last few seconds of Otis Redding's performance. Most of what he'd seen was the back of the singer's head as he received from the judges' compliments. But he had got a look at his face as he'd walked past to the backstage area. It hadn't occurred to him at the time, but yeah – Elvis was right.

'Shit, yeah. So, maybe that wasn't a hit list? Maybe someone was tryin' to bribe one of the judges to get the people in the photos in to the final?'

Elvis peered over his sunglasses to look Sanchez in the eye. 'Yeah?' he said. 'So if it was a bribe, where was the fuckin' money?'

Sanchez felt his cheeks reddening a little. 'Er, oh yeah,' he blustered. 'Must have been a hit list.'

'That's my reckoning,' the King said wearily. 'Though, even a hit list often has a deposit of cash with it.' He paused for a moment, before adding, 'There's definitely some strange shit goin' down here today. An' I don't like it.'

'Me either.'

'Lucky you took that goddam envelope back to reception.' He paused again, as if suddenly remembering that Sanchez was a serial liar, and just as likely to have thrown the envelope in a trash can somewhere. 'You did take it back, didn't ya?' he asked suspiciously.

'Oh yeah. Sure. 'Course I did. Mind you, wasn't a minute too soon. As I was on my way here, that guy Claude Balls who was supposed to have my room showed up at reception.'

'Did he make you?'

'Nah! I got the fuck outta there. Guy was huge.'

'Big fucker, huh?'

'Yeah. An' ugly. Looked like he'd make a good hitman.'

'That bein' the case, Sanchez, I suggest you clear your suitcase outta the room before he goes up there lookin' for you.'

'Yeah. I kinda thought that'd be a good idea.' He looked round nervously, then added, 'Thing is, I don't much fancy goin' up there on my lonesome, though. If you know what I mean.'

Elvis shook his head and sighed. Sanchez's cowardice, like his untruthfulness, was legendary back home in Santa

Mondega. The King knew perfectly well that his friend didn't have the guts to go on his own. But for all his friend's character failings he had always been generous, standing Elvis many a free drink in his bar, the Tapioca, over the years. For good reason, mind.

'Ten years today since I saved your sorry ass from those vampires in church, ain't it?' Elvis said.

'Yeah. I ain't forgotten that, neither. But that whole experience always makes me a bit edgy on Halloween. It's kinda why I took this trip. Thought it'd be nice to get out of Santa Mondega, what with all the undead an' that.'

'Come on then,' growled Elvis, heading out into the corridor. 'Let's go get your bag. You can bunk with me, if we can't find ya somewhere else.'

'Thanks, man.' Sanchez, following, was properly grateful.

They reached the elevator at the end of the corridor and Elvis pressed the grey button set in the wall to call it. They waited for little more than a few seconds before the car arrived and the silver doors opened. It looked empty and both men stepped inside. Sanchez turned to his left to press the button for his floor, to be confronted by an unpleasant sight. Slumped in the corner underneath the keypad was the body of a black man in his mid-twenties.

'*Jeez-uss Christ!*' Sanchez shrieked like a girl as he jumped back in shock.

'What floor's your room on, Sanchez?' Elvis asked coolly. He'd seen the corpse too, but reacted in a much calmer fashion than his friend.

'*Fuck!* Fuck, man! Look, he's . . .'

'What fuckin' floor?'

'Seven.'

Ignoring the body, Elvis reached over to press the button for the seventh floor. As the doors closed and the elevator began moving up, Sanchez regained a little of his composure.

He had a dead black guy at his feet. He'd seen plenty of dead people before, most of them in his bar, but the sight of one crumpled up in an elevator had shocked him, as though he'd been confronted by a spider a second after switching on the bedroom light.

Taking a deep breath and ignoring his pounding heart, he looked a little closer at the corpse, which was half-propped against the wall of the car. The guy was wearing a shiny black suit with a red shirt underneath.

'Oh my God! It's Otis Redding!'

'No shit.' Elvis sounded unconcerned, but Sanchez rattled on: 'That Claude Balls guy must have killed him.'

'Or paid someone else to.'

'Jeez.' Wincing with distaste, Sanchez leaned forward to get a better look at the body. 'I reckon his neck's bin broken.' He sniffed the air. 'Smells like he's been shittin' on the dock of the bay too.'

'That ain't funny, man. Matter of fact, it don't even make sense.'

'Short notice. Best I could come up with.'

Elvis shook his head. 'You know, right now jest ain't the time to be thinkin' up wisecracks. When we get to your room, be an idea to walk right past it. This Balls guy might be in there. Jest follow my lead from here.' Elvis was showing an impressive clarity of thought, given the circumstances. 'An' if anyone else tries to get in this elevator we're gonna have to stop them.'

'Because of the smell?'

'Nah, asshole. 'Cause if anyone sees us in here with this corpse we're gonna be prime suspects for killin' him.'

'Aw shit. Muthafucker.'

There was a pinging sound as the elevator reached the seventh floor. The doors slid apart. Immediately Sanchez saw four armed security guards in black suits and all with military haircuts, standing at the end of the passageway. In front of his room. Preparing to bust down the door and barge in.

Elvis put a hand up to cover his face and stepped to one side where he couldn't be seen from the corridor. Then he whispered urgently to Sanchez, 'Press for ground. We gotta get outta here.'

Sanchez heard the instruction but was so busy staring at the security guards that he paid little attention to which button he was reaching for on the keypad.

All four guards looked back to see who was staring at them from the elevator. What they saw was Sanchez reach for the keypad to press the button for the ground floor. *And miss it.* Instead, he prodded his finger into the open eye of the dead Otis Redding impersonator. The shock of prodding something cold and elastic made him leap back. His action had more disastrous effects, however. The corpse slid from its position against the wall and fell to the elevator floor in front of Sanchez, visible to the four men in the corridor.

'*Oh shit.*' Sanchez recovered his senses, located the ground-floor button and pressed it quickly. He was too late. The guards had seen the body and were focusing on it, and on Sanchez. Elvis's face was safely tucked away out of their line of vision, but the sleeve of his gold suit was poking out past the elevator doors.

'Hey, you. *Freeze!*' yelled the nearest member of the security team. He had drawn a handgun with impressive speed and was aiming it at the elevator.

Elvis reached across and shoved Sanchez to the side. 'Get back up against the wall,' he hissed. 'Don't let 'em get a good look at you!'

With horrible slowness the elevator doors began to close as the four security guards came charging down the corridor.

Fifteen

Johnny Cash – or his impersonator, at least – had well over an hour to wait before his audition. He'd been hanging backstage with the other singers, and had impressed everyone with his cool, unflappable confidence. Little did they guess that underneath the laid-back exterior he was shitting himself. A million bucks was at stake. There was nothing for the runner-up, not a cent. It didn't matter how well he had coped with pressure in his career up to now, this was a whole different ball game.

The backstage waiting room was a hive of activity, chock-full of hopefuls dressed as their favourite dead singers. There were comfortable sofas, chairs and beanbags scattered around, and a table laden with drinks and snacks had been set up against each of the four walls. None of which seemed to be helping to calm anyone down. There was more nervous energy and tension in this one room than the rest of the hotel put together.

The person Johnny most envied was Luther, the Otis Redding performer. Lucky bastard. His audition was done and dusted, and now he was off somewhere relaxing, knowing that he was almost certain to make the final. Johnny wished he could do the same, but needed a pick-me-up, a kind of confidence-booster to get him through the agonizing wait before performing. He also wanted to be sure that the other contestants backstage were really as nervous as he was. Not just faking it.

He looked around at the other performers still waiting to audition and picked out his target. Sure enough, Kurt Cobain looked edgy and uneasy from all the waiting, too. He was standing on his own by the exit to the corridor out back, sucking at a tepid can of Sprite through a straw. *Aw, what the fuck*, thought Johnny and headed over to him.

'Yo, Cobain! How goes it, man?' he asked, offering a confident smile that belied his own nervousness.

The ratty-looking singer smiled back, snorting a little Sprite out of his nose. Didn't look like he was used to people approaching him in a friendly manner, and he was in any case probably wary of Johnny's intentions. Kurt looked like an outsider, and appeared to be doing nothing particularly to fit in.

'Be honest, I'm shittin' myself,' he responded honestly.

'Yeah? Well, I may have somethin' that can help with that.'

'For real?'

'Yeah.'

Kurt eyed him suspiciously. 'You ain't gonna try to sell me on Jesus an' the Power of Prayer, are you?' he asked.

'Nah,' Johnny grinned. Ignoring the other's powerful body odour, he leaned in and whispered in his ear, 'Wanna do a line of coke?'

'You got some?'

Jeez-uss, this guy was somethin' else, thought Johnny. 'No, I was just offering,' he said with heavy sarcasm, before adding, ''Course I got some. You in?'

'Yo! Show me the way, buddy.'

Johnny nodded towards the exit and Kurt followed him out into the corridor. They made for the men's washroom on the right and, after a quick look around, Johnny ducked in through the door with Kurt close behind.

The washroom was empty and they headed straight for the second stall. The place was antiseptically clean, and the white-tiled floor looked as if it had recently been mopped. Checking for a final time that they hadn't been followed in, Johnny's eyes darted round the room before he bolted the door shut behind them. The toilet in the stall they had chosen was as clean as the floor outside. Not so much as a drop of piss on the shiny white seat.

Kurt pulled the toilet-seat lid down and stepped aside to allow his companion to do his bit. Johnny produced a small bag of cocaine from one of the front pockets in his pants. He had hoped not to have to resort to the stuff, because he had wanted to perform with a completely clear head, but he had known full well when he slipped the bag of white powder into his pants pocket that morning that he would end up using it.

He opened the bag and watched Kurt's eyes light up, then poured a little of the powder on to the toilet lid. Next, he pulled a straight razor from the breast pocket in his black shirt. He used the blade to divide the powder into four lines each about four inches long. It took him less than thirty seconds, and he could tell his partner in crime was impressed.

'You wanna go first?' he asked.

The answer was an emphatic yes. Kurt was already holding a short red-and-white-striped plastic straw in his hand, ready to go. Minutes earlier, he had been sucking Sprite through the straw. He hadn't dared hope that he would find a much stronger stimulant.

'Step aside, my good man,' he said, with mock formality. Then, crouching down on the tiled floor, he held the end of the straw to one nostril, pressed the other closed with one finger, and quickly set about snorting up the nearest line. He inhaled it in one long sniff, all of it, then sat back on his haunches and blinked a few times. He wiped the end of his nose with the back of his hand and sniffed hard to drag up any remnants of powder that might be loitering at the end of his nostril.

'That is *good* shit, Mister Cash. Oh yeah. *Very* good shit!' he said. Then he held the straw up to Johnny, who took it and, crouching, leaned over to snort up the line nearest to him.

Outside, someone opened the main door to the men's washroom. Johnny heard footsteps walk in, boots clacking on the tiles. He'd just finished snorting up his first line and was blinking furiously while trying to control the urge to shout about how good the coke was.

The person outside walked slowly across the tiled floor of the washroom. Johnny peered under the bottom of the locked door and saw a pair of scuffed black boots walking past the first stall. The boots stopped outside the door behind which he and Kurt Cobain were crouching, like two schoolboys with a tit mag. He glanced at Kurt, who looked as concerned as he was. Being caught by security taking illegal drugs on the premises would result in disqualification from the competition, so it went without saying that they should both stay absolutely quiet. Kurt obviously understood.

Johnny watched with considerable paranoia as the toes of the boots visible in the gap under the door turned to face them. A horrible pause followed. Then there was a gentle thud as the person outside pushed at the door, only to find it locked. Johnny looked over at Kurt who had his hand over the end of his nose, no doubt trying his damnedest not to sniff.

The boots stepped backwards, first the left one, then the right. Johnny had to lean down further to see them as they retreated out of his sight. A second after he lowered his head the door crashed open, its lock busting with a loud crack. It hit Johnny across the forehead and knocked him back. He landed on his ass on the floor beside the toilet. Terrified, both he and Kurt looked up to see a man dressed all in black staring down at them. He was wearing dark sunglasses and had a black hood pulled up over his head.

Kurt spoke up first. 'Hey, man, d'you mind?' he said in an aggrieved whine. 'We coulda been takin' a shit in here!'

The intruder responded in a gravelly voice. 'Yeah? Both of you?'

'Well, *no*.'

'Look, man,' said Johnny, rubbing his forehead where the door had hit him. 'There's plenty of other free stalls, 'kay?'

'Are you Johnny Cash?'

'Yeah.'

'And Kurt Cobain?'

'Yeah, that's him.' Johnny pointed at Kurt.

'Good.'

The guy didn't appear to be in any rush to move to another stall and the situation was becoming a little awkward. Johnny decided to make a peace offering.

'You want some of this coke? We got two lines left.'

'No.'

There was an uncomfortable pause as they waited to see what his next move would be. He just stared down at them from behind his sunglasses. Kurt was still on his knees on the floor on one side of the toilet and Johnny was still sitting on his ass on the other.

The coke had entered Johnny's bloodstream, and it felt like liquid confidence rushing through his veins. He was fucking invincible. Time to get rid of this asshole.

'You don't want any, then d'ya mind closin' the fuckin' door?'

The man ignored him and pointed at Kurt Cobain. 'Come here,' he grated. The voice was frighteningly cold, devoid of any emotion.

Kurt struggled to his feet and frowned. 'Whadda ya wa—'

CRACK!

Without any warning, the man punched Kurt on the end of the nose. The punch was a solid straight jab with his right fist, and it hit with sickening force. The singer's nose exploded in a fountain of blood and he collapsed back on to the floor, banging his head on the toilet lid as he went down.

Johnny watched on in horror as his scruffily dressed

buddy fell. Then he looked back up at the intruder in their stall. The man leaned down, grabbed him by his greasy hair and pulled him to his feet, drawing him right up to eye level.

'Whadda ya want?' Johnny stammered, echoing his companion. He was close enough to his unwelcome guest to see his own reflection in the man's sunglasses. His confidence had evaporated in an instant. He looked terrified.

With his hand still in Johnny's hair, the man twisted his head around slowly and pointed it down at the toilet.

'Sniff up the rest of your shit.'

'Huh?'

'*Sniff it up.*'

As he spoke, he released his grip on Johnny's hair and pushed him down towards the toilet seat. Johnny did as he'd been instructed and got back down on his knees to snort up the two remaining lines of coke. He picked up the red-and-white-striped straw, which was lying where it had fallen on the floor beside the toilet, and placed it at the near end of one of the lines of white powder. His hands were shaking. He had a horrible feeling that the man behind him was going to smash his head down on to the toilet seat cover as soon as he bent down to start vacuuming up the coke.

But shit, what fuckin' option did he have?

He leaned forward slowly and slipped one end of the straw into his left nostril. At that moment, just as he expected, the intruder slammed down hard on the back of his head. The crushing impact of the blow drove the straw right up his nostril and into his skull. He only felt the cold pain of it for a millisecond. Then his nose hit the toilet lid and bone splinters smashed up into his brain, killing him instantly.

Sixteen

Invincible Angus was an angry-looking guy at the best of times. This was not one of those times. His face twitched with rage upon hearing that his room had been given to someone else. On top of that, the receptionist had given him an envelope addressed to him in his guise as Mr Claude Balls, which someone had handed in. That should have lightened his mood, but when she passed it to him, he saw right away that it had been tampered with. Nor was anyone in reception owning up to having opened it. They claimed that the person who had taken his room had handed it to them in that condition.

Now Angus had tortured a great many people in his time. Sometimes for fun, it was true, but quite often to extract information, and through this experience he had learned how to tell when someone was bullshitting him. And the reception staff at the hotel were too damn scared of him to be lying. He was one hundred per cent confident of that. The fact remained, however, that the envelope still contained the photos and the list of names of his targets. It was just the cash that had gone.

Stephie the receptionist nervously informed him that there were no vacancies left and suggested that he head to the nearest bar for a drink – on the house, naturally – while she did what she could to find him a new room. He could tell she was going to do her best because he'd done a damn good job of scaring the shit out of her and the other staff, including the security guys. After all, it was not often that a six-feet-five-inch-tall hitman walked into the hotel to find that the room he'd reserved had been given to someone else.

On his way to the bar, Angus opened the envelope and flicked through the photos, then took a look at the names of the targets on the slip of paper. He had survived as long as he had because he had good instincts, and those instincts had told him from the get-go that this job was all wrong for him. True, most of his employers were assholes – that was a pitfall of his chosen career – but the guy offering this particular assignment was the worst kind. He claimed his name was Julius, but even that was in doubt.

Even by the standards of the murky world of the professional hitman, this Julius came over as being especially untrustworthy. Angus had seen it in his face as soon as they'd met. He oozed deceit, and more than likely he was withholding information. On top of that, he seemed to be of the type that would give the job to more than one hitman, just to ensure the hit was successful. That kind of guy was always bad for business. It meant other hitmen sniffing around, often taking each other out as well as the primary target. And only the last man standing would be paid for the job. *That is, assuming he didn't get double-crossed,* Angus thought angrily. He would normally have turned down an assignment based on these factors, but he had hit a rocky patch financially, so in this case he figured the reward was worth the risk. Yet, since he'd taken the job he'd been struck by a run of bad luck, something that almost always happened when he took on an assignment he didn't like.

But he was convinced of one thing: Julius was slippery, and his motives were unclear. Angus had only agreed to work for him on the condition that he receive a down payment of twenty thousand dollars. He was confident he could carry out the job, but on the off chance that anything went wrong, that twenty grand would pay off a debt he owed to some seriously unpleasant gangland bosses. Successfully completing the hit would bring him another thirty thousand, but without a down payment there was a distinct chance of not getting paid at all. It wasn't a risk he was willing to take.

The other thing that was really playing on his mind, and which had convinced him that this job was either jinxed or a set-up, was the news that the room he'd booked had been given to a guy named Sanchez Garcia. Just 'cause he, Angus, had been a tad late arriving. It was this man who had allegedly returned the envelope to reception. It seemed likely that he now had the cash deposit and knew all the details of the hit. Maybe he was another contract killer?

Turning these things over in his mind, Angus arrived at the bar badly in need of a drink and in a really foul and frustrated frame of mind. And that was when his luck looked like it might be about to change. Sitting at a table in the far corner of the lounge was a small black guy in a purple suit. Angus recognized him right away: Julius, the shifty bastard who had hired him in the first place. A bald-headed little fella who avoided eye contact whenever he was asked a question. Maybe he could explain what the hell was going on, exactly. Or at the very least, cough up another twenty grand.

Angus walked up to Julius's table. On his way he called over to the barmaid, 'Hey, bitch, get me a double Scotch and ice and bring it over.'

Valerie, thoroughly outraged, looked him up and down, having to crane her neck to do so. Her mouth dropped open in a surprised 'oh' when she saw the size of him. Like most people of whom he made demands, she suddenly decided just to do as he asked.

Angus took a chair opposite Julius at the table and sat down heavily. At first, the James Brown impersonator looked surprised to see him but the look passed all too quickly. He picked up a bottle of Shitting Monkey beer from the table and took a sip. Lots of folks did that, tried to look nonchalant when Angus intimidated them. He took vicious pleasure in knowing that despite appearances, Julius was probably about to shit his pants.

The hitman threw the brown envelope containing the photos and hit list on to the table and sat back in his chair staring Julius out, his facial features tense with anger. 'Where's the fuckin' twenty grand?' he snarled. His red goatee quivered as he spoke.

Julius placed his beer back down on the table and swallowed. 'You're late,' he said. If he was intimidated, he didn't show it. 'I've given the job to someone else.'

'*What?*'

'You didn't show up on time. Someone else now has the contract. Maybe you should have listened to me when I stressed the importance of being on time.'

'I ain't barely listenin' to you *now*, you boring fuck.'

'Well, that's *your* problem.'

Angus was clenching his fists in frustration. 'Muthafucker,' he rumbled, staring hard at the singer.

'Sorry, man. You snooze, you lose.'

Angus leaned over the table and right into Julius's personal space. 'You know, I ain't all the way convinced that you are who you say you are anyway. So watch how you speak to me, asshole.'

At that moment, Valerie arrived at the table, stopping short at Angus's shoulder. Leaning over him, she placed a small round silver tray on the table. It had his double Scotch-and-ice on it. The ice was melting fast, and making light crackling and hissing sounds that punctuated the silence between the two men.

'I'll get this,' Julius offered generously. His expression managed to combine insouciance with insincerity.

'Did it look to you like I was gonna pay?'

Julius leaned across the table and handed ten dollars to Valerie with a friendly smile. She took the money and placed it in a black pouch on the front of her skirt. Then she had the good sense to beat a hasty retreat back behind the bar.

'Thanks,' said Angus grudgingly, picking up the glass and taking a sip. The ice cubes rocked forward and pressed against his goatee. He wiped his mouth dry with the back of one hand as he put the glass back down on the tray. 'So – what the fuck happened to my twenty grand? Reckon you owe me that at least, for draggin' me all the way out here.'

'I don't know what your game is, Mister Balls,' – Julius stressed the name with heavy sarcasm – 'but the twenty grand was in the envelope. Leastways, it *was* when I slipped it under your room door. Way I see it, you now owe me twenty grand.'

'Go fuck yourself. Girl on the desk told me the room was given to a guy name of Sanchez Garcia. Why the fuck's *he* here?'

For the second time Julius looked genuinely surprised. 'Who's he?'

'That's what *I* wanna know. He the man you gave the job to?'

'Shit, I don't know the *actual* name of the guy I gave the job to. Only that he's known to most people as the Bourbon Kid. He doesn't tend to give his real name out.'

'The Bourbon Kid, huh? That muthafucker. Well, has he done the job yet? 'Cause I'm here now and I'm ready to get started.'

Julius sighed, then shrugged his shoulders carelessly. 'If his reputation is anythin' to go by, the job will be done in about ten minutes.'

'Well, we'll just see about that.' Angus picked up his Scotch and downed the rest of it, taking in the ice cubes and crunching them hard between his teeth, as though trying to impress Julius with his tolerance of cold temperatures. Then he slammed the glass back down on the tray and stood up.

'I'll find this Sanchez Garcia guy and get my twenty grand back. Then I'll finish the job I came here to do.' There was considerable menace in the way he said the word 'finish'.

'Good luck with that.'

Angus shook his head at Julius. Little prick wasn't even bothered. His suspicions that this man wasn't worth getting mixed up with had been confirmed. He wasn't exactly sure with whom he should be angriest as he turned and stormed off back to the lobby. But taking out his fury on Julius seemed like a waste of time. Sanchez Garcia was a better target for his frustration.

It was time to come up with a new plan.

Seventeen

Sanchez was overwhelmed by the foul smell coming from Otis Redding's corpse. The sight of the body had already made him nauseous, and the stench in the confined space of the elevator only made it worse. And the corpse appeared to be staring right at him. Freaky bastard eyes it had, as well. He tried to look anywhere but at those eyes, but no matter where he looked he could see them staring at him, feel the glare burning into him. And every time he glanced back, the eyes seemed to have opened even wider. He felt an overwhelming urge to slap Otis round the face and yell at him to stop staring, but he had a feeling Elvis wouldn't approve.

He also tried to remind himself that there were more serious matters to be concerned about at the current time.

As the elevator car descended to the ground floor Sanchez hoped and prayed that Elvis had a plan to get them out of their predicament. When it came to disposing of dead bodies or distancing oneself from a murder, surely Elvis was extremely well qualified? After all, he did this for a living. There had to be a textbook method of dealing with this kind of situation.

'Fuck, man. The fuck we do now?' Sanchez asked. He couldn't hide his desperate need for Elvis to take control of things.

'Help me lift him up,' said Elvis. He reached down, dug a hand under the corpse's right armpit and hauled one side of it up.

After a moment's hesitation, Sanchez grabbed the left arm

and pulled. 'What we doin'?' he asked.

'You seen that film, *Weekend at Bernie's*?'

'Yeah.'

'Well, we're doin' that.'

'We're takin' him *water skiing*?'

'No, dumbass. We're just gonna pretend like he's drunk and we're carryin' him round. Then we'll dump his body where no one'll find it. If there ain't no dead body we can't be accused of killing him. Right now, those security guys who saw us don't know he ain't just drunk. If we can hide the body before they find us, we just tell 'em he was some drunk guy in the elevator an' he got off on the second floor.'

Sanchez loved Elvis. The King's plan was pretty shit, but it was way better than anything he could have come up with himself in such a short space of time. And since right now all Sanchez could think about was slapping the corpse around the face, it was a relief to know his buddy was in control. Elvis was just so damned cool, and he never panicked over anything. He wasn't especially clever or cunning, but he was incredibly confident and had all the qualities of a born leader. Everyone he met warmed to him at once, and nearly all of them would do anything to make him like them. His approval and friendship were the two things about him that most people coveted, no one more so than Sanchez.

Once they had lifted Otis Redding to his feet, they each wrapped one of his arms around their shoulders to give the impression of a drunk being supported by two friends. It was a blessing that he wasn't visibly bleeding from anywhere. He seemed to just have a broken neck and a big mess in his pants. The injury added to his drunken look, because the slightest movement from Sanchez or Elvis caused his head to sway one way or the other. Of course, the first thing that happened was that the head lolled over to rest on Sanchez's right shoulder, the sightless eyes staring up at the bar owner. *Bastard*.

The elevator reached the ground floor and the door slowly

opened, with a slight grating noise. It sounded deafening to Sanchez and he prayed no one was around. No such luck. There were two people waiting in the corridor outside, an elderly couple, probably both in their seventies and both smartly dressed, as if they were heading to church. The man wore a well-cut grey suit and his wife had on a conservative blue dress. No doubt their stay in the hotel was a big deal to them and they wanted to look their best. At first they looked shocked at the sight of Elvis and Sanchez manoeuvring Otis Redding out of the elevator. The corpse's feet were dragging along the floor. As they passed the old couple Elvis winked at the woman.

'It's okay, ma'am,' he said reassuringly, his rich, deep voice adding warmth to his smile. 'He just kinda overdid the booze.'

The old woman smiled, both she and her husband laughed politely as they stepped into the elevator. They stood and watched Sanchez and Elvis dragging Otis Redding down the corridor while they waited for the doors to close. Such a charming young man. And what a good friend to his incapacitated companion. Then the smell hit them.

Sanchez and Elvis passed a few more hotel guests as they headed in the direction of the lobby. Elvis was always quick to tell everyone they met that Otis was just drunk. He succeeded in convincing them and even making most of them laugh, albeit quietly so they didn't wake up what they thought was a drunken Otis Redding impersonator.

'Where we goin', man?' Sanchez asked, his voice taking on a whining tone. 'This dude is gettin' fuckin' heavy!'

'In there,' said Elvis, pointing at a door on the right-hand side of the corridor. It was a grey door with a small plate on it showing a black stickman, signifying that it was the men's washroom. Sanchez, as always, didn't quite catch on to the plan.

'What? You need a piss?' he asked.

'No, Sanchez,' his friend said wearily. 'We can stash him in one of the stalls. No one'll find him for hours.'

'Oh. Yeah. Good plan. What with him smellin' of shit an' all.'

They dragged the corpse over to the door and then Sanchez backed into it, leading the way in. Otis and Elvis followed, the latter checking up and down the corridor to make sure no one was watching them. It seemed that they had timed it well, for their curious entry went unnoticed.

Sanchez was relieved to see that the washroom appeared to be empty. It was a large room, about forty feet long by fifteen wide. On the wall to the left was a line of eight urinals, and on the opposite side was a row of six toilet stalls. At the far end of the room were three washbasins with mirrors above them.

Sanchez was relieved to see that there wasn't anyone in there taking a piss and, from the lack of noise, it seemed a safe bet that no one was taking a shit in any of the stalls, either. There was a shitty smell in the air, but he was pretty sure they had brought that in with them.

'Which stall we goin' ta put him in?' he asked.

'First one. You think I want to carry this guy any longer'n I have to?'

Sanchez led the way, backing into the door of the first stall they came to. Elvis followed and then held Otis Redding up on his own while Sanchez pulled the toilet lid down so that they could sit the corpse on it. Elvis manhandled the body on to the lid and then the two of them spent about a minute trying to position the corpse so that it would sit upright and not fall to one side. Eventually, after both had stood carefully for about twenty seconds with their hands at the ready in case it slipped, they decided the body was secure and would only fall if nudged.

'Hoo!' sighed Sanchez. 'I could use a piss after all that.'

'Good. You go take a piss and I'll lock this door from the

inside and climb out over it.'

'Cool.'

Sanchez walked out of the stall and went over to the nearest urinal on the opposite wall. He heard Elvis bolt the door shut behind him, and then heard him mumble something that sounded like *Shit! I didn't think this through.*

As he began pissing into the urinal, it occurred to Sanchez that in order to climb out of a stall the first thing a person would do was stand on the toilet. Elvis wouldn't be able to do that because Otis Redding was sitting on it. He heard a fair bit of noise as his friend attempted to climb out over the door. The crashing and rattling sounds were accompanied by a fair amount of cussing, too.

Eventually Sanchez finished, zipped up his pants and turned to see Elvis jump to the floor behind him and begin dusting his gold jacket off, checking it for any stains on the shoulders. Sanchez headed over to the three washbasins at the far end of the room, turned on the faucet on the middle one and began rinsing his homebrew off his hands.

'Sanchez,' Elvis called out from back down the room. Sanchez looked up into the mirror above the basin and saw Elvis looking into the second stall, next to the one in which they had stashed Otis Redding.

'Yeah Whassup?'

'Guess you need to take a look at this.' Elvis was staring into the second stall.

'The fuck is it? A giant turd?'

'Worse'n that.'

There was, surprisingly, a note of concern in Elvis's voice, so Sanchez turned off the faucet and shook his hands dry. Then he walked over to Elvis. Before he'd even reached the second stall, he saw that they had a new problem.

'Hey, what's that on the floor?' he asked.

'Blood,' said Elvis.

'Blood? From Otis Redding?'

'Nah.'

There was a small pool of blood seeping out from underneath the door of the stall, which was half open. Slowly but steadily, the pool was growing with each passing second. Sanchez walked a little more tentatively towards Elvis, and when he reached him, he peered around the door.

'Holy fuckin' shit!'

What Elvis had discovered was two more corpses. A guy who looked like a hobo was propped up against the wall at the side of the toilet. The other guy, dressed all in black, was lying flat on his back on the floor with his feet up on the toilet seat. Blood was weeping out from a wound at the back of his head, which accounted for the expanding pool that had spread to outside the stall.

'Fuckin' blood wasn't there just now, when we came in,' Sanchez pointed out, shakily. The feeling of nausea had come back with a vengeance.

'Reckon I knocked one o' these guys over as I was climbin' out the stall.'

'Shit. What the fuck is goin' on in this place?' Sanchez was used to seeing murders in his bar, the Tapioca, but an expensive, respectable hotel ought to have been different. There were corpses everywhere you looked in this place.

The dead guy up against the wall was wearing a scruffy blue sweater and ripped jeans. His face was covered in blood, which appeared to have come mostly from a broken nose and some missing teeth. His greasy blond hair was also stained with streaks of dark red, clotting it together. The gruesome sight was made worse by the fact that his eyes, although open, had rolled up in his head, showing only the whites. *Still, at least he wasn't a gawper like Otis Redding.* Sanchez didn't waste too much time looking at him. The other guy on the floor was a little older with a head of thick dark hair. His eyes had rolled up in his skull too, and his hair was a mess. As Sanchez was looking down at him, Elvis placed a hand on his shoulder.

'Figured out who they are?'

'Huh?'

'Kurt Cobain an' Johnny Cash. Two of the guys on that hit list you had.' Of course he was right. Sanchez couldn't believe he hadn't spotted it sooner.

'Shit. That Balls fella must have offed these guys too. Wow.'

'Yeah. We need to get the fuck outta here, Sanchez. We're now in a washroom with the first three victims from the hit list. Anyone finds us in here, specially after we just been seen draggin' ole Otis around, we're gonna be in deep shit.'

Right again. This wasn't the best place to be hanging around in, and although they were innocent of any wrongdoing, they were prime suspects. What with Elvis being a professional hitman, and that.

But before they had a chance to make an exit, they heard the door to the washroom open. Elvis grabbed Sanchez by the arm and dragged him into stall three. He pulled the door shut behind them and pushed the other man back towards the toilet. The terrified bar owner knew not to say anything, but even so Elvis put his finger to his lips and shook his head. Sanchez found this annoying. He knew to stay quiet. He started to say so, but just then they heard the sound of two men's footsteps on the tiled floor of the washroom. As he heard them walk towards the urinals, Sanchez hoped their visitors wouldn't see the blood seeping out from stall two and decide to investigate.

Eighteen

Emily had spent years building up to this, her big moment: the chance to make a name for herself and earn a contract to perform as a star at the Hotel Pasadena. She wished her mother were with her to share the excitement. Having her around would have helped to control her nerves too.

Her mother, Angelina, had been a successful travelling cabaret performer for many years, and Emily's earliest memories were of wanting to be just like her, to command an audience the way her mother did. As a young girl, she had seen a lot of the world thanks to her mother's travelling. They had spent months at a time on cruise ships, or settled in at a hotel or casino for a season. It had been a wonderful upbringing during which she had met thousands of interesting people from all walks of life. She had fond memories of hanging out with hotel staff and seeing how impressed they were by her mother's singing. Angelina sang beautifully and had a wonderful vocal range. This versatility enabled her to perform many old classic songs in a voice almost identical to the original artist's, no matter how difficult. In venues where she was allowed more freedom, however, she was more than capable of singing her own interpretation of a song.

She had encouraged Emily from childhood to follow in her footsteps, and had been an assiduous tutor. Above all, Emily remembered how she would stand in the wings, watching her mother sing, and wishing she could be just like her. Now was her chance.

Their time on the road together had come to an end two years ago. Angelina had fallen sick with what at first was thought to be a throat infection, but turned out to be far worse. After months of trying to sing, but either being unable to, or putting in substandard performances, she discovered she had cancer of the throat. She was forty-seven. Both of them were devastated.

Emily immediately took over as the breadwinner, but almost every cent she earned ended up being spent on caring for her mother. And it just wasn't enough. Worse still, her own singing career was badly curtailed because Angelina was too sick to travel. So for the last year, Emily had worked every dive-bar singing contest east of Little Rock in hope of securing that elusive big break. And when she wasn't singing, she worked in fast-food joints to help make ends meet.

With hope born of desperation, Emily knew that now was her chance to prove she had what it took to follow in her mother's footsteps. Almost better than that, if she could win the *Back From the Dead* contest, then their money worries would be over. And she'd be a star. Just like Mom. Her mother had been rock-like in her support, urging her to go for it, and with that in mind, and despite her nervousness, she felt an enormous sense of pride as she waited for her turn onstage. The feeling was tempered by her sadness at knowing her mother would not see her perform.

She watched sympathetically from the wings at one side of the stage as a John Lennon impersonator murdered 'Imagine'. She couldn't have hoped for a better act to follow, even though, she did genuinely feel bad for him. She'd seen how nervous he had been before he went onstage. He had obviously let his nerves get the better of him, because he hit a bum note in the first line of the song. There had been some dire performances during the show, but his was possibly the worst. Nor was he helped by the fact that the judges let him carry on singing long after they should have called an end to his performance. Many better singers had been stopped after twenty or thirty seconds. This poor hopeful got to sing for almost as long as Otis Redding, just so the audience could enjoy his misery for a little longer than was necessary.

Once he'd finished, the judges were understandably scathing. Emily winced at the hurtful things they came out with.

'Honey, my *cat* sings like that,' was the worst comment from the normally sympathetic Lucinda.

Not to be outdone, Candy followed with, 'My cat sings *better* than that!'

Nigel administered the *coup de grace* by sighing wearily, 'I think *my* cat just hung itself.'

Maybe the spiteful remarks were a blessing in disguise, for Emily was relieved to see that the audience felt sorry for the guy. His nerves had done him enough damage without the judges adding to his woes. So it was a relief to hear large sections of the audience booing the judges' comments with gusto. Even so, there was no doubt about it: John Lennon would not be making it into the final.

As the crestfallen Beatle impersonator walked offstage, he smiled at Emily briefly. She could see he was on the verge of tears.

'You'll get 'em next time,' she said, offering a comforting look.

'Think I'm gonna find Nigel Powell's cat and borrow its rope.'

It seemed inappropriate to laugh at his joke, but also rude not to, so Emily maintained her sympathetic smile and looked down at her shoes to avoid any further eye contact.

On the stage, Nina Forina, the show's presenter, was busy working the audience, getting ready to announce that Emily was up next. Nina was a glamorous blonde in her early thirties. She was wearing a long shiny silver dress that showed off just how thin she was, giving the impression that she had no feminine curves at all beneath it. She also sported the obligatory orange tan, perhaps from the same source as Nigel Powell's.

As Nina chattered away to the watching crowd, Emily caught sight of a man standing in the shadows to her left, near the edge of the stage. He was staring at her, transfixed by something about her. She was flattered at first, but there was a deeply unsettling quality to the way he was staring. He seemed unaware that she had noticed him staring, and every time she looked away she knew that if she were to glance back he would still be directing that fixed stare at her.

After a while, she realized that he wasn't staring so much at her as at *her dress*. Rattled, she glanced down to check that she didn't have some kind of ghastly stain on the front of her frock. Everything appeared to be in order. Her shoes seemed fine, too. They were still shining brightly, for she had polished them less than half an hour earlier. They were an important part of her outfit, and she took a quick look over each shoulder in turn as she kicked her heels back one at a time, just to check that there was nothing stuck to the soles. They were as clean as they could be.

Emily was nervous enough without the stranger gawping at her, and partly to ease her nerves she decided to flick her long brown pigtails too, even though the man wasn't looking at them. She had taken great care to tie her hair up in plaits that hung down in front of her shoulders. She was sure she still looked exactly as she wanted. But her admirer – if that was what he was – was undermining her confidence, intentionally or not. She had checked her appearance in the dressing-room mirror about a hundred times to make sure she hadn't missed anything. So why was this weirdo staring?

She glanced over at him yet again. He was still staring at her blue dress. This time, however, when she looked at him, she saw his eyes move down. Now he appeared to be checking out her shoes, too. *That's it*, she thought. *This guy needs to be put in his place*. Politely, but firmly. She decided that the best thing to do would be to try to engage him in conversation in order to break the ice. Maybe then she'd find out why he was acting so creepy.

'Kinda bright, aren't they?' she called over to him.

The man looked up and stared directly into her eyes. She offered a smile in the hope that it would be reciprocated. It wasn't. Instead, he stepped out of the shadows he had been sheltering in. Emily couldn't help feeling a little uneasy. This guy was creepy. Worse, his presence wasn't exactly what she needed just before one of the most important performances of her life. His all-dark clothing made it seem as though he brought the shadows with him as he stepped towards her. As he moved out of the shadows, Emily saw that he was wearing black combat pants and a black leather jacket with a hood hanging at the back. He walked past her, and as he did so he pulled a pair of dark sunglasses from a front pocket on his jacket and slipped them on, hiding his eyes.

And then he was gone.

Emily was glad to see the back of him. She made an immediate decision to put him out of her mind and regain her focus on giving the performance of her life. This was made all the easier for her when, within a moment or two of his disappearance, she heard Nina Forina enthusiastically announce that her turn to perform had come at last. 'Ladies and gentlemen, please welcome our next performer, Emily Shannon!'

Emily walked out on to the stage, her bright red shoes positively glowing as she walked. She stopped centre stage, next to the presenter. Immediately everyone in the audience began applauding, for it was obvious from her outfit who she was supposed to be.

Nina announced it for anyone who hadn't worked it out for themselves. 'Emily is now going to perform 'Over The Rainbow' from the film *The Wizard of Oz*. Please put your hands together for – *Judy . . . Garland*.'

Nineteen

Emily's performance of 'Over The Rainbow' put Nigel Powell in a good mood. The girl had the voice of an angel. Her performance had been breathtaking, and had rightly earned her the longest and loudest standing ovation of the day so far. She had stolen the show, just as he had expected she would. He and his two colleagues on the judging panel had been only too willing to lavish vast amounts of gushing praise on her, as well. She hadn't let him down. He had handpicked her to be one of the five finalists, and secretly he hoped she would be the outright winner of the contest.

Powell's benign mood that followed her performance did not last long, however. Shortly after Emily had departed, Tommy, the head of security, signalled to him from one side of the stage. Something was wrong. But what? He called a twenty-minute recess to deal with the problem. He hoped Tommy wasn't making a fuss over nothing.

Having left the stage, Powell strode down a long corridor towards his office. Tommy seemed to be in a hurry, leading the way from a yard ahead. They were halfway there and still the security man hadn't briefed his boss as to the reasons why he had been dragged away from judging the *Back From the Dead* contestants. Powell began to feel irritated.

The corridor leading to his office was empty, but given the unscheduled break, many of the audience were likely to head to the bars, restrooms or the casino, there was every chance the area would soon be flooded with noisy guests.

Tommy ushered his employer along the corridor. This just made Powell even angrier. Who was Tommy to be ushering him along?'

'Why are we hurrying?' he asked, failing to mask his irritation.

'I don't want anyone in earshot, boss.'

'This had better be important, Tommy. I can't go stopping the show every time you want a chat. We're on a fucking tight deadline, you know,' Powell complained.

He still wasn't quite sure why he was hurrying, but from a yard ahead Tommy kept on waving at him to keep up. It made him feel like an assassination target being shepherded to a safe place by a bodyguard, and he fervently hoped that wasn't the case. The security man was picking up speed now, and even broke into a light jog as he called back to answer him.

'Yeah, I know. A lot's happened though, boss.'

'Tell.'

'We think Otis Redding is dead.'

Powell stopped in his tracks and watched Tommy run on a few more steps before realizing that his employer had come to a dead stop behind him. Tommy turned and gestured to him to keep moving.

'Come on, boss!'

'Otis Redding?'

'Yeah.'

'No.'

'Yeah. I'm serious. He's dead. I sent four guys up to that Sanchez Garcia's room, just like you asked. While they were up there, they saw two guys in an elevator with a dead body. They think it was Otis Redding.'

A couple of young audience members ran past Powell from behind, almost knocking into him as they rushed to be the first to get to the bar during the recess. Realizing that they were most likely going to be the first of many, he resumed walking briskly along the corridor to his office, catching up with Tommy, who this time chose to stay alongside him rather than rush on ahead.

'Did we get the guys in the elevator?' Powell asked.

'Not yet.'

'Anyone else see the body? We could have a panic on our hands if word gets out.'

'So far we reckon not, but my guys are on it right now.'

The other's face almost contorted into a frown. Fortunately, the ultra-high levels of Botox in his face prevented him from revealing to the security man just how concerned he was. His voice was the only thing that gave him away.

'Shit. So that Mystic broad was right. This bloke in seven-thirteen. He really is here to kill off the finalists?'

'Looks that way. There was another man with him, apparently, but none of my guys got a look at him.'

'Interesting.' Powell pondered what Annabel de Frugyn had said to him earlier when she was making her hit-and-miss predictions. 'That Mystic Lady, she said he'd have been hired by one of the contestants. We'll need to keep an eye out for any erratic behaviour from the other contestants.'

As he spoke, he noticed that Tommy was wincing. Either he had a stitch from the brisk walking, or there was another problem.

'What?' he asked, trying to frown.

'That ain't all, boss. There's a reason we gotta go to your office.'

'Which is?'

'There's a big scary guy in there.'

'What? What in the fuck is a big scary guy doing in my office?'

'Waitin' to speak to you.'

The door to Powell's office was set back from the passageway, in an alcove. As they turned into it, Tommy reached for the door handle, Before his hand touched it, Powell grabbed hold of his shoulder to slow him down.

'What's he want to speak to me about?'

'Sanchez Garcia.'

'Jesus. Do I really have time for this shit?' The frustration in his voice was becoming more evident with every word.

'Yeah. I reckon so. Like I said, this guy is kinda scary.'

'Does he have horns sticking out of his head? Is he bright red and carrying a large pitchfork?'

'No.'

'Then he doesn't scare me.'

Tommy, aware of his employer's growing irritation, tried to calm him in readiness for what was to come. 'Do you think you could just try a little harder to stay calm, boss?' he suggested.

'Sure,' said Powell. ''Cause right now I'm not trying at all.' Then he barged Tommy aside and pulled a card from his jacket pocket. He swiped it through the reader next to the door handle and watched the small red light on it turn to green. Shaking his head disapprovingly at the hapless security man, he turned the handle on the door. It sprung open easily, as it always did, swinging inwards into the office.

Powell strode in confidently, hoping to make a powerful impression on his waiting guest. He was greeted by the sight of a giant of a man seated in *his* chair, behind *his* desk, smoking one of *his* cigars. The man was wearing a long grey trench coat with a filthy black T-shirt underneath it. He had thick red hair and a wiry goatee. His well-worn, rugged face looked like it could take a punch, and had done many times in the past. Powell glanced at Tommy and rolled his eyes, then walked into the room and sat down opposite the man. Tommy dutifully followed him in, closed the door behind them and stood guard.

The hotel owner was immediately aware of an aura of arrogance and disdain coming from the man sitting at his desk. He responded with indifference.

'You've got two minutes. What can I do for you?' he

asked, politely enough.

'I want you to give me twenty thousand dollars.'

'No. Next question.' He stared hard at the intruder before adding, 'One and three-quarter minutes.'

His guest took the refusal in his stride. 'You know you gotta psycho in your hotel, runnin' round killin' off the contestants in your show?'

'Yes, I do. And my guys are dealing with it now. I expect them to have captured this sicko inside the next ten minutes.'

'Yeah? An' d'you know who he is?'

The questioning was irritating Powell. 'Yes. Do *you?*'

'I might.'

'Well, who do you think it is?'

'You go first.'

'Why should I?'

''Cause I don't reckon you know.'

Finding the conversation quite tiresome, Powell backed down first. 'Okay. I believe his name is Sanchez Garcia,' he said, sighing wearily. His boredom threshold was not high at the best of times, and this guy was already getting tedious.

The red-haired man puffed on his cigar, then took it from his mouth and inspected the end to see how the ash was building. When he was satisfied that it wasn't in need of a tap over the carpet, he looked back at Powell with a smug smile.

'That's right. But here's the real question. Do you know who this Garcia guy is?'

'Does it matter?'

'It does kinda make a difference.'

'Go on then. Enlighten me.'

'Sanchez Garcia is better known as the Bourbon Kid.'

If he was expecting a reaction, he didn't get it. Powell leaned back in his chair and called over to Tommy, who was standing by the door with his hands clasped together in front of his waist.

'Tommy, who's the Bourbon Kid?'

'Probably the biggest mass serial killer in living history, sir. A psycho with a drink problem. Basically, someone you don't want on your tail.'

'Uh huh.' Nigel turned back to the man sitting in his chair. 'And who are you?'

'They call me Invincible Angus.'

'And why do they call you that?'

'Because it's my name.'

'I see. And you want me to give you twenty thousand dollars to kill this Sanchez Garcia guy, who apparently, according to Tommy, is the biggest mass serial killer in history.'

Tommy coughed. 'Actually, I said *living* history.'

His boss tried to frown. 'What's the difference?'

'Well – uh – one's living and the other ain't.'

'Do you even know what you're talking about half the time?'

'No, sir.'

'Then shut up.' Powell turned back to Angus. Despite his impatience to rejoin the show, his interest was piqued. 'So this Bourbon Kid, he's a mass murderer. I think we've established that, right?'

'Right.'

Powell turned back to the security man. 'Okay. Hold on. Tommy, find out how your guys are doing in their hunt for this Bourbon Garcia guy.'

'Yes, sir.' He pulled a small walkie-talkie from where it hung on his belt by his right hip. He pressed a button, raised the device to his mouth, and spoke into it.

'Sandy. This is Tommy. Over.'

A few seconds passed before a voice crackled through the walkie-talkie. It was loud enough for everyone in the office to hear.

'This is Sandy. We got problems here, boss.'

'What's up? I got Mister Powell here with me. We need an update.'

'You're not gonna like this.'

'Try me.'

'Thing is, Tyrone an' me are in the men's washroom on the ground floor and we've just found Otis Redding in one of the stalls. He's definitely dead. Neck's broken, looks like.'

'Any sign of the guys who did it?'

'No, but that ain't all. We got two other bodies in here. Kurt Cobain and Johnny Cash are dead too. And they got banged up way worse than Otis.'

In the office, Powell's mood darkened. He had now lost three of his five finalists. This was bad. Tommy spoke into the walkie-talkie once more.

'Okay, keep looking for these guys. They can't have gotten far.'

'Sure thing, Tom – *OH SHIT!*' Sandy's voice sounded panicked, and his reply was punctuated by a crashing sound

Tommy spoke urgently into his handset. 'Sandy, what the fuck's that?'

The other man didn't respond. What they heard from Tommy's radio was what sounded like an almighty ruckus. For the next ten seconds, the airwaves were littered with the sound of punches connecting with flesh, with agonized yelps and Sandy's attempts at shouting out a commentary on what was happening. It sounded like he and Tyrone were being attacked, but his voice came through muffled by all the background noise. Eventually the signal went dead.

Tommy tried to get him back. 'Sandy? *Sandy?* You still there? What the fuck's happening there?'

For twenty seconds or so they waited for a response from Sandy. Or even Tyrone. None came. Suddenly, Powell was wishing he'd asked Annabel de Frugyn a hell of a lot more questions. Taking a deep breath, he nodded at Tommy.

'Go and get me twenty thousand dollars for this guy here,' he said, pointing at the man sitting opposite him.

Angus, grinning, tapped some ash from his cigar on to

Nigel's desk. 'The price just went up to fifty,' he said with a wink.

Powell realized at once that he didn't have time to bargain. 'Get him fifty,' he ordered Tommy. The security man nodded, then slipped quietly out of the door, closing it behind him.

'Good to know you've seen the light,' said Angus, puffing on his cigar and maintaining his smug look. 'Should've listened to me in the first place, though, shouldn't ya?'

'I'm not even listening to you now.'

'Well, that's your right, I guess. Just get me the goddam cash.'

Powell shook his head, wagging a finger at Angus. 'No deal. You kill this Sanchez guy and whomever else he's got with him. Do it however you like. All I ask is that you do it outside of my hotel. I don't need any more dead bodies turning up. Find 'em, catch 'em, then take 'em out to the desert and kill 'em. Then bury the fuckers out there. When you get back, there'll be fifty grand waiting for you. And I want a Polaroid.'

'An' I want twenty now.'

'No deal. It's not like you won't be able to find me when the job's done.'

The refusal to pay anything up front, however small the amount, was Powell's way of establishing who was boss. Angus might well be a man to be feared. But if he was going to do a job for Nigel Powell, then he would be treated like any other member of the hotel staff. He would have to earn the money first.

The hitman obviously didn't like it. And he made his dissatisfaction clear by the way he stubbed his cigar out on the antique oak desk. Even after it was extinguished he continued twisting it down hard between his fingers, eyeballing Powell the whole time. His face twitched down one side as if he had a fishhook caught in the corner of his mouth, pulling at it. Once he'd regained control of his face he stood up, and his new employer finally understood what Tommy had meant about him being a big scary guy. The man was a fucking giant.

Whoever this Sanchez Garcia guy was, he was in big trouble.

Twenty

The last time Sanchez had found himself huddled out of sight, scared shitless, while Elvis saved the day, he'd been in a church, using a schoolkid as a human shield while his friend shot down the bad guys with a weapon shaped like a guitar. That was exactly ten years ago. This time round, the King simply used his fists. Inside ninety seconds, the brawny security guards were sprawled on the tile floor of the washroom, unconscious and bloody. He'd saved Sanchez's ass once again.

With a combination of speed, skill and brute force, the King had disarmed and knocked out the two security guards, Sandy and Tyrone. Sanchez had stayed in the stall with his eyes closed through most of the assault, although he had already conjured up an exaggerated version of events to tell everyone when he got back to the Tapioca. The important thing was that Elvis had done the job, and done it in style. When the noise of the fight finally came to an end, Sanchez opened one eye and then the other. Elvis was standing just outside the stall with his back to him.

The security guards were splayed across the floor, in the pool of blood still seeping out from stall two. It was hard to tell whether any of the blood staining their black suits was their own. The side of the nearest security guard's head was pressed to the floor tiles, dribbling blood from a nasty nosebleed. The other guy's head was out of Sanchez's view from where he was cowering.

'C'mon, Sanchez! For fuck's sake gimme a hand moving

these two, will ya?' Elvis yelled at him. He had begun dragging the nearer of the security guards towards the third stall, but it was clear he needed some help if he was to get the job done quickly, before anyone else showed up.

'Wow. You really took 'em both out, huh?' Sanchez said redundantly, failing to mask a note of surprise in his voice.

'What the fuck didja expect?'

'Well – y'know. They were armed.'

Elvis threw the first unconscious guard on to the floor of the stall at Sanchez's feet and then threw a disapproving look at Santa Mondega's most cowardly bar owner.

'Yeah, an' you an' me will *both* be armed in a minute, Sanchez. We got two handguns now. Sure hope we don't have to fuckin' use 'em, 'cause my instincts are tellin' me you couldn't even hit your own ass.' He paused, then added, 'An' Lord knows, it's a big enough target.'

Sanchez ignored the comment. Instead, he grabbed the guy Elvis had dropped under the armpits and dragged the body into the corner of the stall next to the toilet, where he did his best to sit it upright. He was becoming a pro at this.

'Uh – like, maybe it'd be best if you had both guns?' he suggested. Elvis was probably a better shot with his weaker hand than Sanchez would ever be with his stronger right hand. And on top of that, he had nerve enough to shoot someone without question or hesitation. Sanchez was liable to flinch if faced with a situation that required him to fire a weapon at someone.

Elvis didn't reply immediately. He was backing into the stall, dragging the second security man with him.

'No chance,' he said, letting the unconscious man slump to the floor. 'It's one each. If we get separated an' you're on your own, you're gonna need a piece, even if it's just for show.'

The two of them shoved the second guy into the corner on the other side of the toilet from his colleague. When they were done, Sanchez took a look at the two unconscious guards and had a rare idea. It had dawned on him that he and Elvis weren't exactly going to be hard to spot if anyone was looking for them. He was wearing his loud red Hawaiian shirt, while the King sported a bright gold jacket and a pair of large gold-rimmed sunglasses.

'We could swap clothes with these guys, couldn't we?' Sanchez suggested. 'Reckon we could sneak out easily then.'

Elvis looked hard at Sanchez and sighed. Then he shook his head disapprovingly. 'You are pretty fuckin' dumb, Sanchez, ya know that? These guys both just ended up in all that blood on the floor. It's all over the backs of their jackets and their pants. You wanna walk out of here in a black suit that's covered in blood 'cause you reckon it'd be more discreet, then be my guest. Personally, I'd rather just have a gun and a pair of *cojones.*' He held out one of the pistols that he had taken from the security guards. 'Here, take it. Now all you need are some *cojones.*'

Sanchez took the gun tentatively. He looked like he was holding the tail of a snake while trying to avoid being bitten by it. Elvis shook his head again, failing to conceal his disgust.

'Aw, fer fuck's sake! Just tuck it in the back of your pants and cover it with your shirt. You can find some room for it in those pants of yours, can't you?'

Sanchez ignored the latest reference to the size of his butt and did as he was told. The gun fitted tightly in the waistband, the cold steel of the barrel wedged nicely between the sweaty cheeks of his ass. Time was short. They needed to get out of the washroom as soon as possible.

'So, what now?' he asked.

'We get the fuck outta here. Prob'ly best if we avoid the lobby – too many people around who might spot us. My guess is, if we take a left turn outta here, we'll be headin' towards the back of the hotel. There's bound to be a fire door there. We can head out through that an' into the parkin' lot. Then I reckon we got about two minutes to get to my car and get the fuck outta here.'

'Cool,' said Sanchez. 'You're leadin' the way, right?'

'Right. We hit any trouble, you point that gun at the bad guys and fire, okay.'

'Yeah, sure.'

'You cool?'

'Cool as I'll ever be.'

Elvis grimaced. 'Yeah. Right. Follow me. Reckon we're already short of time.'

He tucked his gun down the back of his black pants, where it was hidden by his shiny gold jacket. It looked like it fitted a lot snugger than Sanchez's did. He led the way to the door and pulled it open slightly. He peered carefully one way down the corridor. Sanchez watched over his shoulder. There seemed to be no one in sight. Satisfied, Elvis took a step out and turned to check the passageway in the other direction.

THUD!

Before Sanchez could react, a tall man in a long grey trench coat stepped into view. He had blindsided Elvis with a blow to the back of the neck that had sent him crashing to his knees. The man loomed over him and hit him again on the back of the head, even harder this time, with the barrel of the pistol he was holding. Elvis slumped to the floor in a heap, out cold.

Shit! thought Sanchez. *Grab your gun and fire.*

Knowing that time wasn't on his side, he pulled the gun out of the back of his pants. It came out much easier than it had gone in, mostly because it was now slightly lubricated by the sweat from his ass. Fumbling for the safety catch, he took aim at the man standing over Elvis. He recognized the guy straight away. It was the giant hitman whose room and twenty grand he had taken.

Invincible Angus didn't flinch as he turned and saw the bar owner aiming a gun at him. Sanchez was doing all the flinching. He closed his eyes as he squeezed the trigger, wincing at the knowledge that there was a loud bang on the way.

A loud bang did indeed follow.

Unfortunately, Sanchez had only succeeded in firing the gun at the ceiling. The force of the recoil sent him flying backwards, banging his head against the wall behind him. The blow hurt like hell, and was swiftly followed by the world blurring out of focus as he slid down the wall.

He was unconscious by the time he slumped to the floor.

Twenty-One

Julius finished off his performance of 'Get Up I Feel Like Being A Sex Machine' with a trademark James Brown 'heh!' noise. He'd attempted the splits at the end of the dance routine, but had barely made it a third of the way down. Now he stood motionless in a sort of half-squat with one arm outstretched, pointing at the judges.

Even so, the audience loved it and the judges (knowing that he was on their shortlist of five to appear in the final) showered him with gushing praise, particularly Nigel Powell, who congratulated him on being the most energetic performer in the show so far.

Julius's exertions had put a great strain on his tight purple suit. The pants had come close to ripping at the back after his attempt at the splits and the resultant half-squat. He now found himself lapping up the adulation from the crowd while feeling greatly relieved at having escaped the embarrassment of splitting his pants in two.

After suitably outstaying his welcome, he headed off via the side of the stage, waving vigorously at the audience as he went. On his way out to the corridor, he strutted past the remaining contestants who still had to audition. *What a bunch of suckers. The poor saps had no idea that they hadn't a chance of winning.* They parted for him like the Red Sea, and many congratulated him on his performance. But now that it was over, he just wanted to be away from the others. They would all be eliminated from the contest soon, so being polite to them offered little benefit. His chances of winning the competition were high after his great performance. All he needed to know now was whether the Bourbon Kid had done his part. Had – uh – *disposed of* the other four finalists.

Julius was positively bouncing along the beige carpet in the yellow corridor as he made his way to the elevator at the end. By the time he reached it, he was just starting to come back down to earth after the high of performing for the judges. There wasn't another person in sight, most likely because almost all the guests were crammed into the concert hall watching the show. He reached out to the button on the wall and pressed it to call the elevator. The shiny silver doors opened straight away and he stepped inside. As he went to press the button for the eighth floor he noticed flecks of blood on the keypad. He looked down and saw a small pool of blood. The sight of it brought a smile to his face. This was probably the Bourbon Kid's handiwork. Someone had been seriously wounded, at the least, in this elevator. *Killed*, with any luck. He pressed the button for floor eight, then turned and faced out into the corridor he had just left.

To be greeted by the sight of his new accomplice.

The Bourbon Kid was walking along the corridor towards the elevator, looking as sinister as ever. The dark hood on his jacket was up over his head and beneath it Julius could see that he was still wearing his dark shades. Indoors. The funereal outfit really did mark him out as a fearsome prospect. The man exuded evil without even trying. *Great guy to have on your side when you need to kill four innocent people*, Julius thought to himself. He pressed another button on the elevator's keypad to keep the doors open and let his hired gun join him inside. In doing so he managed to get a patch of sticky blood on the end of his finger. He quickly wiped it on his pants leg.

'Eighth floor okay with you?' Julius asked as the Kid stepped in.

'Makes no difference.'

The doors closed in front of them and the elevator began to move upwards. As soon as it did, Julius breathed a huge sigh of relief and pulled the thick dark wig off his head. His bald head was sweating after his time under the spotlight, and it was pleasing to feel some cool air on it at last.

'This fuckin' thing's itchy as hell, y'know,' he said, shaking the wig as if it were riddled with insects.

'Quit your fuckin' moaning,' replied the Kid.

'What's with you?' Julius paused. 'Actually, never mind. Like I care. Is it all done?'

'I'm all done.'

'So they're all dead? *Already?*'

'No.'

'No? Who's still alive?'

'Dorothy.'

'Who the fuck is Dorothy?'

'Judy Garland.'

'What happened? She get away from you?'

'No.'

'What then?'

'I don't kill Dorothys.'

''Scuse me?'

'I don't kill Dorothys.'

'Bull*shit*. You kill anything.'

'Not Dorothys.'

'Why not? What fuckin' difference does it make?'

'I have my reasons.'

'Which are?'

'None of your fuckin' business.'

Julius stood in the elevator looking at his reflection in the metal doors. His bright purple James Brown costume still looked the business. Next to his reflection was that of the dark and shady figure of the Bourbon Kid, who was also staring straight ahead at the silver elevator doors. With his eyes hidden behind his dark sunglasses, his face betrayed not an ounce of emotion.

Julius couldn't conceal his frustration, or his bewilderment at this sudden turn of events. 'Let me get this straight,' he said, his voice close to shaking with fury. 'You kill *anyone* and *anything*, no matter what age, race or sex, but when it comes to Dorothy from *The Wizard of Oz*, you suddenly get a conscience?'

'That's about the size of it, yeah. You gotta problem with that?'

''Course I gotta fuckin' problem with that!' Julius, realizing that he was raising his voice, chose to lower it slightly before continuing. 'She's the main threat to me winnin' this competition. If she's in the final that's it. Game over. I *have* to win this show, and she's the only one left in it that can sing better'n me.'

'I got another plan.' The Kid's voice was deepening with every syllable.

'Well now, that's somethin', I guess. What is it?'

'Learn to sing better.'

The elevator stopped and the doors opened. As he stepped out, Julius rounded angrily on the other man. 'You're a real fuckin' comedian, you know that?'

The Kid pressed the button for the ground floor and stepped back to the centre of the elevator.

'Where the fuck d'you think you're goin'?' Julius asked.

'My work is done.'

As the elevator doors began to close Julius took a step forward and reached his left hand out to hold the doors open.

'You know you don't get paid for killin' three of them, right? The job was for all four,' he pointed out.

'Don't care.'

'Well, that's real good – 'cause I'm gonna have to pay the whole fifty grand to someone else, and all they'll have to do is kill Judy Garland.'

The Kid shook his head slowly. 'No one touches her. Not today.' The sound of his voice was pure gravel.

'Sorry buddy, but she's history. Even if I have to get the fuckin' Wicked Witch of the West to kill her. No way's she winnin' this goddam competition.'

'She might not win it, but she's gonna be in the final.' The Kid gestured with a nod of his head to indicate that Julius let go of the elevator door.

The singer took one last look into the dark sunglasses and shook his head in exasperation. 'I shoulda known not to count on you. You goddam fuckin' idiot!'

The Kid reached inside his leather jacket. Julius considered the consequences of what that might mean. Cigarettes, maybe. Or a weapon. Most likely a weapon. With that in mind he wisely let go of the door, allowing it to close.

All the exhilaration had now left Julius, evaporated like dew in the desert. Even though his wigless head had cooled, he began to sweat. *Shit! Fuckin' godamighty shit!* He realized that things had now taken a disastrous turn for the worse. The Judy Garland impersonator was still alive – for now, at least. But Julius needed her out of the picture before the final started.

'Out of the picture' meaning 'dead'.

Twenty-Two

Sanchez's eyelids felt as though they had been stuck together with peanut butter. He opened them slowly, one after the other, and blinked a few times. Did he have a hangover? No. But someone had just slapped him around the face. He recognized that feeling. He was kinda used to it. This was a slap from a man, though. He knew that, because his left cheek was stinging a little more than it usually did after a slap. Of greater concern, though, was a throbbing pain at the back of his head. He vaguely remembered now. It was from the self-inflicted blow he'd received when he'd hit it against the wall of the passageway outside the men's washroom. That must have been a while earlier. He blinked again, trying to clear his vision, but it wasn't working. This was in part because he had only just regained consciousness. But it was also because he was bobbing up and down on a pull-out bed in the back of a large and well-appointed camper van of some kind. The bed was fixed to the side wall, and the van was being driven somewhere at high speed.

'Where the fuck am I?' he groaned, having exhausted his powers of observation and deduction.

'Devil's Graveyard,' a voice responded. 'In about ten minutes that pain in your head'll be gone.'

Sanchez sat up straight. Then he realized he couldn't move his hands. He glanced down, and in the darkness could just make out that his wrists were bound together by thick silver-grey duct tape. Looking up again, he saw two security guards from the hotel sitting across from him on the seat that ran along the opposite side of the van. Both men were wearing the standard black suits issued by the hotel. The one directly opposite Sanchez had dark spiky hair and a face only a mother could love. His name badge, which Sanchez could read now that his eyes had adjusted to the low light, declared that he was Tommy Packer, Head of Security. The other guy was a shaven-headed military type. Both were pointing pistols in his direction. The one who had spoken was the dark-haired one, Tommy. The other said nothing, but looked wary. And ready to use his gun.

'You okay, Sanchez?' asked a more familiar voice. Sitting on his left was Elvis.

'My fuckin' head hurts,' Sanchez complained, looking to his friend for some sympathy.

'Yeah. Seems you knocked yourself out.'

'Why would I do that?'

'Because you're a fuckin' moron.'

'Oh. That again.' Forgetting for a moment that his wrists were bound together in front of him, Sanchez had an overwhelming desire to rub the back of his head. His attempt was futile, the best he could do was rub the top of his head with the tape binding his hands together. Further inspection showed that Elvis was in a similar predicament. Sanchez looked back at Tommy for an explanation.

'So what's happenin' now?' he asked.

'You're being taken out to the desert, where you're going to be executed and buried.'

Sanchez gulped. 'Uh, like – is that really necessary? I mean, this is all a big misunderstanding. You told them that, right Elvis?'

'I told 'em, but they don't wanna hear it, man.'

'Oh.' Sanchez couldn't mask his disappointment. Or his alarm. 'You gotta plan to get us out of this?' he asked Elvis hopefully.

'Yeah.'

'Cool. What is it?'

'Well, I ain't gonna tell you the plan while Bert and Ernie are sittin' over there, am I? Ya dumb fuck. Who d'ya think I am? *You?*'

'Oh yeah. Right. Ow, my fuckin' head.'

The van came to a stop at the roadside and Sanchez heard the driver up front climb out. He wasn't visible from the seat in the back, but Sanchez heard him walk round to the double doors at the back of the van, his shoes crunching on the gravel-strewn highway. A moment later the doors were pulled open. Sanchez was disappointed to see Invincible Angus standing there holding two shovels.

'Right, hustle. Everybody out!' the big man ordered.

Sanchez peered out of the open doors. It was dark out on the highway, with the only light coming from the full moon. The desert was a shithole at the best of times, now it was a dark, cold shithole with a chilling breeze. Where there had been only dust, sand and dying plants during the day, there were now rustling noises, squeaks and howls from unseen animals, and flickering shadows.

The two security guards waved their pistols in the direction of the double doors, gesturing for Sanchez and Elvis to exit the van. Elvis got up and jumped out of the back on to the deserted highway outside. Sanchez duly followed, albeit with great trepidation. It was pretty dark in the back of the van and as he jumped out he succeeded in tripping himself up on something and flying face first into Invincible Angus's left shoulder, before crashing to the ground in a heap.

'Nice try,' said Angus laconically. 'Typical hitman. Always tryin' to make a move.'

The two security guards followed Sanchez out. Tommy leaned down, grabbed the bar owner under his right armpit and pulled him up off the ground.

'You sure this guy's a hitman?' he asked doubtfully.

'Don't be fooled by appearances. This guy's lethal. The whole bumbling-idiot thing is all for show,' said Angus coldly.

Elvis protested. 'Are you for real?' he said contemptuously. 'Sanchez is a fuckin' bartender, not a goddam hitman.'

Angus shook his head. 'Nah. No bartender could've executed three men, then taken out two security guards with his bare hands.'

'You dumb fuck. He didn't do any of that.'

'So who did? *You?*' Angus mocked.

'Well, I didn't kill no one, but I did take out the two security guys, seein' as you ask.'

Angus smirked. 'You think I'm stupid? Tell you what, though. I'll give you two a chance to prove which of you is the hitman.' He threw the two shovels down on the ground. 'There ya go, ladies. Grab these an' follow me.'

Sanchez looked down at the shovel. '*Great,*' he said sarcastically. 'Buildin' goddam sandcastles in the desert now, are we? Must be my lucky day.'

Until then, Angus had sounded almost jovial. Now he was irritated. 'You know, sarcasm is a very unattractive feature. And lookin' the way you do, you might wanna tone it down, fatboy.'

Sanchez and Elvis both stooped and, reaching down with their tightly bound wrists, managed to pick up a shovel each. The two security guards watched them warily to make sure neither made any sudden movements.

'Go on,' Tommy ordered, shoving his pistol into Sanchez's back. 'Follow him.' Sanchez and Elvis trailed Invincible Angus off the highway and into the desert with the two security men following behind, occasionally prodding their pistols into their captives' backs.

Angus strode on a good five yards ahead, making his way through a mixture of straggly, scratchy sagebrush and juniper plants that grew to a height of about a foot above the ground.

He was heading towards a particularly desolate-looking area twenty yards or so further into the desert. Sanchez took the opportunity to quiz Elvis about how they were intending to escape.

'So what's the plan?' he whispered.

'We wait.'

'Wait? Wait for what?'

'Somethin' to happen.'

'Great plan. Did it take you long to come up with it?'

'Actually, yes.'

Up ahead of them, Invincible Angus came to a halt in an area of soft dirt and sand, clear of the stunted vegetation. He pointed at the ground.

'Okay, so here's the deal,' he said. 'You two start diggin'. I want a hole big enough to bury one of you. See, fellas, I'm a reasonable guy. I wanna know which one of you is the hitman who took my twenty thousand dollars.'

Elvis shook his head. 'What the fuck you talkin' about, man?'

'There was an envelope with twenty thousand dollars in it. Someone took the twenty thousand out and returned the envelope to reception. Which one of you did it?'

Even the security guards weren't sure what Angus was talking about. Only Sanchez knew that there had been twenty grand in the envelope, because he'd stolen it. And spent it. Tommy spoke up from his spot behind Sanchez.

'What are you talkin' about, man? What twenty grand? Ya gonna get it from Mister Powell when ya've done the job. More than, matter o' fact.'

Angus reached both hands inside his trench coat and pulled out two pistols. He gestured with his head at Tommy and the other guard.

'Step aside.'

Tommy and the other guard stepped back out of the way. Then much to Sanchez's surprise, Invincible Angus fired twice, a single shot from each pistol. The curious thing was, he wasn't aiming at Sanchez and Elvis. Brief yelps were heard from the two security men, followed by the sound of them falling to the ground, courtesy of a bullet in the head from Angus.

'I knew this guy was on our side!' said Sanchez gleefully.

Angus looked over at Elvis. 'Is your friend always this stupid?'

Elvis nodded. ''Fraid so. You get used to it.'

'What?' asked Sanchez. 'What's going on?'

'He's killing off his henchmen to show how evil he is,' said Elvis. 'Guy's a walkin' cliché. Ain't you noticed?'

'Point of fact, that ain't what I'm doin' at all,' Angus protested. 'Those guys didn't know who I am. Thought I was helpin' out their boss. But I got more important business than that. I'm here to kill off some of the contestants in the singin' contest.'

Elvis was not done with goading Angus. 'See, Sanchez? I toldja he was a cliché. He's now tellin' us all the intricate details of his evil plot before he kills us off. Put a grey suit on him, shave his hair off an' you've got Doctor Evil right there.'

'Shut the fuck up!' Angus snapped.

Elvis ignored him. 'What next?' he asked. 'You gonna leave us in some trap, then head off back to the hotel and just *assume* we'll die?'

Angus's face started to twitch as Elvis's baiting began to turn his irritation to rage. 'You listen to me, and listen good,' he growled, aiming his pistols at their chests. 'You two got a choice. One of you can live by tellin' me where my twenty grand is.'

'Shit, man. We don't know,' said Elvis. 'There weren't no twenty grand in the envelope, I swear.'

'He's right,' Sanchez agreed shakily. He didn't know which frightened him more: Angus thinking he knew where the money was, or Elvis finding out that there had been twenty grand in the envelope all along.

'Okay,' said Angus. 'In that case, start diggin' the goddam hole. But when one of you two works out how to get me my twenty grand back, feel free to smack your buddy over the head with your shovel. That happens, then whoever's still standin' gets to come back to the hotel with me to give me my money after we've buried the loser.'

Sanchez looked suspiciously at Elvis. Would the King turn on him? Should Sanchez discover some guts and strike first? Or did Elvis really have a plan to get them out of their dangerous situation?

'Guess we start diggin', then,' Elvis suggested. For a man who was probably going to die real soon, he seemed remarkably unconcerned.

Hampered by their tightly bound wrists, both men awkwardly thrust their shovels into the ground and began scooping up dirt to make a hole. Angus tucked one of his pistols back inside his trench coat and pulled out a pack of cigarettes. As he was taking one out of the packet with his teeth, Sanchez whispered to Elvis.

'Seriously, you got a plan, right?'

'Somethin'll happen, man.'

'How d'ya know?'

'Somethin' always happens.'

'That's it? *Somethin' always happens?* That's your plan?'

'Got a better one?'

'Not yet.'

'Then quit bitchin'.'

'You quit bitchin'.'

Angus had put away the pack of cigarettes and was now lighting his cigarette with a gunmetal Zippo. That done, he took a long drag and tucked his lighter back inside his coat. He looked just about ready to make a decision about who should die first.

'Hey, less talk, more diggin',' he called out, exhaling a

lungful of smoke through his nostrils.

The two captives both thrust their shovels into the grave slowly forming in front of them. They continued to dig for several minutes, eyeing each other suspiciously. Elvis was having the most success with his digging, so his end of the grave was a few inches deeper than Sanchez's. When Elvis's side was almost a foot deep, the alarm on his wristwatch went off, signalling that it was nine o'clock. It was a gentle beeping sound, but it resonated clearly in the silent, wide-open expanse of the desert. Sanchez watched as his friend dropped his shovel into the grave they were digging.

'Hey,' shouted Angus, pointing his pistol at Elvis. 'Pick that up and carry on diggin', you sonofabitch.'

Elvis shook his head. 'Can't,' he said.

'Why not?'

'Somethin's just happened.'

Twenty-Three

The Bourbon Kid wasn't generally in the business of saving lives. Emily-the-Judy-Garland-impersonator probably didn't deserve to have her life saved, come to that. But he wasn't about to stand by and put himself through torture, by letting someone who reminded him of Beth sell her soul to the Devil. And the only way the Kid knew how to deal effectively with any kind of problem was by killing. Which was quite a dilemma.

He had had no problem with killing the other contestants. As far as he was concerned, they had all been willing to sell their souls to the Devil in exchange for fortune and fame, whether they knew it or not. *Losers.* Julius-James Brown was just another desperate wannabe. He was different only because he wanted to win more desperately than the others. Added to that, the Kid didn't like him, so if he won the contest and sold his soul to the Devil, then fine. There was a major stumbling block, though.

Julius wasn't good enough to beat Emily. Not in a million years.

Her Judy Garland impression would wipe the floor with his James Brown routine. Someone had to be found who could beat Emily and so save her from selling her soul to the Devil, assuming that really *was* the fate that befell the winner (he only had Julius's word on that). If someone better than her could be found, then it would screw up Julius's plan and teach the little fuck a lesson for refusing to pay up after the Kid had killed three of his rivals. Normally the Kid would have killed someone over such a matter, but Julius had a little more to him than met the eye. If there really was some undead action to be had at this hotel, then it was Julius who knew the truth about it all. That fact would keep him alive for a little while longer. But it wouldn't help him win the million-dollar prize money and the alleged contract with the Devil. The Kid would rather see that go to someone else. And he knew exactly who that should be.

He found Jacko in the casino area, sitting at a roulette table. The Michael Jackson wannabe stood out like a sore thumb in his ridiculous red leather suit. The casino was fairly quiet because most people were in the concert hall, watching the last few performers in the auditions going through the motions and being abused accordingly by Nigel Powell. The few people standing in between the Kid and Jacko were quick to get out of his way as he strode over to the roulette table. He was still wearing his shades so no one could see his eyes. Not that anyone wanted to.

There were four players seated on stools at the roulette table. Jacko, who was sitting at the end nearest to the Bourbon Kid, had placed a single chip on the number thirteen. A desperate man's bet indeed. The croupier, a silver-haired man probably no older than forty, spun the roulette wheel and then sent a small ball rolling around the rim in the opposite direction to the wheel's spin. Jacko watched intently, but before he had a chance to see the outcome, the Kid placed a hand on his shoulder and twisted him round to face him, eye to eye. Jacko looked surprised to see him again, but greeted him with an enthusiastic smile.

'Hi, man. How ya doin'?' he asked.

'Listen to me, you piece o' shit.'

'Nice to see you again too,' said Jacko reproachfully, looking around at the three other players at the table. They all looked a mite shocked at the Kid's rough manner and uncouth language. But wisely, everyone (including the croupier) chose not to comment and quickly refocused their attention on the roulette wheel.

'You had no intention of entering this singing competition, did ya?' the Kid asked.

'What? Sure I did, man.'

'Bullshit. You just wanted a ride here.' The gravelly tone in the Kid's voice that Jacko had noticed before was back. With a vengeance.

'No way, man. Swear to God. I tried to enter, but it turns out the organizers only allow one person to impersonate a singer. There's already another Michael Jackson here, and he performed before I had a chance to sign up. It just means I can enjoy the show, an' maybe next year I'll get a chance.'

'You're entering this contest. I didn't bring you here just so you could sit in the casino playing roulette with –' he looked at the other players – 'a bunch of ugly losers.' The losers in question bridled, but said nothing. One look at the Kid told them that they were likely to come off worst in any altercation.

Jacko sighed. 'Ain't you heard me? Michael Jackson's already been done. He sang "Beat It". Did good, too.'

'What outfit was he wearin'?'

'Huh?'

'What outfit?'

Jacko seemed surprised by the question. 'Uh – I dunno, it was, uh, the same outfit that Jacko wore in the video.'

'Right. Makes sense, don't it?'

'Yeah. We done?' Jacko asked, turning back to the table to see if he'd won.

At that moment the ball dropped into a pocket in the spinning wheel and the croupier announced the winning number. Black thirteen. Jacko's eyes lit up and he let out a jubilant cheer. He'd placed a chip on number thirteen and had won a tidy sum as a result. As the croupier began scooping in the losing bets and paying out chips to the winners, the Kid grabbed Jacko's shoulder again and turned him round to face him once more. This time there was a considerably higher level of aggression in the way he spun him round.

'You told me earlier you were gonna sing "Earth Song".'

'That's right.'

'So why the red leather outfit from the *Thriller* video?'

'I just like it, is all.'

'Bullshit.'

Jacko looked uneasy. He swallowed hard And said, 'Jeez, man, what *is* your problem?'

'You're goin' onstage in the next twenty minutes or I'm gonna make your life worse'n a livin' hell.'

'Fucksakes, buddy. How many times I gotta tell ya—'

'You're gonna be John Belushi.'

'*What?*'

'John Belushi.'

Jacko looked confused. 'He's a comedian, ain't he?'

'Was.'

'Well, I ain't doin' stand-up.'

'He was a singer, too.'

'John Belushi?' Jacko considered what the Kid had said for a second. Then the light seemed to dawn. 'Oh, yeah, he was in the Blues Brothers, right?'

'Yeah.'

'Man, are you stupid? John Belushi was a white guy!'

'So was Michael Jackson.'

'Maybe so. But I can't do no Blues Brothers number dressed like this.' He gestured at his outfit. 'An' besides, I ain't had time to rehearse.'

'You won't need to.'

The Kid took off his sunglasses and handed them to Jacko. 'Put these on and head to the stage area. I'll meet you there in five minutes with the rest of your costume.' He waited to see if that had sunk in, before adding in characteristically gravelly tones, 'You don't show, I'll find you and make your nose look like the real Michael Jackson's.'

Having made his feelings clear, and having convinced himself that Jacko understood, the Kid turned and headed back out of the casino. Once again the other customers drew back out of his path. This time they could see his eyes. It wasn't an improvement.

Jacko called after him. 'I'm gonna need more than a fucking' costume to qualify for the final, ya know that?'

'I'll take care of it,' was the Kid's parting comment as he vanished from sight behind a crowd of people.

Twenty-Four

As Gabriel gunned the Harley past the road sign that welcomed all newcomers to the Devil's Graveyard, he knew he was in for one hell of a night. He had a date with destiny, no less.

Gabriel Locke was a New Age Disciple, trained by the greatest of God's own bounty hunters to protect the world from evil. As promoters of the Lord's work went, Gabriel didn't look quite as many people would have expected. Not for him the crew-cut, the smiling friendly manner, the cheap blue suit. He was a heavily tattooed biker with a shaved head and a two-inch scar running horizontally below his left eye. If he had looked a little less intimidating, things might have turned out differently for him.

After an early career as a wannabe preacher, he had met a man named Rodeo Rex who had shown him that there was much more to God's work than spreading the word and having faith. There was another side. A *much darker* side. A side that involved killing on behalf of the Lord to protect mankind. Rex had taught him all about hunting down and killing devil worshippers, vampires, werewolves and other undead scum, as well as various other evil sorts who had no place on this earth (and who wouldn't get to heaven anyway).

Most recently, they'd been in Plainview, Texas, wiping out a coven of vampires running an underground casino-cum-all-night buffet. Anyone who lost was allowed to leave the premises as they were likely to return another day, but those who won big never left. Or not alive, anyway. They were served up as food for the immortals instead, which had the advantage of turning them into vampires as well, thus raising recruitment.

So Gabriel, his mentor Rex and a couple of other New Age Disciples had shown up and staked the casino out, before descending on the place one night, armed to the teeth. The vampires had put up a feeble fight, as it turned out. They were typical bloodsuckers who only preyed on the weak; indeed, half of them killed themselves rather than suffer at the hands of Rex's gang. The operation was an incredible success.

But two other significant things had happened during their month-long stay in Plainview. First, they encountered a small, bald-headed black guy in his forties who claimed to be more than two thousand years old. He had shown up out of nowhere and claimed that the Good Lord had sent him to find the Disciples, and charge them with a new mission. This man went by the name of Julius. He was pleasant, well-mannered and well-educated in equal measure. And he knew his stuff when it came to religion.

To most people, a guy claiming to be over two thousand years old would have been considered a liar and a fool, but not to Gabriel. The Good Lord frequently led him to all corners of the earth, bringing him in contact with all kinds of people with claims just as outrageous as Julius's. Gabriel had faith in the Lord, and for that reason he believed in his heart that Julius was telling the truth. So, when the little man asked Rex and his crew to help him carry out a job on behalf of God, fighting the forces of evil, they knew he was a good guy.

Assured of their support, Julius had explained that he needed them to help him lift a curse at the Hotel Pasadena in the Devil's Graveyard. The job had everything they could possibly desire in a mission from God. The undead were involved, there were contracts being signed with the Devil, a talent show featuring impersonators of dead singing stars figured prominently, and, almost as important, there was a

$50,000 reward for assisting Julius in the mission.

Rex had agreed that he and his crew would take the job on – indeed, they couldn't wait for it – but then the second significant thing had occurred in Plainview, Texas. The night after they had successfully wiped out the vampire casino, they paid a visit to the local red-light district. And there they came across a smoky, run-down bar that was hosting an arm-wrestling contest. One man was defeating all comers. A shady-looking character with dark, greasy shoulder-length hair and two-day-old stubble. He looked like a biker type who knew how to handle himself in a tricky situation.

It had come as no surprise when Rex pulled up a seat and drew hands with the man. What followed was an arm-wrestling bout like no other. It had lasted for almost forty minutes, with neither man giving an inch. This had infuriated Rex, for he had never lost an arm-wrestling bout in all his life, or even come close. Word of the extraordinary contest had spread like wildfire and hundreds of people had flocked to the bar to watch the outcome and bet their money on who would triumph.

First one man, then the other, gained the upper hand, but eventually Rex triumphed, as he always had. The other guy seemed to give up, as if his muscles had packed up and gone home. It all happened very suddenly. One moment, the two hands and arms were locked almost immovably, the next Rex slammed his opponent's hand down on to the table and let out a huge roar of victory. But then Gabriel witnessed a strange and unexpected thing. Something he had never seen before. This man whom Rex had defeated refused to let go of the other's hand. Instead, he began to squeeze it tightly.

'What the fuck're ya doin'? Let go, ya fuckin' dickhead,' Rex had yelled.

His opponent hadn't responded. By rights he should have let go and congratulated Rex on his victory. Not this guy, though. This guy had no class. He tightened his grip on Rex's hand. Gabriel and two of his Disciple brothers watched on, unsure what to do. The bones in Rex's hand cracked, one by one. Gabriel remembered seeing an impassive expression on the other man's face as Rex winced and struggled to pull away, desperately trying to grab his opponent with his other hand. But the silent man just swayed back out of reach, maintaining his terrible grip. Rex had always taught Gabriel that a one-on-one fight was the only fair way to do things, so he and the other Disciples stood by and watched.

And they regretted it.

Eventually the other man released his grip, stood up and walked out of the bar without so much as offering his congratulations or an apology for his post-bout actions. Rex picked up his winnings and, cursing horribly, rushed off to the nearest hospital to get his hand fixed. Gabriel had gone with him to offer moral support. His mentor was in agony the likes of which he had never witnessed before. Meanwhile, the two other members of the New Age Disciples, Roderick and Ash, followed after the man who had broken Rex's hand. They planned to exact revenge on him for his assault on their admired leader.

At the hospital, the doctors had been forced to perform emergency surgery on Rex's hand. It had, however, been damaged beyond any surgeon's skill, and they had ended up amputating it and replacing it with a hook. That had been a shock, and not just for Rex. How the hell did you console someone who's just had his hand cut off at the wrist? Gabriel hadn't had the faintest idea what to say. He still remembered vividly Rex's fury at the whole incident. And so it was that, without consulting his distraught boss, Gabriel had made a call to Ash to give him the go-ahead to exact revenge on the man.

Which had only made matters worse.

When Gabriel had called, Ash and Roderick had been sitting in a car in the parking lot of a motel, which had a small diner attached to it. Ash informed Gabriel that the man he and Roderick had followed was driving a black Pontiac Firebird. They had followed him to the motel on the outskirts of Plainview, where he had stopped off for something to eat. They had pulled up in the car park and watched his every move for a few minutes, waiting for Gabriel to call with further instructions from Rex. Gabriel remembered his conversation with Ash only too well, for it was the last time they ever spoke. He had instructed Ash to follow the man into the diner. Ash had done this, but had then been unable to find his target anywhere inside. So with Gabriel's blessing he had returned to the car to wait for the man to reappear.

Gabriel had heard everything that followed through his cell phone. It still haunted his every waking moment, even now, several weeks later.

'Gabe. No sign of the guy in the diner or the motel. Guy on reception says he never saw him,' Ash had said.

'You saw him go in though, right?'

'Yeah, but the reception guy says no one's been in.'

'He must be lying. Check again.'

'Hold on. I gotta get back to the car. Roderick's up to something.'

'Up to what?'

'Hang on. Fuckin' car's shakin', man.'

Gabriel heard the sound of Ash opening the car door.

'Ash. Don't get in!' he had yelled into the phone.

'What the fuck? Rod? *Rod?* Jeeesus! Gabe! *He's fuckin' dead.*'

'Don't get in the car!'

'His throat's been cut. Oh Christ! What the—' He had sounded panicky and desperate on the phone, but the line had gone dead mid-sentence. Gabriel had tried to get him back, but without success. Eventually he had gone out to the motel, and found the car and its grisly contents. Of the stranger there had been no sign.

Some days later, the local police had concluded that the killer was the driver of the Pontiac Firebird. After killing Roderick he had waited in the back seat of their car and slashed open Ash's throat shortly after he had returned to the vehicle.

So it had come about that, with Rex busy constructing himself a new hand and Roderick and Ash dead, Gabriel had the Devil's Graveyard job all to himself. And the word on the street was that the guy who had crushed Rex's hand and then killed the two other Disciples had headed out this way too. There was a distinct possibility that he intended to pick up the cash on offer from Julius for his top-secret mission. So if things went as they should, Gabriel could kill him. He looked forward to that.

The desert wind chilled him to the bone as he rode down the desert highway on his chopped Harley, on which he had had almost every metal part chrome plated, so that it glowed silver in the moonlight. Gabriel had always liked cold weather. It made him feel alive when the skin on his arms tightened up and turned red. For that reason, he rode, even at night, in a black leather jerkin over a sleeveless black T-shirt. He was an accomplished rider, and enjoyed the added thrill of not wearing a helmet or too much other protective gear. His only nod towards safety equipment consisted of a pair of heavy biker boots with chrome buckles, and some black leather pants, although these were more for fashion purposes than protection.

On his right bicep, he had three tattoos of dice, bearing respectively the numbers one, two and three. What he wanted, almost more than anything but had yet to earn, were three similar tattoos on his left bicep bearing the numbers four, five and six, signifying that he was a fully pledged member of the New Age Disciples. Completing his mission would attain these. The back of Gabriel's shaved head bore one other small tattoo of a crucifix. He looked like one murderous sonofabitch.

Which was exactly what Gabriel was. Rex had signed him up for his prowess as a killer, nothing else. The religious side of things was still fairly new to him. Sure, he was enjoying the education, but not as much as he enjoyed the killing. As a younger man he had killed a few people he shouldn't have. Now Rex and the New Age Disciples were educating him in the ways of killing for the right reason. Killing for the good of mankind.

The evening sky had darkened quite suddenly, and the stars were shining brightly as he thundered past Sleepy Joe's Diner, the offbeat sound of the big V-twin's exhaust echoing back from the building. He knew the way to the hotel from there thanks to a map that Julius had given to Rodeo Rex. As Rex was unable to attend himself, he had handed it on to Gabriel, along with the mission. It was a proud moment to be trusted by Rex to carry out such an important assignment on his own. He wanted to prove himself worthy. He'd made that hard for himself by arriving late, but he was close now. The Hotel Pasadena lit up the night sky a few miles down the road. The time for killing was near.

Gabriel was itching to get started. The frustration resulting from all that had happened to his comrades in the last few weeks had built up inside him, and he was ready to unleash it. As it happened, his first opportunity came upon him somewhat earlier than he might have expected.

On the right side of the road about half a mile ahead he saw a ragged figure stumbling towards him. He slowed the bike slightly, dropping the speed from sixty miles an hour down to a more manageable thirty. With his right hand he pulled a dull silver handgun from a custom holster on the side of the bike. As he closed with the figure staggering out of the desert towards him, waving its arms, he took aim and fired.

Even above the noise of the Harley's exhaust, the discharge from the gun made an almighty bang in the still of night. The bullet flew with lethal accuracy into the face of the pedestrian at the side of the road.

Nice shot, Gabriel thought to himself as he rode on past the fallen body. Anything that came walking out of the wasteland in the Devil's Graveyard on Halloween almost certainly deserved to die.

He tucked the pistol into a shoulder holster under his jerkin, ready to use it on any more passers-by he might encounter. A further mile down the highway he saw a camper van parked at the roadside. An evil, righteous grin spread across his scarred face.

His night of killing was about to get interesting.

Back down the highway, the body of the man he'd shot lay cooling where it had fallen, the back of its head blown out, its dark uniform dusty and stained with blood.

So ended the life and all too brief police career of Patrolman Johnny Parks.

Twenty-Five

Jacko watched from the side of the stage as a Frank Sinatra impersonator was given a thorough roasting by the judges. Sinatra's performance had started off shaky and simply gotten worse as it went on. He'd hit a bad note early on while incorrectly singing the line 'I know the end is near' during his rendition of 'My Way'. After that, his voice (and his recollection of the correct lyrics) had completely deserted him. At times he howled like a drowning cat, and in one truly excruciating moment he had started singing in what sounded like Flemish. He finally finished off his performance with an appalling fit of coughing.

Jacko had entered his name with the show's organizers just ten minutes before Sinatra had gone onstage. They had agreed to let him perform last on the condition that he acquired a better outfit than the red leather suit he was wearing. It had been difficult to convince them he was planning to perform a Blues Brothers song, particularly because he didn't even know what song he was going to sing. But they had allowed him to enter, most likely because they figured he'd be one of the entertaining 'freaks'.

Since he had arrived at the area off the stage where the Bourbon Kid was supposed to meet him, he'd seen three performances. They had all been awful. But now, as he witnessed Frank Sinatra being taken apart by the judges, he was the only contestant still to go. He was due onstage within the next two minutes and he still didn't have the Blues

Brothers outfit that the Bourbon Kid had promised him. The Kid's efforts to find a suit were taking longer than Jacko had expected, which wasn't necessarily a bad thing. If the Kid didn't show up with the outfit, he had the perfect excuse not to go up and perform. As things stood currently, he might be going onstage dressed as Michael Jackson wearing a pair of sunglasses. And that, as Blues Brothers outfits went, was somewhat lacking in authenticity.

He hurried back down the steps that led to the stage and walked round to take one last look up and down the passageway to see whether the Kid was on his way. He checked both ways three times before deciding that he was going to have to make a run for it. Eventually, just when he had given up hope, he saw the darkly dressed killer appear at the end of the corridor, coming from the lobby. He was carrying a black suit and white shirt in one hand and a smart slim black clip-on tie in the other. He jogged down the hall to where Jacko was waiting.

'You think you could have cut it a bit finer?' the anxious singer snapped sarcastically. 'I don't even know what fuckin' song I'm s'posed to be singin', and let's face it, at this rate I wouldn't have time to learn the words to "The Chicken Dance".'

'Shut the fuck up and put this on,' growled the Kid. He threw the suit and shirt at Jacko who caught them, then laid them down on the carpet. Then he reluctantly took off his red leather jacket and held it out for the Kid to take. When the latter made no attempt to take it, Jacko eventually dropped it on to the floor at his feet.

'This is a shit plan, you know?' he complained. 'I'm due on in about thirty seconds an' I don't have an act.'

'That's okay,' said the Kid, pulling a small silver object from his hip pocket. 'You got an angle.'

'Yeah? An' what's that?' Jacko asked as he picked up the white shirt and began slipping his arms into the sleeves.

'I got you this.' The Kid held out the six-inch-long silver object he'd drawn from his pocket. Jacko took one look at it and shook his head.

'Oh no. Oh no no no. You surely don't think I'm goin' out there with a harmonica, hopin' to win?'

'Figure you'll be the novelty act. No one else has played an instrument. It'll get you noticed.'

'It'll get me laughed at, is what it'll do.'

'That's a chance I'm willing to take.' The Kid's voice sounded like gravel crunching underfoot.

'Yeah, I'll bet. An' what if I say no?'

'You don't wanna know what I'll do to you if you say no.'

'And what if I suck? I still ain't got a goddam song.'

'You won't. You go onstage and you tell the judges that you're dedicating the song to your wife who died recently. Tell 'em her name was Sally. Then you sing "Mustang Sally". It's a singalong chorus. The audience will sympathize with you even if you're crap. Try an' encourage them to sing along. Then you can play the harmonica and get them to do most of the singing for you.'

Jacko buttoned up the top button on the white shirt and sighed. 'Shit, man. Where did you find this plan? In a box of fuckin' cornflakes?'

The Kid stepped forward, reached out one hand and grabbed him round the throat. 'I'll have a better plan if you get to the final. Which you better had. This was short notice.' With that he let go of Jacko's throat, clipped the black tie he had been holding on to the collar of the shirt, and set it straight.

Jacko went to pick up the suit jacket from the floor. 'So where'd'ya find this outfit, anyway?' he asked.

'Some guy in the lobby was wearing it.'

'What's he wearin' now?'

'Body bag, more'n likely.'

'Nice. A dead guy's suit. An' it's still warm. Just what I always wanted.'

As he began putting on the jacket he heard the announcer call his name. Time to get moving. The Kid hustled him back to the area at the side of the stage. As they arrived, the Frank Sinatra impersonator walked out into the corridor, looking close to tears. He put on a brave face as he drew level with them and nodded at Jacko.

'Good luck, man. They're pretty brutal out there.'

Jacko watched the dejected singer walk off towards the elevator at the end of the passageway. The Kid allowed him to get about ten yards before calling out to him, 'Yo, Sinatra. C'mere.'

Sinatra turned around. He had allowed a small tear to trickle down his right cheek. He was only a young fellow, maybe in his late teens, and rejection, with its shock and disappointment, was probably a new experience for him. In need of some comfort, he started walking back towards Jacko and the Kid, hoping they might be about to offer him a few words of encouragement.

'Whassup, man?' he asked, stopping a yard in front of the Bourbon Kid.

The Kid punched him on the chin. The blow knocked him out cold on his feet. He wobbled for a second with a dazed look on his face before falling backwards. As he fell towards the floor the Kid reached out and grabbed hold of his black fedora by its brim. There was a loud thud as Sinatra's head smacked down on to the carpeted floor.

Unconcerned, the Kid turned and placed the hat on Jacko's head, stepped back, then reached out and tilted it slightly to one side. The transformation from Michael Jackson to Blues Brother was almost complete. *Apart from the pants.* Time had run out and Jacko was going to have to go onstage with the red leather pants on. Still, the change had taken place in less than ninety seconds.

'Yeah, you look okay, man,' said the Kid. "'Cept we really need to do somethin' about those fuckin' red pants for the final.'

'I reckon,' said Jacko, shrugging. 'They, like, don't really go with the outfit, do they?'

'They don't go with any fuckin' thing. You look a prick in them at any time.'

'Thanks. Wish me luck, huh?'

'You don't need luck.' The Kid handed him the harmonica. 'Go strut your stuff.'

Jacko took a deep breath and then, with his new outfit on and a harmonica in his hands that he'd never played before, he hurried back to the side of the stage. Once there, he paused for a few seconds to catch his breath, then walked onstage and into the lights. His impersonation of the Blues Brothers might turn out to be disastrous, but at least he sort of looked the part from the waist up. Plus, he had a gimmick. None of the other contestants had played an instrument. If he could show the judges he could play the harmonica half decently, he might just sneak his way into the final.

Twenty-Six

Sanchez wasn't sure what to make of Elvis's sudden decision to drop his shovel. He was even less sure what to make of his friend's gnomic remark that 'somethin'' had 'happened'. What was the meaning of it? It had to be part of a plan, but what kind of plan? One that involved both of them escaping, he hoped. He certainly wasn't happy about the possibility that Elvis might be planning to double-cross him.

Yet if the plan was to confuse Invincible Angus, then it was definitely working. The hitman looked genuinely unsettled by Elvis's sudden claim that something had happened. The right side of his face was twitching and he was visibly grinding his teeth. The man was wound up tight as a coilspring and his self-control pushed to its limit. His eyes opened wide and he pointed his pistol at Elvis's head.

'Pick up that goddam shovel and start diggin' again or I'll blow a fuckin' hole through your fuckin' head right now,' he ordered menacingly.

Elvis showed little concern, and even less interest. He seemed somewhat distracted. 'Look, Twitchy, we need to get the hell out of here,' he said. In the moonlight, the King's face revealed a growing sense of anticipation. Sanchez was as confused as Angus. *What was Elvis up to? And was Sanchez supposed to be in on it?*

'I'm gonna count to three,' said Angus. 'And if you ain't holdin' that shovel and diggin', you'll leave me with no choice. One . . .'

Sanchez decided it was time to take a part. Elvis had played a hand and might well be relying on him to come up with something ingenious. Looking towards Angus, he called out, 'Look behind ya,' pointing to the ground behind the hitman's left leg.

'*Oh fer Chrissakes!*' Angus shook his head and looked at Elvis. 'Is this guy for real? That's, like, the oldest trick in the book. How in the hell is *he* supposed to be a world-famous hitman?'

'Okay,' said Elvis. 'Then look behind me.'

At that point even Sanchez was confused. Whatever their plan was supposed to be, it appeared to be incredibly lame. 'Look behind you' was bad enough, but if Elvis was now playing along by telling everyone to look behind him, then they really were clutching at straws. Even so, Sanchez decided to go along with it, hoping to God it really was all part of a plan. Still holding his shovel awkwardly in his bound hands, he turned round to take a look behind his friend. At first, he was unable to see much in the dark, other than the dark shapes of the two dead security guards on the ground. Then, in the graveyard quiet that had followed Elvis's suggestion, he suddenly heard something.

A rumbling noise. The sound of earth being disturbed, as if hundreds of moles were burrowing up from under the ground. Out of the corner of his eye he saw movement near the dead security guard behind Elvis. The ground started to erupt with small mounds of dirt and sand, spitting dust and small stones into the air. Sanchez felt a clod of loose earth land on his shoe. It had come from within the grave that he and Elvis had been digging. He turned round and leaned over the shallow hole to get a closer look at where it had come from. The rumbling noises seemed to be coming from all around, but the nearest sounds were definitely coming from the grave. Specks of dirt were flying up into the air from it. Something was coming up through the ground.

'The fuck is it?' Angus called over to them. He could plainly hear the noise, which seemed to be growing louder by the second.

Still looking down into the grave, Sanchez stared hard at the small stones and specks of dirt flying up. With only the intermittent light of the moon to see by, he wasn't sure if his eyes were deceiving him or not. Then something pale punched its way out through the soil.

A hand.

An old, decayed hand with dirt wedged beneath its short, broken fingernails. Its fingers were moving, reaching out for something to grab hold of, a hand fighting its way out of the ground. Sanchez looked back up at Angus, who was pointing his pistol at him.

'It's a fuckin' hand!' he shouted.

'What?'

It had taken him a lot longer than it should have, but Sanchez had finally realized exactly what it was that Elvis had been trying to warn them about. Something *was* happening, right enough. Yet another thing the Mystic fuckin' Lady had failed to predict, he thought inconsequentially.

'Oh my God! Behind you!' he suddenly yelled. He was staring at the ground behind Angus, and he really *had* seen something. And this was more than just a hand. What Sanchez saw was a decaying corpse in the process of dragging itself out of the sand and dirt. The upper half of its body was already above the surface and one of its arms was outstretched, reaching for the calf of Angus's left leg. Its face was a vile mess of torn and decaying flesh. Its body was still covered by rags of clothing that hid no more than half of its skeletal torso. The creature still had hair (albeit grey and full of dirt), eyes and teeth, but any fat its body might once have had appeared to have been used up during its underground hibernation. Its black, rabid eyes revealed an insane hunger. A hunger for human flesh.

That was just the start of it. As Angus finally woke up to the fact that something really was going on and turned to take a look, two more patches of dirt erupted within a few feet of each other on either side of him. Bodies were rising up from shallow graves in the desert. Bodies of all the dead people who had been buried there over the last hundred years.

The real *Back From the Dead* show was just beginning, an annual killfest for the undead. And the first course looked likely to be Sanchez, Elvis and Invincible Angus. These grossly deformed, flesh-eating members of the undead had been in hibernation for a whole year.

And they looked damned hungry.

Twenty-Seven

By the time the last performer hit the stage for his audition, most of the other contestants had become incredibly anxious. Every one of them wanted to know if he or she had made it through to the final. For those who had performed early, the wait was unbearable. Many of them had sought refuge in one of the hotel's bars for a drink to calm their nerves before the finalists were announced. Others had returned to their rooms to try to snatch some rest. An unlucky few had been killed, and one other, Elvis, had been taken for a ride out in the desert.

One of the few who had decided to watch the last guy perform was Emily. She was not as anxious as most of the other entrants because she knew that her place in the final was guaranteed. She'd known for months that all she would have to do was to turn up and not make a mess of the audition. Having successfully overcome that hurdle she had since been offering support to the other contestants who she knew had no chance of making it into the final. Her support was genuinely well meant. She supposed that it made her feel a little better about it all, the whole sham.

The guy onstage dressed as one of the Blues Brothers – well, his upper half, anyway – didn't look like he'd be too much of a threat, and he also seemed a touch nervous. Remembering how nerve-racked she had been when she had performed, Emily's heart went out to him. He hadn't done much to help himself by wearing red leather pants, either. *Poor guy.* She watched from the wings as he nervously twiddled with a harmonica while Nina Forina asked him a few questions. Emily had been lucky enough not to be grilled by the presenter before she sang. Generally, if Nina asked a contestant to tell the audience a bit about themselves, it meant the contestant was either some kind of a freak, or had a sob story to tell.

'So, Jacko, are you nervous?' Nina asked, placing a perfectly manicured orange hand on his shoulder.

'Yeah, a little bit,' he mumbled quietly.

'Do you have any friends or family in the audience?'

'Uh – no. My only friend was my wife Sally, but she died recently.'

The audience let out a concerted and sympathetic 'Aaah'.

'I am so sorry,' said Nina, offering a look that might have been sympathetic had Botox not intervened. 'How did she die?'

'Huh?'

'Your wife. Sally. What was the cause of her tragic death? Or is it too painful to talk about?'

To Emily, Jacko seemed uneasy with the questioning, almost as though he didn't know the answers. 'Uh, yeah – I mean, yes, it was painful. She was eaten by a leopard.'

'What?'

'A leopard.'

The audience gasped as one. Recognizing at once that the interview had gone on long enough, Nina turned back to the audience and boomed into her microphone. 'Okay, that's a sad, sad story. But on that note, ladies and gentlemen, please put your hands together for . . . *the Blues Brother*!'

Emily watched as the Blues Brother stood rooted to the spot, not moving, just taking deep breaths. *Oh dear*, she thought, *he's dried*. The applause had ended and nearly twenty seconds of eerie silence passed before Jacko finally began to sing. His song of choice was 'Mustang Sally', though he struggled to get the first line past his lips.

'Mustang Sally,

Someone better slow your Mustang down.'

If he hadn't had a microphone in front of him, the judges (who were no more than thirty feet away) would barely have heard him. Which was just as well because, if the second line was anything to go by, he seemed to be getting most of the words wrong. Like someone singing along to a tune on their car stereo, he appeared to be mumbling a little whenever he was unsure of the words.

Emily tiptoed to the edge of the stage to get a closer look, keeping herself hidden behind the gigantic red curtain that was drawn back to the side of the stage. She thought she was alone, until she noticed someone else watching from the wings. He was standing a yard or so to her left, against a wall that had been painted a deep black. She hadn't seen him until she was up close, for, like a chameleon, he blended into the dark wall.

She recognized him as the strange man she had seen earlier in the day, just before she had gone onstage. He was still wearing the black leather jacket with the dark hood hanging round his shoulders. This truly was a man who could slip in and out of shadows virtually undetected. Yet, although she found him unsettling, Emily seized on this second opportunity to talk to the strange individual.

'Did you lend him your shades?' she asked, nodding over at the Blues Brother on the stage.

The man had been so engrossed in watching Jacko perform that he hadn't noticed her arrival next to him. His initial glare implied that he didn't welcome her approach, but his look softened a little when he recognized her.

'Yeah. Needs all the help he can get.'

'The first few lines are the worst. Then you get your confidence.'

'Right.' There was deep scepticism in the gravelly voice.

Emily *was* right, however. Despite starting hesitantly, Jacko improved with each line, becoming a little louder and more confident with every word he sang. And when he came to the harmonica parts, he shone. The boy could play. Suddenly the audience began to perk up and clap along.

'Told you,' said Emily. 'Doing okay now, isn't he?'

'He's better than you, that's for sure.'

Emily was taken aback as much by the uncalled-for aggression of the remark as by its brutality. 'Excuse me?' she bridled.

'You were shit. Why don't you go home? You ain't going to win.'

'I've as much right to be here as anyone else.' Despite herself she was becoming angry, and a light flush spread across her cheeks.

'Your audition was a phoney,' the dark stranger added.

Emily felt her cheeks turn a gentle crimson colour as the flush spread. It wasn't pleasant to hear someone point out, rather loudly, that her path to the final had been preordained. For a second, it made her doubt her own talent.

'I don't know what you're talking about,' she stammered, looking for a way to escape the conversation.

'The final is rigged. And in case you ain't noticed, three of the original line-up for the final have disappeared. Seems someone doesn't like the idea of people cheating. Why don't you just do everyone a favour and get the fuck back to Kansas?' He looked hard at her, his eyes even more unnerving than sunglasses. She didn't believe that three of her fellow finalists had disappeared – he was just saying it to upset her.

He was succeeding, too. Emily swallowed hard to hold back the onrush of a flood of tears. It wasn't pleasant at all to be spoken to in such a manner. What was this guy's problem? She'd never done him any harm. Onstage, Jacko was now in his element, scorching through a harmonica solo that had the entire audience on its feet.

'You're very rude,' she blurted out before turning away from the dark-clad stranger and moving to her right, until she was actually treading on the bottom of the dark red curtain. She decided that she would ignore him. Instead, she would concentrate on what the judges had to say about the Blues Brother.

After an ovation from the crowd that lasted a good minute, the panel of three judges gave their opinions. The first two, Lucinda Brown and Candy Perez, offered politely positive comments that drew cheers from the audience. Finally it came to the turn of the judge in the middle in the loud white suit, Nigel Powell, the judge whose opinion counted most. He looked a great deal more irritated than he had earlier, when Emily had performed. He was no doubt eager to take a break, too.

'Well, what can I say, Jacko?' he started. 'Your singing was mediocre at best.' The crowd booed and he leaned back and half-turned to look at them. 'Well it was!' he protested. 'However, your harmonica playing was excellent.' The audience stopped booing and began cheering. When the noise died down sufficiently, Powell carried on. 'But the point of this show is proving that you can sing, and for me that didn't really sound like the Blues Brothers. Without the harmonica, that was probably not even average.'

There were more boos from the crowd, and out of the corner of her eye Emily noted a touch of agitation on the face of the man standing next to her. In fact, he looked about ready to kill someone, so in the interests of self-preservation she slipped away and headed back to the safety of the dressing room on the eighth floor. At least there, she figured, she would be among friends like Johnny Cash, Otis Redding, Kurt Cobain and James Brown.

Twenty-Eight

Invincible Angus fired his pistol and all hell broke loose. Literally. Mutant creatures were climbing out of the ground all around him. One of them grabbed hold of his pants leg as it pulled itself up, which was the cue for him to start shooting wildly in all directions. It was also the cue for Elvis and Sanchez to make their escape.

'Run!' yelled the King.

He needn't have bothered. Sanchez had already dropped the shovel, turned and started heading back to the roadside, at what was, for him, a crisp jog, running as best as he could considering his wrists were bound together with tape. He'd managed to avoid the outstretched arms of a couple of creatures that had surfaced behind him, and luck was still on his side. The bodies of the two security guards had attracted the zombies' attention. They were easy prey: recently killed, still warm, and unable to fight back.

Angus, on the other side of the grave that he had made Sanchez and Elvis dig, had rather more of a problem on his hands. There were no corpses on his side of the grave, so all the zombies near him were reaching out and grasping for him. Although he'd shot the first one in the head, they were springing up all around him. Not that Sanchez gave a fuck. Served the dickwad right.

There were no zombies between Sanchez and the van at the roadside, and he and Elvis charged towards it as fast as they could. Sanchez found running difficult at the best of times, but it was proving particularly tricky with his hands stuck out in front of him. Making a virtue of the situation, he raised his hands in front of his face, closed his eyes and prayed to any kind of god who might be listening that the van was unlocked and that the keys were in the ignition. And if there happened to be an untouched meatball sub on the front seat, then so much the better.

They were within a few yards of the road when a small glimmer of light approaching on the highway in the distance offered them some hope. A single headlight appeared about half a mile down the road. Sanchez looked at Elvis. He'd seen it too, and knew it was their best bet.

It would, they hoped, be slightly safer on the road because the chances of any of the loathsome, half-rotted creatures buried beneath it breaking through the asphalt were slim. But their luck ran out before they reached it, as a hand burst out of the dirt at Sanchez's feet and grabbed his left ankle. The check to his progress was enough to make him stumble, and he lost his footing, falling heavily to the ground and hitting himself in the face with his bound hands. It was lucky for the bar owner that Elvis, although now a yard or two ahead, wasn't the type to ditch a friend just because there were half-rotting undead creatures climbing out of the ground. Hearing Sanchez fall, he stopped to see what had happened.

'Fuck, Sanchez! You got a big fuckin' hand on your ankle!' He was staring down at his friend's foot where the grey-skinned, almost skeletal hand was gripping his ankle tightly. Attached to the hand by a rotting arm, rising up out of the sand and dirt, was the upper half of a giant of a zombie. It had a head twice the size of any normal man's. Its skin was a dark ashen colour that looked as though it had been covered in hot tar. Its eyes were yellow and glowed brightly in the darkness. Had Sanchez seen it he would almost certainly have fainted from terror.

Still mercifully unaware of what had grabbed him, Sanchez

was far more concerned with trying to free his ankle from its hand. He heaved hard with all the power of his leg muscles, but the monster's strength was far greater. It was trying to pull his foot towards its mouth as it climbed out of its former grave. If the other zombies looked hungry, then this one looked like it could eat the terrified bar owner whole, without spitting out the bones. Its gaping mouth was enormous, revealing a set of large yellow teeth set in shrunken, bleeding gums and a pair of huge tonsils at the back of its throat. Its bright yellow eyes were agape at the sight of Sanchez's plump leg in its hand.

Elvis reached out, grabbed his friend's bound hands and pulled as hard as he could. Now the King was strong, but the giant muthafucker on Sanchez's leg was a shitload stronger, so his attempt was in vain.

'C'mon, ya fuckin' wimp! You can make it!' he yelled down at Sanchez.

The wimp wasn't convinced. He had now seen the thing that had hold of him.

'Fuck! FUCK!' he screamed. 'I can't get it off. I can't get it off!' He had never been so terrified. He'd been scared by a great many things in his time, from tiny spiders right through to gangs of vampires and werewolves, but this beat the lot. It was the first time anything of such a size had attacked him and tried to eat his leg. Nor were Elvis's attempts to pull him away achieving much. Sanchez had been unfortunate enough to have been grabbed by the Hulk Hogan of zombies. A giant of incredible strength. To make matters worse, three more zombies had climbed out of the ground and were now bearing down on them. They had given up on trying to get their teeth into the corpses of the two security guards, which were already swamped beneath a swarm of decaying undead.

'Elvis! Shit! Help me, man, fer fuck's sake!' Sanchez screamed desperately.

'I'm trying, man. Can't you kick it, or somethin'? Or sit on the muthafucker?'

Sanchez turned to see the giant zombie was now more than halfway out of the ground and was lifting him up by his ankle to destabilize him, readying itself to take a bite out of his leg. He was on the point of letting his bowels open to run riot down his leg towards the creature's mouth when . . .

BOOM!

Startled, he looked up to the road where the noise had come from. As he did so he felt the zombie's grip on his ankle slacken. He scrambled to his feet, desperate to escape the unstable ground. The zombie was still holding him – he could feel its cold fingers around his flesh – but he was now able to kick his leg free. A glance down revealed that the creature's hand was no longer attached to the rest of its body. Its arm had been blown off at the elbow, courtesy of a shot fired by the rider of the motorcycle now drawing to a stop on the highway.

Elvis, still holding Sanchez's hands, hauled the tubby bar owner towards him. Then, suddenly embarrassed, they quickly dropped their grip as the motorcycle covered the last few yards, the rider blipping the throttle as he changed down through the gears. Both rushed to the edge of the road to greet their saviour. The motorbike rolled up alongside them and came to a halt. The rider blipped the throttle a last time, then killed the engine. In the sudden silence, he kicked down the sidestand, leaned the Harley on it, and stepped off. Even Elvis, who was not small, could see he was a giant of a man. Ignoring Sanchez and Elvis, he strode past them, drew a .357 Dan Wesson PPC from a shoulder holster, aimed it at the middle zombie of the three approaching them, and fired a single shot into its face. The sound, and the sight of their companion's disintegrating head, startled the two others on either side. They stopped dead in their tracks and then began slowly to back away, waiting to see if the massive biker was going to fire at them again. Instead, he turned his attention to the giant mutant that was still halfway out of the ground, and now had only one arm. He pulled a handful of bullets out of a pocket in his black leather pants and calmly reloaded his heavyweight revolver. Then he fired a shot into the zombie's face, killing it stone dead. Destroying the biggest enemy early in the piece always had the desired effect. The others backed away and headed back towards the two dead security guards and Invincible Angus, who was still fighting off a whole bunch of creatures in the dark, by the shallow, freshly dug grave. *Tough shit*, thought Sanchez.

The man with the massive handgun turned back to Elvis and Sanchez.

"Kay, let's get the fuck outta here,' he said. 'This is only gonna get worse.' He didn't seem remotely concerned about the hitman battling away in the distance. Apart from anything else, there were now too many resurrected zombies for a lone man with a single handgun to attempt a rescue. Angus was going to have to shift for himself.

'Amen to that!' said Sanchez, looking to the heavens and giving quiet thanks. He was, fitfully, a deeply religious man, although only at times that suited him. In other words, when he was in deep shit.

To his surprise, the big biker walked up to Elvis and the pair of them grinned at each other. The King, having succeeded in ripping off the duct tape that had bound his hands together, slapped hands with the other man.

'Yo, Gabriel, man, how's it goin'?' Elvis asked with a smile. It was plain that the two of them were old friends.

'Been worse. Whatcha been up to?'

'Not much. Kinda dead around here.'

'Yeah. Need a ride?'

'You betcha.'

Gabriel climbed back on to the big Harley-Davidson chopper, kicked the propstand up and fired up the engine. Elvis climbed on to the long leather-upholstered seat behind him. Gabriel looked over at Sanchez, who was praying that he too would be offered a ride, although he didn't see how.

'C'mon, lardass. Get on,' he ordered, gesturing that Sanchez should climb aboard and sit in front of him on the few inches of the seat still available between Gabriel and the massive fuel tank. The bar owner didn't need to be told twice and somehow managed to get a leg over the bike and squeeze himself in on the front of the seat, Gabriel's long arms reaching round him to the controls. It wasn't even slightly comfortable, but it was a dam' sight better than being left in the desert with a bunch of decaying, long-dead freaks.

'What the fuck are those goddamn things?' he asked, nodding at the zombies by the shallow grave that were still fighting to get a bite of Invincible Angus.

'If I ain't mistaken, they're ghouls, or maybe zombies. I wouldn't worry if I was you – Invincible Angus'll take care of 'em,' said Gabriel, revving the bike's engine. Sure enough, the hitman's distant cursing was occasionally punctuated by shots.

'You know Angus?'

'Sure. Now hold on.'

The chopper pulled away and cruised off down the highway, the torque of the big V-twin coping effortlessly with the extra load. With the desert wind blowing sand and all kinds of insects into his face, Sanchez decided it would be best to keep his mouth shut to avoid the intake of unwanted food. He listened as best he could to Elvis and Gabriel as they conducted a quick catch-up, yelling at each other above the beat of the engine and the roar of the wind as the Harley powered through the night.

'What brings you out this way, Gabe?' Elvis shouted from the rear.

'Rex sent me. There's an undead problem round these parts. Guess you noticed. I'm here to fix it.'

Holy shit! thought Sanchez. He'd only known Gabriel for a minute and was already in awe of him.

'You've come here just to fight the undead?' he heard

Elvis ask.

'That's one reason. I also gotta kill some singers.'

'Reckon someone may have killed them singers for you.'

'One less job then, I guess. Give me time to focus on some more personal business I gotta attend to.'

'Like what?'

'You hear about Roderick an' Ash?'

'Yeah, man. Real sorry 'bout that.'

'Well, the guy who killed 'em is rumoured to have headed out this way. Reckon I'll have time to go lookin' for him.'

Sanchez listened in on the shouted conversation for the rest of the journey back to the hotel. It sounded like the dead bodies he'd seen earlier in the day were just the tip of the iceberg.

Twenty-Nine

Invincible Angus was doing an impressive job of fighting off the zombie creatures. Over the years he had fought men and women of all different shapes and sizes, wielding all kinds of different weapons, so he knew how to handle himself in a fight. And even though he had been surprised to find zombies attacking him, he was disciplined enough to put that out of his mind and concentrate on killing the fuckers. There would be time later to reflect on exactly what they were doing out here in the desert. For now, survival came top of his agenda.

He had figured out pretty early that these creatures had a surprisingly high level of intelligence. In most of the zombie movies he'd seen, they tended to stumble around in a dazed fashion with their arms outstretched, mumbling words like 'Brains' over and over. But these were different, at least a couple of notches above that kind of nonsense. They attacked strategically. They knew to steer clear of his pistol. In fact, the sneaky bastards only ever attacked him when his back was turned, so he had to keep spinning around. He managed to gun down four of them, but pretty soon he found that all the spinning was making him dizzy. He'd only be able to keep whizzing around for so long before one of them would catch him off guard.

The really unexpected thing, however, was that not all of them were intent on killing him. When one particularly bony, tattered creature crawled along the ground and then jumped on his back, he expected it to try to take a bite out of his neck.

But the sneaky little bastard actually pushed its hand in the coat pocket of his trench coat. *What the fuck?* At first, Angus couldn't work out what the thing was after.

To his utter dismay, by the time he'd shaken it off, the zombie had snagged the keys to his van, right out of his pocket. Sneaky fucker. As the other zombies continued circling him, the sneaky one ran off limpingly towards the van, followed by another wearing what looked like a very dirty and badly torn pink dress. If Angus didn't get a grip on the situation, he had a feeling he was about to watch two undead, brainless freaks hijack his pride and joy. This was entirely unexpected, and extremely unwelcome.

'Get outta there, you miserable fucks!' he yelled after them.

Why Angus wasted his time calling after them was anyone's guess. They weren't going to respond. Worse still, he should have been running after them, but instead, he stood rooted to the spot as other creatures circled him, finding himself mesmerized by the sight of two fuckin' zombies getting into his beloved giant blue camper van and closing the doors.

If they knew how to drive and actually pulled away, his chances of escape would, for all practical purposes, vanish. When he heard the engine splutter into life he knew he had one option: batter his way through the swarming monsters and get to the van before it drove off. The noise of the engine starting was followed a few seconds later by the sound of CD player in the van bursting into life. Angus's face dropped. He charged at two zombies who were standing between him and the van, knocking them aside more easily than he had expected. Then he started running as fast as he could, shooting down or kicking away any zombie rash or stupid enough to get in his path. No fucking way were those bastard zombies gonna make off with his van and his CD of Tom Jones's greatest hits.

'Get the fuck outta there! That's my fuckin' van, you fuckin' muthafuckers! I'm gonna kill you! Again!'

Angus's cries were to no avail. As the zombies pulled away and zoomed down the highway, he heard the chorus of 'Delilah' blaring out from the van's speakers.

Bastard thievin' undead pricks!

Angus's van was one of his most valuable possessions, but his Tom Jones CD was priceless. *A signed edition from the man himself.* If he had been angry before, he was absolutely seething now. Unfortunately for him, he still had a bunch of zombies to fight off before he could even think about following the van back down the highway to the Hotel Pasadena.

Thirty

The Bourbon Kid waited for Jacko to finish waving at the audience. The Blues Brothers impersonation hadn't gone down as well as he'd hoped. Emily Shannon, the Judy Garland impersonator, was way better. And having just briefly met her, the Kid was pretty sure he'd made a bad first impression. In trying to convince her to quit the show and not perform in the final, all he had succeeded in doing was upsetting her and making her dislike him. That would have been okay if she'd followed his advice and quit the show, but it didn't look like she had. This left him with an uneasy feeling. Something he hadn't felt in a long time. Guilt. He felt guilty about upsetting her. He couldn't get his head around the reasons it was bothering him.

It had been ten years to the day that he had effectively deserted Beth, the one true love in his life. Emily looked so much like Beth. They were even dressed exactly the same, for fuck's sake. And Emily had that pleasant way about her, the same fresh-faced innocence Beth had possessed. What the hell was this all about? Was it some sort of sign? A chance to make amends for the wrongdoings of ten years ago? A chance to get things right? If he righted the wrongs this time and saved Emily, would it ease his conscience?

The memory of his mother's face flashed through his mind. He saw himself, aged sixteen, standing over her as he fired bullets into her chest. Then he remembered the grinning face of Kione, the vampire who had raped his mother and turned her into one of his own kind. That sonofabitch was still alive, albeit in a permanent state of torture, hanging from a ceiling in the Kid's apartment back home, ripe for being tortured again upon his return. And maybe that's where he was best off? Back home? Maiming and torturing? That's what he did best. Particularly when it mattered.

'You okay?' Jacko asked.

The Kid had barely noticed that his Blues Brothers-impersonating sidekick was standing next to him at the side of the stage. He snapped out of his more maudlin thoughts and looked at the idiot in the red leather pants and black suit jacket. He'd pinned his hopes on this buffoon. *What a fuckin' waste of time.*

'I'm done,' he said to Jacko. 'You can keep the sunglasses. Good luck in the final. If you get there.'

'Huh?'

The plan to spare Emily from winning the competition hadn't worked. The Kid had done all he could to stop her from the inevitable, but she seemed hell-bent on ignoring him and putting herself in danger by winning the competition and signing the ill-fated contract. The Kid's talents were best used elsewhere. Everyone he'd met in the Hotel Pasadena was a fucking idiot, a lousy cheat, or a murderous slimeball. Time to leave.

Leaving a baffled-looking Jacko behind he headed to the reception desk. By the time he got there his mood had become so foul that he pulled a gun on the receptionist. He made it very clear to her that he wanted his car keys handed over to him, rather than have a valet drive the car round to one of the hotel's entrances. It took less than thirty seconds for her to locate his keys and hand them over.

The parking lot at the rear was jam-packed with buses that had shipped in hordes of fools from out of town. These were all parked at the rear, so he was pleased to find his black Firebird parked in the front row of cars just a few yards back from the hotel's rear exit.

He opened the driver's-side door and was just about to climb in when he saw a chopped Harley-Davidson cruise around the side of the hotel from the front drive. It caught his attention because the rider was carrying not one but two passengers, one on the seat in front of him, the other behind him. And he recognized them all.

He sat down behind the steering wheel and quietly closed the driver's door. What were these three jokers doing at the hotel? And why were they together? The first one he recognized was the fat bastard at the front – Sanchez, the bartender from the Tapioca in Santa Mondega. Behind him was the rider, a huge, shaven-headed biker, and behind him Elvis, a hitman from the same town. Two of this trio had been intrinsically linked to the Kid's night of evil a decade ago. When he had gone to church to pick up his younger brother up from a late-night service, he'd arrived to find Elvis and Sanchez there with a bunch of dead vampires. Elvis and a preacher named Rex had killed the vampires and apparently, hard though it was to believe, Sanchez had shielded his brother from the vampire attacks. That's what they'd told him anyway, and he had no reason not to believe them.

The third man on the Harley, driving the bike sandwiched between Sanchez and Elvis, was its owner, Gabriel Locke. A New Age Disciple and probably a pretty decent guy, but given what had happened in Plainview recently, probably a bit pissed with the Kid. Murderous, even.

He watched the three of them climb off the chopper and head over to the fire exit at the rear of the hotel. Sanchez the buffoon tried to open the door a few times before realizing it only opened from the inside. Then the three of them headed back round to the front of the hotel.

But why were they here? Elvis was a hitman, but might well be there to sing in the show. Sanchez was a buffoon, not worth worrying about, but Locke – he might well be there to do the job the Kid had quit on. *The job that involved killing Emily.* He would want to ensure that Julius won the show and signed the contract. Yet Gabriel Locke was a religious type, of a kind, which meant that he would probably try to avoid killing Emily. Wouldn't he?

The Kid opened his car door and got out. He drew a pack of cigarettes from his jacket pocket and pulled one out with his teeth. Then he sat back on the hood of his car and sucked on the end of it. It lit up brightly in the cold night air. There was some thinking to be done. What exactly was going on in this hotel? And in the desert that surrounded it?

As he sat looking up at the moon, he heard another vehicle approach. Its tyres were screeching as if it were racing around a banked concrete track at high speed. In a moment it appeared around the same corner from where the Harley chopper had arrived. It was a large blue camper van, almost long enough to be classed as a bus, and it was travelling so fast that it nearly tipped over as it sped around the corner of the hotel. The Kid couldn't make out a face on the driver, but the van careered over towards him and slammed to a stop outside the fire exit. At once the doors flew open and two dark figures jumped out from either side of it. They rushed to the fire exit and tried the door, much as the Kid had seen Sanchez do just a few minutes earlier. They too were unsuccessful.

Then they turned and saw him where he sat on the hood of his car. That was when he spotted that their eyes were glowing. One had red eyes, the other yellow, and they shone with a sinister phosphorescence in the dark night.

Undead muthafuckers.

The Bourbon Kid put his cigarette carefully down on the hood, slid forward off the Firebird and walked towards the two creatures. He heard them hiss at him, and then they tentatively approached, fanning out one either side of him, both eager for flesh.

The Kid had to consider the facts of the situation. He

only had two bullets left, and they were far too valuable to waste on killing a pair of zombies. So, as he walked towards them, he reached his right hand into the left side of his jacket for another weapon.

The nearest zombie appeared to be wearing a tattered old polo-neck sweater, which had once been white but was now grey with filth. It also had on a pair of ruined pants, one leg of which was almost entirely missing, and, incongruously, a broken pair of heavy black-rimmed glasses. It looked like the hungrier of the two, and the Kid readied himself for it to attack first. It duly did, and as it charged towards him he swung his right arm back-handed across its throat. His hand now held a bone-handled knife with an eight-inch blade. It sliced the zombie's throat open and, as its head fell forward, blood seeped out and ran down its chest. The dying zombie fell to its knees, a rasping, gravelly sound escaping from the wound in its throat.

Its partner, a female, was wearing a horrendously dirty pink dress. It had long, straggly grey hair and a face only half-covered in skin. The sight of her comrade falling to his knees stunned her momentarily and the Kid took advantage, lunging forward with his blade and thrusting it deep into the pink dress at chest height. The blade slid in through the rotting flesh with ease and he pulled it downwards in an effort to slice the ribcage right open. The flesh was soft like butter in some places, but tough like gristle in others. After he'd slashed an incision about eight inches long the zombie, like its partner, collapsed forward and fell to the ground before the Kid could pull the knife back out. It slipped from his hand, the blade caught somewhere in the zombie's ribcage.

Both creatures were now effectively dead but, to the Kid's annoyance, the second one had landed awkwardly on his knife. Turning the creature over with his foot, he bent down, grabbed the knife's protruding handle and yanked it out of the corpse. Blood spurted in all directions, some of it spraying on to his hand. Of far greater concern to him was the state of the knife. Due to the impact of the handle against the ground, the blade had bent almost at right angles to the handle. He took a look at it. Besides being bent it was covered in zombie guts. The knife was ruined, and he tossed it to the ground in frustration.

Another weapon gone.

Not only was he now down to his last two bullets, but he had no knives left. If ever there was a sign that he should head home, this was it. But as he turned to head back to his car where his cigarette was burning away on the hood he spotted something on the first zombie's polo-neck sweater. It looked like a cloth patch. He bent down and took a closer look at it. Sewn into the patch in black lettering was a name.

Buddy Holly.

He turned back to the corpse in the once-pink dress. It had flopped back on to its front, so he used his foot again to turn it over. It too had a nametag, this time sewn on to the right breast of the dress. He grabbed it and took a closer look. Again, a name he recognized.

Dusty Springfield.

Thirty-One

The escape from the zombies was still fresh in Sanchez's mind when, having parked the bike, the three of them eventually entered the hotel. The night ride would normally have been exhilarating, but after the horrors of what he'd just seen in the desert, it seemed completely inconsequential. He was still coming to terms with the fact that he'd just been digging a shallow grave for himself and his friend, and had seen two men coldly executed. And that had taken place before the undead showed up, climbing out of the ground and trying to eat him. With all these thoughts running through his mind, it was a decidedly sombre Sanchez who followed Gabriel and Elvis into the hotel lobby and through to the bar.

Gabriel's huge, bulky frame, leather biker gear, shaved head and tattoos made him stand out from all the other hotel guests. From his own experience as a bartender, Sanchez knew Gabriel would be served quickly. Never keep the big, nasty-looking fuckers waiting.

'Three bottles a beer,' Gabriel called out to the girl behind the bar. Valerie took one look at him and, muttering something under her breath, quickly turned to the small fridge behind her. She grabbed three bottles of Shitting Monkey, flicked the caps off with an opener hanging from a key chain on her belt, and placed the bottles on the bar.

Gabriel tossed a fifty-dollar bill at her, picked up the beers and turned to Elvis and Sanchez. 'Let's get us a table and talk through why we're all here.' He nodded at Elvis. 'You can start by tellin' me who Invincible Angus was hired to kill.'

'Sure thing, Gabe.'

Sanchez took a look around the bar. The layout of the place, with its widely scattered tables, made private conversations less likely to be overheard. And this was definitely going to be a private conversation.

There was a raised area at the end furthest from the bar. Elsewhere in the room, many of the tables had one or two people sitting at each, but here they were all empty. Elvis led the way towards one in the corner. A large black speaker on the wall a few feet above the table played gentle background music, which would help to mask their conversation from anyone who might be interested in what a huge biker, an Elvis impersonator, and a chubby bar owner might have to say.

Sanchez seated himself next to Elvis in one of two cream-coloured armchairs. Their backs were to the bar, while Gabriel relaxed on the other side of the table with his back to the wall. He seemed to want to be sure that he could see all that went on in the bar. His eyes constantly darted back and forth, looking for anything of interest or out of the ordinary. After checking out all of the other drinkers (of which there were about twenty seated around the place) for any potential danger, he picked up the nearest beer and held it out to the others.

'*Salud*,' he said. Elvis and Sanchez followed suit, and all three men chinked their bottles together. Then each took a swig of beer.

'So,' said Gabriel, after swallowing a huge mouthful of beer. 'D'ya know why Angus was here?'

Sanchez had no idea. It was a question best left to Elvis.

'Well,' the King began uneasily. 'We don't *exactly* know. Sanchez here ended up bein' given Angus's room an' found a hit list in an envelope. There weren't nothin' to say who it was from. Just photos of the four targets.'

Gabriel placed his beer down on the table. 'Let me guess.

He was supposed to kill Otis Redding, Kurt Cobain, Johnny Cash and Judy Garland, right?'

Sanchez was impressed. This guy was a whole lot better than the Mystic Lady. 'Whoa! How the fuck d'ya know that?'

'I think Angus was my back-up guy.'

'Your what?'

'He said "back-up guy", numbnuts,' Elvis chipped in dismissively. 'What are ya, deaf, as well as plain dumb?'

'Right,' said Gabriel. 'He was my back-up. That hit was supposed to be mine. These four people in the photos were due to be martyrs. Killed for the good of mankind. When I didn't make it here on time, the guy who hired me would have switched the job to Angus as back-up. Kinda like emergency cover.'

Gabriel stopped, picked up his beer and took another swallow. He paused reflectively, before continuing, 'Y'see Angus was one of the best hitmen in the world some years back, but he's gotta gamblin' problem. Makes him unreliable. He owes a lotta people a lotta money and it's clouded his judgement. He gets real personal about being paid up front, an' that means he often ends up shootin' the messenger rather than takin' the goddam job. Real tetchy fella these days.'

'Gamblin', huh?' said Sanchez, tutting. 'What a loser. How much does he owe?'

'His business, I figure,' said Gabriel, picking up his bottle of beer and taking another swig.

'I guess,' said Elvis, taking a pull at his own beer bottle. 'But why d'ya say those four people're martyrs? An' who's the guy who wants 'em dead?'

Gabriel leaned forward and lowered his voice. 'The guy who wants them killed is the Godfather of Soul.'

Sanchez frowned. 'Nah. You've lost me.'

'He means James Brown, ya dipshit,' Elvis snapped.

'Huh? James Brown? Why? Just to win a singin' contest?

Kinda extreme, ain't it?'

Gabriel continued, his voice still hushed. 'Ain't too extreme at all. Not for what's at stake.'

'You mean the prize money?'

'No, I mean the souls of many innocent people. James Brown, or Julius, as he's better known, is here on behalf of God.'

A peculiarly heavy silence greeted this last piece of information. Even Elvis looked like he was having doubts about this. Speaking slowly and distinctly, he drawled at Gabriel, 'Why's a man a God payin' to have contestants in a TV singin' competition killed? That don't seem right. Don't make no kinda sense, man, whichever way ya slice it.'

''Cept it's much more'n a singin' competition,' Gabriel replied. 'You ever seen the film *Crossroads*?'

Sanchez had. It was a favourite of his. 'Britney Spears? Good fuckin' movie, man.'

'No, it ain't. It's shit. An' I ain't talkin' about no Britney Spears bullshit. I'm talking about the Ralph Macchio movie.'

'Macchio? The Karate Kid?'

'Yeah. He did a film called *Crossroads*, back in the eighties.'

'Uh-huh,' Elvis said. 'I saw it.'

'Remember what it was about?' Gabriel asked.

'Road movie. Had Steve Vai in it.'

'Who?' asked Sanchez. He was having great difficulty in relating to what seemed to be an increasingly confusing conversation.

'Steve Vai. One o' the greatest guitarists of all time. I jammed with him once, some years back.'

That at least was something Sanchez could relate to. 'Cool,' he said. 'Reckon you kin get him to play at the Tapioca?'

Gabriel rocked his beer bottle on the table to get their attention again.

'Listen up. What I'm getting' at is this. That movie,

Crossroads, was based on an urban legend 'bout a guitar player name of Robert Johnson. Rumour is that, back in the nineteen-thirties, he sold his soul to the Devil. In exchange, Satan gave him the ability to play guitar better than any man on earth. Basically, this Robert Johnson guy was the first musician or singer ever to sell his soul. Thousands've done it since.'

'Yeah, I saw Bart Simpson do it once,' said Sanchez, agreeing.

Gabriel sighed. 'Can't you get him to shut the fuck up?' he asked Elvis.

'Sure,' said Elvis, glaring at Sanchez. 'But I still don't get what all this Robert Johnson stuff's got to do with what's goin' on here.'

'Because it's pretty much exactly what's happenin' here. An' it's happened every year of the *Back From the Dead* show. The winner gets a million-dollar singin' contract. When they sign it, they're signin' away their soul.'

'To Nigel Powell?' asked Elvis.

'Nope. To the Devil.'

'Does Powell know 'bout this?'

'Yeah. He's in on it. See, he sold his soul to the Devil years ago in exchange for immortality, an' this hotel and its casino.'

'Sweet deal,' Sanchez remarked.

Gabriel shook his head. 'Ain't really. In return, he's gotta get someone new to sell their soul to the Devil every Halloween. An' that's what the winner of this competition is doin'. Sellin' their soul to Satan in exchange for wealth an' fame. 'Cept they don't know that, o' course.'

Sanchez frowned. 'It's all kinda far-fetched. Sounds like bullshit to me.'

'An' zombies?' said Gabriel sternly. 'D'ya believe in them? Or are they a bit fuckin' far-fetched too?'

Sanchez had to admit the big biker had a point. 'Yeah,'

he said. 'See what ya mean. But why kill the four singers? I don't get it.'

'Me either,' said Elvis.

'I'm just gettin' to that part.'

'Like, can you get to it a bit quicker, man?'

Gabriel looked irritated. 'Okay,' he said heavily. 'First off, this show is rigged. The whole damn' shootin' match.'

Elvis slammed his beer bottle down on the table. 'I fuckin' knew it! I toldya, Sanchez, didn't I?'

Gabriel ignored him and carried on. 'Five singers were selected for the final months ago. In secret – only they an' Powell know, But only the four best singers are bein' killed. Like I say, they're martyrs. They're better off dead than winnin' this competition and sellin' their souls to the Devil.'

Sanchez, still confused, couldn't help interrupting. 'So the four best singers are dead. Surely that just means that the fifth best singer wins it and signs the contract?'

Gabriel's face burst into a big beaming smile. 'Boy, you catch on quick, fat guy. Yeah, that's right. An'   Julius – the James Brown impersonator – is the fifth best singer here. So, with the other four gone he's got a pretty dam' good chance of winnin'.'

'And sellin' his soul to the Devil?' Elvis queried the logic of it. 'Why would he wanna do that?'

'It's a sacrifice.'

'No shit.'

'But it's one he can make.' He suddenly seemed to change the subject. 'D'ya know what this hotel is built on?'

'The desert?' Sanchez suggested, redundantly.

'Nope. It's built on top of a gateway to Hell.'

Sanchez looked down nervously at the black hardwood floor and lifted his feet up. 'Shit. I thought it was kinda warm in here,' he said.

Elvis slapped him on the back of the head and signalled for Gabriel to carry on.

'Julius's soul belongs to God. He signs that contract, he's sellin' somethin' he don't own, so the contract's gonna be null an' void. And if Powell ain't got someone to sell their soul by the end of the witchin' hour on Halloween, his hotel an' him will go straight to Hell. This fuckin' place, an' everyone in it, will sink down under the ground like it was never here.'

'What's so special about Julius?' Elvis asked. 'Don't God own everyone's soul?'

Gabriel downed the rest of his beer in one long swallow before giving his answer. 'Julius is the forgotten thirteenth Apostle.'

There followed an even more uneasy pause as both Elvis and Sanchez waited to see if he was serious. Eventually the King spoke. 'You sure 'bout that?'

'Rex believes it. If Rex reckons it's so, it's good enough for me.'

Elvis nodded. He and Rodeo Rex went back years. They had done some serious jobs together over that time and were good buddies.

'No shit. If Rex believes it, I'm with ya, but that still don't explain why the goddam hotel's gonna sink into the depths of Hell. Just 'cause this Julius guy's an Apostle.'

'Look, man,' said Gabriel. He was growing impatient with having to justify everything. 'I don't know 'xactly how it works, do I? I didn't write the Bible. An' last I heard, God wasn't callin' me up, askin' for advice.'

'It's still all kinda far-fetched, though, ain't it?' said Sanchez, plaintively .

'Listen, buddy. One of the basic – "tenets", they call 'em – one o' the first tenets of religion an' God an' all that stuff, is faith. You gotta have faith.' He sighed, trying to sound reasonable. 'I b'lieve we just saw zombies comin' outta the ground an' tryin' ta eat people tonight. That tells me that there is such a thing as life after death, if'n ya can call that life. An' that means there's gotta be a God. Far's I'm concerned, God has sent one of his guys, Julius, over here to save us all again. I'm not gonna sit around complainin' that I'm not bein' given the full facts. I suggest you do the same. Those without faith will be the first to go when things turn ugly.'

'Gotcha,' said Sanchez. 'But while you're helpin' the thirteenth Apostle to send this place to Hell, I'm gonna get a cab outta here. You comin', Elvis?'

Gabriel shook his head. 'Wouldn't do that, if I were you.'

'Why the fuck not?'

'First off, you won't get a cab. An' you won't find a single cop that'll come to this hotel, neither. Right now there are zombies risin' up outta the ground all over the desert, an' they're all headin' this way. They'll be here in less than an hour. You walk out that door 'fore they get here, an' you're gonna be eaten alive.'

'Lemme see if I've got this right. You're sayin' we should wait here for them to arrive? Shit, man, that's just as stupid.'

'Yes, it is.' To Sanchez's shock, another man's voice suddenly spoke from behind him. 'Gabriel,' it continued. 'Come with me. You're just in time.'

Smiling broadly, the massive biker got up from his seat. Sanchez and Elvis both turned to see who he was looking at. Behind them, wearing his bright purple suit, stood Julius. The James Brown impersonator.

Thirty-Two

Nigel Powell was always a little uptight on Halloween. Actually, that was an understatement, for in reality it was without doubt the most stressful day of the year.

For starters, the *Back From The Dead* contest took a heck of a lot of organizing. The schedule was tight, and there were lots of performers to see, some good, some bad and others so downright awful it would be funny, if it weren't Powell's money that paid for them to be here. Getting the show finished by the deadline of one o'clock the following morning was the toughest part. No one else seemed to appreciate the urgency of finishing on time.

So far, this year had been worse than ever. There was something untoward going on. People had tried to fix the competition before – that is, fix it without knowing that Powell had already had it fixed – but this year someone was having one hell of a good crack at it. Powell had three dead contestants already. He also had a psychotic assassin with the ridiculous name 'Invincible Angus' working for him. 'Angus', for Chrissakes. What was this? Fucking *Braveheart*?

At least Angus had proved to be useful. The red-haired assassin had apparently captured both the guy who was killing off the contestants and the person who'd hired him. Powell hoped that he had taken them out into the desert and executed them, as agreed. In the interests of obtaining some confirmation of this, he headed for the men's washroom on the ground floor. Once there, he was pleased to find Cleveland, one of his security team, guarding the entrance. He was a big, muscular black guy who took no shit from anyone. The perfect person to stop anyone from getting into the washroom, no matter how badly they needed a piss.

Powell had hired Cleveland on Tommy's recommendation. Apparently, he had spent time as a prisoner of war and had been traumatized by the whole experience. As a result, after his release he had been unable to continue to serve as a soldier, but was perfect in a less demanding role as a security guard in a hotel. As he approached him, Powell noticed he was eating an ice cream. A strawberry ice cream in a cone, by the look of it. He was about to take a lick of it when he saw his boss approaching. Discreetly, he lowered it to his side.

'Cleveland. Hi. How's it going in there?' Powell asked.

'All good, sir.'

'Is the mess cleaned up?'

Cleveland lowered his voice. 'Almost, sir. The bodies have been moved. Sandy's in there now, just cleanin' the floors and stuff.'

'Good, good. Is Tommy here?'

'No, sir.'

'Do you know where he is?'

'In the desert, sir.'

Powell frowned. 'What's he doing there? I told him to stay here.'

'He's gone with that Angus fella to make sure he kills the two guys who made the mess in the washroom, sir.'

'Well, I'm not sure that was necessary, but I suppose Tommy knows what he's doing.'

'Yes sir.'

Powell had hoped to get a look at the men responsible for murdering three of the singers he had hand picked for the final. Were they other contestants? Members of the audience? Or just bastards trying to ruin the show for their own benefit, or even for their own amusement? Tommy was supposed to be here to tell him who they were. Still, maybe Cleveland would know. 'Did you see the two guys responsible for the – uh – mess?'

'Yes, sir.'

'What did they look like?'

'I didn't notice.'

'You didn't *notice*? How come?'

''Cause I didn't.'

Powell was rapidly revising his formerly good opinion of Cleveland. The man was turning out to be even dumber than most of the other security guards in the hotel. He was all brawn and little else. Where once he might have been a fine and enterprising soldier, he was now a brain-dead muscle man, seemingly devoid of intelligence or personality.

Powell tried a different line of questioning. 'Okay. So, do we know how Kurt Cobain and Johnny Cash died?'

'You mean the singers?'

'No, I mean the planets.' God, this was so exasperating. 'Of course, I mean the fucking singers.'

'Well, Kurt Cobain's death was drug-related. Johnny Cash was just old, I guess.'

Powell stared hard at Cleveland to see if he was being serious, or was trying to make fun of him. Eventually he decided the answer was neither. Cleveland was just a dumbass. This assessment was backed up by the way the security guard was staring vacantly at the wall opposite him, with his mouth slightly open.

'Okay,' said Powell, a hint of irritation creeping into his voice. 'What about Sandy? Can he say who these guys were and what they did to Cash and Cobain?'

'I can't speak for Sandy, sir.'

'*Cleveland*.'

'Yes sir.'

'You're an idiot.'

'Yes sir.'

'And I'm taking your ice cream.' He reached out and snatched the ice cream cone right out of Cleveland's hand. He took a big lick of it, right in front of the disappointed-looking security guard, then snapped, 'Right. Now get out of my fucking way.'

'Yes sir.'

The burly guard stepped aside and pushed the door open to let his boss walk through it. Powell was pleased to see that, inside, the washroom was virtually spotless. That was largely thanks to Sandy, a typically brutish-looking guy with dark cropped hair. He had a mop in his hand and had just finished cleaning the blood off the floor. He saw Powell enter and nodded his head.

'Hi, boss,' he said.

'Good evening, Sandy,' the hotel owner replied, looking down at the floor. There was no sign of blood anywhere. 'Looks like you've done a good job.'

'Thanks.'

'Here, I got you this.' He held out the ice-cream cone, which Sandy accepted tentatively with his free hand.

'Looks kinda like Cleveland's,' he said.

'Well, it's not.'

'Okay. Thanks.'

'So, tell me what happened here earlier. You were talking on the radio to Tommy and the line went dead. I was concerned.'

'Someone jumped me an' Tyrone. All happened real quick. We came in here, saw the bodies in the stalls and called Tommy. Next thing, someone just came outta nowhere. I really dunno what happened.'

'How's your head?'

'It's better.'

'Did Tommy tell you who the guys were that jumped you?'

Sandy took a lick of the ice cream. 'Nah. I was still out

cold when they took them two away.'

'Uh-huh. What about Tyrone?'

'He went with Tommy. Out to the desert. Least, that's what Cleveland says.'

'Yeah, well . . . Cleveland thinks that Johnny Cash died of old age. What do you think?'

Sandy took another lick of the ice cream. He seemed to be thoroughly savouring the taste of it. 'Me? I reckon someone put Johnny Cash's nose through his brain, boss. Last time I checked, old age don't do that.'

'I agree. What about Cobain?'

'Yeah, that was drug-related.'

'*What?*'

'There was cocaine everywhere, and he had blood pissin' out of his mouth, nose, ears – you name it.'

Powell walked past Sandy and peered through the open doors of the toilet stalls to see if they were still showing any evidence of violence. All of them were empty and spotlessly clean. Sandy really had done a good job.

When he reached the last stall, Powell looked up at the mirror above the nearest washbasins on the far wall. He saw his own reflection staring back at him. Behind that, he could see Sandy with his mop, wiping it around the floor by the first stall. Then, suddenly, he saw another figure.

Behind Sandy stood a tall black man wearing a red suit, a red bowler hat and pointed red shoes, grinning at him. Powell's heart jumped into his mouth. He whirled around.

'Sandy,' he said urgently. 'You've done a good job. I'm grateful. You can go now.'

'I ain't quite done, boss.'

'It doesn't matter. Go on. Get out. Leave the mop and bucket. I'll finish up.'

'Yeah? You sure?'

'Take that *fucking* ice cream and get the *fuck* out.'

Startled by the venom in his employer's voice, Sandy

leaned the mop against the wall by the door and walked out, licking the ice cream lovingly as he went.

Powell turned back to face the mirror. Once again, he saw behind him the black man in the red suit and hat. The man walked towards him.

'Having a little trouble this year, Nigel?' he asked. His voice was dark and rich in tone, oozing urbanity tinged with irony, like an aural rendition of a quizzically raised eyebrow.

'Nothing I can't handle.' In contrast, Powell sounded almost surly.

'Really? Are you sure?'

'Yeah. It's all done now. Just some dickwad trying to fix the contest. If only they knew what the winner really got, huh? Don't suppose they'd be trying to rig it, would they?'

The tall man's yellow-coloured eyes lit up. He threw his head back and bellowed out a hearty laugh. 'You know, you grow more uptight every year, Nigel.'

'And you love that, I suppose?'

'I love *chaos*. You know that.'

The man was now standing right behind Powell. Looking over his shoulder into the mirror, grinning at him, his warm breath blowing lightly on to the back of the hotel owner's neck. He had a neatly trimmed, tight, black goatee beard. Which, on either side of his mouth, joined an equally neat moustache. Powell wanted to be rid of him as soon as possible. He wasn't a fun person to hang out with. In fact, he was bad news in every conceivable way.

'Nice beard,' he said sarcastically.

'Very kind of you to say so,' the man replied. 'You know, *you're* only one facelift away from having a beard of your own.'

'Well maybe I'll consider it – when they come back into fashion,' Powell replied with even heavier sarcasm. 'Have you got a contract for me, or what?'

'But of course.'

'Well, just leave it by the washbasin, please.' He did not add, as he would have liked to: 'And then get out.'

The Man in Red reached inside his jacket and pulled out an inch-thick wad of paper. It was good-quality paper, white, standard business-letter size, and densely printed in black ink. He placed it beside the washbasin next to Powell's left hand.

'You know, you're not out of the woods yet, Nigel,' he said.

'How's that?'

'A man has arrived in the hotel, and he's trying to ruin your show. The clock is ticking. Tick-tock, tick-tock, tick-tock.'

'What man?' Powell turned around sharply, only to find that the Man in Red had disappeared. He turned back to face the mirror and his visitor's reflection appeared behind him once more. Grinning. 'What man?' he repeated.

'You know I can't help you. Those are the rules. But I can tell you that there's a man out there trying to destroy your show. A man of God. I can't interfere with that. You had best keep that contract in a safe place. Don't let it fall into the wrong hands, hmm?'

'Well, can you at least tell me who it is that's fucking with my show? Is it this Bourbon Kid guy? Did you send him?'

The Man in Red laughed again. 'I'm on your side, naturally. I'm not sending anyone to mess up your plans. I like your casino. It's a fun place. You just have to keep a lookout for someone who's been sent by the Man Upstairs. That's who you have to worry about.'

'So this Bourbon Kid guy works for God?'

'Ha-ha-ha! No, no, no. Oh dear me, no. The Bourbon Kid, he doesn't work for either side. Strange fish, that one. You must look closer than that. He's not the one you have to worry about.'

'So who is?'

'Haven't you figured it out yet?'

'No. I'm not that clever. Obviously.'

'Then you'd better wise up fast, my friend. You're running out of finalists. At the last count, you had only two left.'

Powell was struggling to keep his cool. The arrival of this man with his grinning face had unnerved him, though this was by no means the first time they had met. 'Why don't I just get some random nobody to sign the contract this year?' he suggested.

'Oh, no, no, no, *no*! That simply wouldn't do,' said the Man in Red. 'This contract has to be earned. *You know that.* I want it to go to someone with talent. Someone desperate for fame and fortune. Someone who will do almost anything for it, no matter what the cost.'

'You finished?' Nigel asked impatiently.

The Man in Red smirked. 'No. There is one other thing, although it may seem trivial in the circumstances.'

'What is it?'

'They have run out of ham sandwiches in the casino.'

'So eat the tuna.'

Without waiting for a response, he looked down at the contract lying on the faux-marble surround of the washbasin. It was the same contract the Man in Red brought him every year. He picked it up and looked back up at the mirror. His visitor had vanished. *Shit.*

Powell glanced down at the contract again. According to his now departed visitor, there was someone in the hotel desperate to ruin his show. Who the fuck was it? And why? He only had two finalists left, James Brown and Judy Garland. The only clue he had was that the person trying to fuck up his show was a man of God.

A *man* of God.

Thirty-Three

Emily had been alone in the dressing room for almost twenty minutes. All five of the finalists were supposed to meet back there after their performances. The other four hadn't showed, and she was becoming increasingly concerned about their whereabouts. Had there been some sort of change to the schedule that she didn't know about? Probably not, but she didn't want to hang around for too long on her own.

Maybe the four guys had decided to go for a drink and had chosen not to invite her? Didn't they like her? Did she smell? Worse than Cobain? It was unlikely, but all kinds of theories were going through her mind, and all were making her a little paranoid. Better to think about something else for a while, she thought, like whether she was doing everything she could to win the competition.

As she sat at the dressing table, she stared at her reflection in the mirror. Should she do something different with her hair for the final? Or stick with the pigtails that the real Judy Garland had worn in the movie *The Wizard of Oz?* Her mother had always said that how you styled your hair was the most important detail, and one that so many other tribute performers overlooked. She was contemplating this and several other matters when there was a knock on the dressing-room door.

'Miss Shannon? You in there?' a man's voice called from the other side. She recognized the voice straight away. It was Nigel Powell's.

'Coming,' she called out.

She got up and opened the door. Powell was standing outside, flanked by two heavies from his security team. Emily smiled nervously and stepped back to allow them to come in. The two guards made no move to enter the room, but Powell walked in without waiting for a verbal invitation. He was still wearing his bright white suit with the black shirt. His hair was still perfectly in place, but something was definitely amiss. He didn't look quite as unruffled as usual. It was clear from the look on his face that he was troubled about something.

'What is it?' she asked, as he closed the door behind him.

'Three of the other finalists have gone down with a stomach complaint. I'm worried that someone may have poisoned them.'

'*What?*' Emily felt her knees go weak. At once she thought back to the last time she'd eaten. It was at breakfast time, when she'd had a bagel and a cup of coffee. Since then she'd been too nervous to eat. 'Oh my God! Are they okay? Do you know what they ate?'

Powell tugged uneasily at his shirt collar. 'No. There's a suspicious character in the hotel somewhere who we suspect is responsible. We're trying to track him down now.'

Emily cast her mind back to a couple of earlier incidents that day. 'I saw a creepy guy at the side of the stage, watching the show. He said he knew it was rigged. He was dressed all in black. Was it him?'

'It just might be. Don't you worry, though. I'm moving you to somewhere safe where he won't be able to get to you.'

Emily felt not only relieved but also (although she wouldn't admit it) excited about the fact that three of her closest rivals were out of the final.

'Which three were poisoned?' she asked.

'It may be four. I can't find the James Brown guy at the moment. The other three are definitely out of the running.'

'Oh dear. Poor souls,' Emily said, with as much sincerity as she could muster.

'Quite. Anyway, would you be so kind as to pack up your stuff and come with me. A bellhop will bring everything from your room. And my apologies for the inconvenience, of course.' He sounded anything but apologetic. But he did sound distracted.

Emily did as he asked, grabbing a few personal belongings from the dressing table and following Powell and the two security guards to the elevator, and from there to a room on the ninth floor. They walked very briskly, and it wasn't hard to pick up on a distinct sense of urgency about the way they eyed with suspicion everyone they passed.

Room 904 was a large and comfortable double room. Emily sat herself down on the king-size bed in the middle and waited for further instruction from Powell. Initially he stayed outside the room, muttering quietly into the ears of his security staff. Emily considered her new surroundings and decided that they were actually much better than the crappy dressing room she had been sharing with the four guys or the single room she had been assigned for her overnight stay. She was still busy admiring the size of her new room when Powell stepped in and approached her.

'I've set two of my security guards to stand outside in the corridor,' he said. 'They won't let anyone in here but me. But that also means you can't leave this room until the security people tell you it's okay. When the finalists are due to be announced they'll escort you downstairs.'

'Okay.'

'Are you okay, Miss Shannon?'

'I'm fine, thanks – uh – Nigel.' This was the first time she had used his name, and she wondered if that was acceptable. He held so much power, after all.

'Good. I just have to go and work out who my new finalists are going to be, and then we're ready to go.' He leaned down and stroked Emily's bare left arm. There was a light in his eyes that made her feel a little uncomfortable. Where he had been reassuring and gentlemanly before, for a moment he seemed creepy and untrustworthy. He winked, then fixed her with a piercing gaze from his hypnotic blue eyes.

'I think you have a great chance of winning this competition, Emily. You've been the best contestant so far. I've a feeling we'll be seeing a lot more of each other. So unless you lose your voice or –' he gave a surprisingly high-pitched giggle – 'get struck by lightning, you should be planning to stick around for a while.'

He stopped stroking her arm and stepped back. She felt excited at the thought of winning the competition, but also slightly repulsed by this new sleazy side to Nigel Powell. She shrugged it off. After all, he probably hadn't intended to be creepy. He was just trying to be reassuring, surely? She watched as with a pleasant 'See you at the final,' he left the room, closing the door behind him.

Increasingly, it dawned on her that she now had a good chance of winning the show. In spite of her natural caution, her mind filled with the thought of seeing the joy on her sick mother's face when she returned home victorious with a winner's cheque for a million dollars. That money would pay for all the care her mother needed, and it was now so close. It was as good as hers for the taking.

After Powell had left, the two security guards opened the door with a master key and poked their heads into the room, nodding at Emily as if to reassure her that they were outside. They were both pretty bulky nightclub-bouncer types, and she felt a fair degree of reassurance as a result. And, with her closest rivals now out of the picture, she was more and more optimistic about her chances in the final. She longed to call her mother and tell her how she was doing in the show, but she was equally excited at the thought of surprising her by returning home with the winner's cheque. And a big fat contract to perform at the Pasadena.

For half an hour, she sat on the large double bed in the middle of the room. There was no television to watch and no radio to listen to. No two ways about it, the Hotel Pasadena really was a strange place. With no television or radio, it was impossible to keep up with current affairs. Iran might have flattened Rhode Island with an A-bomb, for all she knew.

With nothing to do but sit and consider her situation, Emily began to think a little more deeply about things. She had no way of contacting her mother to tell her how she was doing in the show. What if she had wanted to call to find out how her mother was? She had absolutely no way of contacting anyone outside of the Devil's Graveyard. The telephones in the hotel rooms could only be used to make internal calls, and cell phones couldn't pick up a signal, and so were equally useless. It was kind of creepy, really. Then, as she thought about the three other singers who had allegedly been struck down by a stomach ailment, she began to ask herself more probing questions. Like, how would an ambulance or the police get to this place in an emergency? How could they be contacted? If she were to suffer some kind of poisoning, would help arrive in time?

Then something far more serious struck her. Something she should have thought about before. Why had Nigel Powell moved her to another room? He had said it was for her own safety. Safety from what? *Food poisoning?* Surely that should have meant simply that she would be warned not to eat anything? It shouldn't have meant that she had to move to another room, provided she avoided ordering meals from room service. If there was poisoned food in the hotel, it wouldn't be hunting her down. But the person doing the poisoning just might. Maybe Nigel Powell hadn't briefed her fully about how much danger she was in? And if that was the case, why hadn't he?

As she sat on the end of the bed, now bolt upright with

alarm and with a mass of paranoid thoughts running through her head, she heard a noise outside her room. One of the security guards was talking. With the door closed, it was impossible to make out what was being said. His voice was muffled.

Then she heard a curious sound, like a tyre suddenly and instantly deflating. It too was muffled, but Emily recognized it: a shot from a gun fitted with a silencer. A second muffled gunshot followed, and then came the sound of two bodies slumping to the floor outside.

Emily's worst fears had been realized. Food poisoning was not the reason she had been moved to this secure location, with two security men standing guard outside it. There was a killer on the loose.

And he was outside her room.

Thirty-Four

Angus was in a murderous mood, which was a good thing at the moment. *Since when in the fuck did zombies drive?* The successive waves of brutal attacks from the undead creatures trying to bite lumps out of him had annoyed him considerably, but stealing a man's wheels, by God that made him angry. *Fuckin' angry.*

He'd gunned down six of the zombies, and punched down a good few others that had tried jumping on him. But still they kept on coming. If they weren't rising up through the ground, they were lurching – surprisingly fast – across the desert to get to him. He reminded himself how lucky it was that there were two dead security guards lying on the ground. Those suckers were fast food for zombies.

There were probably twenty of the loathsome things on top of the two, now severely mutilated, bodies, and Angus was well aware that once the poor bastards had been devoured he was *really* going to have his hands full.

He fired a couple more shots into the chests of two of the zombies, then made a break for the highway. Kicking aside any grasping hands reaching for him from below, he soon made it safely on to the asphalt road. At least if he ran along the centre of the highway, he could be reasonably sure nothing was going to reach out and grab him from below. Some of those zombie bastards were incredibly strong, but he doubted any of them were tough enough to climb up through a the layers of rubble, concrete and asphalt of the highway.

He ran along the middle of the road in the direction that led back to the hotel, with a whole bunch of zombies pursuing him from behind. Some, faster than others, caught up with him. They were usually dispatched with a belt in the face from one of his handguns or a bullet in the chest. He had enough ammunition to kill about a hundred of the bastards, although it was a real pain in the butt having to keep reloading his two revolvers.

After running for several minutes, he noticed that the zombies were beginning to keep their distance, always staying about ten yards behind him. *Shit!* These fuckers were smarter than the zombie movies he'd seen had led him to believe. If he was right, they were hanging back, waiting for him to tire himself out. An exhausted, winded Angus would be a darn sight easier to overpower, and these fuckers appeared to know it.

Then his luck turned. Another vehicle appeared on the highway behind him. He saw the road in front of him light up in the headlights of a car heading his way. He looked back over his shoulder and saw a Volkswagen Beetle speeding down the middle of the highway, scattering zombies to the side as they jumped out of its path.

Angus needed to make sure that the driver of the car realized he wasn't one of the undead, and would therefore stop to offer him a ride. So despite his tiring legs, he put in a lung-busting sprint. He managed to pull a further ten yards clear of the chasing pack, and as the Beetle came zipping through them he waved frantically at the driver to stop.

The car slowed up as it drew alongside him. The driver's side window came down and the face of a terrified woman in her forties peered out. She had blonde permed hair and bright red lipstick that was smeared across her face, no doubt caused by trying to do her make-up in the rear-view mirror while attempting to evade the zombies in the road. It was all the excuse Angus needed to take an instant dislike to her.

Although he needed a ride back to the hotel, he didn't need some hysterical bitch thrown into the package.

She looked at him desperately. 'What's going on here?' she asked in a frightened-little-girl voice. The pursuing zombies were almost on them.

Angus pointed one of his pistols at her face and fired. The bullet drilled through her forehead, killing her instantly. She slumped over to the passenger side and the car slowed to a crawl. Angus reached in through the window as he jogged alongside and opened the driver's door from the inside. Half hopping, half running, he jumped in and shoved the woman's body out of the way. Landing clumsily in her seat, he slammed the door shut and checked the wing mirror. The zombies were still racing after him, the first few almost level with the back of the car. He drove his foot down on the gas pedal and the Beetle sped up.

'So long, suckers!' he yelled out of the open window.

A minute further down the road, he stopped the car and pushed the dead woman's body out on to the highway. That would give the zombie bastards something to keep them occupied for a while.

Angus had other business to attend to. He was now as angry as hell, and determined to kill Sanchez, Elvis, Julius, Powell, all zombies and anyone else that pissed him off. One way or another, he was going home with a stack of cash and another few victims to his name.

And his Tom Jones CD.

Thirty-Five

Emily's plan was pretty lame. Indeed, in the long and undistinguished history of bird-brained plans, this one would probably have ranked quite highly – maybe even a place in the Top Ten shitty plans. She had a gunman literally seconds away from bursting into her hotel room, with the very real possibility that he was coming to kill her. So what did she do?

Her first thought was to hide under the bed. But she rapidly discovered that its base rested on four very short legs. Emily was slim, but she wasn't slim enough to squeeze under a bed that was only two inches off the floor. That cut her options down considerably. She looked at the alternatives. Climb out the window? Not enough time. In fact, she didn't even know if the window would open. Then there was the bathroom. She could run in there and hide, but it was a dead end and the only place to hide would be in the shower, behind the curtain. Since none of these were viable options, her split-second decision led her to the closet in the corner of the room.

The cream-coloured closet doors had louvred wooden panels in them to allow ventilation. Emily darted over and jumped inside, closing the doors carefully behind her in order to make as little noise as possible. The closet was empty, and through the louvres, she was able to get a good view of the door into the room.

She could no longer hear anything from the corridor outside. Had the killer left? Was he playing games? It was agony waiting to see what was going to happen. She found herself drawing long, slow breaths in order to keep as quiet as possible.

After about twenty seconds, during which she again contemplated running for the window or the bathroom, the lock on the door clicked. She took a sharp intake of breath.

The closet really was the dumbest place to hide.

Emily looked around wildly for anything to shield or defend herself with. She was the only thing in it, aside from an ironing board against the back, and a steam iron on a small shelf to her left. If she needed something to defend herself from attack, then it was going to have to be the iron.

Holding her breath, she watched the door slowly open. A hand holding a pistol with a silencer on the end of the barrel appeared around the edge of the door. Following it in, after peering around the door, was a man. He was well over six feet tall and had a shaved head. He was wearing black leather pants and a black sleeveless leather jerkin. A biker, by the looks of him, and one with a set of three dice tattooed on one of his arms.

His dark eyes checked every corner, scouring the room to find her. He stepped inside, closing the door gently behind him. Then he walked over towards the bathroom with his gun held in front of him. Emily prayed that he couldn't see her through the wooden slats on the closet door. Instinctively, she stepped silently backwards and pressed herself against the wall. What did he want with her? Why would he want to kill her? It was clear that he wasn't intending to hand her a poisoned doughnut. He was intending to shoot her, she was certain of it. She just wasn't sure why.

He disappeared out of her sight into the bathroom, leaving her suddenly faced with a horrible dilemma. Should she dash out of the closet and make a break for it? Or continue to hide? A decision had to be made quickly. If she chose to continue hiding in the closet, she was going to have to grab the steam iron and prepare to use it. If she decided to run, she was going to have to do so immediately.

Her indecision cost her dearly. She had become lost in thought, not paying attention to what the man was doing. The closet door flew open. She gasped as the giant intruder stepped in front of her aiming his pistol at her chest. He had sneaked up at the side of the closet, then suddenly wrenched the left-hand door open.

'Judy Garland,' he said, smiling a small, thin smile. 'Please come out of the closet.'

He seemed very polite. Maybe he wasn't here to kill her? He stepped aside and gestured with his gun for Emily to move over to the bed. She stumbled out of the closet and walked over to it. The biker guy kept his gun trained on her the whole time. She realized that her chances of escaping were slim while his eyes were on her. But how was she going to distract him?

'Sit down, please,' he requested politely. The man had manners, that much was obvious. But he was also a killer. If she was right, there were two dead security guards outside as proof of that.

'What do you want?' Emily asked. Her heart was racing, and her mouth so dry that she found it difficult to get the words out.

'I've come here to kill you.'

'Oh.' Just as she had feared. The guy *was* going to kill her. So what was he waiting for? 'Now?' she asked tentatively.

'That depends on you.' He was standing directly between her and the door into the corridor, blocking off any futile attempt at escape.

'I really would like to live,' Emily said smiling desperately at him, in the hope of convincing him that she was a warm and lovely person who deserved to be spared.

'Yeah, I bet you would. And you can, if you play ball.'

'I'll play ball.'

'Good. Y'see, you can't win this competition.'

'Why not?'

''Cause someone else has to win it. If you win, a lot of people will die, includin' you. I can't allow that to happen.'

Emily held back the urge to blurt, *'But I have to win. For my mom.'* She opted instead for afar more measured response: 'Okay. So what do I do?'

'Leave. All I gotta do is make my boss think you're dead. So, as long as you get the hell out of here and never come back, I can convince him of that.'

'That's it?'

'Nope. Not quite. I'm gonna need a photo of you lookin' dead. So we're gonna have to mock up a crime scene. I got some of those little packets of ketchup in my pocket. I'm suggestin' you lie on the floor an' we splatter some ketchup on your neck and make it look like I shot you. You cool with that?'

'Do I have a choice?'

'No.'

'Okay. Is this what you did with the other finalists?'

'No. They're dead for real.'

Emily was stunned. 'Oh my God! Seriously?'

'Yep. Not killed by me though. Another guy, name of the Bourbon Kid, killed 'em. I haven't worked out yet why he didn't kill you. But he will if he sees you alive.'

'Is he a creepy-looking guy dressed all in black?'

'Usually. You seen him?'

'A couple of times, yeah. He was pretty rude to me earlier. And he knew the show was fixed.'

'Yeah, well, count yourself lucky I got to you before he did.'

'So who are you?'

'Name's Gabriel. I work for God.' He stood over her and unscrewed the silencer from the muzzle of his handgun. It really did look like he had decided not to kill her. He seemed a lot nicer than he looked, too, although Emily recognized she was probably clutching at straws. Or pissing in the wind. Or something. After all, he'd killed the security guards outside, hadn't he? With what even Emily could see was a pretty small gun once the silencer had been removed.

'That's a tiny little thing, isn't it?' she remarked.

Gabriel smiled. 'I can hardly go chargin' round a hotel blowin' people away with a shotgun, now can I? Small pistol like this is ideal for a discreet hotel-room job.' Then, as if fearing he sounded rather timid, he added, 'I got plenty of hardcore shit stashed elsewhere if I need to take down a fuckin' army, y'know.'

'Uh – okay. I was just saying, is all. It's kinda cute-looking – for a gun. Did you really just – uh – kill those two security guys with that?'

Gabriel looked momentarily surprised, as if he'd forgotten about them. 'Shit, yeah. Can you help me get the bodies in here? I can't leave 'em outside. Someone might see 'em.'

'Sure. Why not?' Emily could hardly refuse. She still hadn't had time to process properly her thoughts about this guy. He was a murderer, and for that reason, and that reason alone, she was going to do what he said. Whether he was a good guy who could genuinely be trusted was still open to debate.

Gabriel walked over to the room door and opened it. Emily watched him look both ways along the corridor. The dead security guards were splayed on the floor right in the middle of the corridor. Not exactly discreet, although there was barely a drop of blood on either body. The logic of using the small handgun had really paid off. Gabriel bent down, grabbed the nearest one under his armpits and, walking backwards, started dragging him back into the room with him. Once inside, he tugged the body Emily's way.

'See if you can get him in that closet,' he suggested, nodding at where she had been hiding only minutes earlier.

She took hold of the body from behind, her arms under its armpits and her hands locked together in front of its chest, and started dragging it towards the closet. It was an almighty struggle for her to move the dead weight at all, and she succeeded only in laying it flat out on its back and backing herself into the closet.

Emily had never touched a corpse before, let alone dragged one across a hotel room floor. This was definitely not how she had seen her weekend mapping out. Just holding a corpse in her arms smashed home the reality of it all. By taking part in this, she was technically an accessory to murder. Collaborating with a killer was not Emily's idea of a good time. Regardless of what Gabriel said and who he claimed to be working for, he had still killed two innocent men. What was to say he didn't really intend killing her at some point?

Gabriel disappeared through the door and back into the corridor to fetch the other security guard. At last, Emily had a few seconds in which to think about the options he had given her. Head home and lose out on the million-dollar prize money on offer and the chance to be everything she had ever wanted to be, or stay and be killed.

She could see that it wasn't really a fair offer at all. Even though this man had been polite and had offered her a chance to live, he was asking her to give up her dream and any chance she might have of making her dying mother's last days as painless and peaceful as possible.

Out of the corner of her eye, she could see the steam iron on the shelf in the closet. If she wanted not only to appear in the final of this show, but also to stay alive, she was going to have to use it. This was her last chance. If she could knock Gabriel out with the iron, then she could get Nigel Powell and the police to protect her from anyone else trying to kill her. She could still win the show. And her mother could still get the care that she needed.

Fuck it, she thought. It was worth the risk.

Thirty-Six

By the time Invincible Angus returned to the Hotel Pasadena, he'd dreamed up at least ten new ways to torture, maim, and eventually kill Sanchez and Elvis. By the way he figured things, those two fuckwits had cost him seventy grand so far, between the missing twenty grand from Julius and Powell's promised payout of fifty Gs. Oh, how he'd make it nice and slow. He just couldn't wait to hear their screams of agony.

Even that, however, didn't compare with what he'd do to the zombie pricks who had tried to bite chunks out of him, ripped his favourite trench coat, and stolen his van and his Tom Jones CD. Those muthafuckers had a one-way ticket to Hell, and he was the guy to deliver it to them.

He stormed up the steps at the front of the hotel. A grey-haired old woman in a heavy, expensive-looking white coat was coming out of the glass doors just as Angus was barrelling in. She was about to light up a cigarette, and in consequence didn't notice Angus's huge frame looming towards her. He pushed in between her and the doors, shouldered her hard and watched with glee as she lost her footing and tumbled down the steps, swallowing the cigarette she had been about to light. God, that felt good. It wasn't enough, though. He was eager for some sort of confrontation with absolutely anyone or anything. The next victim to fall foul of his vile mood would get both barrels. He headed straight to the reception desk.

There was just one receptionist on duty, a blonde young woman who looked to be bored out of her mind. The entire lobby was now deserted. No one was checking in this late in the day. Since the whole weekend was organized around the goddam stupid singing contest, everyone had already arrived. And by now the evening's entertainment was well under way.

Angus placed his hands on the reception desk and leaned over to get a look at the name badge on the receptionist's red vest.

'Belinda,' he said, reading it aloud.

She greeted him with a polite smile. 'That's me. How may I help you, sir?'

'Gimme a key for room seven-thirteen. Now!'

The polite smile disappeared as Belinda began tapping on her keyboard and checking the monitor in front of her.

'Are you Mister Sanchez Garcia?' she asked.

'No, I'm the guy was s'posed to have that room before that Garcia bastard stole it.'

'Then I'm very sorry, sir, but I'm not permitted to issue you with a key.'

Angus pulled one of his revolvers out from inside his trench coat and pointed it at the receptionist's head.

'Now, you listen to me, you fuckin' bitch. I've just been attacked by about a hundred fuckin' zombies that just came up out of the fuckin' ground in the desert. Right out of fuckin' nowhere. And if I ain't mistaken, they were trying to bite chunks out of me. I killed quite a few of 'em with this fuckin' gun.' He waved the weapon in front of her face. 'An' when I ran out of fuckin' bullets I killed a few more with my bare fuckin' hands. I've now reloaded the gun, and I gotta tell you, I am really not in the right frame of mind to hear *"I'm sorry, sir, but I'm a stupid bitch so you can't have the key"* from the likes of you. So whyn't ya just give me the fuckin' key and I won't pretend I mistook you for a fuckin' zombie, and had to blow your fuckin' head off.'

'Will there be anything else, sir?'

'That's all.'

'One moment, please.'

Belinda reached down to her right and into a drawer below the desk. She pulled out a key card and placed it on the counter in front of Angus.

'That's a fucking skeleton key, sir. With that fucking thing you can get into any fucking room you fucking want.'

'Thank you. Oh, an' by the way – those fuckin' zombies are headed this fuckin' way. I suggest you give them less fuckin' shit than you fuckin' gave me. An' ya wanna do somethin' 'bout that potty mouth of yours. Unattractive habit in a young woman.'

'I'll be sure to keep that in mind, sir. Enjoy your fucking stay.'

Angus snatched up the key card and headed out of the lobby and down the corridor towards the elevator. The receptionist watched him, waiting until he was out of earshot before picking up the phone on her desk and dialling a four-digit number. The phone rang twice before it was answered.

'Nigel Powell.'

'Hi, Mr Powell, this is Belinda on reception. A rather unpleasant fuck— ' – she just stopped herself – 'gentleman with a gun and a foul mouth has just been in. I gave him a skeleton key to access any room he wants. It was either that, or he was going to shoot me in the face.'

'I see. I'll get security on it. Give them a description when they call you. Are you okay, Belinda? You should take the rest of the night off.' Powell was always solicitous towards his staff. It wasn't altogether altruistic: replacing people out in the Devil's Graveyard was not the easiest task he could think of.

'Oh, I'm fine thanks, Mister Powell. There's one other thing you should know, though.'

'Yeah? What's that?'

'This guy said he had just come in from the desert where he'd been attacked by about a hundred zombies. He said they were headed this way.'

On the other end of the line Belinda heard her employer let out a deep sigh. 'Shit. They're on their way already, huh? We'd best get this singing contest finished up double quick. The bastards are coming early this year, by the sounds of it, and I don't think any of us want to be snack food. That's what those idiots in the audience are for.'

'Yes, sir.'

Thirty-Seven

Emily grasped the steam iron in her right hand and raised it above her head. She found she was trembling with fear. Was this the right thing to do? Or even sensible?

She waited as Gabriel dragged the other security guard into the room. His back was to her, which was fortunate. She didn't think it would go over so well if he were to see her standing with a steam iron held above her head. He kicked the door closed and began moving backwards towards the closet, stooped over, with his hands under the dead guard's armpits. Towards her.

When he was close enough, she took a deep breath, and, using all her strength and weight, swung the steam iron at the back of his shaved head. And she swung it good.

CLUNK!

The iron hit him squarely on the right side of the back of his head. It caught his right ear, but mostly it connected with a part of his skull, covered only by a very thin layer of skin and stubble. Gabriel went down like a sack of corncobs, falling on top of the body of the security guard he had been dragging along.

Emily peered down at him. He seemed vaguely conscious, if the slight murmuring sounds he was making were anything to go by. She had definitely dazed him, but how badly? She didn't want to kill him, so she held off striking him on the head again, and instead tried to step over the pile of bodies between the bed and the wall, and now blocking her path to the room door. There was the security guard that she had dragged to the edge of the closet. Then there was Gabriel, and underneath him, the second security guard. Muttering a slightly hysterical apology, she stepped gingerly on to the first guard and attempted to take a giant stride over Gabriel and the other guard.

As she reached a leg over Gabriel's body, he snapped into life. The momentary dizziness she had inflicted on him had passed all too quickly. He grabbed her left leg and pulled hard on it, causing her to lose her balance. She tripped and fell to the floor by the bed, narrowly missing striking her head on the wooden bed post. The awkward landing made her drop the steam iron on to the carpet by her side.

'You fuckin' bitch!' she heard Gabriel shout. She had succeeded in riling him up, not knocking him out.

He climbed to his feet behind her. As she tried to get back up, he struck her a heavy blow on the back of her neck with his right fist. She fell flat on her face. She now had an idea of how he had felt when she had whacked him with the iron.

'That was really fuckin' stupid,' he snarled malevolently. She looked sideways and up, to see him rubbing the back of his head where she had hit him.

'I'm sorry. I didn't mean it.'

The biker seemed to have recovered completely from the blow to his head. He crouched down and she felt his knee push into the small of her back, pinning her to the floor.

'I gave you a chance to live, bitch.'

'I know. I'm sorry.'

'*Sorry* ain't gonna get rid of my headache. You goddam fuckin' worthless bitch.'

He pushed her head hard down into the carpet. With his knee in her back as well, she was completely disabled. Then she heard the sound she most dreaded – Gabriel pulling his gun back out from within his jacket. He pressed it into the back of her head. She was now more terrified than ever. She had messed up completely. Hitting him on the head with the steam iron had been stupid. And unnecessary. Although, she thought fleetingly, given the chance she would go back and do it again, only a hell of a lot harder.

'Not nice having a metal object thrust into the back of your head is it?' Gabriel growled. He pushed the barrel of the gun harder into her skull. 'See how it feels? Huh? Pretty fuckin' unpleasant, ain't it?'

'Yes. I'm sorry.' Emily began to sob. 'I'm so sorry.'

'Yeah, you're fuckin' sorry. Well, you had your chance!' With his free hand he grabbed a handful of her hair, lifting her head up a few inches off the carpet. 'For fuck's sake, I was doing you a fuckin' favour!'

He slammed her face into the floor. Her forehead hit first, just saving her nose from taking the brunt of the impact. It still hurt like hell, though. She felt dazed. Again, Gabriel pulled her head up by her hair and then slammed her face back down. Emily felt sick. She couldn't hold back the tears any more. She was about to die, and she'd let her mother down. She felt the barrel of Gabriel's gun press into the back of her head again. She screamed out in pain. Then she heard a metallic click. He had released the safety catch. *This was it.*

She closed her eyes and waited for the moment of truth. How would it feel? How long after the bullet entered her skull would she be able to feel the pain of it?

As these questions and a million other thoughts raced through her mind, she heard an almighty crashing noise from behind. The barrel of Gabriel's gun stopped pressing into the back of her head. This was the moment.

BANG!

She heard the gunshot as clear as day, deafening inside the room. Was this what it felt like to be shot? Or dead? She felt nothing. She felt the same. She felt – wait a second. As far as she could tell, she was still alive and breathing. What the –?

THUD!

In her dazed state she twisted her head and glanced to her left. Gabriel's face swam in and out of her vision. She focused on it and realized that he was lying on his side next to her, staring at her. They looked into each other's eyes. Then Emily watched Gabriel's eyes slowly roll up in his head.

She was still lying prostrate on the carpeted floor, unsure what had happened. There was blood seeping out from beneath Gabriel's head. It was creeping along the cream carpet towards her.

Then, without warning, her feeling of dizziness magnified. She raised her head to look behind her. Standing over her and the dead body of Gabriel was the man in black she had seen earlier in the day. He was holding a pistol in one hand, bluish smoke still drifting hazily from its muzzle. As she slipped out of consciousness, she realized that the man known to the world as the Bourbon Kid had come to her rescue.

And had blown the back of Gabriel's head off.

Thirty-Eight

Nigel Powell was sitting at the desk in his office with his head in his hands, fingers covering his eyes. His frustration was evident. His two fellow judges, Lucinda and Candy, were seated opposite him. Neither of them was particularly bright, but they would have to have been exceptionally stupid not to have picked up on his bad mood very quickly. They waited patiently for him to take his hands away from his face. When he did so, the first thing he saw was Candy's tight white leather jacket. As the day was wearing on, her breasts were coming ever closer to popping out of it. The sight distracted him for little more than five seconds. Lucinda's bright yellow dress caught his eye, reminding him of her presence, so he averted his gaze from Candy's cleavage and looked up at the two women.

'Well, you gonna tell us what's the problem here?' Lucinda asked, rather more combatively than she'd intended. She didn't much like Powell, but she was wary of him. Besides, he paid her handsomely.

The hotel owner puffed out his cheeks. He took turns to look them both in the eye to be certain they could sense his frustration.

'We've lost three of our finalists,' he said bleakly.

'Lost them?' asked Lucinda. The way he'd put it made it sound as though they'd all been rather careless.

'They're dead. Someone assassinated them.'

Candy looked confused. Nigel knew she was considerably

more intelligent than people gave her credit for, but in essence she was still a stereotypical airhead blonde.

'What? Who? Which ones?' she asked.

'We've lost Kurt Cobain, Otis Redding and Johnny Cash.'

'*Oh my God*. What about the other two?' she asked. Her agitation visibly increased the strain on her jacket's zip.

'I've arranged for them to be kept under armed guard,' Powell replied, somewhat pompously. 'I believe one of the other contestants discovered who the five finalists were going to be and hired a hitman to kill them off.'

Lucinda shook her head. 'Man, this is insane. I ain't never told no one who the finalists were goin' to be.'

'Me either,' Candy quickly added.

Lucinda leaned forward over the desk. 'You any idea 'tall who's behind all this shit?' she asked Powell.

'That I *don't* know. The hitman and the guy who hired him were apprehended by another hitman a few hours ago. Him and two guys from security took them out to the desert to kill them, but those three haven't returned. And now I can't get hold of them.'

'Sweet Jesus!' Lucinda yelped loudly. 'What in the hell we gonna do now? Cancel the show?'

Powell shook his head. 'Uh-uh. Like the cliché says, the show must go on. We've just got to find replacements for the three dead guys.' He looked at each of them in turn. 'Any suggestions? We've got about two minutes to decide. I want to get this final up and running as soon as possible. This year is turning into a fucking nightmare. So which three acts do we go for? Who did the audience like?'

Lucinda offered up an idea. 'Whyn't we pick one act each? Seems like a fair idea, yeah?'

Powell shrugged. 'Yeah, I like that. Candy, who do you want?'

Candy looked surprised. 'You want me to name an act

right now?'

'No, I would like you to name one at whatever leisurely pace you think is acceptable. Please ignore my remark about us only having two minutes.'

'Are you being sarcastic?'

'Yes. Clever of you to notice.'

'Fine. In that case, I'll go for that Elvis guy. He was cute.'

'That's not a reason to pick him,' Nigel snapped.

'You said we get one pick each, and he's mine.'

'No way. You're not picking someone just because you have the hots for him.'

'Gimme one reason why I shouldn't pick him. One that isn't personal.'

'Okay. I don't like him. As in, *really* don't like him.'

Candy let out a deep sigh. 'Fine,' she pouted. 'Then I pick Freddie Mercury. You happy?'

'Yes,' said Powell, smiling for the first time. 'He was pretty good, without being too good.' He turned to the other judge: 'Lucinda, what about you?'

Lucinda frowned and considered the question for a moment. 'That Blues Brother guy was good,' she said ruminatively.

'The one with the harmonica? And the red pants?' Candy couldn't hide the scorn in her voice.

'Yeah. I like him. He had somethin' about him.'

Powell pulled a face. 'Really? I thought he was rather a one-trick pony with that whole harmonica thing.'

'We pickin' one each here, or what? I said Blues Brother and I'm stickin' with him.' Lucinda was clearly far more determined than Candy. And Powell didn't have the time to argue.

'Fine,' he said. 'That gives us four finalists. So who shall I pick?' He drummed his fingers on his desk for a few seconds as he cast his mind back to all the singers they'd seen earlier.

'You didn't even see but half the acts,' Lucinda pointed

out. She was right. His constant to and fro-ing during the auditions had meant that he had missed watching many of the contestants.

'True. Everyone I saw was dreadful, too.' Suddenly a name popped into his head. 'I know. While I was in the lobby earlier I heard a lot of audience members raving about a Janis Joplin performer. Seemed to be a body of opinion that she was the highlight of the show. Think I'll go with her.'

Lucinda and Candy both looked stunned. Lucinda spoke up for both of them. 'You didn't even see her!'

'Oh, what does it matter? Judy Garland has this show sewn up anyway. No one's going to beat her. Besides, I think it would be good to have another woman in the final.'

'Yeah, but, trust me, that woman ain't the one,' Lucinda protested.

'Enough already,' said Powell waving a dismissive hand. 'We had one choice each, and she's mine.'

'But . . .'

'No buts, damn you!' he almost shouted, before continuing in a calmer voice. 'That's it. Now let's just get out there and announce it. God knows, this show is running over schedule already. I've got a couple of calls to make. You two can go and tell Nina who we've chosen for the final. Go on. Go. Close the door on your way out, won't you?'

Lucinda and Candy both got up from their seats and headed for the door. As they were leaving, Lucinda tried one last plea. 'Nigel, that Janis Joplin? Seriously, you can't . . .'

'Yes I fucking well can. Now get out!'

Thirty-Nine

Emily opened her eyes. Her vision was blurred and her eyes stung. She was also rapidly becoming aware of a painful throbbing at the front of her forehead. She was lying on a bed staring up at the ceiling. She could feel dried tears on her face, but she couldn't recall crying or remember why her head hurt. She reached a hand up to her forehead, wondering if it was as swollen as it felt.

From somewhere nearby, a voice like cold gravel spoke out. 'How ya feelin'?'

The sound startled her and she sat bolt upright. She regretted it immediately. Her head pounded. There was a man sitting at the end of the bed she was lying on. And from what she could tell, she was no longer in the same room that Nigel Powell had put in her in. She quickly moved her eyes around to take in her new surroundings. The rapid eye movement made her head hurt even more. She was in another hotel room all right. It was similar to the one Nigel Powell had set her up in, only this one was slightly smaller and with a single bed instead of a double. And the creepy guy in black who had been rude to her earlier in the day was sitting at the end of her bed.

'How ya feelin'?' he asked again.

'Who are you? What am I doing here?' she asked him, fearful of what his answer might be.

'Looked like someone was tryin' to kill you,' the man replied laconically.

Emily had a sudden flashback to the moment when she was confronted by Gabriel the biker-gunman. She remembered hitting him with a steam iron and knocking him down. As a ploy for escape, it hadn't worked as well as she'd hoped. Then he had pinned her down and banged her head on the floor a couple of times. Everything was a bit of a blur after that. So how had she ended up with this guy? And what were his intentions?

'What happened? I remember struggling with that biker guy and . . .' She recalled seeing Gabriel's face next to hers on the floor. The way his eyes had stared blankly at her for a second before rolling up into his head. 'What happened to him? Is he dead?'

'I shot him in the head. So yeah, probably.'

'Oh my God!'

Emily was not a supporter of violence, the steam-iron incident notwithstanding. And she certainly wasn't a fan of murder. At the moment, however, all she could think about was how incredibly cool it was to be sitting next to a man who had killed someone just to save her. That only happened in the movies.

'You did that for me?' she blurted out. The pain in her head had left her still a little dazed. She would otherwise never have let her guard down, even momentarily, to let him know exactly what she was thinking.

'Yeah.'

'That's *awesome*.'

As soon as she had uttered the word, she felt her face go scarlet with embarrassment. She rubbed her aching forehead, using her hand to hide the blush on her cheeks as she did so. To hide her confusion, she quickly asked more questions.' But who are you? And why did you kill him?' she asked.

'You ever heard of the Bourbon Kid?'

'Yeah. You mean that psycho guy with the drink problem who kills innocent people? He's a freaking maniac. They should lock him up and . . .' She trailed off. 'That's you, isn't it?' she said softly.

'Yeah.'

'Sorry.'

'I don't generally need a reason to kill someone, but when I walked into your hotel room it looked like the guy was 'bout to kill you. Had a gun pointed at your head.'

'Oh God.' Emily remembered the feeling as Gabriel's gun had pressed against her skull. 'He was going to shoot me, wasn't he?'

'No. He wasn't.'

'Huh?'

'Turns out his gun wasn't loaded. Seems he was just trying to scare you a little.'

Emily put her hand over her mouth. *Gabriel hadn't been so bad after all.* 'Oh God, you must feel so bad about killing him!' she exclaimed.

'No. I'd've killed him anyway.'

Emily frowned. 'Why?'

''Cause, fuck him.'

'Uh – like – okay. So who was he? What was he doing here?'

'Name of Gabriel. He was some sort of preacher.'

'A preacher? Why would a man of God pretend he was going to kill me? It doesn't make any sense.'

'The Lord works in mysterious ways.' Emily looked at him sharply, to see if he as making fun of her. His face was expressionless.

'Like, wow.' She was struggling to take it all in. She rubbed her forehead again. All this thinking was making her head hurt even more. But she was curious to know something else. 'Listen, if I'm not mistaken, when we met earlier you didn't like me very much, so I'm kinda struggling to work out why you saved me from that preacher with the gun.'

'You remind me of someone. Someone I used to care

about.'

'A girlfriend?'

'Somethin' like that.'

'What happened to her?'

'She's in jail. For murder.'

'That figures.'

'What?'

'Sorry. I didn't mean that.'

The Kid looked hard at her. 'That was a well-timed apology,' he growled.

'It's the blow to my head. I didn't mean to speak disrespectfully.'

'Yeah.' He seemed to lose interest for a moment. Then he spoke again, more urgently. 'Look, you gotta get out of this place. There are people tryin' to stop you winnin' this competition. An' they're ready an' willin' to kill you.'

'Why? What's going on? That biker guy – Gabriel, did you say? –he told me that three of the other singers were killed. But Nigel Powell said they had, like, food poisoning, or something. Which is it?'

'They're dead.'

'Poisoned?'

'No. I killed them.'

'*What?* You killed Otis Redding, Kurt Cobain and Johnny Cash?'

'Yeah.'

'Why would you do that?'

'James Brown offered me a lot of money.'

Emily looked stunned. '*Julius?* Why?'

'He wants to win.'

She rubbed her forehead yet again. All this new and frightening information was a lot to take on board with a pounding headache.

'I'm sorry, but I am *really* confused. And my head hurts, which isn't helping me to think straight.' It suddenly occurred to her that she had lost all track of time. 'Oh God, have they announced the finalists yet? How long have I been out? I've got to perform in the final.'

She jumped up from the bed and on to her feet. The sudden movement made her feel dizzy and a little sick, so she quickly sat back down. The Kid stood up and positioned himself neatly between her and the door.

'Listen to me, 'cause this is important,' he said. 'This competition is a joke. Only it ain't a funny one.'

'I know.'

'*No. You don't.* You don't know shit. So shut the fuck up and listen. Seems all the previous winners of this show sold their souls to the Devil when they signed Powell's contract. An' now they're all brain-dead zombies barely able to think for themselves. I just got jumped by Buddy Holly and Dusty Springfield in the parking lot, an' they looked like they'd been decomposin' for quite a while.'

There was a long pause as Emily waited for the Kid to validate his bizarre statement. He didn't.

'What are you talking about? Are you on drugs?' she blurted out at last.

'No. Just don't sing in the final. You need to get the fuck outta here. I'm gettin' out, too. You wanna ride? I'll take you to the next town. Right now this ain't a safe part of the world to be. There's fuckin' undead folks all round this place.'

His ravings were beginning to irritate Emily. 'Undead? I'm sorry, but nothing you're saying makes any sense,' she said with a distinctly schoolmarmish tone to her voice. 'And again, not wishing to be rude, but you are well known to be a psychopath, so when you talk about undead people and deals with the Devil, I'm inclined to think it's because of your – uh – mental problems.'

If she had hoped to provoke him, she failed. 'Just don't win the competition, okay?' he said, the gravel in his voice more evident than ever.

'Look, I'm sorry, I really am. And I thank you for your concern. But it's been my dream to sing for a living, especially at a place like this. And the million-dollar prize money would change my life. It's everything I've worked for my whole life. It's for me, and it's for my mom. I want her to know that everything we did was worth it. She's sick. My mother is sick.' She could hear her voice rising, but decided to continue anyway. 'She only has a few months left to live, and I want to make her last days special. We've got nothing at the moment, and with this money, I could get her properly cared for. And she'd know that I'd finally stepped into her shoes. I haven't come this far only to throw it all away because you think there's ghosts here.'

'So win the contest, but don't sign the contract.'

'No.'

'What?'

Emily shook her head. 'No. If your mother was dying, but you had the chance to keep her alive for a little bit longer, wouldn't you do everything you could?'

'I killed my mother.'

'Oh.' For a moment she was too stunned to speak. Then she plunged on, desperate to explain her situation. 'But –'

'Just. Go. Home. Your mother will understand.'

Something inside Emily snapped. 'Yeah, I'm sure she'll be very sympathetic as she lies there in a shitty care home drawing her last breath. And I can say, "Yeah, sorry, Mother, but I passed up the chance to get you some proper care because a psycho with a drink problem told me I'd be selling my soul to the Devil if I won the show".'

The Kid appeared unruffled by her aggressive sarcasm. 'You *know* this show is rigged.' he replied. 'You were secretly handpicked for the final. Don't get all fuckin' moral about it now.'

Emily raised an eyebrow. 'Oh, *I'm sorry*. Are *you* lecturing *me* about morality?'

'Yes. I am.'

'Well, that's pretty rich. Coming from you, and all. *Excuse me* if I don't think you're quite the right man to sit in judgement on others.' Her tone softened as she continued. 'Look, I'm grateful to you for maybe saving my life and everything, but I have to win this show. It means everything to me. So I'm sorry, but I'm going to sing in the final. The only way you can stop me is by killing me. So make your choice. Either let me out of here, or pull your gun out and finish me off. I'm not afraid to die, you know.'

'Yes you are.'

'I'm not. I'll never be afraid to die for what I believe in.'

The Bourbon Kid reached one hand inside his jacket. 'Okay. Then I guess you've given me no choice.'

Forty

Sanchez wasn't about to admit it to anyone, but he was actually pretty excited about the upcoming announcement of the performers who had made it into the final five in the *Back From The Dead* show. He was hanging backstage with Elvis, watching all the other hopefuls as they waited nervously to be called up onstage to learn their fate.

There was a real mixture of contestants, too, ranging from those who looked exactly like the singers they were impersonating, to those who were just downright freaky. The best was Freddie Mercury, who looked totally convincing. He had on a pair of tight white pants with a red stripe down the sides, and a yellow leather jacket over a plain white singlet. His thick black moustache and goofy teeth added to an imitation that was uncannily accurate. Sanchez hadn't seen him perform in the auditions, but if he had the voice to match the looks he would certainly be a contender.

At the opposite end of the spectrum were some very unconvincing weirdos. One in particular stood out: a midget called Richard whose look and act were modelled on Jimi Hendrix. His outfit consisted of tight black pants, high-heeled boots and a white shirt beneath a purple coat. Unfortunately for him, several other contestants were also named Richard. As a result, people tended to refer to him as Little Richard, which was visibly pissing him off. There was also a Frank Sinatra impersonator with a large white Band-Aid over his nose, who was walking around claiming that his hat had been stolen.

What had really caught Sanchez's interest was the behaviour of Julius, the James Brown impersonator. Could this guy really be the thirteenth Apostle? He looked a little edgy and was eyeing up all the other contestants suspiciously. At one point his gaze met that of Sanchez. Julius smiled and nodded at him and Elvis, probably acknowledging that they were friends of Gabriel. Sanchez nodded back politely. No sense in upsetting one of God's favourite people. Could be a useful ally to have, come Judgement Day. Did he know that Sanchez knew who he was?

That set the bar owner thinking. Would Julius's James Brown impersonation be good enough to get him through? And what about Judy Garland? Had Gabriel – or the other hitman, Angus – successfully eliminated her from the contest? What if her name was called and she didn't show, because she'd been killed? And who would the other finalists be, since at least three, and maybe four, of the original line-up were dead?

In the corner of his eye, he could see Elvis bouncing on the balls of his feet, a little like a boxer psyching himself up for a fight. Making an effort, Sanchez snapped out of his thoughtful state of mind and began making encouraging noises to his friend about how making it to the final was a formality. While Elvis didn't need any boost to his confidence, he probably appreciated the effort.

'Hey, man, whatcha gonna do if you get selected for the final, huh?' Sanchez asked. 'I mean, what if you get through and James Brown don't?'

Elvis was eyeing up the James Brown impersonator much as Sanchez had done moments earlier. He answered Sanchez without taking his eyes off the Godfather of Soul in the bright purple suit.

'I'm damn' sure he'll make it. I don't reckon God put us through the last twenty-four hours only for his Apostle guy not to qualify for the final.'

'Sure hope you're right.'

'I'm right.'

'So where's Gabriel, then? You think he's bumpin' off Judy Garland 'bout now?'

'Well, I guess that'd explain why she ain't here.' Elvis seemed supremely unconcerned.

Sanchez thought about it for a moment. The Judy Garland impersonator had done nothing wrong, from what he could tell. And she'd smiled at him and said hello backstage earlier in the day. None of the other precious bastards had done that. *Wannabe celebrities,* he thought. *They were all in danger of disappearing up their own buttholes.* So far, she seemed like the only one not totally self-obsessed. Even though Sanchez liked Gabriel, and owed him a debt of gratitude for saving him from the zombie mutant folk in the desert, he didn't really like the idea that his new friend was possibly murdering an innocent young woman in cold blood somewhere in the hotel. Especially one who had seemed to smile genuinely at him. Not even his friends usually did that.

He was dwelling on the unpleasantness of the whole situation when a security guard came over and politely asked him to move out of the backstage area. Wishing Elvis the best of luck one last time, Sanchez headed for the area at the side of the stage where he could watch the show from behind the far edge of one of the huge red curtains, which for now were still closed, hiding the stage.

He had barely arrived at his vantage point when the rear of the stage area went dark and a drum roll began to boom out of the sound system. A moment later, the magnified voice of the show's host, Nina Forina, followed the roll of drums.

'Ladies and gentlemen,' she said dramatically. 'Please – put your hands together – for – our judges!'

At that moment, the curtains parted and a spotlight lit up centre stage to reveal the three judges standing proudly in its beam. Sanchez was able to stay tucked out of sight behind the curtain's edge. He had a perfect view of the proceedings. All he was missing was his recliner, a bag of popcorn and a couple of bottles of beer.

Onstage, the three judges stood in the centre and lapped up the adulation from the audience in front of them. After milking the applause for all it was worth, they took their seats on the panel, which was level with Sanchez. Once the cheering and clapping and whistling began to die down, the stage lit up again and Nina Forina walked elegantly to the centre. She stood for a moment, beaming a bright white smile, basking in the last dregs of the audience's applause. Then she held out her arms, and the auditorium finally fell quiet.

'Hello, everyone. Are you ready to find out who our five finalists are?'

'Yeeeaaahhh!'

'I can't hear you. Are you ready to find out who the five finalists are?'

'YEEEAAAHHH!'

Nina clapped along with the roaring crowd, before turning sideways and making a gesture to the back of the stage. The glare of the lights blazing down on her gave Sanchez a view he hadn't been expecting. Her dress was practically transparent. *Jesus.*

All of the shortlisted contestants began filing out on to the stage behind her. There were about a hundred of them, yet on the stage it looked like twice that number. Elvis was one of the first to come out, waving and blowing kisses at the audience. He looked confident enough, unlike Julius who, to Sanchez's surprise, now looked quite nervous.

When the noise eventually died down to a gentle hush, Nina turned back to the panel of judges, now seated at the front of the stage with their backs to the auditorium.

'Nigel, would you please tell us all who the first contestant is to make it into the final five for this evening's show?'

Powell sat looking smug in pride of place between his two female colleagues. His face flashed up on a giant television screen at the back of the stage and, for some reason unknown to Sanchez, it invoked a few screams from a number of young women in the audience. As if looking in a mirror, Powell stared up at the screen and smiled his overly bleached, toothy grin, which shone brightly against his orange tan. After preening for so long that Sanchez started to feel nauseous at the spectacle, he eventually responded to Nina's request.

'I certainly will, Nina,' he said, with a wink that Sanchez found almost equally nauseating. 'The first finalist impressed us all with his showmanship. His singing voice wasn't perhaps the best, but if he picks the right song in the final, he stands a serious chance of winning this competition. Nina, our first finalist is . . .' He paused for a ridiculously long time in order to tease the audience, before announcing, '*Freddie Mercury!*'

The Freddie Mercury impersonator jumped for joy, punching his fist in the air and hissing a quick '*Yesss!*' under his breath. He bounded over to Nina Forina, who hugged him and gave him a perfunctory kiss on the cheek before directing him to stand a few yards behind her on the right. Freddie looked over and, seeing Sanchez, flashed a wide beaming smile at him. Sanchez smiled back, and through gritted teeth muttered the words 'smug' and 'prick' under his breath.

Again, Powell psyched the audience up before announcing Janis Joplin as the second finalist. The delighted performer bounded out of the crowd of contestants at the back of the stage, waving her hands in the air like a hyperactive escapee from a lunatic asylum. She was a hippy chick with long brown hair, wearing pale-tinted sunglasses with circular lenses and a green flowery dress that stopped just above her knees. She hadn't bothered with high-heeled shoes, either, preferring a pair of comfortable white sneakers. The outfit was topped off by a number of strings of beads of varying lengths hanging around her neck, including an enormous yin-yang symbol that bumped against her navel. She shared the obligatory hug and kiss with Nina, to a surprisingly enthusiastic reception from the audience, then took up a place next to Freddie Mercury.

That's two down, thought Sanchez. *Only three spots left. Sure hope that Julius guy gotta decent contingency plan if he don't get picked. Otherwise his whole scheme is fucked.*

Hugely amplified, Powell's mellifluous voice boomed loud and clear for a third time.

'The next contestant through to the final – that's number three of five, remember – is the man with the most hideous pair of red leather pants I've ever seen . . . *the Blues Brother!*'

As the audience roared and stamped their approval, Sanchez saw a black guy dressed as one of the Blues Brothers appear from among the crowd of hopefuls. He was wearing a black suit over a white shirt with a thin black tie, and a pair of sunglasses. On top of his head was what looked distinctly like Frank Sinatra's missing hat. He walked over to Nina Forina, looking, Sanchez thought, somewhat sheepish. She congratulated him with a polite hug and peck on the cheek, and then he walked over to take his place alongside Janis Joplin in the row of finalists. Sanchez scratched his head and tried to make sense of Powell's 'red leather pants' comment. The Blues Brother was wearing a black suit – black jacket, black pants. Maybe the chief judge was colour blind? Which maybe explained why he'd picked a black Blues Brother?

Sanchez had been loyally hoping Elvis would get through, but not having been one of the first three picks meant that his buddy's chances were now looking pretty slim. Ideally, the last two finalists would be Elvis and Julius. Elvis could then deliberately lose in the final, meaning that Julius would only have three others to beat.

Truth was, though, even those were minor considerations. Or distractions. Sanchez's palms were sweating profusely. The knowledge that there were bloodthirsty, flesh-eating zombies on their way to the hotel was bad enough. But knowing that his only chance of getting out of the Devil's Graveyard alive rested on the shoulders of a James Brown impersonator hardly filled him with confidence.

Up on the giant screen, Powell waited for the excited audience to quieten down before announcing the judges' next choice.

'Our fourth finalist blew us all away with his performance earlier. Someone full of energy, and undoubtedly one of the best entertainers in this competition. Ladies and gentlemen, the fourth contestant through to the final is . . . *James Brown!*'

Sanchez felt an overwhelming sense of relief. He also hoped to hell that Julius really was the saviour that Gabriel had predicted. *Guy'd better be who he says he is,* he whispered to himself as Julius appeared out of the crowd of wannabes at the back of the stage. He was bouncing around like a complete lunatic, uttering trademark James Brown 'heh' noises. The plan was still on. *Whatever the fuck the plan actually was.*

Once again the applause gave way to an expectant silence. 'And finally,' Powell announced. 'Our fifth contestant was an absolute certainty to make it into the final after delivering what was probably the best vocal performance of the heats. Ladies and gentlemen, the last contestant through to the final is . . . *Judy Garland!*'

The audience produced an even bigger cheer than they had for any of the four other finalists, only this time it didn't last as long. It began to peter out as it became evident that Judy Garland wasn't onstage. Soon, the crowd's confused murmurings overtook the syncopated smattering of any remaining applause. Everyone started looking around, as if they expected the missing singer to appear from round a corner somewhere or from behind another of the hopeful – and now heavily disappointed – contestants standing at the rear of the stage.

'Judy Garland?' Powell asked hopefully. 'Is Judy Garland still here?'

Nina Forina joined in. 'Judy Garland? Maybe she went back to Kansas?' she said, with a horribly overdone guffaw. An uncomfortable hush descended upon the auditorium. Sanchez took some comfort from the knowledge that he wasn't the only one in the room who came up with crap gags.

He waited to see if Judy Garland appeared from among the crowd of other contestants at the back. Out of the corner of his eye he saw Julius subtly clench his fist in front of his chest in victory. Gabriel must have done the job. Judy Garland would not be making it to the final. Sanchez felt a little guilty about that. Her non-appearance meant that she had almost certainly been brutally murdered, all so that a guy claiming to be the thirteenth Apostle could save a bunch of others (including Sanchez). *Sure it was kinda harsh, but in the best interests of everyone*, the bar owner thought, sententiously.

For a few minutes, confusion reigned as the judges deliberated on what to do. Members of the security team were sent to check the corridors to see if Miss Garland was on her way. As the seconds ticked by and still she didn't show, the audience became restless. A few plastic cups were hurled towards the stage. The security guards were speaking urgently into two-way radios as they darted out into the corridors. The show was in danger of turning into a shambles. One by one, the guards returned with shakes of their heads to indicate that the fifth finalist was nowhere to be seen.

Nigel Powell was going to have to think on his feet, but this was obviously something he was good at. And he knew it. From his seat in the centre of the panel, he gestured for the crowd to calm down, his every move repeated, hugely magnified, on the screen at the back of the stage.

'Okay, ladies and gentlemen, it appears that Dorothy has got lost somewhere on the Yellow Brick Road!'

The audience laughed heartily (in spite of his joke being no better than Nina's earlier effort). When the laughter died down, he carried on. 'So, what we're going to do here is pick the sixth best contestant from the heats. Would you please put your hands together for a performer who surprised us all with his musical talent. Ladies and gentlemen, contestant number five in the final will be . . . *Elvis Presley!'*

Elvis strutted to the front of the stage with the confident swagger of a man whose place in the final had never been in doubt. He blew kisses and waved to the audience. After kissing Nina Forina and grabbing her ass for a good squeeze, he made his way over to the other finalists. He looked over to Sanchez and gave him a thumbs-up with both hands as he took up a spot next to Julius on the end of the row.

Nina, who was blushing after Elvis's inappropriate (though not altogether unwelcome) grab at her tush, raised her microphone to her lips and gestured for the crowd to be quiet.

'Okay everyone,' she yelled. 'We now have our five finalists. Let's please give them all one more round of applause!'

The crowd was up on its feet, loudly cheering, stamping and clapping once more. After a few seconds of cheering, however, Sanchez noticed the volume of noise from the audience go up a few decibels. At first he wondered if someone had fallen over onstage, for it sounded as though the audience had worked itself into an overexcited frenzy. He craned his neck and twisted his head from side to side, hoping to see evidence of some horribly embarrassing pratfall. He'd be sick with disappointment if he'd missed it. There was nothing Sanchez loved more than seeing people trip over in public.

Then he saw the reason for the extra loud cheers.

Out of nowhere, Judy Garland had rushed on to the stage. She looked flustered, but with every step she took towards Nina Forina and every ringing cheer from the audience, she began to regain her composure. This young woman was undoubtedly the crowd's favourite, and by the look of the wide, beaming smile on Powell's face, she was his, too. He stood up from his seat and once again gestured for the audience to be quiet.

When they calmed down, he kept them waiting in silence for a little while longer, before making the announcement they all wanted to hear.

'Okay, folks. Who has a problem with us having *six* finalists this year?'

The crowd went wild. The screams of approval became deafening. Sanchez looked across at Elvis. Elvis looked back at him with a frown of deep concern darkening his face. Julius's chances of being crowned winner with his James Brown impression had just taken a serious knock.

And what had happened to Gabriel?

Forty-One

Emily had come frighteningly close to not making it to the stage on time. She had the Bourbon Kid to thank, she supposed. He'd saved her life, after all. (Well, okay, Gabriel's gun hadn't been loaded. But he could have bludgeoned her to death with it. Or strangled her. Or . . . Emily could rationalize with the best of them, when necessary.) And he hadn't killed her for openly defying him. When he'd reached inside his jacket, she'd feared he might be about to draw out a weapon. Instead, he had pulled out a pack of cigarettes. He was probably capable of killing someone with a cigarette, but he'd chosen not to in her case. Which was a relief. Whichever way you looked at it, he was famous for killing people over pretty trivial matters. Like *nothing,* for instance.

As she stood on the stage reflecting on all that had happened, she became aware that Julius was staring at her. She looked over and nodded to him, offering a half-hearted smile. He glanced at her curiously before flashing a brief and insincere smile in return. If what the Kid had told her was true, Julius had expected her to be dead. No wonder he was looking at her oddly. Emily shivered. She didn't feel safe. There was only one person who could help her. Nigel Powell.

As everyone slowly departed the stage in the wake of the announcement of the finalists, Emily walked tentatively over to the panel of judges. A twenty-minute recess had been called. Many of the audience had deserted their seats and gone off to stretch their legs. Powell's two female companions, Lucinda and Candy, had also left their seats and vanished, which gave Emily a perfect opportunity for a quiet word with Powell.

He smiled at her when he saw her approach. 'Hello, Emily,' he said, getting to his feet. You could say what you liked about Nigel Powell, but he had good manners. When it suited him. 'I thought you weren't going to make it for a minute. You cut it a bit fine there, didn't you?'

'Yes. I'm terribly sorry about that. Actually, I need to speak to you about that. Can I have a quick word with you?'

'Sure. Take a seat.' He gestured for her to sit in the chair to his right and, when she had done so, sat down himself. 'What can I do for you?'

Emily shifted in her chair; it was still warm. 'I've got a headache.'

'I'm sorry to hear it. Would you like me to get you some painkillers?'

'Someone hit me over the head with a gun.' This was not absolutely true, she knew. But it was shorter than launching into a full explanation.

'Excuse me?'

'A gun. A man broke into that room you put me in. He shot both of your security guards dead and then tried to kill me.'

Powell's face looked about as shocked as it could. 'Oh my God. Start from the beginning. Who tried to kill you?'

'He was a big biker guy called Gabriel. Shaved head, arms like tree trunks.'

'Jesus. Where is he now?'

'He's dead. His body's still in the room, with the two security guards.'

'He's dead? Who killed him? You?'

'No. A guy called the Bourbon Kid. He saved me. For reasons that make very little sense to me, really.'

'The Bourbon Kid *saved* you?'

'Yes. And according to him, Julius, the James Brown

impersonator, paid this Gabriel guy to kill me. Apparently the other three finalists – the original finalists, that is – are dead too. Did you know any of this?'

Powell nodded, but made no attempt to explain just what it was that he did know. 'Julius, huh?' he mused. 'I should have known. There was something about him that got under my skin the first time I met him.'

'So you think it's true, then? About him trying to kill all the other finalists?'

Again, he nodded. 'Actually, yes I do.' For a moment, he looked away, apparently lost in thought. Then he turned back to her and said, in his urbane way, 'Thank you for coming and telling me this. I'll have him thrown out of the competition.'

'Are you going to call the police?'

'Of course. The proper authorities should deal with this. They'll throw him in jail. And, I should think, throw away the key.'

Emily breathed a sigh of relief. 'Thank goodness for that. I was really worried about telling you all this.'

'Not at all.' Powell stood up. 'Go mix with the other finalists. Do not say a word about this to anyone, and whatever you do, don't get split off from the herd. Stay in crowds at all times. I'll get rid of Julius and whoever else he may have hired to try to help him rig this contest. You just worry about singing. Because, with him out of the show, you've pretty well got it sewn up now.'

'That's not why I told you this,' Emily said defensively.

'I know. Now run along.' He winked at her. 'People will start to think the show's rigged if they see us chatting like this.'

'Thank you.' Emily got up from the seat and headed for the backstage area. She could see the back of Freddie Mercury's yellow jacket descending a flight of steps so she raced after him. *Safety in numbers*, she told herself, *as long as you stay away from Julius.*

Nigel watched her trot off backstage and thought hard about what she had just told him. So, Julius was the fly in the ointment, the agent of destruction, trying to ruin the show. Quite why, he wasn't sure, but that didn't matter.

James Brown, the Godfather of Soul, would be eliminated before he had a chance to sing in the final.

Forty-Two

The members of the Pasadena Hotel house orchestra had been rehearsing for much of the day. They were therefore extremely disappointed to discover that three of the songs they had been practising were no longer required. At the last minute, Nigel Powell had informed them that they would only play for two of the finalists. The others would be singing along to some karaoke backing music that the house deejay was in the process of downloading from the Internet. Understandably, the musicians were all very frustrated, airing their complaints as they made their way through the hotel corridors to the orchestra pit in front of the stage.

Twenty-four musicians in all, all of them, bar the pianist and the drummer, carrying their instruments, made the long walk from the rehearsal area to the auditorium. A number of them did so in the resentful knowledge that their skills and their instruments were no longer required. They would simply be sitting in the orchestra pit and watching the show. One such was Boris, the backup guitar player. His part had now become redundant. It was his twenty-first birthday, and playing in the show had been going to be the highlight of his musical career to date. But now the senior guitarist, Pablo, would be the only one needed for the two specified songs.

Feeling more than a little downbeat, Boris plodded along at the rear of the group, sulking at his misfortune. As they trailed down the long corridor from the lobby to the stage area, he noticed the orchestra members in front of him begin to part, like the Red Sea before the Children of Israel. He saw, walking towards him through the middle of the gaggle of musicians, a muscular-looking man wearing a black leather jacket with a dark hood pulled up over his head, leaving his face in shadow.

As Boris attempted to step out of the way to allow him to pass, the man reached out and grabbed him by the shoulder.

'Hey, you,' he said in a gravelly voice.

'Yeah, uh – hi,' Boris replied. Something about the man made him feel nervous.

'Bin lookin' for you.'

'*Me?* Why?'

'Guy up in the booth wants a word with you.'

''Bout what?'

'The fuck would I know?'

'Well, I'm supposed to be doing the show any minute.'

'It's *about* the goddam show, man. Guy wants you to do a big solo, or somethin'.'

Boris's eyes lit up. 'Yeah?' But his initial excitement was quickly replaced by suspicion. This was more than likely a practical joke. 'You just said you didn't know what it was about,' he said warily.

'That's 'cause it's a surprise. I didn't wanna ruin it for you.'

'Oh. Right. What's the solo for?'

'Hey, man, I've said way too much already. It's up this way.' He pointed to a stairway running off the corridor on the right, which Boris had passed moments earlier. Not wanting to be forgotten by his fellow orchestra members, he yelled out to them.

'Catch up with you guys, yeah?'

If any of them heard him, they gave no sign of it. They all carried on walking, before turning right through a door that led into the lower area of the auditorium, where the orchestra pit was located.

Boris followed the hooded man over to the stairway. The stranger gestured for him to go up first. The stairway consisted of no more than ten steps but it was unlit and that made it difficult to see where it led. When he reached the top, he found himself in another corridor and began walking along it. Halfway along was a door on the left on which was a plaque bearing the words 'SOUND BOOTH'. As Boris approached the door the hooded man brushed past him.

'In here,' he grunted, pushing the door open.

Boris walked in as the man held the door open. Inside, sitting at a mixing desk in front of a large plate-glass window that looked down on the auditorium below, was the show's deejay. He was a short, fat, balding white guy in his late thirties, wearing a blue tracksuit with white stripes down the sleeves and legs. His ears were covered by some really serious-looking brown headphones, which probably explained why he didn't appear to have heard the two men come in. Boris called over to him. 'Yo, Harry! You wanted to see me?'

Startled, Harry turned and looked at him, pushing the headphones down off his ears, his blotchy red face revealing a look of puzzlement. He shook his head.

'Boris? Nah. Don't think so. Ain't you s'posed to be playin' in the pit?'

Boris turned to the hooded man for an explanation, in time to see a fist coming right at his face. Instinctively he closed his eyes as the full force of the blow crashed into his nose. The last thing he heard was a horrible crunching noise as his nose shattered.

The Bourbon Kid picked up Boris's feet and dragged his unconscious body into the corner of the sound booth. He lifted the young man's guitar from where it had fallen and took a good look at it. It seemed to be in reasonably good shape. There were no visible scratches on it, and no blood from the injury he had inflicted upon the guy's nose. The deejay, who had not stirred from his seat, appeared to be watching with interest, waiting for an explanation.

'Uh, like, what's goin' on, man?' he asked.

'Needed a guitar.'

'Ya couldn't've just asked him if he'd lend it t'ya?'

'I could.'

'But you chose not to?'

'That's right. I want somethin' from you, too.'

'What's that?'

'A Blues Brothers CD. You got one?'

'Yeah.'

'Give it to me.'

'Will I get it back?'

'No.'

Harry couldn't hide the look of disappointment on his face. But he also seemed to have a keen understanding of what would happen to him if he didn't do as the Kid asked. He leaned down and started sifting through a large black case of compact discs on the floor by his right foot. After a few seconds he hooked out a Blues Brothers album and tossed it over to the Kid.

'There y'are. Anythin' else?'

'Yeah. You in charge of the backing music for the finalists?'

'A few of 'em, yeah. House orchestra is playin' two of the songs. I'm puttin' on backing tracks for the other four.'

'Don't play a track for the Blues Brother when he's up.'

Harry looked baffled. 'Huh? I've been told to. I'm playin' "Mustang Sally" for him to sing along to. I've downloaded the track from the Internet.'

The Kid stood his newly acquired guitar against the wall by the door, reached into his jacket and pulled out a dark grey pistol. He waved it at Harry. 'You play that backing track for him, I'm gonna shoot you in the face with this.'

Harry made his mind up very quickly. 'Okay. It'll kill his chances of winnin', though.'

'That's my problem.'

Harry shrugged. 'Okay. Whatever. Is that all?'

'No. I'll be back in five minutes. And I'm gonna want your seat.'

'Great. Look forward to it.'

'Yeah?' A very faint smile appeared on the hooded face. Harry shrank from the sight.

The Kid slid the pistol back into his jacket, picked up the guitar again and reached for the door handle to head out of the sound booth. As he did so, Harry pressed a button on the CD player on his mixing desk. The song 'That's Not My Name' by The Ting Tings began playing.

The Kid stopped on his way out the door.

'You choosin' the music?' he asked.

'Yeah. Cool song this, huh? Really catchy.'

'You takin' requests?'

Harry shook his head. 'No. 'Fraid not, buddy. I got a set playlist worked out.'

'Takin' orders?'

'Er – what d'ya have in mind?'

'"Live and Let Die". Get me in the right frame of mind for later.'

'What's happenin' later?'

'I'm gonna kill someone.'

Harry inhaled sharply and, for a man who normally had a very red face, turned a little pale. He had the good sense not to keep the Kid waiting, however. He spun his chair round and, with the speed inherent in people who don't want to be future murder victims, bent down to the case of CDs on the floor and began frantically rifling through them.

But by the time he'd found the Paul McCartney CD the Bourbon Kid was gone.

Forty-Three

Knowing that there was a horde of partially decomposed undead creatures heading towards the hotel, Nigel Powell made damn sure that the final started as soon as possible. First, and most importantly, he had to ensure that the orchestra knew what songs the finalists were going to perform. There had been some grumbling among the musicians, but Powell had no the patience for it and had made it very clear that what songs were played wasn't up for debate. As things now stood, the orchestra would perform only the songs for Judy Garland and James Brown.

It truly was turning into the most stressful of days. The *Back From The Dead* show was always a nerve-racking time for him, but this year had been a disaster from the start, and now he had the Godfather of Soul running around trying to kill as many of the finalists as he could. So far, Powell hadn't worked out how to make sure the murderous little jerk didn't make it to the final.

After taking care of the music issues and a few other last-minute details, he headed back to the stage area and gave the nod to the stagehand in charge of the curtains. The song "Live and Let Die" by Paul McCartney was playing, but on a signal to the deejay the music was faded out. Once the auditorium was silent again, the curtains parted and Powell appeared onstage to a roar of approval from the watching audience. Without milking the applause as much as usual, he quickly made his way over to his seat on the panel between Lucinda and Candy, who had been waiting patiently for his return. As he sat down he leaned over and whispered in Lucinda's ear.

'I can't wait for this all to be over for another year. This one's really been a show to forget.'

'Sure has,' she mumbled back

'At least things can't get any worse.'

'Oh, they can.'

'I doubt that,' Powell muttered under his breath. He was struggling to hide just how stressed-out the event had made him feel. 'At least it's nearly over now.'

Lucinda shook her head as if she disapproved of something he'd said. Before he had a chance to ask her what she meant by that, his face appeared on the giant monitor at the back of the stage and he thought better of it.

When the crowd had calmed down, Nina Forina stepped into the spotlight centre stage.

'Ladies and gentlemen – the final is about to begin!' she exclaimed, with not altogether forced enthusiasm. The crowd clapped, wolf-whistled, stamped and cheered back at her. After teasing them for a few more seconds, she made the announcement for which they had all been waiting. 'You're a great crowd,' she yelled. 'So please put your hands together for our first finalist, singing "Piece Of My Heart" . . . Here's *Janis Joplin!*'

As more cheers followed and Nina stepped away out of the spotlight, the Janis Joplin impersonator appeared from the wings. She walked timidly to the centre of the stage in her garish green dress and white sneakers. Then she stood and waited beneath the spotlight for the deejay in the booth to put on the backing track for her song.

A brief pause, then a drum beat started, followed by a guitar playing the opening bars of the song. The singer began to wiggle her shoulders and hips. Her movements were not particularly in time to the music, and when she began to sing it became obvious why. Her voice was deep and full of aggression as she practically shouted out the first few lines.

'Didn't I fuckin' make you feel like you were the only fuckin' muthafucker, yeah?

An' didn't I fuckin' give you everythin' that a whore really could, you fuckin' asshole?

Honey, you fuckin' know I did!'

The audience laughed and cheered. The aggressive swearing ruined the song for some, but enhanced it for others. Not having seen her audition, Nigel Powell was the only person surprised by the performance. He leaned over and whispered in Lucinda's ear once more.

'What just happened?'

'We tried to tell you.'

'Tell me what?'

'She has Tourette's.'

Powell began rubbing his forehead in despair. 'Oh, brilliant. That's just perfect. Of *course* she has. Why wouldn't she? I mean, come *on* – if you have Tourette's and it's this bad, you enter a singing competition, don't you?'

'It's worse when she sings, apparently.'

'You have *got* to be kidding me!'

'Shhh,' Lucinda snapped. 'She's getting to the chorus. This is the best bit.'

Powell made a point of ostentatiously covering his ears with his hands, so that no one in the audience would be in any doubt about his disgust at the performance. For the next few minutes what was almost certainly the worst tribute ever to the late Janis Joplin energetically murdered 'Piece Of My Heart', littering it with foul-mouthed obscenities.

When at last she was finished she stood shyly in the spotlight, awaiting the judges' comments. These were somewhat varied.

'I loved it,' said Lucinda enthusiastically. 'But it'll be a tragedy if you win, honey, 'cause the others are all better'n you.'

The most positive thing that Candy could find to say was 'Nice outfit, terrible singing!'

Powell was blunt. 'You suck,' he said. 'You're a disgrace, and I have no idea how or why we put you into the final. Please go away.'

He was quite right, of course. Now that the Tourette's-suffering singer had performed in the final, however, would the audience decide to vote for her en masse, just for her sheer entertainment value? Here was yet another irritation to add to the ever-growing list. At the top of that list was Julius.

In the silence that followed the dejected Janis Joplin impersonator as she slouched offstage, Powell spotted one of his security guards at the side of the stage, trying to catch his attention. It was Sandy. The hotel owner nodded at him, harbouring the cryptic thought, *He knows what needs to be done.*

Forty-Four

Truth was, Sanchez was a good deal more nervous than Elvis. The King had performed onstage countless times before. There were few things he enjoyed more than being in front of an audience. Sanchez, on the other hand, was edgy for all kinds of reasons. If Elvis did great and won the contest, what would it mean? Would the zombies swarm in, and if so, would they try to kill everyone? Or just the people in the audience? And if Elvis lost, and Julius-the-James-Brown-impersonator won, then what would that mean? Would the hotel really crumble and be sucked into the pit of Hell?

Sanchez was not, by any measure, a cerebral man. Nor even a particularly rational one. All the speculation was making him extremely anxious. So he did what he always did when nervous. He headed for the restroom with the intention of filling his hip flask with piss for the next unsuspecting victim. He did this with a certain amount of trepidation, given what he had experienced there, but he was banking on his belief that, in a hotel like the Pasadena, the place would have been restored to order hours ago.

The corridor leading to the men's washroom was deserted, as was most of the rest of the hotel by this time. Everyone seemed to have made for the auditorium in order to watch the final sing-off and the declaration of the winner of the competition. The washroom was empty, too, and Sanchez was pleased to see that someone had come by and cleaned up the mess from earlier. The pool of blood that had spilled out of the stalls and on to the floor was gone, as were the corpses of the dead singers. Almost as important, the horrendous smell had gone too, which was quite a relief. He locked himself away in stall four and, with a remarkably steady hand, began pissing into his silver hip flask. It was a skill he had mastered over the years, and in spite of his nervous state, his aim was dead on. It was a very satisfying piss, too. As he was finishing he heard someone else walk into the washroom and unzip his fly, preparatory to taking a leak at one of the urinals.

Sanchez screwed the lid back on his flask and unlocked the door of the stall, then made his way over to the washbasins to give his hands a quick rinse. He paid little attention to the man pissing at the middle urinal as he placed the flask down beside of one the basins and flicked on the hot faucet. As he began to rinse his hands in the warm water, he noticed out of the corner of his eye that the other man was staring at him. Without wishing to do anything that might suggest he was eyeing up another man who was urinating, Sanchez slyly turned his head to see who it was.

Their eyes met for only a second. As fractional moments of time go, however, it was more than enough. Sanchez grabbed his hip flask and ran for the door, giving the urinals a very wide berth. The man taking a piss was Invincible Angus. And he'd seen and recognized the hapless bar owner.

'Wait up, you fucker!' Angus roared. 'I want my twenty fuckin' grand!'

Sanchez didn't have the twenty grand. All he had was a hip flask full of piss. He'd have to sell a heck of a lot of it to make twenty thousand dollars, and generally speaking, his piss went for about three dollars a shot on a good day.

As he charged out through the washroom door, he heard Angus zipping up his fly. *Now wash your hands!* he thought. But he didn't think that Angus would, somehow.

SHIT!

The washroom door was heavy and didn't instantly

spring shut behind him after he dashed through it. It made a slight creaking sound as it ground slowly to a close. Sanchez didn't have the time to waste pulling it shut behind him. In a blind panic he rushed back towards the main reception area. It was a good fifty-yard run to reach the glass double doors at the end of the corridor that led to the lobby. And when it came to running, Sanchez was about as fast as he looked. Which wasn't very fast at all.

He reached the glass doors, slammed into the left-hand one and barged it open. In his panicked state, his legs weren't following the instructions from his brain as quickly as he would have liked. He lost his footing and fell through the open doorway and on to the floor in the reception area. As he climbed back to his feet he saw that, back down the corridor, Invincible Angus had come out of the washroom and was aiming a gun at him. Without waiting to watch him squeeze the trigger, Sanchez took a quick look around for his best escape route.

BANG!

Angus raced out of the washroom without bothering to wash his hands after hastily curtailing his piss. He first looked left, then right where, in the distance, he could see Sanchez getting up from the floor. The fat bastard had obviously tripped over after flying through the glass double doors at the end. Angus wasted no time in pulling his gun from inside his long trench coat and pointing it down the corridor at the troublesome, thieving little jerk. Without taking time to aim accurately, he fired a shot.

BANG!

The glass in the left-hand door shattered. The bullet had gone right through it and looked like it might have caught Sanchez in the shoulder, because the tubby bastard spun around just after climbing to his feet. If he had been hit, it couldn't have been much more than a graze, because he didn't stay around to chance a second shot. Angus saw him dart off to the corridor on the left that led to the bar. He immediately set off after him. No way he was he going to let the thieving dickwad get away from him again.

He raced down the corridor in pursuit. When he reached the doors at the end he leapt through the frame of the one that had been destroyed by his shot. His boots crunched down on a sprinkling of glass on the floor on the other side. Feeling several shards sink into his boot he readjusted his landing, bouncing into a kind of triple jump. Once he was sure he was clear of all the glass he glanced down at the heel of his right boot and saw a large shard of glass sticking out of it. Stopping momentarily, he reached down and pulled it out. Fortunately the heel was thick and the glass hadn't penetrated through to his foot. He tossed the shard of glass aside and watched it slide across the marble floor. It stopped just short of the front entrance, for some poor unfortunate to step on later.

The reception area was completely empty. Not a soul in sight. Although it seemed odd that there were no receptionists on duty, Angus took account of the fact that he'd warned them earlier about the army of zombies headed their way. He had also just fired a bullet into the reception area. Combined, those two factors probably had a good deal to do with the lack of people around the place. He glanced about wildly to find Sanchez. The fat fuck had gotten quite a head start on him now.

Catching Sanchez was his top priority. He needed to know where the bastard had stashed his twenty grand, and if that wasn't possible, then killing him would be a pretty good consolation prize. If he got his cash advance back, then he would have enough to pay back a decent chunk of the debts he owed. And maybe there was still a chance of claiming the fifty thousand dollars from Nigel Powell for killing Sanchez. But first he needed to catch him. Where the hell had he gone?

Charging off down the corridor towards the bar, Angus

was surprised to find that Sanchez was already out of sight. The corridor ran on for about fifty yards before opening up into a large hall area with the bar off to the right. He figured Sanchez must have made it to the end and headed for the bar.

When Angus reached the end of the corridor he once again found no one in sight. The hall was completely empty now that everyone had headed into the auditorium for the final. In the bar on the right all the tables and chairs were unoccupied. The only living thing that remained was a lone bartender wiping down the bartop, a blond-haired young man in his early twenties wearing the standard uniform of black pants, white shirt and red vest.

'Where the fuck'd he go?' Angus bellowed at him.

The bartender didn't answer, but tilted his head towards a door behind the bar. Angus nodded at him and ran over to the side of the bar where a section of the bartop was hinged to let staff come and go. He lifted the flap, letting it crash down onto the top, and ran through the gap in the bar. With rather more care he slowly pushed open the door at the back of the bar that led to the kitchen. He peered through it, wary of being ambushed by Sanchez. Had he known of the other man's legendary cowardice he wouldn't have bothered, but caution was something he'd learned very early on in his career as a hitman.

The kitchen was also empty. The staff had all gone, most likely to watch the show. They had left behind a godalmighty mess, though. Six-foot-high food trolleys were scattered around intermittently, and there were numerous worktops still covered in food, dirty plates and cutlery. But there was no sign of Sanchez.

Angus looked around the room for any other escape routes Sanchez might have taken. There was only one other exit from the kitchen, over on the far wall to Angus's left. It was a white door with a circular glass porthole set in it at eye level. Watching his step, he carefully but swiftly crept over to it, holding his pistol at the ready in case Sanchez showed his face. When he reached the door, he turned the handle only to find it was locked. That could mean one of two things. Either Sanchez had gone through it and locked the door from the other side. Which was unlikely.

It was far more probable that his quarry was still in the kitchen. Somewhere.

Forty-Five

Just a few hours earlier, Emily had felt quite comfortable about being in the final. Armed with the knowledge that the four other finalists had also been pre-selected, she felt less guilty about how she'd come to be there. She had got to know Johnny Cash, Kurt Cobain, Otis Redding and even James Brown reasonably well. But with the first three dead and the fourth, James Brown, most likely responsible for their murders, she had some new finalists to meet. Freddie Mercury and Janis Joplin had been friendly and welcoming, and she had hit it off with them both straight away. She was also fairly confident that she could beat them.

The two new finalists to whom she had not yet introduced herself were Elvis and the Blues Brother. Right now, Elvis was out on the stage, singing for all he was worth. Acutely aware that she needed to stay among people, in case she was targeted by the killer, Emily took the opportunity to introduce herself to the Blues Brother. She'd seen him making for the backstage area a minute or two earlier, so she headed back there to find him.

She found him alone, sitting in one of the well-upholstered chairs in the corner, eating some chicken wings from a paper plate on his lap. There was a coffee table in front of him and another comfortable chair on the other side of it. As the chair was empty, Emily wandered over to introduce herself, though she hesitated for a moment. He was still wearing his sunglasses, so it was hard to tell whether or not he welcomed her approach.

'Hi, I'm Emily,' she said, smiling and holding out a hand.

The Blues Brother had a mouthful of chicken and hurriedly swallowed the last few chunks. 'Hi, I'm Jacko,' he said pleasantly. 'I won't shake your hand, if that's okay. Got greasy fingers.'

'Sure,' said Emily, withdrawing her outstretched hand. 'Mind if I sit down?' She gestured to the chair opposite him.

'Sure.' Jacko placed his paper plate, now empty except for a few gnawed bones, down on the coffee table between them and picked up a napkin to wipe his hands.

Emily sat down. 'You nervous?'

Jacko shrugged. 'Not really. You?'

'A little.' She wished she could see his eyes. 'You did a great job earlier.'

'Thanks. You too. Been singin' a long time, I bet.'

'Yeah. Got the bug from watching my mom sing in clubs when I was a kid.'

Jacko half-smiled. 'You never lose the scent that fills your nostrils, that first time you watch someone great perform in a club, do ya? If they put you under their spell, you'll never get rid of the urge to do it yourself, to feel it in your lungs, that scent from the club, the one that reminds you of the performance, huh?'

'That's it exactly.'

'Yeah. I know. Shame people like Nigel Powell will never get that. He's just a suit, trying to recreate that scent and sell it. This show, it ain't got that scent. What they got here is a smell that came straight out of a can.'

'Yeah, I guess. But it'd be cool to win, though, wouldn't it?'

'You think?'

'Well, yeah. Don't you?'

'Hey, it's always nice to win. But it ain't the end of the world if you don't.'

Emily really couldn't figure this guy out. "Kay then, what about the money? The money'd be nice, right?'

Jacko finished wiping his hands and put the napkin back on the coffee table. 'That why you're here? The money?'

'Well, no. Not just the money.'

'Fame too, huh?' There was nothing aggressive about the way he spoke. He just somehow made it sound as though Emily's pursuit of fame and fortune was rather shallow.

'Don't get me wrong,' she said defensively. 'The recognition would be nice, but the money is important. It's for my mother. She's real sick, and the money would really help.'

Jacko smiled and nodded. 'Sure. Know what you mean. Family's important. Gotta take care of 'em, even if it means compromisin' your values, right?'

'How do you mean, compromising my values?' She could feel the beginnings of a blush warming her cheeks.

Jacko airily waved a hand around the space, somehow indicating the entire auditorium and everyone and everything in it. 'Is this really why you started singin'?' he asked. 'So you could win a talent show and make easy money?'

'You're kinda direct, aren't you?'

'I don't mean to offend. Just wonderin' if this is what you got into music for?'

'Well, it's either this or touring round the bars and clubs, earning just enough to get by, isn't it?'

Jacko took off his sunglasses. 'It's an honourable way to make a livin',' he said, smiling.

'Yes, it is. But it won't make you rich, will it?'

'So, it's just about the money, then?'

Emily shook her head and smiled. He was quite a tease, this Jacko fella. 'It does seem like it sometimes,' she admitted softly. 'But in all honesty I just love to perform in front of an audience. What's your excuse? Why are you singing?'

Jacko stared up at the ceiling. 'I lost my way. Forgot all about why I got into music in the first place. This here, this show, it's just a shortcut to money and adulation. Not exactly payin' your dues, is it?'

'So it's kinda like selling out, huh?' Emily said dryly.

'That's exactly what it's like.'

'So you'd rather be out working the club circuit?'

Jacko sighed. 'Yeah. I'd love to go back to the club circuit. Smoky bars, that's where the magic really happens. Performin' just so you can pay for your next meal, knowin' that if you suck, your audience'll let you know about it.' He pointed in the direction of the auditorium. 'That audience out there, they'd cheer a monkey with a banjo if it had a sob story. Playin' in clubs, now that's really livin'.'

He was right, and Emily knew it. 'I agree with you,' she said. 'Those were some of the happiest times of my life, working the club circuit. I'd love to go back to it one day and just sing my own stuff, you know? Not be impersonating someone else. That would be awesome. Maybe if I do well here, I'll get that opportunity. At the moment though, people want to hear me do Judy Garland.'

'So you're sellin' out.'

'We all are, aren't we?'

'Yes, we are. But you can only sell the family gold once.'

'How's that?'

'Once you sell out, there's no goin' back. You can't buy back your credibility if you never had it in the first place.'

'I paid my dues in the clubs,' Emily said defensively.

'Me too, but now look at us. Performin' as other people. It ain't how I saw my career pannin' out. I mean, look at me. I'm the ultimate loser. The Blues Brothers were little more than a tribute band themselves, and here I am impersonatin' a tribute act. That's about as low as it gets, ain't it?'

He sounded genuinely regretful about the way things had worked out for him. For the first time, Emily began to reflect on the fact that she'd passed up her dream of being a singer in her own right, to chase the dollar as a Judy Garland impersonator.

If she won this competition, that was how she'd always be known. If she made it big as a reality-show star, she'd never have credibility as anything else. She would always be known as the girl who sang like Judy Garland. But that was the price she would have to pay for the success she wanted. There was no sense in getting down about it.

'It's not all bad, Jacko,' she said, trying to sound optimistic. 'If you win, you can make all your dreams come true. You could go back to singing in the clubs and you wouldn't have to worry about money any more.'

Jacko slipped his sunglasses back on. 'Y'know, dreams do come true, Emily,' he said, standing up. 'But they don't come for free.' He smiled down at her and said, 'I gotta go freshen up, I'm on in a minute. Nice talkin' to you.'

Emily thought back to her earlier conversation with the Bourbon Kid. He'd talked about how the winner of this show would be selling his soul to the Devil. Now she understood what he meant. It was metaphorical, obviously.

Wasn't it?

Forty-Six

Elvis stood before the panel, eyeing the three judges in turn. He had just given his all-time best performance of 'You're The Devil In Disguise' and was waiting for their reaction. He was probably as anxious as he ever got. Which was not very.

The plan had been to underperform the song a little to give Julius a better chance of winning the show with his James Brown routine, but when it came to the crunch, *he'd thought, Fuck Julius*. Elvis didn't even know the guy. Why should he give a fuck just because the guy was supposedly the thirteenth Apostle and was going to rid the place of all the goddam flesh-eating zombies outside? Hell, the other finalists weren't going to make it easy for him, so why should the King? And besides, if the undead did swarm into the hotel, Elvis was one of those most likely to make it out in one piece. In his time he'd seen vampires, werewolves and now zombies and survived 'em all, baby. Still in one piece, and still cool.

Like the pro he was, Elvis had given his performance everything. The vocals had been spot on, the swivelling hips had sent the women in the audience crazy and the sneer – well, that was all his own. Candy was the first judge to pass comment. She leaned forward, squeezing her breasts together so tightly that there was almost a race on to see which would pop out first: Elvis's eyes, or her nipples.

'Elvis honey, I think I'm in love with you. That was just awesome. I gotta tell you, those dance moves got just about every woman in here goin' weak at the knees. Congratulations.

I reckon you've just put yourself in contention to win this competition!' The crowd cheered and stamped, the noise only fading as Lucinda began to pass judgement.

She was equally enthusiastic. 'You da man, Elvis. *You da man!*' she yelled, jigging her head from side to side and pointing randomly around the stage. Again the audience bayed their approval.

It was perhaps inevitable that the only negative comments should come from Nigel Powell, who was making a very good job of looking deeply underwhelmed. 'Well, it was *okay*,' he began, inducing jeers from the audience. 'Well, it *was*. Elvis impersonators are two-a-penny on the nightclub circuit. It was good, sure, but I don't think it was good enough to win the whole show. Truth is, you don't really deserve to be on this stage with the other finalists. Good luck, though.'

Elvis headed off to the side of the stage with his usual panache, waving at the audience and blowing kisses at any of the prettier women with whom he could make eye contact. When he made it offstage to the side area behind the curtain he was slightly surprised, if not disappointed, to see that Sanchez had disappeared. *Had the fat bastard even seen him sing? Or had he slunk off somewhere for an enchilada?*

He decided to hang around behind the giant red curtain to wait for Sanchez to return. Freddie Mercury was announced, and bounded onstage enthusiastically for his performance. Just then, the Judy Garland impersonator sidled up alongside Elvis and briefly touched his right arm to gain his attention.

'Hi, I'm Emily. I just wanted to say I thought you were great,' she said. 'Really strong vocals and your dance moves were so-o-o cool. Are they off the cuff? Or do you rehearse a lot?'

Elvis shrugged nonchalantly. 'All improvised,' he said.

'Well, you know who really thinks you're cool?' Emily said, tapping his arm again.

'Who?' On the whole, Elvis believed that everyone

thought he was cool. On the whole he was right, too.

'Janis Joplin,' she whispered.

'Huh?'

'I think she kinda likes you.'

'Yeah? Where is she?'

'Backstage. Why don't you go back and say hi?'

'You kiddin' me?'

Emily laughed. 'No, but she's kinda nervous about approaching you herself. Because, well, you know, she's got that problem.'

'What problem?'

'The Tourette's. She's not great at meeting new people. She even called me a – ' Emily blushed ' – an extremely unladylike word when I congratulated her on her performance.'

'Oh yeah. That. Actually, I kinda like a woman with a dirty mouth.' Behind them, they heard Freddie Mercury begin belting out an impressive rendition of the Queen song 'Who Wants To Live Forever?'

'Cool,' said Emily. 'Why don't I introduce you?'

'Sure thing. Bring her up here.'

Emily disappeared backstage and left Elvis alone to watch the guy impersonating the late lead singer of Queen. By the time he had finished his performance and was standing before the judges, Emily had returned with a rather nervous-looking Janis Joplin. Elvis liked the look of Janis. She was kinda kooky and despite seeming rather timid, he knew that once she opened her mouth she was liable to start spouting all kinds of filth. *Just his kind of chick.*

'Hi again, Elvis,' said Emily smiling. 'What's your real name, by the way?'

'Elvis.'

'Wow. That's sort of handy, isn't it?'

'Guess so.' There was no doubt: the man oozed nonchalant cool.

'Well. I'd like to introduce you to my friend, Janis Joplin.'

Elvis could see that Janis was extremely nervous about meeting him. But being as confident with women as he was in everything else, he reached out and took hold of her left hand. He lifted it to his mouth and gently kissed the back of it.

'Pleased ta meetcha, Janis. What's your real name?'

'CUNT!' yelled Janis.

Elvis frowned. 'That's kinda misfortunate. What were your folks thinkin' when they came up with that?'

'No no, sorry,' Janis stammered. 'My real name is Janis. I didn't mean the . . . the – that. It's just a nervous reaction I have.'

'Well, I'm mighty pleased to meetcha,' said Elvis, looking her right in the eye.

'Pleased to meet ya too, SHITHEAD!'

Emily intervened in the blossoming courtship. 'Ssshhh,' she whispered. 'The judging panel's giving Freddie Mercury his comments.'

All three judges gave Freddie the thumbs up, Powell even going so far as to tell him he'd been the best performer so far.

'Wow,' said Emily thoughtfully. 'They really liked him, didn't they?'

Elvis looked at her. It occurred to him that she was a sweet, innocent and extremely pleasant young woman. Not his type, of course – Janis Joplin and her foul mouth were more his kind of thing – but he couldn't help feeling glad that Emily had made it to the final and had not been assassinated by Gabriel. Not yet, anyway.

'Y'know somethin', Emily?' he said. 'You're all right.'

'Thanks,' she said, flustered by his sudden compliment.

'WHORE!' yelled Janis, immediately following it with a quiet 'Sorry.'

Elvis smirked. Janis was a real laugh. *Definitely his kind of girl.* He continued to look at Emily for a few seconds, however, because he didn't want Janis to see that he was finding her affliction amusing. Once more he turned on the charm. 'Well, Emily, much as me an' Janis here were both excellent, an' ol' Freddie Mercury seems to've done okay, I still reckon you'll walk away with it. If you're as good as everyone says, then you'll clean up.'

Emily smiled her appreciation, then rubbed her forehead. 'Thanks. I've a splitting headache, though.'

Janis reached out and touched the other girl's forehead. 'Shit! You've got a fuckin' big lump there. What happened?' she asked.

'If you must know, I had my head smashed repeatedly on the floor of my hotel room by a guy who tried to kill me.'

Elvis felt a cold shiver run down his spine. *So Gabriel had tried to off her?*

'How'd it happen?' he asked.

'This big shaven-headed biker guy tried to kill me, but before he could finish the job another guy came to my rescue and shot him dead. To be honest, I'm still kind of dazed about it all, and not just from having my head beaten against the floor.'

'Oh.' Elvis's deeply non-committal response concealed his confusion at this latest turn of events. So Gabriel was dead and Sanchez was missing. Elvis had some thinking to do. What was going on? And as he rubbed his hand on Janis Joplin's ass, another question struck him. *Was ol' Janis wearin' any panties?*

As Elvis was pondering the answers to all of these important questions, Freddie Mercury bounded off the stage and came over to join them. There was a broad smile across his face, as he was unable to hide the excitement he wanted to share with them.

'Wow, did ya hear that?' he asked them. 'They said I was the best so far!'

'Good for you. Congratulations,' said Emily.

'FUCKBAG!' yelled Janis.

'She thinks you're good, too,' Elvis said in Janis's defence.

'Thanks.' said Freddie. 'Who's up next, anyway?'

Elvis looked around. 'S'posed to be that Blues Brother guy. Can't see him nowhere, though.

He looked thoughtfully at Emily for a moment, before adding softly, 'Maybe he's gone missin', too?'

Forty-Seven

Invincible Angus's eyes scoured the kitchen. The place was a mess, as though it had been abandoned by staff caught out by a fire drill. Metal tables on castors were scattered around, kitchen utensils littering the work surfaces. Remains of food, sauces and flour covered everything. There were tall steel trolleys with trays on them scattered around too. And a smell like something had died in there permeated everything, although it was more likely to be rotten meat.

The state of the kitchen was unimportant, however. Foremost in Angus's thoughts was finding out where that weasel Sanchez was hiding. All he needed to do was stand still for a moment, look around and listen. With any luck, an answer to the question of Sanchez's whereabouts would soon present itself.

And it did.

In the near corner thirty feet or so in front of him, Angus could see a large metal door that looked as though it led into a walk-in fridge or freezer. He'd ignored it on his first scout around the room, assuming that Sanchez wouldn't be stupid enough to hide in such an obvious dead end. But as he thought back to how the fat little bastard had knocked himself out when trying to fire a handgun earlier in the day, it made perfect sense. Sanchez was a buffoon, and undoubtedly dumb enough to hide in a room with only one way in or out.

It was then that Angus noticed the clinching evidence. On the floor outside the metal door was a small pool of blood.

Closer inspection showed that a trail of it led from the door through which he had entered from the bar. He must have winged Sanchez with the bullet he'd fired through the glass door into the lobby. The trail led all the way from the bar door to the pool outside the metal door, where it came to an abrupt end.

Shame it's so easy, he thought with a grin.

Soft-footed, Angus followed the trail of blood, doing his best not to be heard. He stopped outside the door and leaned up against it with his ear pressed to the cold metal. There was no sound from within. He reached over to the large metal handle and slowly pulled at it. It was spring-loaded and flicked up in his hand, permitting the door to open slightly. He became even more cautious, for there was a possibility that Sanchez might now be armed. Very slowly, while standing back out of harm's way, he grabbed the handle and pulled the door open.

No one charged out. He cocked his head, listening. Still nothing. He carefully stepped round the open door and stood just inside the entrance, pointing his gun into what was clearly, from its temperature, a walk-in freezer.

There was a light mist inside the cold store that made it difficult to see clearly, but he could make out three ceiling-high racks of shelves containing boxes and bags full of food and separated by aisles. Condensation was running down the walls and the whole place had an uncomfortably damp, clinging feel to it. There were also a few pig carcasses hanging from the ceiling. No sign of Sanchez, though. Angus took a look along the floor and saw that the trail of blood continued. It led round to the aisle on the far left. That was to be expected, as it was the part of the freezer farthest from the door.

He walked slowly over to the left-hand rack and peered around it. There was a long row of headless pig carcasses hanging from the ceiling. The trail of blood on the floor continued past them. It occurred to Angus that there was something a little odd about this trail of blood. It didn't look like it had dripped to the floor from someone running or walking. It was smeared across the floor in an unbroken line, as if Sanchez had been crawling along the floor on his stomach. Angus stepped carefully round the first butchered pig, his finger taking up first pressure on the trigger of his gun. The smell in this particular part of the freezer was especially repugnant. Rotten meat that had no doubt been kept for too long, although it had to be pretty bad to overcome the effect of freezing. Either that, or Sanchez was in there and had shit his pants.

The aisle was no more than twenty feet long. Sanchez didn't seem to be anywhere in sight. Still checking all round him for a potential ambush, Angus followed the trail of blood until it came to a sudden stop a few feet from the end of the aisle. He stopped and looked around. For the trail to have ended, Sanchez must have climbed. The shelves on either side of the aisle were stacked high with boxes. Against the wall in the far corner, jutting out from behind the last box on the bottom shelf, was exactly what Angus was looking for. A pair of highly polished slip-on shoes poked out. As he crept closer he realized that the owner's feet were still in the shoes.

He stepped around the last pig carcass and jumped out in front of the shoes, his gun aimed and ready to fire. What he was faced with was not at all what he had been expecting. He lowered his pistol, frowning, completely nonplussed by what he saw. The owner of the shoes was a man, but this guy was already dead. And half-frozen, too. It wasn't Sanchez. So who the fuck was it? There was frozen blood all over the man's face and neck. The blood stopped when it reached a red and black neckerchief below his chin. Angus reached inside the man's grey suit jacket and found a driver's licence. He pulled it out and peered closely at it through the cold mist. The photo of the owner matched the bloody, messed-up face of the corpse.

'Just who the fuck is Jonah Clementine?' Angus whispered aloud.

He had barely finished asking himself the question when the freezer door slammed shut behind him.

Shit! Sanchez!

Sanchez had been cowering for his life beneath one of the wheeled metal tables in the kitchen. He had found one that had a white tablecloth overhanging all four sides almost to the floor, and had crept underneath it. To his relief the cloth covered everything, bar his feet. Even they would only be seen if someone were to lean down to take a closer look.

It had come as an almighty relief to him when Angus finally succumbed to his hunch and followed the streaks of blood on the floor into the walk-in freezer. For a few terrifying moments Sanchez had been unsure what the vengeful hitman was going to do. He was not a clever man, and had certainly never been described as cunning. Sneaky, yes. Devious and untruthful, certainly. Weaselly, most definitely. But cunning? Hell, no.

He had seen the trail of blood and had gambled on Angus following it into the freezer. Finally, one of his gambles had paid off. When his life was on the line, Sanchez's ability to weasel out of just about anything took on levels of genius reserved only for the likes of Einstein. Naturally, his moments of genius were usually followed by an overwhelming sense of smugness and a powerful desire to gloat, which, as history had proved on many occasions before, were virtually always followed by some sort of comeuppance. It was a lesson he had signally failed to learn over the years.

Crawling out from his hiding place, he tiptoed over to the freezer door and slammed it shut. During his long and undistinguished career on the fringes of the catering industry, Sanchez had often come across this type of walk-in freezer, and he knew that, for some reason, they could never be opened from the inside. Quite why, he had no idea. Maybe it was in case the food came to life at night and tried to escape?

Who knew? Either way, it was something for which he was profoundly grateful. From behind the door he heard Angus's voice utter a single word.

'*Fuck!*'

Sanchez shouted triumphantly back through the metal door. 'Have an *ice* time in there, loser!'

At once the muted voice of the trapped killer yelled back, 'You're fuckin' dead, dirtbag!'

'Hey man, *chill out!*' Unable to rein back on either his gloating or his lame jokes, Sanchez launched into a hip-swivelling dance normally reserved for the privacy of his own home. He incorporated some face-pulling at the freezer door into his dance moves, revelling in the fact that he'd outwitted a world-famous hitman. He couldn't help himself, his celebration reaching new heights of smugness and self-congratulation because he knew that Angus was on the other side of a locked steel door, and could do nothing about it.

BANG!

Sanchez saw a spark fly from the door handle and heard a small click. On the other side of the door, Angus was shooting at the lock.

Fuck!

The triumphalist dance came to an abrupt end. Sanchez wisely took to his heels and ran for his life.

Forty-Eight

Jacko was backstage, taking deep breaths in readiness for his imminent performance of 'Mustang Sally'. He was wearing the Bourbon Kid's dark sunglasses, the Frank Sinatra impersonator's hat, and a suit that had belonged to someone who was probably dead. He was alone in the backstage area now. Everyone else had moved off to better positions in order to watch the finalists perform. With the seconds ticking down before he was due onstage, the Bourbon Kid finally reappeared through a door at the back of the room.

'I was beginnin' to think you'd gone home,' said Jacko. The Kid walked up to him holding a smart black Fender guitar in his right hand.

'Here,' he grated, holding the instrument out. 'Use this.'

Jacko took the guitar in both hands. 'You're kiddin', right?'

'You can play this in the final.'

'But there ain't no need. They got a karaoke track for me to sing along to this time. I don't even need the harmonica.'

'You ain't singin' "Mustang Sally" this time.'

'Yeah I am.'

'Try it. See how long ya live.' The voice chipped at Jacko's nerves like gravel on new paint. He stood the guitar up on the floor and allowed the neck to rest against his left leg to keep it from falling over. Then he took the sunglasses off and looked the Kid in the eye. 'Like, I thought you wanted me to win this? I almost know half the words to "Mustang Sally".

Why'd I sing somethin' different now? Shit, man, I'm due on in about a minute!'

'I cancelled the karaoke track. You're gonna play a guitar solo this time.'

Jacko tucked the sunglasses away in the breast pocket of his black suit jacket and picked the guitar up to take a good look at it.

'This thing even tuned?' he whined.

'How the fuck would I know?'

Jacko grabbed the black strap on the guitar and lifted it over his head, allowing it to rest around his shoulders. Then he strummed a chord and began twiddling the machine heads on the headstock at the end of the neck.

'See? You're a goddam natural,' said the Kid, patting him on the shoulder.

Jacko groaned. 'This is, like, the worst plan ever, man.'

'Maybe. But if it works out you'll be signin' your name on that winner's contract later on.'

'You'd like that, wouldn't you?'

'Yeah.'

'What if I lose?'

'I'll kill you.'

'Right. No pressure, then?'

'Put the shades on. You're due on in a minute.'

Jacko pulled the sunglasses back out of his jacket pocket and slipped them on.

'So, what am I gonna sing now? I already told the organizers I was doin' "Mustang Sally" again.'

The Kid reached inside his jacket as if to pull out a gun. Only this time he drew out a CD. *The Blues Brothers Greatest Hits*. He held it up in front of Jacko's face and pointed to the track listing on the back of the case.

'Track three.'

Jacko ran his eyes down the listing, stopped at track number three, and slowly read what it said. Then he peered over his dark glasses at the Kid.

'*You sonofabitch*.'

'Yeah.'

Forty-Nine

Emily was itching to get out onstage and perform. Jacko was due up next, then her, and last of all would be James Brown for the finish. She felt confident that she could outperform the three singers who had already been up. Janis Joplin had been an out-and-out disaster. Elvis and Freddie Mercury had both been impressive, but if she was on form she was sure she would beat them. James Brown would no doubt be a danger to her chances of winning, though not necessarily because of his singing. The Godfather of Soul was super-bad and liable to pull a weapon on her. Not the kind of guy she wanted to bump into in a dark corridor. The unknown quantity was the Blues Brother, Jacko, now only seconds away from performing. In fact, Nina Forina was standing centre stage, ready to announce him.

'Ladies and gentlemen,' her voice echoed out round the auditorium once more. 'Please put your hands together for our fourth performer in the final. Singing "Mustang Sally", it's . . . *the Blues Brother!*'

The crowd afforded Jacko a very substantial round of applause, and even a few wolf whistles. His earlier performance with the harmonica had been extremely well received, particularly because he had managed to get some audience participation going. So when he walked onstage with a black guitar hanging from a strap around his shoulders, the applause doubled in volume and the whistles were drowned out by cheers and foot-stamping. Watching Jacko while a technician hooked his guitar up to an amp, Emily guessed that if he had felt under pressure before, then it must be ten times worse now. Even if he had told her earlier that he wasn't nervous, surely he had to be? Everyone was before a big performance, and this one was a potential career-changer.

The sound of applause eventually died away, to be followed by – silence. The expected backing track never arrived. The speakers all around the auditorium remained dead.

Jacko stepped up to the microphone in the spotlight at centre stage and spoke softly into it. 'Uh – like, at the last minute I've kinda decided to do a different song.' He cleared his throat as a low muttering began to rise from the crowd in front of him. 'I'm goin' without a backin' track too, but' – he looked down at the orchestra pit below him – 'if anyone in the band wants to join in as the song goes on, then be my guest.'

Emily's mouth fell open. Had he lost his mind? The crowd seemed to echo her thoughts. The muttering in the audience grew louder, and in the orchestra pit in front of the stage the musicians looked quizzically at each other, readying themselves to play in case a chance to join in should arise.

And then Jacko began to play his guitar.

He looked nervous, and was clearly deep in concentration as he plucked slowly at the strings. And what the hell was he playing?

Emily found herself joined by the other surviving finalists, each as curious as she was. It made fascinating viewing. Was this guy, this Blues Brother, throwing away his chances of winning? Or was this an exceptionally cunning ploy to win over the audience, and maybe the judges too?

After playing a few fairly decent chords to the stunned audience before him, Jacko launched into the first lines of the song.

'Come on
Yo people, we're all gonna go . . . '

Emily recognized the tune, although she found herself,

and not for the first time during the show, unconvinced that the lyrics were correct. She'd heard the tune played many times in various bars, usually by Blues Brothers tribute bands. It was 'Sweet Home Chicago'. Jacko confirmed it for her as he hit the end of the first verse.

'Back to that dirty old place
They call Chicago . . . '

Whatever else Jacko may have lacked, it wasn't nerve. He carried on playing away on his guitar and singing reasonably competently. He wasn't generating the same level of enthusiasm from the audience as he had with his earlier performance of 'Mustang Sally', however. But this crowd liked him, if only for his eccentricity; they weren't going to boo him unless he did something really stupid.

Freddie Mercury seemed to speak for everyone when he whispered loudly, 'What the fuck's he doin'?'

'That's "Sweet Home Chicago",' said Emily.

'Shit, I know that, but it's just him an' a guitar. What was he thinkin'? Guy's blown it.'

Emily looked around at the other finalists, wondering what they thought. They were all there except for James Brown. He'd disappeared off somewhere again, thank God, and was still missing. Elvis and Janis were still there, although they weren't really paying too much attention. They seemed more wrapped up in each other than in anything that was happening onstage. Elvis was whispering something in Janis's ear and she was looking back at him and frowning, as though she couldn't hear what he was saying. Eventually he sighed, drew a breath and shouted out loud: 'I said, d'ya wanna go somewhere for a fuck!' Emily watched Janis nod her head frantically, beaming a wide smile back at the King. Then the two of them swiftly disappeared in the direction of the backstage area. Emily chuckled to herself before turning back to watch Jacko committing 'competition suicide' onstage.

He was about a minute into his act when something

unexpected happened. From the orchestra pit below, the drummer began to add a little backing beat, tapping on the snare drum. It served as a catalyst for the other orchestra members to pluck up the nerve to join in. After the disappointment of learning that they would only be playing for two of the finalists, Jacko's invitation for them to play along had lifted their spirits. The pianist began tickling the ivories on his grand piano, then one of the saxes joined in, followed by the other guitarist, Pablo, and even a couple of the violinists. Gradually the sound came together and swelled, echoing Jacko's guitar and harmonizing with his singing. Within seconds, the entire orchestra was playing along with considerable verve.

The introduction of the orchestra suddenly brought the crowd to life and they were once more back on their feet, clapping and swaying to the music. Emily looked on in wonder as Jacko's confidence grew. He started to strum away vigorously on his guitar, his hips began to swivel and his voice became stronger and more self-assured. As the song slid into its long musical solo he began to act as conductor for the orchestra below, nodding at whomever he wanted to take on the meat of the tune. One minute it was the saxophones and trumpets, then the pianist, then back to Jacko, now wailing away on the stolen Fender.

And the audience loved it.

Emily found herself tapping her feet to the music. She too was enjoying herself. The thought crossed her mind that Jacko might actually be one heck of a tough act to follow, but she sternly reminded herself that she could only do her best and hope that it would be enough.

As the Blues Brother's and the orchestra's performance began to reach a crescendo that no doubt signalled the song's climax, Emily felt someone grab her right arm. Startled, she turned round to see the Bourbon Kid, who had a tight grip on her.

'Wanna word with ya,' he said baldly.

'Uh, sure.'

He nodded at Freddie Mercury. 'In private.'

The Kid had most probably saved her life earlier, so it was only fair that she should indulge him with a minute of her time. Maintaining his grip on her arm, he led her down the steps and through the door into the corridor behind the stage. Then he led her a few feet along the corridor, out of the sight and hearing of anyone in the backstage area.

'What is it?' she asked.

'Listen, if you figure you're gonna win, can't you just hit a bum note, or somethin'? Know that you coulda won, but choose not to?' His voice was as gravelly as ever, but now it carried a note of urgency.

Emily shook her head. 'We've already been through this. I'm sorry. I need the money. And I also need to know that I'm good enough to win this. I told you before, this isn't just for me. My mother's sick. I need the prize money.'

'Okay, then how 'bout this? If you win, you just don't sign the contract. They'll give it to someone else. I'll kill whoever that is an' get you the money that way.'

Emily shivered. 'I'm sorry. No. I want to know that I'm good enough to win this, and I don't want anyone else to die in order for me to get the money. In fact, I don't want anyone else to die, whatever the reason. There's been too much killing already. And besides, I wouldn't accept a prize I hadn't won, nor money stolen from someone who'd been . . . who'd been— '

The Kid squeezed her arm a little tighter. 'I got one bullet left in my gun. Don't make me use it on you. I wouldn't wanna do that.'

'Then don't.'

'I'll let you sing. But I can't let you win.'

Emily stepped back away from him, shrugging her arm free of his hand. 'Well, that's up to you,' she said. She remembered everything she'd talked about with Jacko and knew she had to do this. Then she turned her back on the Kid and headed back to the stage to prepare for her final performance of 'Over The Rainbow'.

As she walked away, she wondered if the Kid's last bullet was about to slam into her back.

Fifty

Sanchez was breathing pretty heavily as he made his way to the stage area to find Elvis. His escape from Invincible Angus had taken its toll. His lungs weren't used to the effort required for running, and his legs felt like jelly. Normally he would have had to sit down and take a breather after expending so much energy. On this occasion, though, fear-fuelled adrenalin kept him on his feet. The knowledge that the hitman might already have shot his way out of the freezer kept his heart pounding and his feet moving.

Ahead of him, as he hurried down the corridor that led to the entrance at the back of the stage, he saw the Judy Garland impersonator engaged in what looked like a heated conversation with a shady-looking fella in a hooded leather jacket. Their argument came to an end when Emily turned away and walked back towards the stage area, and the man stormed off past Sanchez towards the lobby. The guy looked familiar, but Sanchez didn't have time to dwell on whether he knew him or not. He was so out of breath he was practically seeing double. And he had more important things to worry about than checking out some other creep in a hotel stiff with them. He turned left through the doorway to the stage area and saw Emily climbing the steps up to the side of the stage.

'Is the final over yet?' he asked breathlessly as he caught up with her.

Surprised, she turned and smiled at him. 'Oh, hi. No, not quite. The Blues Brother has just finished and I'm up next.'

'Great. How'd ol' Elvis do?'

'He did good. I reckon he's in with a chance.'

'Cool. What about the others? How'd they all do?'

'Yeah, everyone did okay.' After her run-in with the Bourbon Kid, she didn't have the energy to explain about Janis Joplin.

What Sanchez really wanted to know was how Julius had got on in the contest. Was the thirteenth Apostle going to win and save the day? Or what?

'An' James Brown? How'd he do?'

'He hasn't been up yet. Powell changed the order of the show at the last minute, so he's going up last now.'

'Yeah? Why the change?'

'I've really no idea. But it means I'm on a bit sooner, which is fine with me. I'm getting pretty nervous.'

Dimly, Sanchez realized that he needed to find something encouraging to say. The girl was okay, so he tried to stifle his usual negative attitude and find something to say that would reassure her.

'Well, best of luck when you're up there,' he piped, offering a sickly smile. 'Just make sure you beat that smug asshole Freddie Mercury.'

Emily prodded Sanchez in the arm and nodded her head towards the curtain by the side of the stage. Freddie Mercury was standing there, just within earshot. It looked like he hadn't heard what Sanchez had said because he smiled at them both as they approached him.

'Hey, Emily, c'mon,' Freddie said. 'We was beginning to think you were goin' to miss the final. You're up in a minute, girl.'

'Shush,' said Emily, pointing at the stage.

Freddie Mercury turned and looked where Emily was pointing. Sanchez peered round him. On the stage, Jacko was standing before the judges. Lucinda gave her opinion of his performance first.

'Well, well, well,' she said. 'Man, that was somethin' *else*! I ain't seen nothin' like that *in years!* Boy, *you a star!*' From behind her, the crowd vociferously endorsed her approval. Then Candy passed judgement. 'Well now, Mr Blues Brother, that was brilliant. Just *brilliant*. I wasn't sure where you were going with it to start with, but in the end you gave what was without doubt my favourite performance of the evening. Congratulations!'

Finally, from his seat in between the two female judges, Nigel Powell offered his all-important opinion.

'Let me just say,' he began dismissively, 'that first up, I don't approve of your changing the song at the last minute.' The audience immediately began booing and Powell quickly gestured with his hands for them to quiet down. 'No, wait. Seriously,' he went on, 'it isn't fair on the other contestants when you play fast-and-loose like that. And I don't remember you asking anyone's permission to play your guitar in the final.' The booing from the auditorium became louder and more aggressive. Powell remained unflustered by it. 'But,' he said, raising his voice above the din, 'I've got to admit – you were excellent.' The boos changed to cheers and whistles in an instant. Up on the giant screen Powell looked like he had more to add, but he quickly thought better of it and waved Jacko off the stage.

The young singer departed to a standing ovation far greater than that accorded to any of the previous contestants. He reached the side of the stage and ducked behind the red curtain, to be greeted by Emily and Freddie Mercury. Emily gave him an enthusiastic hug and a kiss on the cheek.

'Wow! I only hope I can do half as well as that,' she said generously. 'You were awesome. Really you were. Well done.'

Sanchez watched from a few feet away, wondering what this would mean for the competition. Even Freddie Mercury was looking seriously troubled by the reception the Blues Brother had been accorded. Julius was going to have to do exceptionally well if he was going to beat the rest, and Judy Garland, the favourite, hadn't even been up yet. And where in the hell was Elvis?

The answer was not long in coming. 'Yo, Sanchez, you're back,' Elvis's voice called out from behind him. Sanchez turned and saw his friend walking towards him with his arm around Janis Joplin's waist. Her hair was a mess and her clothing somewhat disarranged. They had clearly, and recently, just engaged in frantic sex.

'Yo, Elvis,' Sanchez whispered back, anxious not to draw too much attention to himself. 'That Invisible Angus guy? He's back.'

Elvis took his arm from Janis's waist. 'Where ya been, man?' he asked, walking over with a frown on his face.

'The guy just chased me all round the fuckin' hotel. I locked him in some kinda goddam freezer, but when I left he was tryin' to shoot his way out of it.'

'Good. Let him. He comes anywhere near me again an' I'll kick his fuckin' ass.' He rubbed the back of his head where Angus had cold-cocked him earlier 'Sonofabitch has got it coming.'

'He's got a gun,' Sanchez pointed out. 'Mebbe two.'

'I don't fuckin' care. Fuck him. And the horse he rode in on.'

Janis Joplin stepped forward and joined them. 'Yeah, fuck him. Fuckin' muthafuckin' asshole bastard.'

Sanchez smiled politely at Janis. 'Ya kinda have trouble controllin' that, don'cha?'

'That ain't the Tourette's,' said Janis. 'If Elvis don't like the guy, I don't fuckin' like him either. Muthafucker.'

Their conversation was interrupted by the voice of Nina Forina announcing Emily. 'Ladies and gentlemen!' she boomed. 'Singing the classic song "Over The Rainbow", h-e-e-e-e-ere's Judy Garland!'

There was another massive round of applause and cheers

from the crowd. Sanchez watched Emily take a deep breath. Then she bounded on to the stage.

Show time.

Fifty-One

Julius felt uneasy. Rigging the *Back From The Dead* show so that he won had been a lot harder than it should have been. First, Angus hadn't showed up on time. Then the Bourbon Kid had taken on the job, but, after a bright start, had refused to kill the Judy Garland impersonator. For personal reasons. What were the chances of that? And then Gabriel had turned up to save the day.

That hadn't worked out either. Emily was still alive and Gabriel was nowhere to be seen. Julius had a horrible feeling that the Bourbon Kid had carried out his thinly veiled threat to protect Emily. In which case, it was entirely probable that Gabriel was dead. And if that were the case, Julius reflected, there was a distinct possibility that his plans had been compromised.

The schedule for the final had initially earmarked him to perform fourth out of the six, but word had filtered through backstage that he was now due on last. No explanation had been given for this. As soon as he'd heard the news, delivered to him by some junior nobody from the show's production team, he became paranoid that his plot might have been discovered. When, seconds later, he overheard two burly security guards asking the Blues Brother whether he'd seen 'that scumbag James Brown anywhere' he decided to make a hasty exit from the backstage area. His plan had been compromised, he was certain of it.

So, in the interests of keeping his plan (and himself) alive,

Julius had headed down to the casino in the lower floor of the hotel shortly after Janis Joplin had performed. His intention was to hang out down there until the last possible minute before his performance. He hadn't told a soul where he was going, and he hoped to God that he could avoid being spotted by any CCTV cameras. That wouldn't be easy for someone walking around in a purple suit with wide-flared pants. To give himself a slightly better chance of going unrecognized, he took his black wig off and tucked it inside his shirtfront. Tufts of it poked out, giving the impression that he had the world's hairiest chest.

Once inside the casino, he looked for the busiest area where he could go and mingle with the crowd. One roulette table stood out from the rest. There was a bunch of people gathered around it, making a lot of noise. He headed over to it and wormed his way into the middle of the crowd.

'What's goin' on here?' he asked a small Chinese woman sporting a black eye.

'Mystic Lady. She win thousands of dollars!' the woman replied.

'*Mystic Lady?*'

'Yes yes. Mystic Lady.' The Chinese woman nodded vigorously and pointed at an elderly, grey-haired woman seated at the roulette table. She appeared to be the only person playing, but she had a mountain of chips in front of her, and everyone's eyes were on her. 'She see future. Make big wager. Win *huge!*'

Julius threaded his way through the crowd until he was just behind the Mystic Lady person. She had placed a stack of yellow chips on red. The crowd fell silent as the rather depressed-looking croupier spun the wheel. Once it had completed its first full revolution he took a deep breath, nodded at the Mystic Lady and then with a deft flick of his hand, cast the small white ball into the wheel, against the direction of rotation. Julius leaned over her shoulder to watch the outcome. Everyone seemed to be holding their breath, so that all that could be heard was the rattling of the ball as it ran round the wheel. Eventually the wheel began to slow and the ball dropped down to nestle in one of the numbered pockets. When the wheel had slowed sufficiently, there were gasps from the watching audience, followed by cheers as the croupier called out wearily, 'Red, number twelve!' The ball had settled in the number twelve pocket, which just happened to be red, exactly as the Mystic Lady had predicted.

While the croupier was counting out yet more chips to add to her pile, the old woman turned around on her stool and looked directly at Julius. She stared hard at him for a few seconds. He wasn't sure what her reasons were for staring, but he decided to break the silence.

'Congratulations,' he said, intending to comment politely on her good fortune

'Julius?'

It shocked him that she should know his name because he didn't recall ever having met her before. Maybe she really did have mystical powers and could see the future, as the bruised Chinese woman had suggested.

'Yeah. How d'ya know my name?' he asked.

'*They're coming for you.*'

'What? Who?'

'Them.' The Mystic Lady nodded at the casino entrance behind Julius. He turned and looked. Four burly men in black suits had come down the stairs from the hotel and were looking around the casino. It was obvious they were members of the security team. They must have seen him on CCTV. He needed to get out before they spotted him in the crowd. He looked back at the Mystic Lady to see if she knew what else was coming his way.

'What do I do?' he asked.

'You're a James Brown impersonator.'

'No! Not, what do I *do*. I mean how do I get outta

here?'

'Stairs, elevator. Your choice. And now, if you don't mind,' she added primly, 'I've a roulette wheel to play.' With that, she swivelled on her stool until she was facing the table again.

Julius looked around for an exit. The Mystic Lady was right. *Stairs or elevator*. The four security men were standing just inside the casino's entrance, itself just a few yards from the foot of the stairs, which ruled that option out. It would have to be the elevator, over on the far wall. He hadn't been spotted yet, so he began edging his way over to it, trying to keep the people crowding round the roulette table between him and the entrance.

The nearer he got to the elevator, the thinner the crowd and the greater the chance that he'd be seen and recognized. In the end he had to make a break for it, but without drawing attention to himself by *looking* as though he was making a break for it. So he settled for walking at a brisk pace in mincing steps, which probably looked ridiculous, although that was the least of his concerns. When he reached the metal doors, he pressed the button on the wall to call the elevator. He didn't dare look back to see whether he'd been spotted by the security guards.

The elevator seemed to take an eternity to arrive. He kept pressing the button, muttering 'C'mon, c'mon!' under his breath. He could hear the machinery churning away behind the wall. It sounded worn out, but eventually the grinding noise came to an end. An extremely loud pinging sound followed, and the metallic-silver doors slid slowly open. Julius darted inside and reached for the keypad on the wall. He pressed the first button that his fingers reached, which was for the tenth floor. Then he stood as close as possible to the side wall to avoid being seen by the four heavies from security.

After what seemed like another eternity, the doors began to close slowly. He felt growing relief with every inch that it moved. He was going to make it. But when the doors were just an inch or two away from meeting the frame, a hand appeared in the gap. A large hand with coarse black hairs covering the back of it. He was doomed. The doors reopened and a large, crop-headed white man wearing a black suit stepped into the elevator.

'Julius, I assume?' he said.

Julius didn't respond. Three other security guards stepped into the elevator with him. The first guy reached over to the keypad and pressed the button for the ground floor. Then he looked down at Julius and smiled.

'I sure hope you got your bucket and spade with you, pal. We're takin' you on a trip out to the desert. Kinda sandy there.'

As the doors slid shut behind the four men, Julius's heart sank. The guy who had pressed the button for the ground floor put an arm around his shoulder and gripped him tightly, pulling him into the middle of the elevator.

'Why so down, buddy?' he asked. His three companions sniggered. Julius contemplated his fate. How in hell, he wondered, was he going to get out of this mess?

The elevator moved smoothly up to the ground floor, issuing its obligatory pinging noise as it reached its destination. The doors slid open and Julius saw a man standing in the corridor right outside. He was facing the elevator with his head bowed. His clothing was dark and he had a hood pulled up over his head, concealing his face. Even so, Julius had no difficulty in recognizing him.

One of the security guards stepped out of the elevator and into a world of trouble. The Bourbon Kid grabbed him and in an instant spun him round and drove his right arm up behind his back. A loud crack followed. Before the guard could make a noise, the Kid spun him back and smashed the heel of his free hand into his captive's forehead, jolting his neck back sharply.

Another, much louder, crack followed.

The Kid dropped the man's body to the floor. Then he looked up at the three other guards in the elevator carriage. All their swagger and bravado had evaporated.

'Anyone else gettin' off on this floor?' he asked in his usual unpleasant, grating tone.

Julius watched all three of his captors step back and hold their hands up in surrender. One of them reached forward and began tapping on the buttons to make the doors close. *Pussies.*

So the Bourbon Kid was watching his back after all, Julius thought. He stepped out of the elevator and turned back to face the three surviving security guards.

'Thanks,' he said, smiling. 'That was fun. We should do it again some time.' The doors closed and the elevator resumed its ascent. Julius turned back to the Bourbon Kid.

'I knew you wouldn't let me down. God will reward you for this. You just went halfway to being absolved of your sins.'

The Kid lowered the hood on his jacket, reached out his left hand and grabbed Julius's face, squeezing his cheeks hard. 'I ain't on your side, fuckwad.'

'Maybe you are and you just don't know it.'

'Nope. Pretty dam' sure I ain't.'

'But secretly you wish you were?'

The Kid squeezed Julius's face even harder, then raised his arm and lifted him off his feet, hauling him away from the elevator doors. The two of them were now in the middle of the corridor, looking at each other eye to eye, although Julius's feet were about six inches off the ground.

'Listen, fuckwit,' said the Kid. 'I wanna know the exact truth 'bout you and why you wanna win this contest so bad. I've seen the zombie muthafuckers that used to be singers hoverin' around outside, an' I reckon you know what that's all about. Where do you fit in? An' can you *really* beat Judy Garland?'

'Okay . . . ' Julius began. Before he could continue, the Kid raised the index finger on his right hand to silence him.

'One more thing,' he said in his gravelly voice. 'You say one word I don't think is one hundred per cent true, I'll break your goddam neck. You think about that 'fore you say anythin'. *One word.*'

Julius swallowed hard. He was just about to open his mouth to speak when the elevator made its pinging noise again. He glanced to his left and saw the metal doors opening once more. The three security guards had come straight back down and were about to exit the carriage. Their faces revealed identical looks of shock at the sight of Julius and the Kid still present in the corridor, with the corpse of the fourth guard at their feet. The Kid turned his head slowly to look at them. There was an awkward moment as the three of them stared back, realizing they had come back down a touch too hastily. The one nearest the keypad promptly pressed one of the buttons and the doors slowly closed again.

The Kid turned back to Julius and pulled his face in close. 'You wanna be in that final, start talkin'.'

Fifty-Two

Nigel Powell was finally starting to enjoy himself. Emily's performance of 'Over The Rainbow' was even better than the one she had given in the auditions. With the orchestra behind her she excelled, growing in confidence with every word she sang.

There wasn't an empty seat in the auditorium. No one slipped out to the washrooms. No one sneaked off to the bar for a late drink. No one ducked out for a snatched cigarette. The entire audience remained absolutely silent throughout the song, not wanting to miss – or, worse, spoil – a second of it. Unlike the boisterous performances of the other contestants, which had brought the mass of people to their feet, singing along and dancing in the aisles, this was something to be savoured. Awed, the crowd simply sat and enjoyed the beauty of Emily's voice. Her elegance and grace shone through in a contest which, in Powell's view, had been marred by a series of tasteless lapses. Janis Joplin's swearing, Elvis's gyrating, Jacko's song-and-dance nonsense, and Julius's attempts to have all the other finalists killed, among other things. At last the stage had been graced by someone who had no gimmicks and no angles, just talent.

When the last notes of Emily's song died away, the audience rose as one and applauded loudly. Cameras flashed, people cheered and whistled, the entire orchestra jumped to their feet crying '*Brava! Brava!*' Even the three members of the judging panel stood up, clapping wildly. To his left and right

Nigel saw tears shining on both of his colleagues' cheeks. If this girl didn't win, something was wrong.

As, old-fashionedly, Emily curtsied to the audience, Nigel felt a great wave of relief. This would, he hoped, be the last performance of the evening. Julius would by now have been escorted from the hotel by security, soon to be digging his own grave in the Devil's Graveyard. Happy times indeed.

When the applause finally died down, Emily stood shyly before the judges, who had sat down again, and waited for their assessment. Candy was the first to speak up. Wiping tears from her eyes, she half gulped, half sniffed out the words, finding her breath as best she could.

'Brilliant! Just *brilliant*! Best performance of the night,' she gushed tearfully.

Lucinda was equally flattering. 'A star is born! You were awesome, baby. You couldn'a done more. No one could, you ask me. Congratulations, honey – an' then some.'

And finally a deathly hush fell all around as Powell took his turn to speak. For once he got to his feet, looked directly at the anxious singer, and said smoothly, 'Emily. That, my dear, was just incredible. I don't know of anyone in the world who could have sung that better than you.' He paused, then added, 'And I include the late Miss Garland.'

At once the crowd started shouting out every kind of support. Initially, just one or two drunken fans yelled out their appreciation, but soon the whole audience was screaming like a crowd at a football game. Powell continued paying Emily compliments, but the huge noise drowned him out until he gave up and just waved her offstage with a gleaming smile and a kiss blown from his outstretched hand.

With a spring in her step, Emily left the stage. Nina Forina returned to her place in the spotlight and addressed the audience.

'Okay, everyone! Quiet please!' she shouted. She had to wait for another thirty seconds for the crowd eventually to quieten down enough for her to continue. 'It's time for our final contestant, the absolutely last finalist in the *Back From the Dead* show. Ladies and gentlemen, please put your hands together for the Godfather of Soul – *Ja-a-a-a-a-mes Brown*!'

Powell watched with interest as the James Brown fans in the audience began clapping and cheering. Would Julius show up? He thought not. He certainly hoped not.

Nina was looking around, expecting the last finalist to appear from the side of the stage. She looked both ways, and her face beginning to betray a feeling of mild concern. Powell waited for her to realize that Julius wasn't going to show. When, some seconds later, she duly did, she looked to him for a signal as to what she should do. Smiling in an especially self-satisfied way, he leaned forward to speak into his microphone. It was time to tell the audience to start voting for their favourite acts using the keypad on their seat. James Brown wasn't going to appear.

And then, just as he opened his mouth to speak, Julius bounded out on to the stage. He flashed his enormous smile at the judges and then walked over to join Nina.

Nigel Powell was inwardly fuming. How had this devious bastard managed to make it onstage? Security would be held accountable for this. Yet knowing that his face was visible on the giant screen, he had to watch on with a forced smile as Nina skipped back into the shadows and Julius stepped up to the mike.

'Heh! Is everybody ready to party one more time?' he yelled into the mike.

The audience roared back an emphatic 'YEAH!'

The show wasn't over yet.

Fifty-Three

Sanchez was more uptight, more on edge than any of the finalists. Only minutes earlier, he had locked a psychotic, ginger-haired, pony-tailed gunman in a walk-in freezer. And that psycho was liable to reappear at any moment, bent on exacting his revenge. There was, too, the small matter of the zombies in the desert now heading towards the hotel with the intention of eating everyone alive.

If he believed everything that he had been told, then his hopes of getting out alive rested entirely on the shoulders of Julius, a James Brown impersonator – and possible thirteenth Apostle. If Julius won the show, then – allegedly – some kind of curse would be broken. Even so, Sanchez still hadn't forgotten that Gabriel had made some passing remark about the hotel sinking into the pits of Hell if Julius signed the contract. Whichever way he looked at it, none of it was good. And all the answers were due in the next half-hour.

By the time he heard Nina Forina announce that the last singer was due onstage, his nerves were absolutely fried. It didn't help that the singer in question, Julius, took an age to show up. But just when it looked like he'd bugged out, he appeared from the wings, grinning like a fool.

Sanchez was hanging with Elvis and the other singers at the side of the stage, eagerly anticipating Julius's performance. He didn't disappoint. His song of choice was 'I Got You (I Feel Good)'. Like the Blues Brother and Emily, he had the advantage of backing from the orchestra. Jacko had got the musicians warmed up with his rendition of 'Sweet Home Chicago', and Emily's sublime singing had lifted their playing to new heights. Now, brimming with confidence, they offered very able support to Julius.

Where Emily had her beautiful voice, Elvis his charisma, Janis her amusingly inappropriate swearing, the Blues Brother his guitar and Freddie Mercury his uncanny resemblance to the late subject of his impersonation, Julius had some fantastically energetic dance moves. During his routine he covered every inch of the stage. By the time he was halfway through the song he was sweating liberally. He did the splits a few times, bouncing right back up each time without using his hands to help him. He strutted around, banging his head with his hands in time to the music, and when he wasn't singing, he filled his performance with shrieks and screams. Every 'Heh!' or 'Ooow!' he yelled seemed to excite the audience further. As they had been with several of the other performances, they were up on their feet in the aisles, banging their heads and dancing along to the music. It wasn't just the audience, either. The brass section of the orchestra seemed really to have entered into the spirit of the performance.

Sanchez kept half an eye on the judges, trying to gauge their reactions. Lucinda Brown was swaying and clapping in time to the beat, clearly enjoying herself. Beside her, Nigel Powell was giving little away. His face didn't move much at the best of times, but if his body language was a guide then he didn't seem to be too impressed. He sat with his arms folded and his lips pursed tightly together. On the other side of him, Candy Perez was smiling and waving first one and then the other arm up and down in the air, in some sort of dance move that made her look as though she was climbing an invisible ladder. Sanchez watched intently as the movement of her arms made her tightly constrained breasts move up and down one at a time. *Jesus!* he thought to himself. *One of 'em's gonna pop out any minute!'*

As he studied the gap at the top of her tight, partly zipped-up jacket, he was convinced that he could see a nipple popping out over the top. He opened his eyes wide and started nudging Elvis, who was standing on his right.

'Shit, man – look!' he whispered. 'Reckon I can see one a Candy's nipples!'

He expected his friend to thank him for the heads-up. Instead he heard a woman's voice. 'Thanks, that's nice,' it said, rather coolly.

At once Sanchez realized that it wasn't Elvis he'd been nudging, but Emily. He looked around and saw Elvis behind him talking with Janis Joplin. He felt his cheeks redden slightly with embarrassment.

'Uh – sorry,' he mumbled. 'Thought you were someone else.'

'That's okay,' said Emily with a chuckle.

'YO, ELVIS!' Sanchez shouted over the music to his friend. 'QUICK! I RECKON I CAN SEE OL' CANDY'S NIPPLE!'

Ditching Janis in mid-conversation, Elvis came over. He peered over Sanchez's shoulder, squinting at Candy to see for himself whether his friend was right. After a few seconds he nodded his head.

'Nice.'

Whether or not Julius's performance was good enough to win the show, Sanchez would never know. He and Elvis spent the last minute or so of the song with their eyes glued to Candy's protruding nipple.

Sanchez had been a big fan of Candy Perez since she had topped the charts with a song called 'I Love Chubbies'. He had once tacked a poster of her up on the wall in the Tapioca. It had stayed up for nearly an hour before someone stole it. He'd been very bitter about the theft at the time, but now all was forgiven. Whoever had stolen it could keep it, for all he cared. He had something far better now: the sight of Candy's nipple for ever stored in his photographic memory.

Just thinking about it was making him light-headed. With all that had gone on during the day, he hadn't had time to eat, and the food craving, coupled with the sight of Candy, was making him feel dizzy.

When Julius finished his performance and everyone (including Candy) stopped jigging up and down, Sanchez felt a twinge of disappointment. But he applauded and cheered louder than he had done for any of the previous acts.

'Didja see that?' he said, nudging Elvis again. 'Fuckin' awesome. Practically saw her whole tit, man! Awesome!'

'Elvis is back there,' Emily replied.

'Uh? Oh.' He felt his cheeks reddening again. Elvis was back talking to Janis Joplin. 'Sorry. Thought you were him.'

'I know.'

'Didja see that, though? Amazin', wasn't it? She's got fantastic tits.'

'Elvis is still back there.' A distinctly frosty note had crept into Emily's voice.

'Yeah, I know. But I gotta share this with someone, so just pretend you're a guy for a minute, will ya? Jeez, it ain't too much to ask, is it?'

Emily laughed. 'You want me to act like a guy? Okay.' She stood deep in thought for a moment, before piping up. 'You know I saw her in the shower earlier?'

'What?'

'Yeah. She was, like, totally naked, and with another woman. They were making out.'

Sanchez heard what Emily said and started to feel even dizzier. His legs went weak and suddenly, although he could still distantly hear Emily's voice, he couldn't see her.

'Sanchez? I was just kidding. I made that up. I was just trying to be a guy for a minute, like you asked. Sanchez? *Sanchez?*' She repeated his name several times before suddenly raising her voice and calling out, 'Hey, can someone get a paramedic? I think this guy's fainted.'

Fifty-Four

The bar had been empty for most of the last hour. The young bartender, Donovan, had had very little to do other than clean glasses and stack them on shelves. The rest of the bar and kitchen staff had vanished. He was the poor sucker left behind to mop the floors and wipe down the tables.

The only excitement had occurred a half-hour or so earlier, when, after hearing a shot some distance away, he had allowed a short, fat, Mexican-looking fella through to the kitchen area. A few moments later he had waved a gunman through after him. He wasn't quite sure what had gone on in the kitchen, but the tubby little fella had come rushing back out a few minutes later and run off in the direction from which he had come. The angry-looking dude in the trench coat had yet to reappear.

When the grim-faced man in the black hooded leather jacket approached the bar, Donovan recognized him straight away. He was smart enough, too, just to hand over an unopened bottle of Sam Cougar and a shot glass, without even waiting to be asked. He had been watching from the back of the bar earlier when the Kid had killed Jonah Clementine, so he knew not to be awkward.

The Kid looked at Donovan. The guy was too terrified to mess with him. He was just the kind of bartender needed at the current time. He'd serve the drinks and then get the fuck outta sight. The Kid appreciated that kind of service. He accepted the bottle and glass with a nod, and perched himself on a high stool at the bar. By way of payment, he decided not to kill Donovan. Instead, he reached into his jacket, took out a pack of cigarettes and shook one free. He placed it between his lips and drew on it. The bartender watched in horrified admiration as the end of the cigarette glowed and lit. *How fuckin' cool is that?* he thought, before busying himself with wiping glasses well away from the bartop.

The Kid sat and drank the bourbon. It was good stuff; in fact, it was so good that he probably drank a little more than he should. Then he dropped the remains of his cigarette on the floor, slipped off the stool and began making his way back to the reception area. He carried the bottle along with him, trailing it loosely in one hand and taking occasional swigs on the way. He had a lot on his mind. Like whom he was about to kill with his last bullet. The decision was dependent on a number of factors, but with only one shot at his disposal, his decision about whose brains to blow out was going to have to be dead right. And his aim was going to have to be good.

He had just allowed Julius to live, despite learning the truth about him. But he'd come to the conclusion that the James Brown impersonator had a chance of winning the show, and so long as Emily didn't win and sign that poisoned contract, he didn't give a damn what the outcome might be. He was ready to do whatever it took to achieve the result he wanted, and if that meant shooting someone then he'd do it without hesitation. Or regret.

When he got back to the lobby at the front entrance of the hotel he found it deserted. It had been quiet earlier when he had made his way through to the bar, but now, at half after midnight, the emptiness was oppressive. There was something strange about it, too. No night staff on the reception desk. No bellhop manning the entrance. All the phones, keyboards, pens and papers on the reception desk had been packed away, the computers shut down and the monitors covered. The whole place looked as if it had been uninhabited for weeks, or even months, as though the staff had left on summer vacation and closed the place down. In fact, they were most likely all in the auditorium, awaiting the result of the singing contest.

The Kid took a swig of Sam Cougar, then stood completely still. Listening. He possessed a sixth sense way beyond that of most mortal men. He could feel something was about to happen.

Something evil was near at hand. Even after drinking as much bourbon as he had, he could sense it. He wiped his mouth with the back of one hand, reached inside his jacket and pulled out the dark grey handgun. He began turning slowly around on the spot. The alcohol was beginning to kick in, leaving him a little unsteady on his feet as he kept turning with the gun aimed at the walls, watching, waiting for something to appear.

Finally he heard a noise.

The noise had been there all along, it had just taken him a while to notice it. It was a dull low-pitched scratching sound coming from the glass doors at the hotel entrance. It was pitch dark outside and with the lights on in the lobby, it was impossible to see beyond the doors. As soon as he'd become aware of it, the scratching sound grew louder. Then it was joined by a low hissing noise.

As he listened to the sounds and tried to figure out what they were, the muffled voice of Nina Forina drifted into the reception area. The singing had finished and she was thanking the audience for voting. No doubt the result was soon to follow. The Kid needed to be up in the sound booth with his gun trained on the stage. But first he had to know what the hell was making the noise outside?

He moved slowly towards the glass double doors at the front entrance. His boots crunched on some broken glass on the marble floor as he walked. There was a large crimson-coloured mat printed with the hotel's name on the floor in front of the doors. He stepped on to it, silencing his footsteps. He took five more steps towards the doors. The scratching and hissing were definitely coming from outside, because the sounds grew louder with every step he took. And the closer he got, the more the hissing began to sound like whispers. Voices whispering to him. He couldn't make out what they were saying.

Then, when he was little more than a foot from the glass, the hideously deformed face of a woman slammed into the door in front of him. Typically, he didn't flinch. Instead, he looked closely at the thing. The skin on its face was black and looked coarse, like sandpaper. The creature might once have been white-skinned, but now it had a complexion that suggested the whole head had been scalded by boiling water and then thrust into a pit of tar. Its red, bloodshot eyes leered at the Kid and its open mouth made biting motions at him through the glass, as if it hadn't eaten for a year. As indeed it hadn't.

The Kid set the bottle of Sam Cougar down on the crimson mat and stepped right up to the glass door. He raised one hand to his forehead to block out the light from the chandelier on the ceiling behind him and peered through the glass at the face pressing against the glass door. It was most definitely that of an undead creature of some kind; he'd have worked that out quickly enough even if he hadn't killed two of the things in the parking lot earlier. But how many of its kind were out there? It was hard to tell. There were definitely others moving around outside, beyond the locked doors, but it was impossible to get much of a look at them. The only way to tell for sure would be to turn out the lobby lights.

With Nina's commentary whipping the audience up into a muffled frenzy somewhere behind him, the Kid knew that he didn't have much time. The results would be announced soon. He tucked his handgun down into a deep pocket on his right thigh. It slipped in snugly with the butt sticking out at the top, from where it could be quickly drawn. Then he headed over to the reception desk. Reaching it, he slammed the palm of his right hand down on the counter and, almost as part of the same movement, vaulted over it. On the wall behind the desk was a panel of light switches, three across and three down. He flipped all nine switches down, instantly plunging the entire lobby and reception area into darkness.

Then he turned and took a look back at the glass entrance doors. It was clear now just how dangerous the situation was. There were zombies everywhere. They were clawing at the doors, desperately trying to clamber over each other to get to the front, with others behind them cramming on to the steps leading up to the entrance. The doors were made of heavy armoured glass and secured by steel bolts top and bottom, as well as a substantial steel lock in the centre, where they met, but they weren't going to hold the filthy creatures back for long.

The Kid vaulted the reception desk again and walked back over to the crimson mat by the entrance doors. He had not even got within a yard of the glass before the zombies had worked themselves into a frenzy, each one eyeing him up for its first kill. The sight of his warm, living flesh drove them crazy. Ignoring them, he stood close enough to the doors to get a good look around outside. There wasn't time to count them all, but it was a pretty safe bet that there were several hundred zombies outside, baying for blood and desperately fighting to get in.

He picked up the bottle of bourbon from the floor and pressed it to his lips, taking a large mouthful and swallowing it in one. Then he reached inside his jacket and drew out a soft pack of cigarettes. He put the pack to his mouth and pulled one out with his teeth. It was the last smoke in the pack, so he tossed the empty wrapper on to the mat at his feet. The Bourbon Kid had never been in the business of backing away from any kind of fight, but he had to take into account the fact that he was outnumbered by maybe five hundred to one. Further, he only had one round left in his gun. And that shot was intended for someone else. Someone who was going to be in range very soon.

With that in mind, he drew hard on his cigarette and watched it light up of its own accord. The smoke filled his lungs for a few seconds before he blew it out in the direction of the zombies. The swirling cloud blew up against the glass doors and then drifted in a blue haze towards the ceiling. The gesture seemed to anger the creatures at the doors even further, for their lunging and scrabbling grew more frantic. The doors began to shake violently. He turned his back and headed towards the corridor that led to the sound booth. The results of the *Back From the Dead* show were about to be announced, and he had to be up in the deejay's sound booth.

Ready to line up his target.

Fifty-Five

Sanchez could feel cold liquid splashing on to his face. He opened his eyes and blinked them a few times, before wiping away the water trickling into them. It dawned on him that he was half-reclining in a comfortable armchair and that there was a small crowd of people looking down at him. He recognized the nearest figure. It was Emily, and she was holding a small plastic bottle of water in her hand. He could also hear a familiar voice was calling out his name. 'Sanchez? You okay?' It was Elvis. He sat up and blinked a few more times. He caught sight of Elvis's gold jacket glowing just behind Emily. 'Where am I?' he asked.

'You're in that room backstage. Ya passed out, man. Just went down and banged your head on the floor.'

That seemed to be right. The back of Sanchez's head was throbbing and it hurt like hell. 'How'd that happen?' he asked.

Emily handed him the half-empty bottle of water. 'We were just, you know, talking,' she said, 'and all of a sudden you went pale and fell down.'

'Oh.' Sanchez couldn't think of anything to say. Then a thought struck him. 'Hey! Is the show over yet? Who won?'

Elvis leaned over him, peering over his gold-rimmed sunglasses. 'Hell, you've only been out for five minutes or so, man. They ain't announced the winner yet.'

'Cool. What did the judges think of Julius? Last thing I remember, he'd just finished his song. It's all a blank after that.'

'You shoulda seen what happened,' said Elvis. 'Man, it was fuckin' hilarious.'

'Why?'

'Well, first up, Lucinda says he's great. She loves him.'

'Yeah! Good.'

'Yeah, but then ol' Agent Orange Powell tells him he sucks ass.'

'Muthafucker.'

'Yep. But then it gets good. See, Candy Perez gets up, an' she says he's brilliant.'

'She's a good judge.'

'She sure as hell is. She even tries to gee the crowd up a bit by wavin' her arms around. But you'll never guess what happened then.'

'What?' asked Sanchez, rubbing the large bump that had formed on the back of his head.

'That tight white jacket thing she's got on? Well, what with her wavin' her arms an' stuff, the zip slips down and BAM! *Her tits fall out!* You shoulda seen it, man. Funnier'n hell. They got it up there on the big screen, an' everythin'. That woman's got a *helluva* rack!'

Sanchez felt a wave of dizziness sweep over him. Faintly he heard Emily's concerned voice. 'He's passing out again. Sanchez, are you okay? *Sanchez?*'

He awoke again several minutes later, to yet more water being splashed on his face.

'What happened?' he croaked feebly.

'You passed out again,' said Elvis.

'Again? How many times is that?'

'Twice, man. We tried to get you a doctor, but there ain't no staff on duty at reception no more. Seems like they've all deserted the place an' gone home.'

'Ow, my head! Why's my fuckin' head hurt?'

'You fell down an' hit your head just after Julius did his

James Brown thing.'

'Oh yeah, right. What did the judges say about him?'

Emily and Elvis looked at each other. Then Emily spoke. 'They said he was good.'

'Right. That's good.'

'MUTHAFUCKERS!' It was not difficult to tell from this that Janis was still in the backstage room with them. 'They're about to announce the winner,' she said, tugging at the sleeve of Elvis's jacket.

The King looked back at Sanchez. 'You feel up to watchin' the result?'

'Shit, yeah.'

'Well then, haul that fat ass up!'

Elvis hurried off after Janis, leaving Sanchez with Emily. She held a hand out to him. He took it gladly and she hauled him out of the chair and on to his feet. The sudden movement brought a minor rush of blood to his head and he felt a little dizzy again.

'How's your head?' she asked.

'Kinda hurts a bit. Throbs, ya know? But I'll be okay,' he said bravely. He was still seeing stars, but his head was gradually clearing. Emily took his hand and pulled him towards the door that led to the stage area.

'Come on, we'll miss the result,' she said.

Sanchez tugged his hand away from hers and stopped for a moment. The blow to his head seemed to be giving him all kinds of strange thoughts. Emily looked back at him. 'What is it?' she asked.

He stood and rubbed the bump on his head. Should he tell her what he was thinking or not? *Fuck it, yeah. It couldn't hurt.*

'Uh, Emily?' he said tentatively. 'I don't really know what's gonna happen when they announce the winner of this show. But,' he paused and took a deep breath. 'If my buddy Elvis ain't the winner, then I gotta hope it's you. You're the best one here, and ya really deserve it.'

A beautiful smile lit up the girl's face. 'Thank you,' she said. 'You're the first person to say that and sound like you genuinely mean it.'

Sanchez shrugged. 'Well, y'know,' he mumbled, as embarrassment began to overtake him.

Emily grabbed his hand again and pulled him towards the steps that led up to the stage. 'Come on, Sanchez. We'll miss the result if we're not careful.'

'Yeah, okay.' Then he had a sudden flashback. 'Were you tellin' me something about Candy Perez earlier?'

Emily laughed, but didn't answer. She led him up the stairs until they came out behind the large red curtain across the stage. As they crossed to the side, Nina Forina stood centre stage waiting for the curtains to part, with the panel of judges in front of her. At the side of the stage, by the curtain's edge, Elvis and Janis had joined Julius, Jacko and Freddie Mercury.

A drum roll began to sound from the orchestra pit, working up to a crescendo. Seconds later, the curtains parted and Nina stepped forward into the spotlight. The audience began cheering. Sanchez looked down at his wristwatch. It was almost one o'clock in the morning. The witching hour was nearly over. Where the hell were the zombies? And Angus, for that matter?

While he was contemplating the answers to these worrying questions, he gazed out at the auditorium. Every seat was full, men and women of all ages waiting excitedly for what was to come. All undoubtedly oblivious to the fact that what was to come probably involved a lot of bloodshed.

Looking up to the gallery, Sanchez saw the deejay flicking switches in his glass booth. There was someone else in the booth with him. Sanchez squinted. His eyes were still plagued with occasional flashes and black dots from the blow to his head when he had knocked himself out cold. But he'd seen something. Were his eyes deceiving him? He couldn't decide whether his eyes were playing tricks, or there really was a gunman in the booth with the deejay. He blinked a few times, trying to clear his vision, to see if he had imagined it. But he hadn't. Standing next to the deejay was a man dressed in black with a hood pulled up over his head. He was holding at his side something that looked like a pistol.

Sanchez was on the point of grabbing Emily's arm to draw her attention to the sinister figure in the deejay's booth, when the gunman suddenly ducked down into the shadows. It wasn't the first time Sanchez had seen this man. Who was he? And what was he doing in the deejay's sound booth?

With a gun.

Fifty-Six

Emily felt more nervous than she had the first time she had ever auditioned. The feeling was even worse than the first occasion on which she had performed in public. In fact, this topped just about any experience of her life, as far as nervousness went.

Nina Forina stood before the audience waiting for a signal from Nigel Powell. Emily was sure that he was teasing the audience by taking his time to wait for them to be quiet. Eventually, and before a riot started, Emily saw him give Nina the nod she had been waiting for. After that, she waited a further few seconds for total quiet from the crowd. Then she spoke again.

'Okay, everyone. OKAY! I'm extremely pleased to announce that I have the results of the *Back From the Dead* singing competition right here in my hand.'

She was speaking the literal truth. In her hand she held a small shiny gold envelope. The eyes of everyone in the auditorium seemed to be glued to it. Emily's fate was in that envelope. Her mother's medical care rested on the result tucked inside it.

As the crowd began to grow restless, Nina racked the pressure up another notch by opening the envelope agonizingly slowly and then coyly peering inside it. Emily could just make out a small rectangle of white card in the envelope. It was too far away for her to be able to read what was written on it, but Nina took a long look. After pulling it halfway out of the envelope, she glanced back up at the audience. This sent a whole bunch of them off into a screaming fit worthy of a Beatles concert, *circa* 1964. After savouring the moment for just a little longer than was necessary, she finally drew out the whole card. Emily craned her neck to see if she could get a good look. Nina was no fool, however. Like a poker player, she kept the card close to her chest, peering downwards to take a sneaky look at the results. After a long moment, her eyes opened wide. Since her face was there for all to see on the giant screen behind her, everyone saw her expression. She let out a small gasp and put her hand to her chest as if she were short of breath from the shock of what she had seen. Emily wondered what that look might mean. It might mean that the result was a genuine surprise, and since she was the favourite, that wasn't good news. Alternatively, the show's host might just be faking the shock to keep the audience guessing. Either way, Emily felt as though she would never breathe again.

More screams and yells from the restless and by now thoroughly over-excited mob followed, and after gesturing for them to quieten down, Nina cleared her throat.

'Ladies and gentlemen, the results of the *Back From the Dead* singing contest are as follows. In sixth place is . . . *Freddie Mercury*.'

There were gasps of surprise from the audience. Although he hadn't been one of the favourites to win, most people had expected him to finish higher than sixth. Freddie walked onstage and waved at the audience, who applauded him loudly. From behind her, Emily heard someone (who sounded uncannily like Sanchez) mutter something that sounded like, 'Serves the bastard right. Smug prick.'

Freddie made his way over to Nina, kissed her on the cheek and took up a place on the raised area at the back of the stage. Partly out of politeness, and partly from disappointment, the crowd applauded with some vigour. But, like Emily, what they really wanted was to know the names of the top five, particularly the top name of all. People began calling out the names of their favourite performers to show their support. Nina waited for them to quieten down before continuing with the results.

'Ladies and gentlemen, please put your hands together for the contestant who finished in fifth place.' She looked down at the card she was holding in her hand. Emily was sure it wasn't really necessary for her to look at the card again, but it kept the audience guessing for a few seconds longer. Then she announced loudly, 'Here we go . . . *Janis Joplin!*'

The crowd cheered, clapped, shouted their favourite swear words and gasped in equal measure, as a slightly disappointed Janis walked onstage. She waved politely, kissed Nina on the cheek, shouted 'Muthafuckers!' at the audience, and then walked away to take up her place next to Freddie Mercury at the rear of the stage.

Once again the auditorium fell into a hushed expectation. Among the little group at the side of the stage the tension was almost unbearable. Emily was watching how all the remaining finalists were coping. Julius was wiping his sweaty hands against his suit. Why was he still here? Nigel Powell had promised to have him thrown out. Somehow he had managed to avoid that, and Powell had obviously decided not to ban him from competing. Why was that? she wondered.

The Blues Brother, Jacko, was giving very little away, his eyes well hidden behind his sunglasses. Elvis, for all his self-confidence, seemed a little nervy, in Emily's opinion. His jaw was working, as though chewing imaginary gum. The only person at the side of the stage who didn't seem concerned about the result was Sanchez. He was staring at Candy Perez. He'd overheard someone backstage say that her tits were liable to fall out 'again'. He wasn't quite sure what that 'again' meant, but if there was a sniff of a chance of an appearance of Candy's finest, he wasn't going to avert his eyes for more than a second at a time.

Again Nina waited for the audience to quieten before

announcing the next disappointed contestant. *Or loser*, Emily thought.

'Ladies and gentlemen, in fourth place, please put your hands together for . . . *Elvis Presley!*'

Elvis looked livid. His lips were pursed and his fists tightly clenched. The gold-rimmed sunglasses probably hid just how furious he actually was. He strutted on to the stage with an angry swagger, staring over at Nigel Powell with a trademark sneer. He managed a half-hearted wave at the crowd, but blanked Nina altogether on his way to the losers' podium at the back to join Freddie and Janis.

Now only three remained.

'So – we're down to the final three,' Nina announced once the applause had died away. 'Who thinks the Blues Brother will win?'

A loud cheer went up from the crowd.

'Anyone favour Judy Garland?'

Another huge cheer.

'Yeah? Then what about James Brown?'

Once more there was a riotous cheer from the audience. If one thing was clear, it was that the result was going to be close. Emily couldn't gauge from the audience's reaction which act was the most popular. Had the crowd cheered as loudly for her as they had for Julius and Jacko? It was impossible to tell.

What followed was a shock. Nina looked down at the card in her hand once more and bit her lip. Then she smiled, nervously.

'Let's have a big round of applause for our third-placed contestant . . . *James Brown!*'

There was a momentary gasp from the entire audience, followed by loud cheers and then a roar of applause. Emily saw Julius's mouth drop open. He looked utterly dumbfounded, and for a moment could only stand in stunned silence. Emily felt a huge surge of excitement. Her dream was so close now.

In less than a minute she would know if she had won. She stepped aside from Julius as he walked onstage. She didn't want to be anywhere within stabbing distance of the man who had tried to have her killed. As he passed, Jacko patted Julius on the back and spoke for Emily when he said quietly, 'Tough shit, fuckface.'

From his spot behind Emily, Sanchez watched with interest. Hearing that Julius hadn't won snapped him out of his hypnotic trance. He had been concentrating so hard on Candy's breasts, trying to use the force of his will to bring them out, that he'd not been paying sufficient attention to Nina's announcements. But on hearing that Julius had only come third he looked to see how the James Brown impersonator was taking it. Badly, Sanchez reckoned. He was standing stock still, doing a passable imitation of a stunned mullet. Jacko patted him on the back and said something, whereupon Sanchez decided to offer his won thoughts.

'You gotta go up onstage with the rest o' the losers,' he whispered in Julius's ear.

The devastated singer appeared not to hear him, so Sanchez shoved him in the back hard enough to propel him out from behind the curtain and on to the stage. Julius walked towards Nina with a half-hearted wave at the audience. His body language hinted that he was far more disappointed than the other losers. Unlike Elvis, however, he did manage to plant a kiss on Nina's cheek. Then he too took up his place at the rear of the stage, on the end of the line next to Elvis.

Now thoroughly alert – or as alert as he could ever be – Sanchez thought hard about what this might mean. *What the fuck happens now?* he muttered to himself. He tried to grab Elvis's attention by standing on tiptoe and discreetly waving his hands, but the King was obviously still coming to terms with not winning the competition and wasn't making eye contact with anyone.

Again the applause died down, and again Nina spoke up.

'Ladies and gentlemen,' she began seriously. 'There are two contestants left. Can we have them both onstage, please?'

Sanchez watched Emily and Jacko walk out on to the stage to a chorus of cheers from the audience. They took up places on either side of Nina, who kissed each of them on the cheek. She had now replaced the card bearing the results in the gold envelope so that no one could see it.

'Okay – quiet please, everyone,' she yelled.

Once more the crowd gradually fell into an expectant hush, though it was punctuated by the occasional shouted comments from a few drunken lowlifes. And then Nina announced the result.

'The winner – yes, *winner* – of the *Back From the Dead* contest is . . . '

Fifty-Seven

Sanchez had no idea what to do. *Julius hadn't won.* HAD. NOT. WON.

He had plenty of time to dwell on this serious complication because almost a full minute had passed since Nina had announced 'The winner – yes, *winner* – of the *Back From the Dead* contest is . . . ' A seemingly never-ending drum roll swelled under her announcement and kept on going in a continuous roar of sound. Sanchez half expected to see a giant Battery Bunny in the orchestra pit, tapping away at the snare drum, because the tattoo was showing no sign of coming to an end. It just kept going. He looked at his watch again. That contract had to be signed by 1:00 a.m.

It was now 12:55.

The entire audience was going crazy, shouting out encouragement to whichever of the two remaining acts they favoured, as well as abuse at the drummer. Then suddenly the drum roll crashed to an end. A hush descended upon the auditorium. Nina finished her announcement.

' . . . *the Blues Brother!*'

The audience roared its approval. Nina, who was holding the hands of both finalists, raised Jacko's hand into the air to signify his victory. Standing on Nina's right, he smiled and waved his right hand in acknowledgement, thanking the audience for their votes. On Nina's left, Emily hung her head in disappointment. Then, graciously, she let go of Nina's hand and walked across to Jacko. She gave him a congratulatory hug, then stepped back to join the crowd of losers at the back of the stage.

Sanchez shook his head and turned his thoughts to what might happen next. Julius was supposed to be the one signing the contract. But Julius hadn't won, and he could hardly push Jacko out of the way and sign the contract himself. So what was he going to do? If the answer was nothing, did Elvis have a plan? Because Sanchez was ready to go home. Like, now.

He frantically waved a hand at Elvis again, trying to grab his attention. It was time to get the fuck out of the hotel. Elvis finally noticed his friend's desperate wave and nodded back at him. With any luck he was thinking the same thing. Grabbing hold of Janis Joplin by the arm, he whispered something in her ear, and then the pair of them headed offstage to join Sanchez.

'You ready to get the fuck outta here?' Sanchez asked.

'Dam' right,' said Elvis. 'Let's just hold on one minute, though. See what Julius does.'

Sanchez was anxious to get away from the place, the faster and farther the better. Now that he had Elvis with him, he reckoned his chances of getting out alive had improved considerably. Deciding that he no longer gave a fuck about events on the stage, he headed over to the flight of steps down to the corridor that led to the reception area. As he was making his way down the steps he heard the sound of glass breaking. It came from the lobby. A cold blast of air followed it. *A window must have broken somewhere near by.* When he reached the foot of the steps he heard the sound of footsteps, lots of them, heading his way. Moving fast.

He stopped and peered round the edge of the doorway, looking towards reception. His jaw dropped open and he felt his heart miss a beat. The zombie creatures from the desert had crashed through the glass double doors at the entrance and were swarming into the hotel in their hundreds. They darted off in all different directions, looking for human flesh to feast on. Sanchez turned and ran back up the steps to the stage area. He wasn't happy about being an appetizer. And as appetizers went, he was big enough to share. At once his cowardly instincts came to the fore and he did what he did best – ran from trouble.

Elvis and Janis were standing at the top of the steps with their backs to him, watching the proceedings on the stage. Nigel Powell had left his seat on the panel and was holding what could only be the contract in both of his hands. The shock of seeing the zombies had rendered Sanchez temporarily speechless. He stood behind Elvis and took a few deep breaths. The King hadn't noticed him. He was talking to Janis.

'Soon as someone signs that contract, we gotta get the fuck outta here, babe,' Sanchez heard him say.

'Don't you wanna see the encore?' Janis asked.

'Nah, we gotta go. That guy who's won is about to sign a contract with the Devil. Gonna sell his soul. Be damned all to hell.'

'*What?*'

'I'm serious, babe. There's a buncha fuckin' zombies headin' this way, too. They'll kill us all, 'less we can get ol' James Brown there to sign that goddam contract.'

'But the Blues Brother won fair and square,' Janis protested.

Sanchez finally got his voice back and blurted out what he'd seen. 'Elvis! The zombies! They're already here! They're in the fuckin' hotel!'

Elvis turned round and looked at Sanchez, then glanced down at his watch. 'Shit! It's twelve fifty-seven.'

Sanchez looked over at the stage. 'If Jacko signs the contract, then the zombies'll stay an' kill us all, yeah?'

Elvis nodded. 'That's how Gabriel told it.'

'But if he don't sign it by one o'clock, then this fuckin' hotel sinks into Hell, an' we're all dead, right?'

'Again, correct.'

'So why're we still here?'

''Cause if Julius signs it, we might be okay.'

'What happens if Julius signs it? I don't recall Gabriel bein' very clear about that part.'

'Fuck, man, ya do ask some goddam questions,' Elvis said exasperatedly. 'Listen, I ain't sure, but Julius is the only one can break the curse. Whatever the fuck the curse is.'

Janis looked at the pair of them as though they were certified lunatics. 'What the – *shit, fuck, muthafucker* – are you two talkin' about?'

'Ain't no time to explain,' said Elvis. 'We gotta stop that guy from signin'!'

'Too late,' said Janis quietly, pointing at the stage.

Nigel Powell was now standing centre stage with the Blues Brother, facing the audience. Powell was holding the deadly contract, Jacko a ballpoint pen. *Ready to sign an agreement with the Devil. Selling his soul.*

Jacko took off his sunglasses and tucked them into the breast pocket of his jacket. Then he reached out a hand and took hold of one end of the contract in Powell's hands. He held the pen up, signalling that he was looking for the appropriate place to sign.

Elvis shook his head and looked away, unable to watch. 'Poor bastard,' He sighed. 'He'll be damned all to hell.'

'Better him than me,' mumbled Sanchez. They watched as Powell took a look at his own wristwatch. His eyes betrayed how eager he was to see some ink on paper. It was a beast of a contract, nearly two inches thick. There was no time for Jacko to read it. *Just sign it,* seemed to be the overwhelming message. As Jacko brought his pen up to paper ready to sign his life away, Sanchez and Elvis stood frozen, wondering what would happen. And what to do.

At that moment, Sanchez heard a noise behind him. He looked back and saw two zombies run past the foot of the stairs from the corridor below. *Those fuckers're goin' to be everywhere in a minute*, he thought. He looked back at the stage.

In time to see Julius finally make his move.

From his place at the back of the stage among the losers, the purple-suited singer charged forward towards Jacko and Powell. 'STOP!' he yelled. *'Don't sign it!'*

He barged past Nina Forina, almost knocking her off her feet. Seeing him coming, Powell tried to hurry Jacko along.

'Ignore him. Quick, sign it!' he urged.

From somewhere high up in the auditorium there came the sound of more glass shattering. It was not as loud as the noise Sanchez had heard a minute earlier, but even so it startled him. He turned in the direction of the sound, in time to see the glass at the front of the deejay's sound booth fragment and shower down on the audience below, like a river of ice crystals.

Down on the stage, Julius reached out and grabbed the collar of Jacko's suit jacket, trying to pull him back before he signed the contract. He had the handful of black cloth in his grip for less than a second before a gunshot rang out.

BANG!

Sanchez watched on in paralysed horror as Julius's head exploded. A neat hole appeared in his forehead. A fraction of a second later the back of his head opened up and a cloud of blood and brains sprayed out over a wide area of the stage. There was a particularly unpleasant sound as a huge chunk of soft, wet matter splattered on to the front of Nina Forina's silver dress. Scarlet specks flew up into her face and she screamed out loud in shock and terror. The high-pitched scream served as the catalyst for a thousand others from horrified onlookers in the audience.

Sanchez looked first at Julius's lifeless body as it fell to the floor of the stage. It made a loathsome thudding sound as it crashed to the floorboards. From the ruined head blood pumped out on to the stage and down over what was left of the singer's face. His wig, dislodged by the shot, lay in a pool of it, gradually soaking it up. For a few seconds his dead eyes stared across the stage directly at Sanchez, before rolling up in his head, leaving only the whites exposed. *That's about the fifth fuckin' time that's happened today,* thought Sanchez, inconsequentially. Sickened, and extremely scared, he looked up at the gunman in the deejay's booth. Now that his head had cleared, he recognized him as the darkly dressed guy with the hood pulled up over his head, the shadow of it covering much of his face. Sanchez had passed him in a corridor earlier, and seen him up in the deejay's booth just before the results were announced. *That's a guy I won't forget in a hurry,* he thought.

He tugged violently at Elvis's gold jacket and pointed up at the sound booth. 'That guy just shot Julius!'

'Yeah? No shit, Sherlock.'

'D'ya think he's dead?'

'With his brains all over the goddam stage, I guess I'd have say of course he's fuckin' dead. Dumbass.'

'But he's the thirteenth Apostle!'

Understandably, Janis Joplin still looked confused. 'What?' she asked.

'He was the thirteenth Apostle,' Sanchez gabbled, pointing at Julius's corpse. 'He was the only one coulda have saved us all, and now he's dead. We're all fucked!'

Janis frowned. 'Don't be an asshole. That'd make him more'n two thousand years old.'

'I'm willin' to believe it,' said Sanchez.

'Yeah? But he looks about thirty. Thirty-five at most.'

'Well, he would, wouldn't he? He's an Apostle.'

Janis clearly wasn't buying it. 'So do Apostles get, like, free anti-ageing cream from the drugstore?'

'They might.' Sanchez wasn't at all sure where all this was leading.

'Kinda a shame, then, he didn't think to pick up any hair restorer while he was there.'

Sanchez frowned. When she wasn't swearing at him or anyone else, Janis could be pretty sarcastic. 'Look,' he tried again, 'we were told by a guy who knows about these things. Weren't we?' he looked to Elvis for support.

'Yeah. But, I dunno, man. Maybe it was all bullshit?'

'But Gabriel believed it.'

'Yeah, but he'da believed Joan Rivers was twenty-one if ya'd told him.'

Sanchez suddenly felt very worried. As well as scared. Had Gabriel been duped by Julius? 'So is there a thirteenth Apostle or ain't there?' he thought aloud.

'Doubt it,' said Janis. 'Though I did read about one once. I'm sure he's buried in Africa, or something.'

'Maybe it's that guy?' said Elvis, pointing at Jacko, who had now signed his name on the contract that Powell had held out to him.

By now it was hard to hear what anyone was saying. Most of the audience were screaming. In fact, pretty much everyone on the stage except Powell and Jacko was running around screaming at the sight of Julius's body, as well as the thought that the gunman up in the booth might fire again. At them.

Then, as the audience members began fleeing the auditorium, they found that they had something new to scream about. There was no escape. Zombies swarmed in from all the exits. Blocking the way out.

The carnage was only just beginning.

Fifty-Eight

Nigel Powell looked at his wristwatch. 12:59 a.m. Now that was cutting it fine. The show had been a disaster. He promised himself he'd never allow it to run this late again. Better security was required for next year. And a tighter running schedule. Still, it was over now. Jacko had signed his name on the contract. Show over.

Next year, there would be no place for James Brown impersonators. Julius had come closer than anyone to fucking up the show. But who was he? And why had he been so desperate to win? As he considered possible answers, another question popped into Powell's head. *Who the fuck had shot Julius?* Sure, he himself had ordered security to find him and take him on a one-way trip to the desert. But that had been earlier. He hadn't given orders to anyone on the security detail to pull a firearm and shoot if Julius made a lunge for the contract. Well, he'd order a full review of proceedings later. For now he was just relieved to have another sucker sign his contract with the Devil.

He had to concede that Jacko's calm demeanour was impressive. The young singer had been unfazed at seeing Julius gunned down. And even now, with the zombies beginning to rip the crowd in the auditorium to pieces, he seemed remarkably unconcerned. Both he and Powell had a few spots of blood from Julius's shattered head on their clothes. The hotel owner's white suit was ruined. Jacko's black jacket hid the stains pretty well. Still, Powell could live with a ruined suit. It would be better than swapping places with Jacko. He knew what was coming next for the winning finalist, and it wasn't going to be pretty.

'I'm sorry about that,' he said, nodding at the bloodied corpse just behind them. His distaste was only too evident. 'But congratulations on winning the show. Well deserved.'

'Thanks,' Jacko replied, smiling. 'Been a strange kinda day, ain't it?'

'It certainly has.' Powell turned his attention towards a couple of security guards who were loitering at the back. Like everyone else on the stage, they were staring in horrified disbelief at the zombies attacking the audience.

'Hey you guys!' he called to them. 'Stay onstage, yeah? The zombies won't come up here.'

He looked out at the auditorium. The zombies were sprawling in through every exit, clawing at screaming members of the audience, biting chunks of flesh out of them. It was a horrific sight, but one that Powell was used to. He'd seen it many times before. The zombies liked to attack in numbers and were singling out vulnerable fans who had been separated from the groups that had managed to stick together. Three or four of the loathsome, decaying creatures would gang up and attack each individual. There were terrified high-pitched screams from women who were having their arms and legs ripped off by gangs of the mutant flesh eaters. Young men too, shrieked like children as zombies gouged out their eyes, bit into their legs and ripped off their clothing.

Watching dispassionately, Powell breathed a sigh of relief as he thought about how the show had been cut so close to the deadline of 1:00 a.m. He gazed on the massacre for a few seconds, allowing himself a thin smile, before turning back to Jacko.

'Don't mind the ghouls,' he said. 'Those – things – will be on their way once they see that you've signed the contract.'

'I ain't so sure,' said Jacko coolly, peering out at the

carnage in the auditorium.

As the originator, owner, promoter and chief judge of the show, Powell had always found that each year the winner would inevitably be a little shocked by the appearance of the undead and the bloody mayhem they brought with them. He remembered the previous year's winner, a Dusty Springfield impersonator. She had screamed the place down, becoming really quite hysterical. He had been unable to calm her and had been greatly relieved when the Man in Red had stepped out of the audience. He had reached into her chest and ripped out her soul. Nasty business, really. But inevitable.

The arrival of Powell's evil acquaintance from the mirror always signified an end to the evening's proceedings. Once again he looked at his watch, then smiled at Jacko. Any second now the Man in Red would silently materialize from some dark corner, reach into Jacko's chest with his ghostly hands and remove his soul. The fact that the singer wasn't screaming in panic like most of the previous winners was making things much easier for Nigel Powell.

Eventually, right on cue as Powell's wristwatch emitted a tiny chime to signify one o'clock and the end of the witching hour, the Man in Red appeared at the back of the stage, grinning like a kid let loose in a candy store. Jacko had his back to him, and so didn't see him approaching. Powell did his best to keep the Blues Brother distracted as the big black man with the big white grin and the sharp red suit and hat sidled up to them.

'You know,' said Powell affably, placing a hand on Jacko's shoulder, 'I personally thought Judy Garland was going to win, but you really did the Blues Brothers proud with that cover of "Sweet Home Chicago".'

'Cover, *my ass!*' Jacko scoffed.

'Excuse me?' said Powell. Jacko's aloof, even arrogant, attitude since winning had him somewhat perplexed. 'What do you mean?'

'*Cover*? Pah. That was no cover version. The Blues Brothers covered it. Not me.' He shrugged his shoulder to dislodge the other man's hand.

'Huh?' Powell was confused. 'How do you mean? "Sweet Home Chicago" was a Blues Brothers song, wasn't it? Sure it was – I saw them sing it in the movie.'

'Yeah, you did. But they didn't write it.'

'Ah. Right. I see what you're getting at. So who did?'

Jacko took off his hat and placed it on Powell's head, pushing it down firmly. Then he winked at his new employer.

'*I* wrote "Sweet Home Chicago",' he said.

The hotel owner stood rooted to the spot, trying to fathom what Jacko could possibly mean. Then an icy chill swept through him and his face dropped. He looked down at the bulky contract in his hand and quickly flicked through the pages to the end. When he got to the last page he fixed his eyes on the signature at the bottom. The name that Jacko had signed stood out. Each letter of it was like a knife thrust to Powell's heart.

Robert Leroy Johnson

He looked back up at the young man standing before him. Only now Jacko was not alone. Elvis, Sanchez and Janis had all drifted over to see what was going on. Even more worryingly, the Man in Red had joined them and was now standing with his arm around Jacko's shoulder.

'Good to see you again, Mister Johnson,' he said, grinning at Jacko.

Powell was stunned. He looked at Jacko, unable to mask his shock. '*You're* Robert Johnson? The Blues Man?'

'The very same.'

'But . . . but, didn't you sell your soul to the Devil about a hundred years ago?'

The Man in Red took his arm from around Jacko's shoulders and placed one hand on Nigel Powell's left shoulder. 'Yes sir, he did. Back in 1931.' Despite his broad grin, his words were as cold as steel.

Powell's hands began to shake. 'Then this contract is null and void. You can't sell *him* something that he already owns!'

Jacko winked at him again. 'Been nice knowin' ya. Gotta be goin' now, son.'

Fifty-Nine

Sanchez had seen some crazy shit in his time. The revelation that Jacko the Blues Brother was actually none other than Robert Johnson, the guy who had sold his soul to the Devil in the nineteen-thirties, was quite a story. But, taking into consideration that only minutes earlier he had believed that there was a surviving thirteenth Apostle who made a living impersonating James Brown, he was willing to accept that it was possible.

He'd encountered vampires and werewolves in his time running a bar in Santa Mondega, which had prepared him for just about anything. But this – this was all getting to be too much. Especially the introduction of zombies into his world. Right now he was only yards away from a whole bunch of them. These fuckers were savages. He watched as two of them played tug-of-war with some unfortunate guy in a polyester tracksuit, each with its teeth in a different part of their victim, growling as they pulled him this way and that. Being up on stage, viewing the pandemonium from a safe distance, was like watching a horror movie. Except that here it was the audience being slaughtered while the 'actors' – those up on the stage – looked on. The result, however, was that Sanchez felt safe, sort of. For the moment.

There was also a big, rather sinister-looking black man in a sleek red suit with a red derby on his head, standing with Nigel Powell and Jacko. Considering all that was going on, this guy seemed ridiculously happy. He had a huge grin across his face. Powell had quite the opposite. The achingly bright white smile had been wiped from his face, and his tan seemed to have faded from orange to a kind of dirty beige.

All of the surviving finalists were now standing centre stage, watching Powell. He appeared to be gasping for breath, as if suffering a heart attack.

'I ain't sure what the fuck is goin' on here, man,' Elvis said. 'Who's the big guy in red? An' where in hell did he come from?'

Sanchez shrugged. 'Looks like a black Santa to me.'

'Yeah? Or maybe he's the Devil?' Elvis had a point. He could be. With all the other mayhem going on, and the rumours that the winning contract belonged to Satan, it was a possibility.

'In that case, can we just get the fuck outta here?' Sanchez pleaded.

'Just hold on a while. See what happens. Seems safe enough up here for now.'

Sanchez wasn't going anywhere without Elvis, and his buddy did seem to be right. The zombies were keeping clear of the stage. It was, he thought, the safest place to be in a hotel that really wasn't safe to be in.

The Man in Red standing with Powell and Jacko turned round. He looked at Sanchez and Elvis and the other singers. Then he winked at Sanchez and walked away, back towards the rear of the stage from where he had come.

'Who the hell was that?' Sanchez asked aloud for anyone to answer.

Nigel Powell responded, quietly, almost to himself. 'We're all fucked,' he said. 'Doomed all to hell.' Raising his voice, he almost shouted, 'Hell, d'you hear me?'

'Pardon me?'

Sanchez had been hoping that Powell might be able to show them a way out. After all, it could only be a matter of time before the zombies below stopped ripping limbs off the screaming audience members and started climbing their way up to the stage. There were already a few of them in the orchestra pit tearing the musicians to pieces. Instruments were squeaking and honking as band members tried in vain to fight back. The tuba player, in particular, was honking for all he was worth in the hope of keeping the creatures at bay with the deep bass blare from his giant instrument.

For once, everyone else looked more terrified than Sanchez, with two exceptions. Elvis remained the epitome of cool, as always, and Jacko too seemed completely unfazed by what was happening. While waiting for one of the two to offer a suggestion about how they should escape, Sanchez heard the cacophony of zombies and their victims suddenly drowned out by music. And this time it wasn't the tuba. Blaring out through the speakers around the auditorium was the Paul McCartney CD that the deejay had played earlier. The screaming audience below were being drowned out by McCartney and a chorus of burping frogs singing 'We All Stand Together'. Fuckin' run in terror together, more likely, thought Sanchez. If ever there was a sign indicating what he should do, this was it.

'That's it. I'm gettin' the fuck outta here!' he declared, hoping desperately that someone else would agree, and then take the lead.

'Just hold on one second,' Elvis snapped back. He walked up to Powell and stopped in front of him. 'So, how do we get outta this shit, huh?' he asked, prodding the other man in the chest.

'I . . . I'm not sure,' Powell stammered. 'I think . . . I guess the safest place to be is up here on stage. Maybe they won't come up here.'

Elvis looked unimpressed, his mouth twisting into a sneer the King himself would have admired. 'Yeah? An' what was it you said to me earlier?' he asked.

'What? I don't know. Now's hardly the time for this.'

'You said I don't deserve to be on this stage.'

'Big deal. Get over it, already.'

'I have. But you know what?'

'What?'

'Now *you* don't deserve to be on this stage.' He leaned back, and then with all his strength drove his right fist into the shocked face of Nigel Powell. It connected with full fury right on the end of its target's nose. There was a sickening crunch and a spray of blood as the impact of the blow knocked the show's deviser and chief judge off his feet. It sent him flying back off the edge of the stage into the orchestra pit below. He landed in the middle of a melee of zombies and half-eaten musicians, torn-off limbs and ripped-out entrails. The expression on his face was one of the purest terror. Never had an orange-skinned man looked so pale.

The zombies allowed him one agonized scream before he vanished beneath a pack of them, to be eagerly devoured. They seemed to know who he was. In the dim recesses of their rotting brains, they knew that this man had tricked many of them into selling their own souls to the Devil in exchange for what they had thought would be money and fame. The rest were hapless audience members from past shows who had become zombies through being killed by them. He was finally getting his comeuppance. From a horde of undead creatures who despised him.

Elvis turned back to face Sanchez and the few remaining survivors. The stage was still free of zombies, but that would surely change. Soon.

'Yo, Johnson!' Elvis yelled at Jacko. 'Get us the fuck outta here!'

The Blues Man grinned at him. 'Sure thing. Be a pleasure. Follow me.'

Sixty

Nina Forina, Candy Perez and Lucinda Brown had long since left the stage, trying to make a break for it with a few of the security guards. Occasionally, shots punctuated the din as the guards tried to fight their way through the frenzied ghouls. Sanchez could have followed them, but he reckoned that sticking with Elvis and Jacko had to be a better option. The Blues Man led the way off the side of the stage, from where they had all watched the results in what seemed like an earlier life. Sanchez and the others followed on behind. The tubby bar owner cunningly weaselled his way in right behind Jacko and just in front of Elvis, clearly the safest place to be. Janis Joplin was behind Elvis, desperately clinging on to his hand. Emily was behind her, and finally, bringing up the rear, came Freddie Mercury. The only person left behind on the stage was Julius. His corpse was still lying on the boards where it had fallen, blood oozing from the fatal head wound.

As Sanchez followed Jacko down the stairs to the corridor that led to the lobby, he saw one of the undead creatures charging towards them. It stopped at the foot of the steps, blocking their path to the corridor. Half of its face had rotted away, making it hard to tell what it had looked like when alive. It was a face that had probably once belonged to a young man who had wanted nothing more than to be a famous and successful singer. Now it was a decomposing mask of evil, bereft of a soul, twisted with its desperate desire to feed on human flesh. Judging from its tattered, rotting clothes, it had once been the owner of a smart suit not unlike Jacko's. But where his suit was clean and well pressed, the zombie's was torn and filthy, covered in mould and dirt and blood.

The hideous creature stood stock still in front of Jacko and the two of them eyeballed each other for a moment. The zombie seemed to recognize him; indeed, it seemed not to want to bite chunks out of him. It was, however, quick to turn its ruined gaze on the very edible midriff Sanchez kept barely concealed beneath his red Hawaiian shirt.

Repelled yet faintly fascinated, Sanchez watched on, trembling at the stand-off that had developed. Eventually, Jacko raised a hand to the zombie and shook his head. 'These folks are with me. Let 'em be.'

There was an awkward few seconds during which the zombie snarled at him, apparently considering what he had said. All that could be heard were the dwindling screams of the remaining audience members and incessant burping of frogs on the Paul McCartney track. But, eventually the zombie stopped snarling at them, turned its back and ran off down the corridor towards the rear of the hotel.

That's a result, thought Sanchez.

Jacko led the way into the corridor and beckoned the others to follow him towards the lobby. Sanchez peered around the corner into the corridor and immediately noticed that it was fairly packed with blood-crazed zombies in the process of attacking any audience members, security guards, judges and singers who had tried to escape. The putrid stink of the zombies mingled with the coppery smell of fresh blood in a scent that no one was likely to bottle as Charnel No.5 any time soon.

'Look,' yelled Sanchez. 'There's Little Richard.'

'Nah, that's Jimi Hendrix,' said Elvis.

They were both right. Sanchez looked on in horror at what was happening. Over by the opposite wall, Richard, the diminutive Jimi Hendrix impersonator, was being eaten alive, legs first, by a pair of zombies. He was still alive and screaming in agony. Elvis was quick to shove his buddy in the back and out into the hall.

'C'mon, fatso,' he muttered. 'We ain't got all fuckin' day!'

'The fuckers're eatin' him alive!' Sanchez couldn't stop himself from staring at the dreadful sight.

'Fuck him,' said Elvis, heartlessly. 'He ain't nothin' but the starter. You'll be the goddam main course, if you don't get your fat ass outta here!'

Sanchez took the hint. He hurried along the corridor behind Jacko, staying as close to him as possible and thanking his lucky stars that the guy had some sort of influence over the zombies. There were around twenty of the mutant creatures in the corridor ahead of them, lined out along both walls. They were respecting Jacko's order to stay back, but they were also visibly itching to reach out and take a grab at anyone who stepped away from the group. The King followed on behind him, waving his fists at anything that looked like it might dare to lunge at Sanchez. Janis Joplin kept a tight hold on the back of Elvis's gold jacket, meanwhile shouting all kinds of obscenities at the watching zombies.

At the rear, Emily and Freddie Mercury were the most vulnerable. Emily's stupid bright red shoes weren't made for running. The heel on the left shoe broke loose as she hurried along, one hand clutching the back of Janis's dress. Freddie was constantly knocking into her from behind and it was his stepping on her feet that had caused her shoe to break.

Emily found it hard to focus on moving ahead, knowing that a zombie might lunge at her from behind or the side at any time. The creatures were all willing to back off when Jacko – or Robert Johnson, she supposed she should call him – ushered them away, but by the time the end of the line of fleeing singers reached them the memory of his warning had fled their raddled brains. As the escapees approached the glass doors – one shattered by Angus's bullet – into the reception area, one of the deformed figures made a lunge for Freddie Mercury. Emily, trying to concentrate on not looking at the zombies, kept her eyes fixed on the glass doors and a glimpse of the exit. She didn't notice initially when one particularly large zombie grabbed Freddie from behind and smothered his mouth with its thick bony hand. But she heard his muffled cries for help.

She turned and stared in horror as the hideous, semi-naked giant began to drag Freddie back down the corridor. He was frantically kicking his feet in his desperate attempts to escape, but his plight was spotted by a few other zombies, which immediately leapt upon him. With Paul McCartney's 'Frog Chorus' almost drowning out the loathsome noises they made, the zombies began devouring him bloody mouthful by mouthful as the largest of them carried him back towards the stairs that led to the stage area.

Up ahead, Sanchez could see that the exit was within reach. He looked back to check that Elvis was still behind him. He was. Survival was looking like a possibility. Relieved that the zombies now all seemed to be behind them, he shouted over the frogs' din to Elvis. "Least the hotel ain't plummeted into the depths of Hell like Gabriel said it would!'

'Don't tempt fate!' Elvis yelled back above the din.

But the tubby bar owner's gift for tempting fate had not deserted him. Within a second of Elvis's warning, Sanchez saw a large crack appear in the floor of the corridor behind them, accompanied by a drawn-out creaking noise. It was only an inch or two wide and probably not very deep, but it was racing towards them from its starting spot about fifty feet behind them, tearing the carpet apart. The floor was breaking open like a hatching egg. Zombies dived away from it, jumping towards the walls.

At the back of the line of would-be escapers, Emily saw it too. Slabs of plaster from the walls and ceiling were coming loose, too. The corridor was beginning to shake like some mad fairground ride. Emily looked back one last time and saw Freddie Mercury's feet vanishing down a side corridor towards the stage in the hands of a group of zombies. She didn't know which was more horrifying, the fact that Freddie was being eaten alive, or that the floor was about to split in two.

Undoubtedly this was as terrified as she had ever been, and she was now cursing herself for not having followed the Bourbon Kid's advice. She couldn't help but wonder what had become of him. He was one of those guys who seemed to know no fear, who always fought everything head on. Just the kind of man she needed right now. She hoped desperately that she would spot him somewhere, amidst the havoc.

Unfortunately for Emily, bringing up the rear with Freddie now gone left her as the most vulnerable. Being at the end of the line meant that a number of flesh-hungry zombies were eyeing her up. At least there were no longer quite as many of them to contend with. A bunch of them had dashed off to the stage area with the screaming Freddie Mercury, while the sight of the floor splitting in two had scared off several of the others.

A second, extremely loud creaking noise drowned out the singing frogs. This time it wasn't just the floor splitting in two. The entire corridor tipped over to one side, causing everyone to slide over with it and crash against the side wall. All five of the surviving escapees stumbled and lost hold of each other. Emily suffered worst. Her right shoe came off, and since the other had a broken heel, she flicked that off too. Her plain white ankle socks offered no grip whatsoever on the weirdly tilted floor. She lost her footing completely and toppled over on to the large crack in the floor, which was now almost four inches across. And it was slowly widening.

One of the zombies that had been standing back against the wall grabbed hold of Emily by her hair. Its crusty black fingers grasped one of her pigtails and pulled hard. Then its other hand grabbed her beneath her left armpit and pulled her up towards its mouth. She turned her head and looked the creature in the eyes. One of its eye sockets was completely empty. It had barely any skin on the top of its head and its one good eye was red at the centre, the yellowing white bloodshot. The skin on what was left of its face was charred and coarse, and in its gaping mouth she could see that its gums had rotted away. But its teeth were still there. They were jagged and sharp and canted at different angles, like those of a crocodile.

Once it had dragged her to her feet and pulled her back, away from the others, it displayed a level of cunning that Emily would not have expected from a zombie. Releasing its grip on her pigtail it placed its right hand over her mouth to prevent her from screaming out for help.

She struggled with the deformed monster. Although it was stronger than her, it too was also fighting to keep a steady foothold in the listing, crumbling passageway. Emily managed to spin herself around and elbow it in the head. The blow knocked it slightly off balance and she was able to free herself from its grip. As soon as she had knocked its horribly coarse hand away from her mouth she screamed out for help. It was a futile effort.

Paul McCartney's frog chorus was still in full swing and the constant burping noises drowned out her cry. Worse, Emily suddenly found herself in the desperate position of having at least six zombies between her and Janis Joplin, who hadn't even noticed that the girl dressed as Dorothy was no longer behind her.

Before Emily could decide what best to do, a hand grabbed her left shoulder from behind and she heard a familiar gravelly voice. It was a voice that struck fear into most people, but in Emily it instilled nothing but hope and relief.

'How many more times am I gonna have to rescue your ass?'

She turned her head. Her heart soared, and she was immediately overcome by a feeling that everything would be all right when she saw the Bourbon Kid behind her. He had the dark hood on his jacket pulled up over his head, a sure sign that he was in full-on killing mode. He also held a large pistol in one hand. He was pointing it at three zombies coming from the direction of the auditorium in an attempt to scare them off. They held back, but were clearly only waiting for a chance to pounce. Emily took stock of the situation. They were in a decaying, crazily tilted corridor with three zombies behind them and six between them and the reception area, and an enormous crack in the floor that was growing wider by the second. The Kid began pulling her back down the corridor in the direction she had just come from, towards the three zombies. The nearest potential escape route was via the lobby, but she had a strong feeling that her best chance of survival lay in following the hooded serial killer.

'I should have listened to you before,' she said apologetically as she edged down the corridor with him. Two large male zombies from the reception end began tentatively following them, wary of the Kid's gun but readying themselves to make a lunge.

'Well, this ain't the time for me to give you the "I told you so" speech,' said the Kid. 'Although, for the record, I did fuckin' tell you.'

'Yeah. I know. Can you just get me out of here and tell me again later?'

'Doin' my best. In a minute, when I shout "Run", you fuckin' run past me down this corridor then turn right at the end an' follow the signs to the fire exit.'

'What are you going to do?'

'Gonna kill these fuckers.'

The Kid was true to his word. A few seconds later he launched himself at the three zombies in front of him, at the same time yelling at Emily to run. With her heart beating wildly Emily rushed through the opening the Kid had created and headed for the end of the corridor. Halfway down it, realizing that there seemed to be no more zombies in front of her, she stopped and looked back. The Kid had two of the filthy creatures all over him and had dropped his gun. It looked as though they were trying to pin him against the wall. Each had a hold of one of his arms, attempting to force him back so that the third zombie could get a clear run at him.

If Emily had learned anything in the last few hours, it was to do as the Kid said. That meant running for the fire exit. Leaving him behind maybe wasn't the bravest thing to do, but her gut instinct was telling her that he'd be okay.

She hoped.

Sixty-One

Invincible Angus's attempts to get out of the walk-in freezer had left him extremely frustrated. (For its part, the freezer had left him extremely cold.) The anger at being outwitted and imprisoned by an imbecile like Sanchez was building inside him. It increased his desire to kill someone, whether Sanchez or simply the next person he saw was of no consequence.

In trying to shoot open the lock from the inside, he had only succeeded in scaring Sanchez away. Firing a round at the metal door had actually turned out to be a none-too-clever idea. The bullet ricocheted off the lock and up into the ceiling. Many more shots like that and Angus might have found himself the unfortunate victim of a gunshot wound, courtesy of his own pistol.

For almost twenty minutes he froze his ass off trying various other ways to bust the lock on the door. First, he tried charging at the door and ramming his shoulder into it. That left him with a bruised shoulder. He then tried hammering on the lock with the butt of his gun. Again, no joy. His third idea was no more productive. As the cold began to affect his rational thinking he set about looking for something inside the freezer that might force the lock open. Since the most useful tool he could find was a chicken drumstick, the outcome was inevitable.

Even though he was wearing his long trench coat and a pair of thick combat pants he was now feeling the cold very badly. With time running out and the chills beginning to cut to the bone he decided to try firing at the lock again. Clearly a more careful approach was required, so he stepped further back out of the way behind the corner of one of the rows of shelving and fired from a distance His hands were shaking with cold which affected his ability to aim his gun with any accuracy. So once again, after firing at the lock, he had to dive for cover as the bullet ricocheted around the inside of the freezer. This time, however, the shot did have a positive outcome, although not quite what had been intended. Just when he thought he had exhausted all his options he heard a voice shout from the kitchen.

'Is someone in there?'

Angus rushed to the door and yelled through it, 'Yeah. Help me! I'm locked in the goddam freezer!'

The sound of footsteps heading towards the freezer door was one of the most welcome he had ever heard. There was a clicking and then the door was pulled open. Angus hurried out, shivering violently. Standing on the other side of the door was the young dark-haired bartender who had gestured to him that Sanchez had run through to the kitchen. He looked both confused and terrified in equal measures. At first Angus assumed that the sight of his pistol had scared the young man, but his face was deathly pale and he looked as though he'd seen a ghost. Angus glanced down at the name badge on his red vest.

'Thanks, uh – Donovan. Thought I was gonna freeze to death in there,' he said, with his teeth chattering. He began dusting the frost off his clothes, only to be confronted by something far worse than the cold. Behind Donovan the door from the bar area into the kitchen burst open, and the hideous form of a pale-skinned male zombie appeared. It wore tattered clothing and had almost no hair, just a pale, putrid scalp to go with its gaunt face and red eyes.

'They're everywhere, man!' Donovan yelled. His voice revealed that he was genuinely terrified. 'They're killing off anyone they can get their hands on. We need to get out of here!'

The zombie arched its shoulders back and hissed at them, revealing a foul set of gnarly teeth. Then it began to shuffle cautiously towards them, eyeing Angus's gun, wary that he might use it.

'It's okay,' said Angus, dusting some frost off his pistol. 'I got a plan. Y'see, they only prey on the weak.'

'So what do we do?' asked Donovan, his voice beginning to crack as hysteria swept over him.

'Survival of the fittest, my friend. They just want an easy meal. One that can't fight back.'

'So? What the fuck're we meant to do? Throw it a turkey drummer?'

'Nah. A wounded bartender.'

Donovan looked confused for a moment. It was a look that almost immediately turned to one of fear and then of despair as Angus turned the gun on him. In one swift movement the killer aimed at the bartender's leg and fired a bullet into his thigh.

'Aaagh! SHIT!' Donovan fell to the floor clutching his right thigh with both hands at the point where the bullet had entered. Blood pumped out and seeped into his dark pants and through his fingers as he tried to stem the flow. A long, low moan escaped him as he rocked back and forth.

Angus looked down at him and shrugged. 'Sorry, man. Like I say, survival of the fittest.' With that, he stepped aside and ducked behind a couple of the metal trolleys to allow the zombie a clear run at Donovan. The creature gratefully homed in on the stricken bartender on the floor, allowing Angus to sneak over to the door. He didn't bother to look back as he headed out into the bar area.

Outside the kitchen, the scene was one of indescribable mass panic. Zombies and humans were running around the bar and the passageway that led to it. The scene resembled a spectacularly bloody riot at a football game. Zombies were chasing hotel guests and jumping on any that became separated from the scattered groups. Angus made a point of waving his pistol about as ostentatiously as possible, hoping that the zombies would think twice about attacking him once they saw it. They didn't have much in the way of brains, but like any other creature they had survival instincts, despite being undead. They did seem to be leaving him alone, no doubt hoping to land some easier meat.

So far unattacked, Angus was able to see that the filthy things were swarming in from the reception area. A quick decision was needed, and so he made it. Head the opposite way and look for another exit. He jogged briskly towards a set of cream-coloured double doors at the far end of the passage. As he did so, the floor began to shake beneath his feet and the walls started to crumble. Slabs of plaster fell from the ceiling. This was plainly no time to hang around.

The doors were about twenty yards away, and between him and them were about six zombies chasing a group of guests who had come to the same conclusion about the best way out. Surprisingly quick-footed, the zombies were picking off the slowest of the guests. Angus, with his pistol held menacingly out in front of him, was able to glide safely through the carnage towards the doors. A petrified-looking, middle-aged blonde woman in a green frock raced through before him, but courteously stopped to hold the doors open for him after she'd passed through them.

The doors led at right angles into a corridor. Faced with the option of turning left or right, Angus took a look both ways. Turning right would mean walking into a dead-end twenty yards further on. The only option was to turn left and run back towards the centre of the hotel and the auditorium. He shoved the woman in the green frock in the back, pushing her into the wall opposite. She hit her face hard and fell to the ground in a heap. Angus wasted no time and began running down the corridor in which there was no sign of a single zombie, though the noise of them attacking screaming victims could be heard quite plainly. Seeing a passageway coming up on the left, Angus made a point of staying close to the right-hand wall. He wanted to ensure that if anything lunged out at him he would be as far away as possible from the opening in which it would be lurking.

As he approached it, he slowed to a steady walking pace, just in case any zombies were waiting to pounce. His gun was cocked and ready to fire. What he actually saw when he reached the turning and glanced down it was a number of zombies in a fight with a guy in a black leather jacket. The man had a hood pulled up over his head. But that wasn't what grabbed Angus's interest most. Between him and the hooded man was the Judy Garland impersonator. She was backing down the corridor towards him.

Up to this point, his day had been one of utter frustration. He'd wasted a lot of time trying to retrieve his twenty thousand dollars from Sanchez, and had blown his opportunity to complete the hit for which Julius had offered to pay him. Here was a chance to carry out the task he had been given, and maybe pick up a cash reward.

It was worth using one bullet on this bitch, wasn't it?

He didn't need to think twice. As the girl turned and began running down the corridor towards him, he took aim and fired a bullet straight into her chest.

The look on her face was priceless. *Total surprise.*

Angus loved to kill. And when the victim was caught completely by surprise, and looked him in the eye after taking a bullet – well, a hit didn't come much sweeter than that.

The man with Judy Garland had taken on three zombies in a fistfight and was making a pretty damn good job of it. Hearing the gunshot he visibly stiffened at the sound. He managed to throw two of the zombies simultaneously to the floor as another one circled, waiting for its chance to attack, biding its time. The hooded man turned and saw Judy Garland slump to the floor. Her legs had buckled at the knees and folded underneath her. She collapsed, landing on her side before falling over on to her back, staring up at the ceiling. Angus could see the face within the man's dark hood. He looked stunned. It was plain that this woman meant something to him, because he seemed momentarily to forget about the third zombie behind him as he watched her legs crumple beneath her. For a split second he looked up at Angus and the two of them exchanged a look. Angus smiled. This guy obviously considered himself a major-league hardass. But he had zombies swarming all round him. As the third zombie pounced on the man from behind, Angus winked at him.

Job done.

Thirty seconds later Angus made it out of the hotel through a fire exit that led to the parking out back. The ground was trembling violently beneath his feet by this time and he was relieved to be out in the open. The building was falling to pieces.

It wouldn't be long before the hotel and its parking lot crumbled into a huge chasm in the ground. Angus wasn't quite sure what had caused the earthquake, and he didn't have time to stop and work it out. He scoured the parking lot for any sign of his camper van, in the hope that the zombies had left the keys (and his Tom Jones CD) inside it. It was nowhere to be seen, and with sections of the lot beginning to crack open and sink into the pits of Hell below, he decided it would be safer just to head for the best car in the lot, which happened to be a black Pontiac Firebird. He fired a bullet through the driver's-side window and unlocked the car from the inside. It took him thirty seconds to hot-wire it, the big V8 engine bursting into life with a deep-throated roar.

A minute later, Angus was back on the highway and heading out of the Devil's Graveyard.

Sixty-Two

The gunshot drowned out the burping frogs, the creaking of the walls, and the horrible sounds of the undead and their victims. And it could mean only one thing. Out of the corner of his eye, the Kid saw Emily stop dead in her tracks. But before he could turn around, he had two zombies to deal with. With one swing of his right arm he caught the nearest one across the head, the back of his fist slamming hard into its skull. The impact sent the zombie crashing into its comrade. They both fell down and rolled, entangling themselves in each other, across the corridor and towards the widening crack in the centre of the floor. On the far side of the crack, up against the wall, the third zombie was still standing back, ready to pounce. The Kid ignored it and turned back to see where the shot had come from.

Emily lay crumpled on the floor. The bullet had hit her in the chest and her legs had buckled under her. She had collapsed into a heap on the floor with blood oozing out of a hole in her chest, staining her blue dress and turning it a horrible colour that looked black from a distance. She stared up at the Kid and he saw in her eyes the fear of death. A small amount of crimson liquid began to trickle from the right corner of her mouth as her lungs filled with blood. But who had fired the bullet?

The Kid looked down the corridor to where it joined another. Standing at the intersection with a gun in his hand was a giant of a man. He had long red hair tied back into a ponytail and a matching goatee. He was dressed much as the Kid himself often was, in dark clothes and a long trench coat, no doubt designed for concealing weapons. Their eyes met briefly, and then the gunman winked at him and disappeared out of sight along the main corridor.

Before the Kid could go to the stricken girl, he felt the third zombie pounce on his back, its bony grey arms clinging tightly round his neck. This creature was thin and wiry and appeared to be wearing little more than a torn pair of grey shorts. The Kid stepped back hard towards the wall behind him, smashing the spine of the creature up against it before it could take a bite out of his neck. Then he spun round and smashed his right fist into its face. The sound of bone cracking followed and its face caved in like putty. Its arms fell helplessly to its side. It was incapable of defending itself, so the Kid hurled it across the crumbling corridor at the other two members of the undead. They were in the process of climbing back to their feet. When the third zombie hit them, they all ended up in a heap on the floor. There were easier victims to prey on than the Kid and the zombies, even with their limited intellect, were quick enough to work that out. He didn't bother to watch them retreat down the corridor towards the auditorium.

Emily was on her back on the floor, struggling for breath, choking. He ran to her. Before he could get to her, another huge tremor from below sent him crashing into the wall. He bounced hard off it and landed on his front at Emily's side. She was staring wide-eyed at the ceiling above, gasping. Getting to his knees, he took hold of her right hand with his. She didn't seem to have much strength left as her life ebbed away. The feel of his hand seemed to wake her from the almost hypnotic trance that had left her staring at the ceiling. She blinked, then stared into the Kid's eyes. Her own eyes were beginning to fill with tears and she choked out a few barely audible words that caused more blood to seep from her mouth.

'I want to go home.'

The Bourbon Kid covered his mouth with his free hand as he felt a lump settle in his throat. She reminded him so much of Beth, the girl he'd loved and lost ten years earlier. The similarities were uncanny. The same clothes, the same kind, generous nature and the sweet innocent face. He watched on as she spluttered out five more words.

'I don't want to die.'

'I know.' Despite the constriction in his throat, his voice had lost its gravelly edge.

Her pigtails had come loose and her hair was a straggly mess. The Kid wiped some stray strands out of her eyes and swept them back across her forehead. Although she was cold to the Kid's touch she was sweating profusely and her breathing was noisy and laboured. Her mouth had filled with blood and she could neither spit it out nor swallow it.

Tears streamed down her cheeks. 'Don't leave me here,' she choked. 'I don't want to die on my own.'

'It's okay. I'm stayin'.'

It didn't seem an appropriate moment to point out that they were minutes away from sinking into the depths of Hell, along with the hotel and everything and everyone in it. For Emily's sake he hoped she'd be dead and her soul gone elsewhere long before that happened. Her hand was rapidly growing colder and her grip on his was weakening. The only thing he could think to do was to squeeze her hand tighter, as if it might help her ignore the pain she was in. And let her know that he was there. He wasn't leaving.

The plaster on the ceiling above them began to crack and crumble as the building shook. The Kid managed to use his free hand to deflect a few chunks of debris away to prevent them from landing on Emily. The dark stain from the bullet wound in her chest fanned out across most of the upper half of her blue dress, while the blood trickling from her mouth tainted the white sleeves.

As the huge crack that bisected the floor in the corridor

began to widen further, Emily's body nearly slipped over the edge and into the smoking pit of Hell below. He pulled her clear of it, to be certain she didn't slide in before she died.

A few seconds later her eyes rolled up into her head and her hand fell totally limp in his. Her breathing ceased, and her body slumped lifeless on the ruined floor.

Sixty-Three

The Hotel Pasadena crumbled at an alarming rate. On the ground level, huge cracks appeared in the ceilings, floors and walls. Sanchez knew that at any second the ceiling might collapse on him, or a huge crack in the floor might swallow him up and send him plummeting into the pits of Hell. As he raced across the lobby towards the front entrance, he prayed that he would make it out in one piece. The desert had never looked so inviting.

He had never been much of a runner, preferring to drive whenever the need arose to travel more than fifty yards. But with his life on the line, he was suddenly a match for a greyhound. Jacko had proved invaluable in leading the way out and keeping the zombies at bay, but now, with the night sky outside visible just a few yards away, Sanchez decided to light the afterburners.

A huge crack in the marble floor of the reception was widening at a frighteningly rapid rate. It ran from the corridor right through the middle of the reception area to the front entrance. As Sanchez made his move to get around Jacko, a particularly violent eruption shook the whole building and the crack in the floor suddenly doubled in width. It was now a good two yards across. The crimson welcome mat by the remains of the entrance doors suddenly disappeared into the chasm. The hotel was, quite literally, splitting in half. In his haste to avoid the smoking fissure and reach the exit, Sanchez accidentally knocked into Jacko as he passed him. The Blues

Man let out a surprised yelp and Sanchez heard him stumble and fall.

There was no time to look back and see if he was okay. Sanchez felt a little bad, but getting himself out of there was his top priority, so once he was past the man who claimed to be Robert Johnson, he just kept on running as fast as his short, pudgy legs would carry him.

He could hear Elvis screaming at him to run faster, and Janis shouting something that sounded like 'fat bastard'. With all that was happening he hardly needed the extra encouragement. He charged through the remains of the glass doors at the front of the hotel and down the concrete steps on to the long driveway out front. Then he kept on running, only glancing back once to see that much of the giant hotel had already sunk into the huge crater that had suddenly appeared in the once beautifully maintained grounds.

Eventually, with not a breath left in him, Sanchez came to a ragged stop at the end of the hotel driveway, underneath the arched welcome sign that spanned the entrance. To right and left, the highway was dark and deserted, but it felt relatively safe. The tremors from behind weren't having any effect this far from the hotel. Doubling over with his hands on his thighs to catch his breath he looked up and was pleased to see that Elvis and Janis had also made it out safely. They both looked relieved, though there was a distinct probability that Janis would begin cussing once she got her breath back. But of Jacko, Emily or Freddie there was no sign.

'The others get out?' Sanchez wheezed.

Janis piped up. 'We got separated from Freddie an' Emily quite early. Maybe they got out another way.'

'What about the blues guy?' Sanchez asked. 'He was still with us just now, wasn't he?'

Elvis, who was not particularly out of breath, and didn't seem to have even a single hair out of place, shook his head disapprovingly at him.

'You mean Robert Johnson? The guy who practically invented the blues?'

'Yeah, him.'

'The guitar legend? The guy who saved us all by keepin' the fuckin' zombies away?'

'Yeah. That guy.'

'You knocked him down into a fuckin' big goddam crack in the floor. I'd say he's suppin' with the Devil right about now.'

Sanchez screwed his face up. This was awkward. A witty remark was required to ease the situation. 'Sure hope he's got a long spoon,' he quipped.

Elvis was decidedly unimpressed. 'A long spoon? The fuck's that got to do with anythin'?'

'Dunno. I'm just sayin',' Sanchez muttered awkwardly.

'Fuck you, Sanchez. Your weasellin' ways have just sent one of the greatest musicians of all time into the pits of Hell. Ain't you got no shame?'

'Rather him than us, right?'

Elvis sighed exasperatedly and turned away. Behind him, Sanchez could hear the noise of the hotel crumbling. It sounded like an iceberg breaking up. The building was almost gone. The penthouse suites on the top floor slowly disappeared out of sight beneath ground level amid a giant cloud of dust and sand. A huge pillar of dust swirled up into the night sky and slowly descended to the ground, like dissipating fireworks. Just then, above the diminishing roar of the disappearing hotel, came the sound of a powerful engine and the horrible clash of inexpertly changed gears.

From round what had been the side of the hotel, a massive blue camper van appeared. It had been left in the parking lot at the rear of the building, but now it was zipping down the drive through the clouds of dust, heading towards Sanchez, Elvis and Janis.

'Hey! Over here!' Elvis shouted, waving at the driver.

The van hurtled towards them, racing ahead of the falling debris and the cracks appearing in the driveway behind it. When it reached the road, the driver pulled it up alongside the three survivors. 'This whole fuckin' day just gets stranger by the minute, don't it?' Sanchez remarked.

The folding door at the front of the camper van hissed as it opened. Then the sound of Tom Jones singing 'It's Not Unusual' blared out from the van's stereo system.

Sanchez rushed to the door, knocking Janis Joplin to one side in his eagerness to be the first to climb aboard the van. When he stepped on board he was astonished to see that the driver was none other than Annabel de Frugyn, the Mystic Lady herself.

'Why, hello, Sanchez,' she croaked, offering him her usual gap-toothed smile.

'Uh – yeah.' For a moment he was completely lost for words. Then 'Hi. Great idea stealin' the van,' he said approvingly. He found it confusing to say anything to the old witch with approval.

'Yeah. I had a premonition that there was some sort of quake imminent, so I scoured the parking lot and found this lovely van with the keys still in the ignition. And a Tom Jones CD, too, signed by the man himself!'

Elvis and Janis followed Sanchez aboard and made their way towards the back of the van. Elvis yelled back at the Mystic Lady.

'Yo, woman! Press that metal to the floor, baby. Let's get the fuck outta here.'

'Sure thing, King,' Annabel simpered in reply. Elvis tended to have that effect on women, even ones as downright peculiar as the Mystic Lady.

Sanchez took a seat just behind Annabel. For a moment he just sat there with his mind in neutral. Then he breathed a huge sigh of relief at having escaped the carnage and destruction. A comfortable cushioned seat had never felt so good, even though his sweaty buttocks did tend to stick to the plastic seat cover. As they sped off down the highway he looked back and watched the final moments of the hotel as it plunged into the pits of Hell. By the time they were half a mile down the road, the Hotel Pasadena was all but gone. To any fresh visitor, it would seem as if it had never existed.

Sobered, he looked up into the rear-view mirror at the top of the windshield. He could see the Mystic Lady's face in it. They smiled at each other. Maybe she wasn't so bad after all.

'You okay, Sanchez?' she asked.

'Been better.'

'Well, we're all safe now. Be back in Santa Mondega 'fore you know it.'

'So long as nothin' else goes wrong.'

'It won't. I can see us getting back with no more dramas.'

'Bein' able to see the future really pays off sometimes, don't it?'

'Certainly did earlier,' Annabel replied. 'I made a killing on the roulette, you know.'

'*Yeah?* 'Cause that tip you gave me sure didn't work out too well. I lost a fuckin' fortune on the wheel when you called red.'

Annabel smiled. 'Funny, that. You know, that was the only time I didn't win all day.'

'*What?*'

'I won almost a hundred thousand dollars today on that roulette wheel. The only call I got wrong was the one when you lost all your money.'

'Thanks a bunch,' said Sanchez, bitterly.

A knowing grin spread across the Mystic Lady's wrinkled face. 'Maybe next time you offer me a drink, you'll think twice about giving me piss,' she suggested.

Goddammit, thought Sanchez. *Shit karma, again.*

After that, he would have preferred to spend the journey

at the back of the van, as far away from Annabel as possible. Unfortunately, Elvis and Janis were in need of some privacy. Sanchez did his best not to be too nosy, but his occasional glances back were greeted by the sight of Janis bent over the pull-out bed with Elvis pounding into her from behind. And Janis wasn't exactly a quiet fuck, either. Energetic sex wasn't moderating her Tourette's much.

The moon and a million stars shone down brightly from the night sky. They lit the desert and the long ribbon of the highway with a pleasant glow, barely hinting at the evil left behind where the hotel had once stood. Sanchez had never been a great admirer of moonlight, but after all he had just been through he took comfort in the sight of it. There had been moments over the past twenty-four hours when he had thought he might never see even simple, natural sights like the glow of the moon and stars again. From his seat behind Annabel the faint glimmer of light allowed him to see a crossroads up ahead, long before it was illuminated by the van's headlights. He didn't recall seeing it on the journey to the hotel, and since it appeared to be without a road sign to provide directions, he hoped Annabel would know which road to take. She slowed the van to a crawl as they approached it. Then she leaned back and looked over her shoulder at Sanchez.

'You know which way we go from here?' she asked.

'Not a fuckin' clue. Straight ahead's probably as good as any.'

'I don't know,' said Annabel dubiously. She was still half turned towards Sanchez, not really watching the road ahead of her. Looking past her at the approaching crossroads, Sanchez spotted a man in a black suit, wearing a fedora, walking down the middle of the road. He would have been hard to spot even in the glare of the van's headlights, had he not been carrying a large white signpost over his shoulder.

'WATCH OUT!' Sanchez yelled.

Annabel whipped back round to face the windshield,

slamming on the brakes as she did so.

'Jesus! Who the hell is that?' she asked.

Sanchez got up and joined her at the front of the van. The signpost the man was carrying had four arms set at right angles to each other, each with a place name lettered on it, though Sanchez couldn't read them.

'I think,' he said softly, 'that's Robert Johnson.' He thought back to the young singer he had known as Jacko, and whom he had met for the first time only a few hours earlier. Somehow, that name no longer seemed to suit him.

Annabel raised an eyebrow. 'The Blues Man?'

'Yeah.'

'The one who sold his soul to the Devil at the crossroads?'

'Yeah. That one. How the hell'd he get here so quickly? Thought I'd killed him back at the hotel.' Seeing her expression, he added hastily, 'Shit, it was an accident.'

'I'm not sure I need to hear about that,' Annabel said primly, shaking her head. 'He was a good sort, you know, was Robert Johnson.'

'How d'ya mean?'

'Well, the spirits are telling me he's about to show us the way home.'

Sanchez watched Johnson prop the sign on the ground and look around for the exact spot to stake it. 'Yeah, he's puttin' the signpost back on the crossroads.'

'Exactly,' said Annabel knowingly.

'Wonder where he found it?' Sanchez thought aloud.

'Where he left it, most likely.'

'You think he took it down?'

'Like I said, he was a good man.'

'How the fuck does stealin' signposts make him a good man?'

Annabel sighed. 'Think about it, Sanchez. That signpost directs people to the Hotel Pasadena. By taking it down and hiding it every Halloween, Robert Johnson has probably saved a heck of a lot of lives. And now he's showing us the way home.'

She pointed up ahead and they both watched as the black man in the suit rammed the signpost down into the loose earth at the roadside, where two arms of the crossroads met. After securing it he twisted it around. Annabel pressed gently on the accelerator and the van slowly approached the crossroads. When they were close enough to get a good look at the signpost they saw the man they believed to be Robert Johnson point up at one of the white-painted arms. It indicated the turning to the right. Lettered in black on the sign was the word 'HOME'.

Annabel flashed the headlights at him by way of thanks and began to turn the steering wheel to the right. As the van came round, Sanchez waved a regretful hand at the Blues Man, in apology for having nudged him into the chasm in the floor of the hotel. Johnson waved back once, then doffed his hat to show no hard feelings. With that last gesture, he disappeared into the night.

The van sped on through the darkness for another hour before the Mystic Lady eventually parked it up at the first motel they came to outside the Devil's Graveyard. Sanchez would finally have somewhere safe to rest his weary head in peace.

And he wouldn't have to continue listening to Janis Joplin screaming 'Fuck me harder, you fuckin' muthafucker!' any more.

Sixty-Four

Breakfast in a motel was all that Sanchez could have wished for. He had lost his luggage and his jacket, all left behind in his room at the Hotel Pasadena. Since the place had now plunged into the depths of Hell, there was every chance that the Devil and his minions were walking around in Sanchez's finest selection of Hawaiian shirts. So he made do with the red one again, even if it was a tad sticky and stale. As for his shorts, he was used to wearing them for weeks at a time in any case, so neither was it any great hardship to pull them on once again.

He sat in a booth by the motel diner's window, tucking into a fried breakfast and occasionally sipping from a mug of steaming hot coffee. As he did so, he reflected on all that had happened in the Devil's Graveyard the day before. Opposite him at the table sat his good buddy Elvis. At least, Sanchez liked to think of Elvis as his buddy. Chances were high, however, that once they were back in Santa Mondega they wouldn't have much contact, unless Elvis came by the Tapioca for a drink. *But, hey,* Sanchez thought, *we kinda bonded a little during yesterday's goings-on.*

Like Sanchez, Elvis was stuck in the same clothes that he'd worn the day before. Yet unlike Sanchez, he looked as cool as ever, somehow making yesterday's dirty clothes look so much less sleazy than did the bar owner. His hair was still unruffled, despite an evening of angry sex with Janis. He did look tired, though – just about ready to nod off to sleep at any minute, Sanchez thought. He'd kept his trademark shades on and was sitting back against the red vinyl-covered bench in the booth, with his legs stretched out over to Sanchez's side of the table.

All the King had in front of him was a plate with a cheeseburger on it, which he hadn't yet touched, and a glass of orange juice.

'That was some fuckin' day yesterday, huh, Sanchez?' he commented.

'Yeah. Not exactly my idea of fun. Reckon next year I'm goin' to stay in Santa Mondega. Gotta be a whole lot safer.'

'Yeah, man. Smart idea.'

Sanchez finished up the last piece of sausage on his plate and wiped his mouth with a napkin, before reaching for his coffee cup.

'Reckon you'll see that Janis Joplin chick again?' he asked Elvis, who was staring out of the window at something in the parking lot.

'Yeah, maybe. She's kinda cool. Say what, though, Sanchez, ya oughta take out that Annabel thing. She's got it bad for you, buddy.'

'She's got somethin' bad, sure enough,' Sanchez grumbled. 'I can smell it every time she's near.'

Elvis laughed politely and continued to stare out of the window. From behind his sunglasses Sanchez saw him raise an eyebrow.

'What's happenin', man?' he asked.

'Yo, Sanchez,' Elvis half-whispered, so that no one within earshot would hear him. 'Check out that black car outside.'

With a squeak from the tortured vinyl, Sanchez twisted his substantial butt round on the bench and peered out of the window to get a look at the car. Sure enough, in the lot outside was a black Pontiac Firebird parked in front of one of the motel rooms. It was rocking wildly from side to side.

'What d'ya reckon's goin' on?' Sanchez asked.

Elvis grinned. 'I reckon,' he said in his lazy drawl, 'yep, I reckon someone's gettin' fucked.'

Sixty-Five

Invincible Angus had spent a thoroughly unsatisfying night in the Safari Motel. After the chaos of the previous day's events, he had ended up without any of the cash he had hoped to pick up. He had successfully gunned down the Judy Garland impersonator, but it hadn't made him any money. He hadn't retrieved his twenty thousand dollars from Sanchez, either.

When he checked into the motel the previous night he'd been somewhat overhasty. Apart from one pistol, he'd left his few remaining possessions, including a box of shells and his spare magazines, in his newly acquired black Pontiac Firebird, which he'd parked in the bay right outside his room. Not a clever thing to do at the best of times, but particularly dumb when the car had no window on the driver's side, on account of him having put a bullet through it. But Halloween had been so hectic, and so frustrating, from start to finish that all he had wanted to do was get a good night's sleep. Now that he'd had that sleep, he was fully alert again.

The motel room he had stayed in was pretty basic, but it sure beat spending the night in Hell, or inside a zombie's stomach, which was probably more or less the same thing. He stepped outside and breathed in a lungful of the fresh, early-morning air. It was good to be alive after all that had happened. That at least was something to be grateful for.

It was then Angus caught sight of what might just prove to be a lucky break. On the other side of the parking lot was the motel diner. Sitting at a booth by the window, stuffing his face full of sausage, was Sanchez fuckin' Garcia. And he had his buddy, the Elvis jerk, with him. These two muthafuckers might still have Angus's twenty grand. And if they didn't? Well, they were still worth killing anyway.

He closed the motel door quietly behind him so as not to draw attention to himself. All he had to do was grab a couple of the loaded magazines he had stupidly left in the car the night before. Then he was going to finish the job of burying those two bastards in the desert. Not even very deep, since they'd be doing the digging.

The morning was surprisingly cold considering how hot it had been the day before. There was a light frost on the car's windshield brought on by the chill of the desert night. As he walked over to the driver's door Angus glanced up at the sun, which was just beginning to show over the horizon. At that low angle its rays were blinding, and he was grateful for the Firebird's dark-tinted windows.

He opened the car door, feeling the chill of the frost on the door handle under his fingers. He lifted his right hand and blew warm air from his mouth on to his fingertips. Those fingers needed warming up in readiness for squeezing the trigger of his gun. He glanced over at the diner again. Sanchez and Elvis didn't seem to have caught sight of him yet. As he climbed into the car he kept his gaze fixed on Sanchez's fat face as he chewed greedily on his breakfast. *That thievin' sonofabitch was gonna be sorry he ever messed with Invincible Angus.*

The black leather seat in the car was ice-cold and he shivered as he sat down on it and pulled the door shut. Still staring at his two intended victims, he reached over blindly to the glove compartment, where he'd stashed the shells and spare magazines the night before. As he did, his hand brushed against something in the passenger seat. He quickly turned his head to see what it was, and reeled back in shock. Slumped next to him in the passenger seat was a corpse.

Judy Garland.

The woman he had shot in the hotel the previous night. She smelt pretty bad, too. The front of her blue and white dress was stained almost black from a dark patch of dried blood where his bullet had smashed into her chest. Her face was hideous, the eyes open but turned up into the head, so that only the whites showed. Her hair was disordered and stiff with blood, the neat pigtails long since gone. The effects of death had drawn her lips back from her teeth in a terrifying rictus that looked like a snarl.

Jesus! he thought. *How in hell had this woman's body come to be in his car?* As soon as he asked himself the question, Angus felt his blood turn to ice. One look in the driver's mirror answered the question for him.

Staring back at him from the rear seat was a dark figure with a hood pulled up over its head.

THE END (perhaps . . .)